Without Family Ties

By Shannon Whitford

iUniverse, Inc.
Bloomington

Without Family Ties

iUniverse books may be ordered through booksellers or by contacting:

iUniverse
1663 Liberty Drive
Bloomington, IN 47403
www.iuniverse.com
1-800-Authors (1-800-288-4677)

Because of the dynamic nature of the Internet, any Web addresses or links contained in this book may have changed since publication and may no longer be valid. The views expressed in this work are solely those of the author and do not necessarily reflect the views of the publisher, and the publisher hereby disclaims any responsibility for them.

ISBN: 978-1-4502-3245-6 (sc)
ISBN: 978-1-4502-3249-4 (ebook)
ISBN: 978-1-4502-3250-0 (dj)

Library of Congress Control Number: 2010907575

Printed in the United States of America

iUniverse rev. date: 6/22/2011

Acknowledgments

My parents set exemplary standards and expectations for all their children. I believe my siblings and I have patterned our lives from the regular displays of love and affection, examples of morals, values, kindness and dignity that our parents displayed and expected of us.

The structure of the core family changes every generation. I was raised in a traditional home with curfews and rules to follow. My father was determined to keep his children close in spite of his personal challenges, discomforts, and a never-ending will to live. His generosity and his enduring love for his family have influenced me in everything I do.

My mother deserves more than a mere mention. Us kids frequently challenged and tested her. She maintained her stance and raised us with good discipline and dignity. Mom's continuous dedication to meet all of her family's needs—many days on less than a few hours of sleep—is commendable.

I must also thank the people at iUniverse for their help and patience in the development of my book.

Contents

Prologue

Love affairs and illegitimate babies have been part of history since the beginning of time. Veterans, rock stars, TV personalities, politicians, and people from all walks of life have fallen into less than desirable and questionable family situations.

It's not true that we always choose to live our lives as we do. Decisions made for us by other people often have effects on the outcome of the remainder of our lives. Because of complacency we become passive and accept these decisions instead of fighting them. We pass on the occasional challenge and ignore opportunities that will improve our lives. We can put up a fight and try to change the outcome, but whether we agree or not with others' choices and decisions, most often, we cannot alter the future.

When Ray Buckley discovered the woman he loved was planning to marry another man, he became devious and almost dangerous in the quest to become her husband. The outcome produced one of the best rock musicians of current times.

Ray Buckley chose a career in the Air Force. It was very lucrative and enabled him to maintain a very stable income for his family. Like any husband and father, Ray was very protective of his family.

Busy lifestyles have made maintaining close family relationships a tedious chore. Years of chemical abuse, misconstrued facts, fame, fortune, and complacency, stymied Ray's son Gary and almost prevented him from discovering the truth about his misconstrued past.

Glen Dornstadt—son, brother, father, grandfather, and Korean War veteran, became involved in a love triangle while serving his time in the Air Force. The outcome of that affair followed him the rest of his life.

Glen's childhood equaled poverty levels. After he enlisted in the Air Force he swore he would never live that way again; however poor judgment and unfortunate circumstances, took him back there once again.

Most of Glen's life was a struggle. He struggled with his relationships, his career choices, his income and most of all his health. Fortunately for Glen, the values and moral he taught his children became a valuable asset to him as he aged. Most of us would be fortunate to have such a good supportive family structure like the one Glen built.

A cloud hovered over Glen most of his adult life. He refused to take any chances on the one solid relationship he had. "Everyone has something in their past to be ashamed of. I hope you'll understand someday," Glen said sternly to daughter as he lay ill. As Glen aged his view of his indiscretions changed. He accepted his mistakes and his past was not something to be ashamed of any longer, but something to be proud of.

Chapter 1
Glen's Past

Glen Dornstadt was often referred to as a flounder. He grew up two hundred feet away from the Susquehanna River. His summers were spent exploring and swimming in the river with his brothers and friends after he completed his daily chores. Niles Dornstadt, Glen's father, felt it was necessary to teach all of his children how to swim, living only 200 feet from the river. The girls didn't spend as much time in the river as the boys, but they were all good swimmers.

One scorching summer afternoon Glen and his brothers heard screams coming from the river. The boys ran to see a small boat capsized off of a nearby island. Seven people were scrambling to hang on to a sinking vessel. Glen and his brothers were able to help three people back to shore. Two others swam to shore themselves, but two were missing. Glen anguished over what more could have been done to save those two people. He was a hero to the people he saved, but to him, losing the other two were inexcusable and a poor performance on his part. Those deaths haunted him the rest of his life.

Glen quit school in eleventh grade from lack of interest. He had dreams to pursue and school interfered. He wasn't a good student so school was not a priority. A career in the military would help him accomplish his dreams a lot faster. In the 1940s and 50s men were expected to enlist in a branch of the service after they completed high school. The Korean conflict was a large attraction for young men and Glen eagerly joined many of his friends and enlisted in the Air Force. Men lied about their age to fulfill enlistment requirements. Birth certificates were changed and never questioned. Like many other enlistees, Glen was only seventeen when he left for basic training in Texas. Enlisting provided men with skills to assist them in finding jobs after they left the service. It was common to re-enlist for an additional two to four years. If you wanted to see the world, you were told to join a branch of the armed forces.

Glen wanted a skill, but he wanted to travel too. Joining the Air Force was a practical solution in accomplishing his goals. He dreamt of being a pilot and the Air Force was his best option—or so he thought. He planned to go places that no one else in his family had ever gone before. Glen and his brother Paul enlisted together. Unfortunately, only Glen returned. Glen found it difficult to talk about Paul's demise. Paul's body was never recovered after his plane was shot down over Korea. Kathryn Dornstadt took Paul's death very hard and displayed his picture many places throughout her house. Once her grandchildren were old enough to talk, they were advised never to mention Paul's name around her.

After his enlistment, Glen's vision problems became evident. His dreams of becoming a pilot were gone but other challenging occupations were readily available. After completing basic training Glen's first stop was London before moving on to Korea. This was a good start on his plans to travel. Every soldier was required to take a special missions training before their assignment in Korea. Glen really didn't want to go to Korea, but he had enlisted knowing that Korea was a probability.

Glen still wanted to be in the air and becoming a paratrooper trainer was his second choice allowing him that opportunity. After only six months in Korea, Glen was sent to Puerto Rico to begin his instructor training. He was a little reluctant at first, but after only a few jumps, he was hooked. In his short career as an instructor, Glen made over three hundred assisted jumps. He loved this part of his military career and often reflected back to that special time in his life.

While in London, Glen became romantically involved with a woman who accepted a ring and promised her future to another man. These individuals became entwined in a bittersweet love triangle involving passion, desire, motivation and deception. In a dramatic retaliation, Ray managed to twist and turn many situations into devious acts and lies that remained with Glen until his passing. The son they created pondered for years about who might be his real father. Only one man would find out the answer to the mystery shortly before his death.

Georgina Steiner never meant to cause lifelong agony and controversy between the two families. Surely she must have realized what turmoil her indiscretions would have on her son.

Like most fathers, Glen taught his children how to tie their shoes, sat with them when they were sick, and played games with them until he was exhausted. His daughter almost suffocated from the hug he gave her after he brutally spanked her for running in front of a moving car. He taught his son the proper stance to hold a baseball bat when he started to play Little League. He taught all of his children how to fight back when they knew they were right. They struggled to maintain civility when he taught them how to drive a standard transmission automobile. He cried when they graduated from school and again when they got married.

Glen remained close with all of his children until his death. He shared his embarrassing past with only a few close relatives and his oldest daughter Dana. His siblings were aware of his relationship failures; however they were not eager to share information when confronted. Dana struggled to search for the truth and closure.

Glen's siblings felt that if he wanted her to know about his past he would have shared that information with her.

Over the year's people have shared miniscule details and information about Glen's past. Eventually secrets are exposed and families are left with a lot of questions and unknown details. Unfortunately, the remainder of the mystery will never be known.

Glen was in a very serious life altering automobile accident in the early 70's. His back was broken and his legs were severely damaged. Other critical health issues not related to Glen's accident were prevalent the last twenty years of his life. In spite of his handicaps, he happily struggled successfully to support his family. With all of his afflictions, Glen remained positive. Showing pain and despair was a weakness that he refused to expose. Like anyone else he had insecurities. His strongest desire was to keep his family close. Calmly and fairly he'd help his children work out their differences to achieve that goal.

It wasn't until his car accident during Dana's senior year of high school that he opened up and shared his secret past with her. A few weeks into his recovery while Dana sat with him at his bedside as he struggled to ask her this question. "Can you keep a secret?" he asked Dana. Assuming it was a secret related to his accident, Dana replied, "Of course Dad."

At first Dana questioned her father's state of mind. She was shocked and surprised as she listened to his story. Glen rarely offered information about his past. He easily maintained Dana's attention as she listened intently as every detail unfolded. He repeated as he spoke softly that this secret was not to be shared with any family member—at least not yet. "Promise me," he said. "Okay Dad, don't worry. Who would I tell?" Dana asked. "No one, absolutely no one," he said.

Dana was convinced at first that he was dreaming or hallucinating and brushed off his stories. As his recovery continued the details got more explicit. Dana finally acknowledged that her father struggled with this secret for many years of his life.

She often wondered why he chose to share his indiscretions with her. It was like opening a faucet. Information flowed smoothly and he held nothing back. Feelings of shock and disbelief overcame Dana as her father discussed many private and intimate details with his own daughter. Every time he spoke of Georgina, he'd shed a tear or two. Taboo—not in today's world, but during Glen's youth, he would have been thought of much differently. Accusations, stories and details are vague, secondhand, and difficult to prove now.

Before his accident he rarely spoke about his time in London. He was there to get paid and perform his job and maybe learn a valuable skill for the future. Training was grueling and crucial for survival, but there was nowhere else he could he apply that experience?

Dana often wondered what kind of valuable life skills you learn from fighting in combat.

Glen's siblings knew miniscule parts of his past, and they too had been sworn to secrecy and were very reluctant to share any information. After Glen's death Dana approached her aunts and uncles about her father's secret past and was hurt when they called her names and told her to stay out of his business. They were stunned that Dana held such little regard for the privacy of her father's past. Why would she want to expose something they had been asked to keep secret?

Glen shared a variety of information with his siblings, but none of them got the same story. Unfortunately, Dana didn't find out until after his death that there were more secrets yet to be revealed. Dana was successful in getting her Uncle Wayne to share a variety of information about Glen's past. The information was interesting but not what Dana was looking for and often not what she was expecting to hear. His oldest sister Ada shared much information of what she knew about Glen's past. At first she was rather hesitant to offer any information, but she eventually opened up and was relieved that someone else knew about Glen's mysterious past. Dana enjoyed every minute she was able to spend with her relatives. Ada attempted to prepare Dana for other information about her father that would probably surface during her search. Most of her information was sad and very vague. Dana made several attempts to find answers to her remaining questions, but it appeared that no one else had any more information to share.

Glen was usually a very calm individual, but when tested, he could change into a tyrant in a second. One time he hurled his son into the refrigerator after Darren was caught lying about what time he came home the previous night. At times Darren might have deserved punishment but not on that particular occasion, and not like that.

Glen had a very sentimental side when he talked about his mother. Glen was rather critical, and not as kind when referring to his father. Niles Dornstadt was always trying to escape reality and responsibility. Niles didn't tolerate Kathryn's nagging even though he probably deserved it. He chose to stay away from home as much as possible. Niles often repeated, "that damn woman is too controlling for me."

Dana never had the opportunity to bond with her grandparents. Kathryn had already passed away before Dana's birth. Niles passed away when she was only three years old. Glen gave Dana a picture from a family wedding where Niles spent a lot of time bonding with his youngest grandchild, who at that time was nearly two years old.

Glen passed away in 1995 leaving behind a questionable legacy. Losing a parent leaves a big emptiness that no one understands until it happens to them. It's a sickening feeling. Knowing Glen was no longer suffering from his ailments helped Dana accept her father's death. Unfortunately Glen had a lot of unresolved secrets from his past that would remain a mystery. All of a sudden, the unknown becomes more important. The memories you have of someone after they have passed on are very different from when they are present with us. Dana was afraid that eventually she'd forget all of those special qualities she loved about her father.

Chapter 2
Finding A Place to Call Home

Myron and Bernice Steiner came to the United States in 1919 during a reign of growth and prosperity. Before they had children the couple saved all of their money to facilitate their move. Their feet weren't even firmly planted in the United States when Bernice discovered she was expecting their first child.

Myron was of average height and had a fair complexion. His blue eyes and big smile caught the attention of just about everyone he met. He was an easy going individual and known to be a prankster. Bernice was a beautiful brunette with a very small frame. She was a very serious person and didn't take pranks and jokes lightly. It was often said that their personalities clashed. Myron said, "You just need to know how to treat her to bring out her beauty."

Three daughters were born in Beaufort, South Carolina. When the depression came along they struggled to raise their children during the worst financial times the United States ever had. Myron lost his job and their income just stopped. Bernice cooked and cleaned for those fortunate enough to be able to pay her with food to feed her family. Myron looked for work daily, but no one was hiring.

It was a tough decision, but the Steiner's decided to return to London. England wasn't exactly prosperous during this time either; however London wasn't suffering from as serious of an economic depression as the United States.

Upon returning to London, Myron and Bernice managed to earn enough money to provide a simple and prosperous life for their daughters. Myron took a job as a stevedore and Bernice cleaned for neighbors and churches. They would soon purchase a suitable house in the southern district of London.

Ellesandra (Ellie), the oldest of the three girls had a bold and rather outspoken personality. She was heavyset and did not inherit the beauty of her mother. Even though she wasn't a beauty queen she married her high school sweetheart immediately upon her high school graduation. Ernest took her to the United States and her family rarely heard from her once she left England.

Joanna, the middle daughter, was very smart, attractive, and more interested in intellect than in men. Eventually a young London doctor conquered Joanna's heart. Unfortunately, it was a continuous struggle for Joanna to maintain her marriage with such a good-looking, charming, and rich man who encountered beautiful women every day. She tired of his carousing and after only a few years of marriage, they divorced.

Then there was the beautiful Georgina, named after her grandfather George and her grandmother Gina. She carried her name well. She had red hair and green eyes and was small in stature, intelligent yet somewhat introverted. She had a serious disposition, yet occasionally there was a mysterious silliness about her. Unaware of her simplistic beauty, she easily ignored whistles and comments from those she considered to be immature idiots.

Chapter 3
New Recruits

Ray Buckley was born and raised in Austin, Texas. From as far back as he could remember his home life was very stressful. He and his siblings fought constantly. His father Tony was a miserable alcoholic. After work he expected his dinner on the table when he walked in the door. Every night he'd retreat to the front porch with his spiked iced tea yelling obscenities and making nasty remarks to anyone who passed by. Ray was much closer to his mother Agnes. Tony called him a mama's boy. Agnes was a big woman with ongoing medical problems. Because of her husband's rude and sarcastic remarks she didn't want to be associated with him any more than necessary. She stayed inside and read books. The neighbors thought she was unfriendly, but in reality, she was just trying to avoid conflict and embarrassing situations. Ray couldn't wait to turn eighteen so he could enlist in the Air Force—it had to be better than his home life.

On the rare occasions that Ray mentioned his family, he'd avoid mentioning how dysfunctional his home life had been. His parents could barely stand to cohabitate. His oldest brother, Tony was in and out of jail for just about every offense imaginable. His brother John was the favorite son and always at the top of his class. He was the first child in his family to go to college. Most parents would have been proud, but his parents felt college was an unneeded burden.

Eventually John became a neurosurgeon and later a teacher at a famous Dallas hospital. Their only daughter Rhoda was the average unassuming child of the family. She was always overshadowed by her three devilish brothers.

Love and affection were rarely displayed, causing Ray to have his own issues in that area. Ray's brothers were just as argumentative as his father, and he was just plain sick of the fighting. It was a miserable place to be, so why would he return home once he joined the Air Force?

Ray began his Air Force career at Lackland Air Force base near San Antonio, Texas. After he completed boot camp, several temporary locations were offered to the new airmen. Some men were choosy and picked their locations. The remaining airmen drew straws to find out where they would be reporting for their first assignment. Ray didn't care where he was sent.

He was lucky and picked London. The men knew their assignments were temporary holding ports until they were needed in Korea, so it didn't matter to most of them where they went.

Correspondence from home was infrequent. Ray never received gifts like the other airmen did. Ray loathed his family and felt that the longer he stayed away, the better.

In early 1946 Ray began his pilot training. The sooner he got to Korea the sooner he could return to the states and get a job with a commercial airline to do what he loved best. Ray had little concept of the training time required in learning how to fly fighters over Korea. Instrument training was tedious, but he picked it up quickly. Mechanical training for "quick fixes" took him much longer to learn. When an emergency arose during combat, making adjustments and repairs to your own aircraft was a matter of life and death. Pilots needed to know how to resolve these problems and do it quickly.

Soldiers, sailors and airmen from every branch of the service frequented E-Jay's Pub in South London. Most men were unmarried, lonely and looking for companionship until they received their orders for Korea. Ray was extremely good-looking and had no problem charming women. His wavy brown hair, deep dark brown eyes, and dimples made Ray a favorite among the ladies. He appeared taller than he was because of his slender build. Ray and his buddies just wanted to make friends with the ladies at E-Jay's. None of them had any intentions of getting involved in any permanent relationships. None of them were planning on taking a British girlfriend home to America. They were all headed to Korea and who knew if they would ever return.

Ray had no intention of getting involved in a romantic relationship, but after a few visits to E'Jay's Pub, he found himself infatuated with Georgina Steiner. She caught the attention of every man she walked past. Georgina didn't try to attract men; she was rather shy and found it difficult to carry on a conversation with strangers. Up until now Ray had only sporadically dated girls. This woman was different. She was the most stunning woman he ever laid his eyes on. All of a sudden it didn't matter what country she came from.

Ray was completely consumed by this young woman who sat quietly alone at her table while her friends mingled and pushed themselves on the other service men. Ray couldn't let her sit alone like that so he bought her a drink and personally delivered it.

"Hi, my name is Ray. You look thirsty. I brought you a white wine. It seems perfect for an angel like you," he said. "Thank you, but I don't usually drink alcohol, however I will try it," Georgina said.

"Do you have a name?" Ray asked. "Yes, it's Georgina Steiner," she offered quietly.

"Are you always this quiet, or are you sad or upset?" he asked. "I am quiet until I get to know someone, then I talk more," she said.

Ray looked for Georgina every night, but she seemed somewhat elusive. Then finally on a weekend break a few weeks after their first encounter, Ray saw her again. "I thought I'd never see you again," he told Georgina. "I didn't know you were looking for me," she said. "I won't lie. You've stolen my heart. I'd really like to get to know you better. Will you take a walk with me? It's too loud in here," Ray said.

"I don't have your heart and I don't think I want to take a walk with you. I barely know you. I could be walking with a crazy man," she quietly replied.

After a few weeks of prompting Georgina, Ray finally got her to open up. She began sharing information about her family and her job. She soon began to feel comfortable with him. He'd often ask her to dance, but she always refused until finally one evening with a look of uncertainty she agreed to dance with him. The first time he held her in his arms, Ray knew she was the woman he wanted to marry. Ray and Georgina continued to date until he received his orders to report to Osan, Korea.

Georgina promised Ray she'd wait for his return. His only request of her was that she stopped visiting the local pubs with her friends. "Women who frequent those places earned themselves names," he informed her. *"No woman of his would be found in those whore dens,"* he thought to himself.

There was no time for long good-byes. Ray gave Georgina his school ring to show his commitment to her; she gave him a locket which contained her picture and a lock of her hair. That was the only memento Ray had of Georgina. He kept her picture with him at all times. Whenever Ray encountered disappointment or discouragement, he'd pull out Georgina's picture and reminisce about his beautiful girlfriend. Ray swore that her picture inspired him to be more careful and to always watch his back. He had someone special waiting his return once he completed his responsibilities in Korea.

Most airmen had a difficult time acclimating to Korea. Media information didn't even come close to relaying how bad it really was there. It's much worse than anyone could ever imagine. The Korean lifestyle was so different from the American's. While in Korea, soldiers and airmen lived on dirt floors, ate and slept in huts or crowded tents, and endured extreme temperatures. Clothing, tools, ammunition, and supplies were extremely limited. Other than that, "a guy could get used to the place," a soldier was heard saying.

Chapter 4
The Commitment

After only a few months, Georgina's lonely days and nights ran together. She did as Ray requested and stayed home. Her friends continued frequenting the local pubs. Every day was increasingly difficult for her while she patiently waited to hear from Ray. A simple Western Union about his impending return or his well-being would suffice. Correspondence was very infrequent. Ray warned her before he left for Korea that it would be a one year minimum assignment. He never promised a return date, nor did he promise to correspond. She expected to receive an occasional letter from him though. Georgina began to wonder whether he would indeed return for her.

On occasions, lower class airmen were offered the opportunity to replace a higher class injured airman if he were willing to serve out the remainder of the injured man's tour. Ray had served seven months of his assigned tour when he was offered the chance to replace a wounded sergeant. He was given six hours to make his decision. It would mean more money, more power, more respect, and eventually, a better place to live, along with control over those who had so frequently put him down. The downside was that his time in Korea would increase to include the sergeant's remaining nine months and the rest of his own tour, placing him in Korea for another fourteen months. It didn't take Ray long to make his decision. He wanted the security that came with the power.

Ray wrote Georgina to inform her of his new assignment. She was excited to have received mail from Ray, but her excitement quickly turned to frustration. That was not what Georgina needed to hear. The past seven months seemed like an eternity. She was hoping he'd be returning in five months. Could she handle fourteen more months of loneliness?

Georgina's coworkers and friends received mail regularly from their enlisted friends and family. Was Ray ignoring her? If he were really interested, wouldn't he have at least taken a short leave between assignments to visit her? A visit would have given her this assurance. Georgina no longer knew where their relationship was headed. She knew very little about Ray's past because he didn't share much personal information with her. His future was even more of a mystery to her. Did he neglect to share his future plans with her because he didn't know if he would return, or did he just avoid the usual information about money, dreams, children and marriage because it was unimportant to him?

Georgina's friends tried to convince her that Ray was sparing her embarrassment. This was the easy way for Ray to tell her that she wasn't in his future any longer. Molly coaxed her to move on and to make herself available again.

Once Ray headed to Korea, getting leave to go back to London was complicated. He didn't care much for paperwork and that would require a lot of time he didn't have. The other airmen had no desire to return to London. They were anxious to return home to the States. Not Ray, he didn't have a reason to go home. He was returning to London for the love of his life when the opportunity allowed.

Georgina was quickly becoming a recluse in her house and Molly couldn't stand by and watch that happen. "Georgina, forget about Ray and go to E-Jay's with me. You don't need to pursue a new relationship, but you need to get out," Molly urged. Georgina swore she would not drink one drop of alcohol. She got tipsy very easy and could not risk embarrassing herself in any way. "Okay, that's fine, I'm just thrilled you've decided to go out," Molly said.

In May of 1947 a new group of enlisted men arrived in London ready to begin their training. Glen Dornstadt was in this new group of talented trainees. He was eager to learn the latest technologies of the time. Like all of the other airmen waiting for reassignment, these men frequented E-Jay's Pub looking for temporary companionship. They danced and romanced the same women as the last group of men had.

Georgina turned away drink offers all night. She responded with various statements explaining her boyfriend's absence. She was quickly getting frustrated and scolded several men. She repeated over and over that she was there to be with her friends for an evening out. These statements worked for most of the men who approached her, but the occasional jerk had to be removed from the pub for harassment.

"Please accept those drinks Georgina, there are several of us here; we can share them," Molly begged. Her night was a disaster. She felt as though she were cheating on Ray. Georgina warned Molly not to ask her out again as her evening was nothing but a bad experience.

Georgina returned to her boring routine of working and staying home in the evenings. Molly often visited with Georgina and begged her to leave the house, but Georgina just didn't seem interested. She was determined to wait for Rays return. "Don't you realize that Ray might never come back?" Molly warned Georgina.

Weeks later Molly tried again. "Please come with me tonight," Molly begged. "I am meeting an airman from the United States Air Force and he is bringing a friend. These men are homesick and they need some companionship. Can't you just go with me tonight and keep them company? It has been a while since you went with me to E-Jay's. What do you say Georgina?" Molly coaxed her.

Georgina thought seriously about her situation and then reluctantly agreed to accompany Molly one more time. "Okay, but we are not leaving E-Jay's, not for any reason except to come home. Understand?" Georgina exclaimed.

"Great, I'm going home to get ready and I'll be back in an hour for you," Molly shared. She turned and rushed out the front door yelling. "Don't be late!" she yelled excitedly.

Molly and Georgina spent the evening getting to know their new friends. Glen Dornstadt and Kenny Umstead were both new in town and had never ventured far from home, let alone another continent. Georgina sat down and gazed in the direction of the men. She was immediately attracted to Glen. He was very good-looking with dark brown hair and blue eyes. He wasn't very tall but he had a very solid build. The two airmen were very respectful, kind, and funny with the girls that first night.

All evening Kenny and Glen treated the ladies like queens. Molly's crush on Glen was evident. She left that night disappointed that Glen was more interested in Georgina than in herself. She'd been in this predicament before, and she wasn't anxious to get involved with another man who would eventually break her heart so she immediately cut ties with both of the airmen. That wasn't what Molly was hoping to accomplish that night.

Guilt overcame Georgina when she found herself attracted to Glen. "*If I really love Ray, I wouldn't find anyone else exciting or interesting*," she thought to herself. Even though she rarely heard from Ray, she felt compelled to stay faithful to him, at least that night. After a few more lonely nights, she began to change her mind. Thoughts of Glen invaded her frequently. Letters from Ray were just about nonexistent. The occasional one that reached her was very brief with little or no information about how much he missed her or when to expect his return. Ray was more interested in his accomplishments than their relationship. Maybe it was time to move on.

Glen was leaving for Korea soon and as hard as he refrained from becoming involved in a serious relationship, his feelings for Georgina were obvious and hard to disguise. Normally, Glen was very strong-willed, but this beauty found his weak spot. Georgina was giving him mixed signals. Glen decided he better ask her out on a date before his departure to Korea. He asked Georgina out for dinner explaining that no commitment was involved. Other men warned him not to get involved. It was unlikely that he'd be able to return to London to maintain a relationship.

Glen was glad he ignored the warning because he and Georgina quickly developed a close relationship. Glen was everything to Georgina that Ray wasn't. He talked non stop about his family. He liked to take long walks, enjoyed candlelight dinners and he frequented the movies. He attended Church with Georgina and her family and enjoyed going to her house to play card games. Ray had little interest in getting to know her family better. All he usually talked about was his job, his career goals and how other airmen were so inefficient.

In no time Ray was only a memory. Her parents warned her to call off her commitment to Ray before she pursed a relationship with Glen. She snubbed their suggestions by saying, "I don't think I have a relationship with Ray any longer. I never hear from him," she relayed.

A month shy of Ray's discharge, Georgina received a letter from him.

Georgina,

I must return home to check on my family. My mother has been asking to see me for a while now. I'm going home to make sure she is okay. I will come back to London for you as soon as I possibly can. Please know you are in my heart and thoughts daily. I will be in touch

with you, when time allows. When I return we
will plan our future together.

Ray didn't even sign his letter. He was so vague that Georgina
was confused about what it was that she found in him to enter
into a relationship. She hoped he wasn't planning to return and
that he was just informing her of his discharge. Why couldn't he
find time to write more often? Why was he so mysterious? All of
a sudden, she was questioning everything about Ray. Georgina
was certain she no longer wanted Ray in her life. Her decision was
solid. People change; feelings change; and new people come into
our lives. Georgina still liked Ray but Glen took over her heart.
How could Ray expect her to still love him after months of little
or no communication?

Chapter 5
The Bad News

Ray planned a short visit to Texas with his family. Many changes took place the four years he was gone and he needed to make sure everyone was okay. Ray needed to make sure everything at home was under control. Then he'd visit with Georgina in London to ask her hand in marriage before he returned to Korea to take care of discharge formalities. There was nothing to keep him in Texas.

Family and friends were disappointed that Ray was in such a hurry to leave. He hadn't been home in four years and his friends wanted to spend some time with him. All he wanted to do was leave again. Joel Barns, Ray's best friend from school, waited anxiously for Ray's return. Joel hoped to introduce Ray to his wife and new baby. Ray revealed he was in a hurry to get to London where he had left his heart. "You know Ray, if this woman truly loves you, she'll wait just a few more days for your return," Joel told him. For the next half hour Ray and Joel talked about their relationships, their jobs, and their experiences over the past four years. Joel begged Ray to change his mind about leaving so soon, but Ray was focused on returning to London to marry Georgina.

Years of absence didn't change anything between Ray and his father. Tony Sr. was eager to pick up where he had left off with his son years earlier. Tony had a difficult time talking to any of his children without shouting and arguing. This was Tony's only way of communicating. He was a lazy, jealous person, who was always ready to put down those he considered to be do-gooders. His own sons suffered worse than anyone.

"I suppose you think because you served our country that makes you better than the rest of us, don't you, boy?" Tony Sr. said.

"Dad, I don't want to argue with you. I haven't been home for a long time. After only one day you're already starting fights. Can't you just relax for once? I came home for some peace and relaxation. Korea was very stressful. If this is what I must endure while staying here, I may as well leave for London today," Ray said.

Angrily Tony Buckley stood up, kicked his chair back against the wall, slammed his hand down on the table and then pointed his finger at Ray. "Well son, if you expect any pity from me, there's the door. You can leave now, but don't you cry to me about how tough life is. You don't know what tough is," Tony shouted.

A distant weak voice from the back of the house could be heard crying, "Don't you chase him away you bastard! He just got home. Give me a chance to spend time with him and catch up on his years of service to our Country," Agnes Buckley cried.

"Ah, you just shut up back there. Nobody wants to talk to you," Tony Sr. said.

"Dad, stop," Ray said. "I won't stay for long. I need to make sure Mom is seeing a doctor and getting proper medical care. I'm going to visit a few friends and then stop by Uncle Clay's gravesite," he explained.

Clay died in a terrible truck accident while Ray was in Korea. Clay was much closer to Ray's age than Tony Sr.'s, and they were more like brothers than uncle and nephew.

Clay was Tony Sr.'s youngest brother. Tony raised his brother after his mother passed away at a young age. Losing Clay was like losing one of his own children.

"I've been thinking son, you're right about fighting; I'd feel terrible if something were to happen to you, like what happened to your Uncle Clay. I still feel the pain every time I hear his name. You can stay as long as you like. Look, I even fixed up your room for your visit. No one else uses it and I want to you stay here a while. I'm sorry about arguing with you. Things aren't too good here and I just needed someone to take out my frustrations on. I guess you walked through the door at the wrong time," Tony Sr. said.

"Thanks Dad, I appreciate your honesty. Either way I'm not staying for long. I have a lovely girlfriend in London waiting for me. Here, look at her picture," Ray said proudly. He had a lot of love to share with Georgina. He almost couldn't remember why he had returned home. He had hoped that since he was away for so long his family would be eager to see him and welcome him home. After his exposure to how other men's families treated them, Ray had hoped his family had changed. When he discovered that nothing had changed, he tired of them quickly.

He would soon visit with Georgina and make her his wife. Ray decided they would stay in London. He could handle living anywhere, as long as Georgina was by his side. There was no reason for him to return to Texas. During the past four years of service to his country his daily thoughts of Georgina got him through some pretty bad situations. Ray didn't care if he ever returned to the United States. He'd leave that decision up to Georgina. As soon as Ray had definite travel plans he sent Georgina the following telegram:

My Beautiful Princess:

My flight arrives Tuesday at 6:40 PM. I hope
I can depend on you for a ride to the Graystone
Hotel where I have reservations. I can't wait to
see your smiling face.

Forever yours, Ray

When Ray arrived, he never anticipated what was about
to happen. He hoped Georgina would run into his open arms.
Instead, her parents accompanied her. All of a sudden he had
a bad feeling of awkwardness and fear. Ray was baffled about
his cool greeting. He had many questions as to why she had
responded as she did. He certainly wouldn't take advantage of
her. Georgina's lack of excitement and enthusiasm concerned him.
Something just wasn't right. Once again that awful cramping
began in his stomach.

"Ray, it was very difficult for me waiting for your return. I
stayed home as much as possible, but I was lonely, so I went out
with my friends," Georgina said.

"That's okay. I understand. You can't stay home all the time,"
Ray said.

"No Ray, you don't understand. I met someone else while you
were gone. I wrote you daily waiting to hear something from you,
but you never responded. I didn't know if you were dead or alive. I
thought maybe you were ignoring my letters. When I didn't hear
from you, I decided you weren't interested any longer. Just in case
you were still interested, I didn't want to give you any reason to
get discouraged, so I was very careful about what I said in those
letters. I think the world of you, and I've read how easily enlisted
men give up when someone they love ends a relationship. I have
heard of soldiers throwing themselves in front of firing lines. I
couldn't live with myself if something like that happened to you,"
Georgina shared.

"I'm sorry Ray but I can't see you anymore. I have been dating another man and he'll be returning soon. He has visited me twice in the last two years. I receive letters from him regularly. You didn't come back even once. I wasn't sure if you and I still had a relationship. I know it's difficult for you to open up and to share your feelings, but you could have written to me more often. Maybe if I knew of your plans, or your intentions, I might have remained faithful to you. I have nothing else to say," Georgina said.

"I never told you the relationship was over. I would have informed you of that, if that were the case. I thought we had an agreement. I love you, this can't be the end. I won't let it be the end. I can't believe you're ending our relationship like this. It's not easy being an officer in the Air Force. I thought you understood our relationship would continue when I returned. How did you expect me to continue to pursue you when I was over three thousand miles away? Distance and time were against me. I had tons of paperwork to complete and you wanted me to drop everything and find time to write to you? I didn't know you wanted me to ignore my country's security and cater to your needs instead! How was I to know that you were planning on ruining my future if I choose to protect my country? Sorry that I am faithful and committed to the United States. I guess its best that I find out now how dedicated and committed you are instead of finding out after we're married. I'm not good at expressing my feelings, so I don't know what else to say," Ray said shaking.

"I didn't know you were still interested? How long did you expect me to wait to hear from you? I haven't heard from you in months, except for that letter telling me you were going home. I didn't know when you planned to return, if ever. I'm sorry, but my mind is made up," Georgina said, no longer able to look Ray in the face.

"You go then. I don't want to impose on you. I'll find a ride to the Graystone. Just know that I don't give up easily. Oh and here, this picture belongs to you. It was the inspiration that carried me through the last few years of hell and torment. I especially want to thank you for not notifying me of your decision. Your picture might have saved my life. Before you go, can I ask one final question? I think you owe that much to me," Ray said with a stutter and a weak voice.

"What is your question?" Georgina asked hesitantly.

"What's your new boyfriend's name? I want to meet him. I want to make sure he's going to take care of you. I need to know for peace of mind," Ray said.

"No, Georgina. You don't have to answer that question," Myron said. "Let's go," Bernice said.

"Wait," Georgina said. "I'll answer his question. He's right, I did accept his ring and told him I would wait," Georgina said. "My new boyfriend is Glen Dornstadt from Pennsylvania. He's in the Air Force too. He likes it here, and he is willing to live in London.

I know so much more about him than I ever knew about you, Ray. I know he has four brothers and three sisters. I also know his father was in Germany during World War I. His parents met there while his father served his country. The grandparents and their daughters hid soldiers in an underground cellar while Russians searched their house looking for infiltrators. Glen's father was one of those soldiers. He fell in love with Kathryn. She helped take care of him. They didn't even speak the same language, but they got past that barrier. He promised to take her back to the States if he ever got out of Germany alive. They headed back to the US with a new baby and hardly any money. They found a home in Pennsylvania, and the rest is history," Georgina informed Ray.

She started to shake and cry as she yelled at Ray, "and I don't know anything like that about you. Damn you Ray, why didn't you share that kind of information with me?

"We can talk, and I will share all of that information with you. We had so little time together. I just wanted to learn about you. I didn't know you wanted to talk about my family history. I didn't know that was important to you. I only cared about you, not about my family," Ray said shaking.

"You don't get it, do you Ray? We had that opportunity. You didn't care about our families. All you ever talked about was how to make yourself look better to your troops. I knew about all of your trainings. I heard every nasty comment you made about your fellow officers. You never asked about my past or my family. You never talked about your parents or Texas. Learning about each other wasn't important to you. You never opened up to me about yourself. Glen told me all about himself and his family. I fell in love with him because of his sincerity and his desire to share information with me about his past, and his love of his family. He's not shy when it comes to expressing his love to me. I'm just not interested in maintaining a relationship with you any longer. I want you to leave now," Georgina said.

Ray was on the next flight out of London. He was in shock and his stomach was killing him. He had absolutely no desire to return home after his discharge. His father's comments would tear right through him if he returned home empty-handed. There had to be a way that he could make Georgina's information work to his advantage. *"That Glen guy—the other man—he is in the Air Force too, and he's a traitor. You just don't do that to a fellow airman. I know people who will help me ruin that traitor's life forever. He'll be sorry he ever interfered with another man's woman,"* Ray promised himself.

As soon as his discharge was final, Ray planned to return home to Texas, but probably not for long. He had a lot of time to think during that long trip back to Korea to finalize his release from his camp and then return to his main base in North Carolina. He had lots of time to formulate a plan to win Georgina back, and if that meant re-enlisting, then he would do so. What other choice did he have?

Chapter 6
Pulling Rank

On a bright sunny morning six weeks after his release, Ray paid a visit to Pope Air Force base near Fayetteville, NC. Technical Sergeant John Sawyer eagerly greeted him. Ray had a good feeling about the impending meeting. Hopefully, it was going to be very productive for him.

"So you're thinking of re-enlisting?" Sergeant Sawyer asked.

"Yes, but I'd prefer not to go back to Korea. Is there any way you can guarantee that I won't be sent back to that hellhole?" Ray asked.

"You surprise me Ray. You of all people should know there are no guarantees in the Air Force. I can write that guarantee, but you know that a guarantee is not worth the paper it is written on, especially if you have angered the wrong person," Sawyer said, turning away from Ray. "Why don't we get the paperwork out of the way and once again you can be a proud airman in the Air Force. You'll need to go through a four-week retraining and then you'll return to your old rank of airman first class. How does that sound to you?" Sergeant Sawyer asked.

"Great, I'm in," Ray said.

It didn't take Ray long to move up in rank. He was eager to continue learning about securing the United States borders and civilians. There was no time to goof off and Ray was going to make sure that enlistees under him felt the same way.

Ray developed a stomach ailment soon after his first enlistment. Whatever he was suffering from was getting worse. Anxiety and stress caused his condition to leave him in a great deal of pain. His cramping and diarrhea was escalating quickly and Ray claimed his relationship complications with Georgina were to blame. His treatments had become ineffective.

Now that he was back in the Air Force Ray needed to find out about Glen Dornstadt. He became nervous and had a difficult time concentrating while he waited to receive Glen's records.

Glen had spent only a few months in Korea when he was suddenly transferred to Puerto Rico for training to instruct other airman on how to parachute out of airplanes and helicopters. This was crucial for survival in war time. Even though Glen loved his position in the Air Force, like most airmen, when the time came he was ready to sign his discharge papers and get on with his life.

Glen sent Georgina a postcard informing her that he didn't know how long it would take to complete his final paperwork, but as soon as he was done he was going home to see his family. He gave her an approximate time period when to expect his return to London.

Glen was eager to return to Pennsylvania. His mother and father were still married, but his father wasn't home much. On his occasional visits home he'd stay long enough to mend some fences, clean up and repair his small farm and have a drink with old friends. Niles had a difficult time staying sober long enough to complete the much needed repairs. He'd often fight with his wife and children and then leave abruptly. His family rarely knew his location but he always returned home when he needed money and a place to sleep. Before Glen enlisted he promised his Mother he'd come home every chance he had. Guilty feelings of neglect overcame him once he started visiting with Georgina on his leaves. Finally after a two year absence Glen needed to check in on his Mother for peace of mind.

Glen's desire to take care of his mother was a quality that Georgina admired. She knew that if Glen was that considerate with his family, he would be that way with her too.

Glen returned home to discover his Mother's health deteriorating. All of his younger brothers except Kevin were now enlisted in a branch of the service. Kevin was still in school and had very little money to help his ailing mother with her house. Kathryn Dornstadt was a small stocky, fifty-five-year-old woman with a deep German accent and a strong will. She was your typical devoted mother and grandmother with nine children and many grandchildren, but no one was taking care of her? Because of Kathryn's serious health problems, her worthless husband and her inability to work, her large home needed multiple repairs. Glen didn't have much money, but his mother had always been there for him when he had needed her. Now she needed his help and he wasn't going to let her down.

"I'm only going to stay a little while, Mom. I'm going to get your house cleaned and your garden started and then I'll be leaving again. I met a wonderful woman while I was training in London and we've become very close. I'd like to get to know her better. If I have my way she will become my bride. I'm certain you'll love her as much as I do. I will bring her home to meet you as soon as I can. I promised her if we get married we'll live in London," Glen shared.

Kathryn Dornstadt was pleased for her son, but sad that he was leaving again. She wanted the best for all of her children. It would be wonderful to see Glen happy, but she didn't want to see him move to London.

"Glen, why don't you bring her to Pennsylvania to live?" Kathryn asked weakly

"I'd love to, Mom, but I promised her she wouldn't have to leave London. She has agreed to come to the States to meet my family, and maybe someday try living here. For now, it's on her terms, and when she's ready, we'll give it a try," Glen said.

That's not what Kathryn wanted to hear but she couldn't make those choices for her son; she had to let him go.

"Glen I want you to be happy. I hope she takes good care of you. You will be such a good man with the right woman. You are the most generous out of all of my children. You are easy to talk to and I can't bear the thought of someone hurting you. She won't do that, will she?" Kathryn questioned.

"No Mom, she is very sweet. She and I are so much alike; we share the same desires in life," Glen assured his mother. "I hope she feels the same way Glen. You deserve the best," Kathryn said.

After nearly three weeks at home with his mother, Glen made arrangements to return to London. His plane was scheduled to leave early Monday morning. Before Glen left he promised his mother he'd visit with each of his sisters. He told them about his situation and that he would be leaving for London on Monday. He promised to keep in touch. With the exception of Kevin, his brothers were scattered all over the country and not easy to locate. Glen promised his mother that he would make an effort to reach them once he was settled in London.

Glen returned home from visiting his sisters on Sunday evening. He packed his belongings and spent what seemed like hours saying good-bye to his mother. There was no one else in the world he loved more than her. Leaving her so soon was very difficult for him.

Sunday evening while double-checking his travel plans, a brown Jeep pulled up to the front of the house. A man dressed in an Air Force uniform knocked at the door. "Are you lost?" Glen asked the man. "I don't think so," he said. "I believe you are who I am looking for?"

"No, not me, I don't think so; I am no longer enlisted," Glen said. "I have been out of the Air Force for almost four weeks. I am the only one of my brother's who was in the Air Force, I'm sure you have the wrong address," Glen shared.

"Are you Glen Dornstadt?" the airman asked. If you are, I have orders to pick you up and take you to your base in North Carolina. I don't know why or who made the request; I am just following my orders. You must come with me right away," the airman warned.

"This is ridiculous. I am going to miss my plane to London. My flight leaves early tomorrow morning," Glen said told the airman.

"Not anymore," the officer said. "Your reservations were canceled, you are coming with me." "Okay, but I'll need to send a telegram to my friend in London. She will be waiting for me at the airport, and if I am not there, she will be worried," Glen said in a stern low voice.

"Look, I was sent to retrieve you as fast as possible. Can't we do this after we arrive in North Carolina?" the airman asked. "No way," Glen said. "I know how the Air Force works. If I don't do this first, I may not be given the opportunity to notify my friend once I arrive. This is your choice, let me send her a telegram or I'm not returning with you. I am not the property of the United States Air Force any longer, so what can they do to me?" Glen asked.

"Okay, but make it quick," he warned.

My Dearest Georgina,

I'm sorry to inform you that I ran into some complications with the Air Force. I have been instructed to return to my base in North Carolina. There must be some unfinished paperwork for me to sign in order to finalize my discharge. I will be in touch with you as soon as I can reschedule my flight to London.

Love, Glen.

Georgina was disappointed again. "What's up with these enlisted men? Glen has ruined all of your plans for a welcome home party. The food is prepared, and the decorations are in place and we don't have anything to celebrate," Bernice stated.

"We'll just have to wait and have the party for him when he finally returns," Georgina said to her mother. Once again Bernice was very concerned for her daughter. She remembered the difficult times Georgina went through while courting Ray and the amount of time she spent waiting for him. Many nights Georgina cried herself to sleep. Georgina finally appeared happy with Glen. Now this! Bernice prayed that this was just a very temporary setback.

"Georgina has been through enough with American men," Bernice said to Myron. "This one better not disappoint her too," she relayed.

"Well, maybe she's better off. She should stick to dating local fellows," Myron said.

When Glen arrived in North Carolina he was informed that his discharged had been revoked. "They don't do this in the Air Force," Glen insisted. "Since we have so many injured enlistees and not enough new recruits joining our forces, we are revoking discharges. You will be serving at least another two years with us," the officer informed him.

Georgina waited patiently to hear some news from Glen. She wrote him letters and even sent his Mother a telegram.

Dear Mrs. Dornstadt

My name is Georgina Steiner. I am Glen's girlfriend from London. Can you tell me how to find Glen? He seemed to leave in a rush and I am concerned for his safety. Do you have an address where I can reach him? Please help me. Anything you can tell me will be appreciated.

Sincerely,
Georgina Steiner

Unfortunately, because of Kathryn's weak knowledge of the written English language, Georgina's telegram went unanswered. Kathryn couldn't identify that piece of mail from her other mail and she disposed of it. Georgina never received a reply.

Finally about six weeks later on a beautiful day came a knock at the Steiner's door. It was a telegram for Georgina.

Dear Georgina,

I am so sorry about my lack of communications. Because there is a shortage of new recruits during an active war, and my prior outstanding performance, the Air Force has revoked my discharge. I have been assigned an additional two years of service. "So much for good performance" I will be in touch with you, as soon as possible. Please be patient. I don't like this interruption any more than you do.

I miss you terribly and can't wait till we meet again.

Love, Glen

Glen was all too familiar with Georgina's disgust with Ray's lack of communications and cancellation of plans. Glen wasn't about to let that happen to her again.

Myron didn't buy Glen's excuse. As far as he knew, the Air Force couldn't just revoke his discharge like that. After all, Glen had served his entire four year commitment. This was just another disrespectful American soldier hurting his little girl. Didn't any of these men have any morals? Georgina was going to get hurt again, and he couldn't bear telling her that this was just a poor excuse to end their relationship.

Hearing Glen's news made the rest of the Steiner's happy, especially Bernice. Georgina no longer questioned Glen's intentions. At least he had a good reason for his absence and Georgina was relieved that Glen was okay. He just wouldn't do this to her intentionally. Breathing a sigh of relief, Georgina went for a walk in the park to expel some of her excitement. All of a sudden Georgina heard a familiar man's voice calling her. She turned around to see Ray Buckley coming directly towards her.

"Ray, what are you doing here?" she asked.

"With Glen out of our way now, I intend to spend some well-deserved time together with you. I am hoping you will see it's me that you really love. Glen was just filling a void while I was gone. Let me prove that to you. I can't forget you Georgina. Give me a chance to spark your memory. You'll find that you have always loved me," Ray said.

"Ray, tell me you didn't have anything to do with Glen being recalled to duty in the Air Force. Tell me the truth, because none of this makes sense to me. Glen signed all of his discharge papers; how could he be forced to serve another two years?" Georgina asked.

"Let's not talk about Glen. Let's get to know each other again. If you'll just give me the opportunity, I will make you the happiest woman alive, but you've got to forget Glen and give me another chance," Ray said.

"I don't want you. Don't you understand that? I want Glen. You stay away from me," Georgina said.

"You're not listening to me. Let's try courting all over again. I know we can get as close as we were before I went to Korea. If I must open up and tell you about my past, then I will do so. I'll tell you anything you want to know," Ray said.

Chapter 7
Despair

Glen was instructed to report to Osan Air Force base in Korea. Once he arrived he discovered he was assigned to a remote camp so far away from civilization it would take days to receive goods, medical services, and mail. The area was pristine, untouched by the horrors of war. He was very distraught about this location. He knew he would have very little opportunity to get mail out to Georgina. He must have really angered someone to be sent to such a remote location.

After 4 weeks at this location he was transferred to a camp 40 miles south of Seoul. This was where he expected to go to battle, yet he was assigned to desk duty. Although he wasn't fighting in battles, he was surrounded by the effects of the war.

Stories depicting poor living conditions in Korea during the conflict were somewhat true, but much worse than reported. Most soldiers saw only the most unfortunate and destitute citizens. Battles, fighting, and explosive events were held far away from the wealthy and progressive people of Korea. Only a few lucky soldiers would witness such prosperity. The majority of Koreans had very little in assets and most had absolutely nothing. Necessities that we take for granted—clean running water, finished floors, beds, doctors, and hospitals—were an unknown commodity to most Koreans.

Soldiers left Korea with undiagnosed mental afflictions. Many exhibited symptoms of anguish, despair, and depression. A soldier knew there was nothing or very little he could do to change the lives of these very poor, destitute people. Repeated suggestions to seek safety and to leave were shrugged off by people so dedicated to their country that abdicating was not a choice. Heartache and despair were observed everywhere. People only knew the poor life. They were content to live the only way they knew. Still, these poor citizens were always willing to give everything they had to the soldiers who helped them. Guilt kept many a starving soldier from taking food from struggling civilians, but at times, food was a welcome offering.

Maintaining communications with family from a combat area was difficult. Phone service was terrible and only used for emergencies. Most often it was days between mail service.

For some reason after only two months, Glen's assignment in Korea was cancelled. He was ordered to return to North Carolina and assigned another desk position. He was confused about all of these transfers but he was relieved to get out of Korea. Correspondence with his family and Georgina could now resume. He sent out mail at least twice a week, but he rarely, if ever received mail. When he did, it was usually from home. Why wasn't Georgina writing back to him?

Glen finally received a letter from Georgina informing him of the party she had planned for his return to London. She mentioned that she would hold on to the decorations for his eventual return. Feelings of guilt flooded Glen. *"She went all out for me, and I let her down"*.

Glen knew that his revoked discharge was a farce and a payback for angering the wrong person. This was not how the Air Force operated, and someone had created a lot of favors and pulled many strings to do this to him. Eventually he would get to the bottom of this evil act—when he had a free moment.

During the Korean conflict, soldiers were paid good money to re-enlist. They were offered incentives and rewarded with an additional fourteen days of leave per year. Initially Glen was not offered these incentives, but his persistence paid off and he eventually received his incentives. Glen planned to schedule leave as soon as possible to go to London and maybe coax Georgina to come back with him. He was also going to make inquiries regarding his re-assignment. Glen wrote to Georgina and informed her to be ready to go to the States on a few days' notice. Glen never received a response to his request. He was well aware that Georgina might not be interested in traveling home with him any longer. He couldn't take a chance on leaving her behind if she was still interested in him, and in meeting his family. Cost was not important to him, but Georgina was.

Glen didn't know that while he was planning to make Georgina his bride, Ray was making his move to steal her back.

Saturday morning when Georgina and her mother made their regular trip to the food store a familiar voice greeted them. "Good morning ladies, it's so nice to come upon such a lovely site. How would you like to join me for lunch?" Ray inquired. Georgina stood in disbelief and reminded him, "I can't Ray, I'm waiting for Glen to return."

"Georgina," Ray said, "I know you don't have feelings for me any longer, but I am going to be in London possibly for the next two years on a special mission, and I am also here for medical care. You might as well get used to seeing me around. There's a doctor in London who specializes in stomach ailments for veterans. He will be treating my illness. Since I am in London anyhow, why don't we make the best of my time here and renew our friendship? If you won't join me for lunch today: how about dinner tomorrow night?" Ray urged.

"Absolutely not, you're a scoundrel. I know you had Glen's discharge revoked. You did this against his wishes and I can't trust you. No, I am not going to go to dinner with you. Not now. Not ever. So save your breath, and don't ask me again," Georgina relayed in an annoyed tone.

Ray couldn't let Georgina's attitude frustrate him. That familiar pain in his stomach was returning. Now Ray was certain this situation was the root of his sickness. There had to be some way to trick Georgina into meeting him away from her home and family. Ray enlisted the imagination of his friend Joe Kisko. Joe was the most scandalous and devious person Ray knew.

Georgina was an aid at Saints of Mercy Hospital in the Village of Highspire, south of London. She walked four blocks every day to catch the bus to work. Most days she arrived home by four thirty PM. On occasions, she'd work three to four hours later through the dinner hour.

One evening Bernice was getting worried when, by nine PM she still hadn't heard from her daughter, and she didn't get off of the last bus for the night. Bernice went down the street to E-Jay's Pub to look for her daughter. When she didn't find her there she called the hospital to see if Georgina was still working.

"This is Bernice Steiner," she said when the phone was answered. "Can you direct me to the third floor?" she asked. When the person answered, Bernice asked, "Could you tell me what time Georgina left from work?" A nurse replied, "I'm sure her usual time of three forty-five PM."

"Oh, I see. Well, can you tell me if she left with anyone or if she mentioned that she was stopping some where? I am her mother, and she is not home yet," Bernice informed her. If you can hold for a minute Mrs. Steiner, I will ask around to see if anyone knows where she might have gone. I'll be right back, okay?" the soft female voice said in a concerned tone. "That will work my dear," Bernice responded with hope in her voice.

After a few minutes a very concerned nurse replied. "Mrs. Steiner I am sorry. No one saw her leave, and no one heard her mention anything out of the ordinary. If we hear anything we will be in touch with you."

Bernice Steiner was worried. This was so unlike her daughter. She's never done anything like this before. Bernice decided to visit Scotland Yard to report a possible missing person. When she arrived the officers were busy with serious crimes and problems. After two hours, an investigator listened to her concerns.

"Now let me get this straight to make sure I have all of the information correct. We have a twenty-three-year-old attractive female with lots of friends? It is only one AM; don't you think this is a bit premature? She will probably be home when you get there," the officer said.

"I don't think so Officer Brody. She doesn't have any transportation home unless she walks, and that would be at least six miles for her, and it's only thirty-five degrees outside. That is not like her at all. If you can't do your job sir, maybe I need to speak to your superior," Bernice said. With that, she proceeded to walk right through the door into the captain's office.

"Where is he?" she asked. "He doesn't come in until seven AM, Mrs. Steiner. Why don't you go home, and if Georgina isn't home in the morning, come back, and we'll talk," Officer Brody said.

"You don't understand, Mr. Brody. If she is not there now, she won't be home in the morning; I can almost guarantee that," Bernice relayed. "Well it's your choice Mrs. Steiner. You can wait here until morning or go home and get some sleep," Officer Brody said sternly. "I'll be back at 6:30 AM, Bernice said in an irritated voice.

Ray Buckley had tricked Georgina. He coaxed his friend Alex Packer into asking Molly out for a date. He urged her to bring a friend because he had a friend who just wanted someone to dine with for the evening. They'd meet at the Crossfire Restaurant at five thirty PM for the Friday night buffet and dance. Alex's friend did not show up. Ray happened to be dining at the Crossfire with a very glamorous woman. She had on a long, sleek, red dress with a bit of cleavage showing. She wore silver dangly earrings, and her blond hair was tossed in a bun on her head. Georgina turned her back to Ray. She didn't want him to see her. Unfortunately, seeing Ray with another woman really hurt. *"I don't understand this; I should be happy for him,"* Georgina told herself. Eventually Ray and his date approached Georgina's table.

"Good evening Georgina. I'd like you to meet my friend Rachel Harris," Ray said. "Hello, good seeing you again Ray," Georgina said. The women both glanced at each other and said "hi" at the same time. "You ladies have a good evening now. Rachel and I must be on our way," Ray snickered.

"Wow, imagine that. I didn't think he'd get over you so fast. It looks like he found a real beauty," Molly said. "Well, I hope she makes him happy," Georgina sighed.

A short time later Ray returned by himself. He sat at the bar alone. Eventually he went over to the table where Georgina was seated and asked if he could sit with them. Reluctantly, Georgina allowed Ray to join them for a drink. Georgina discovered she was enjoying Ray's company. It was the first step in his plan to win Georgina back. Ray continued to buy drinks for both women so it wouldn't look like he was playing favorites. Georgina was having such a good time with Ray that she lost track of time. It had been months since she let down her guard and relaxed. Tonight she was going to forget about Glen.

Georgina arrived home at two thirty AM., unaware that her parents were worried about her; she went straight to her room and planned to sleep in late the next morning. When Bernice Steiner finally returned home from Scotland Yard, she noticed that Georgina's bedroom door was closed. Bernice was positive that it was open when she left. When Bernice opened the bedroom door she found Georgina sound asleep. Bernice was surprised and rather upset with her daughter's lack of communication and disregard for her parents concern.

Bernice woke up Georgina for an explanation. Georgina was sure that she had told her parents that she would be late, so she wasn't worried about the time she had come home. Bernice was certain that Georgina had not informed her that she would be late.

"Mom," Georgina said, "I told you two nights ago I was going out with Molly and some friends. Can we discuss this in the morning? I am really tired," Georgina said. "You bet we will!" Bernice said, as she headed to her bedroom upset.

"Bernice, I thought I told you to mind your own business," Myron said. "When she wakes, I want an explanation as to why we weren't told about her plans," Bernice said.

"You should have waited until morning after you've both had some rest before you badgered her and played detective. Food and rest always make for a better conversation," Myron said.

In the morning Georgina approached the kitchen with apprehension. "Mom, Dad, I am really sorry for worrying you like that last night. I am positive I told you about my plans. I haven't heard from Glen for several weeks now, and I know I'm not thinking straight. Maybe I thought I told you and forgot. Anyhow, last night I was with Molly and her friend Alex. Ray was dining there, so he joined us. Ray makes me realize how much I miss Glen," Georgina reassured her parents.

"I think you have made the right choice. Ray is a nice man, but how could you go wrong with Glen? He's a real gentleman. I'm sorry for being so hard on you, I was just worried about you," Bernice scolded her daughter.

A few months went by and there was still no correspondence from Glen. Georgina was losing hope. She wondered if something had happened to Glen. She decided to go to the American embassy to find out what she could about him. Maybe Ray was right— maybe soldiers get so involved in their duties that they just lose track of time and neglect their loved ones.

The American embassy said they would let her know if they received any information about Glen.

The next morning, Ray Buckley knocked on the Steiners' door. "Good morning beautiful. How is your day going so far? I meant to ask you, do you and Glen have any wedding plans or hasn't your relationship gone that far yet?" Ray asked. "The Air Force took him away from me before we got that far. He only has eight more months, and he'll be back; I just know it," Georgina said.

"Don't you remember how long it was that I went without hearing from you? You told me that sometimes it is difficult to find time to write. You said you were so busy that time just flies by and before you know it, you have lost another day, another week, and another month. Well I assume that must hold true for Glen too," Georgina stated.

"Well you haven't asked what has brought me here, so I must tell you. The American embassy has sent me to inform you that Glen was injured in an accident almost three months ago. His prognosis is not good. He has serious wounds to both legs and shoulders. He also suffered minor head and chest injuries. He will be months in recovery, and to make matters worse for you, they moved him to Walter Reed Hospital in Washington, D.C." Ray said solemnly.

"I want to go visit him! Do you know how much money I will need to get there? Then I will need enough to stay in a hotel and then more money to get back home? Ray, I need your help," Georgina said. "I'll need somewhere to stay. Maybe I could get a job there and I would be able to visit with him every day, and when he gets better, we could get married," Georgina said.

"Whoa, wait a minute, not so fast." Ray said. This plan was going to backfire on him. When he heard Georgina had gone to the embassy for information, he thought he had had it all worked out. Up until now this plan had sounded like a good idea. It would be too bad if it all came crashing down on him. "*I need to come up with a quick solution. What else can I tell her to keep them apart,*" Ray thought.

"Georgina, don't rush into anything yet. I need to make sure he's going to stay at Walter Reed. I don't believe you would even recognize Glen, and I don't think he would recognize you either. His head injuries have caused him memory problems. Why don't you wait a few months? I'll keep you posted on his prognosis. In the meantime, I'll be traveling back and forth from London to

North Carolina on a regular schedule and I'll be able to give you updates," Ray said.

"Why do you go back and forth so much?" Georgina said. "I'm involved in a special forces investigation. I can't tell you anything about it. This investigation requires a lot traveling in order for me to report new security information. I expect this will take months. I'm sorry to bring you bad new. I must be going now. Try and have a good day," Ray shared.

Georgina was beside herself. She felt terrible for Glen. "I can't believe all of this," she told her mother. "Something just isn't right. I don't know why, but I think Ray is lying to me. I wish I knew how to contact Glen's family. Maybe they could keep me informed about his condition," Georgina said to her mother.

Just as Georgina thought she had made the decision to go to the States, she received a Western Union telegram from the American embassy in London.

Dear Ms. Steiner;

Per your inquiry regarding Glen Dornstadt:
our investigation has been completed. No record
of him exists anywhere in Europe. However, an
Airman that fits your description is listed on the
Raleigh, North Carolina roster. There have been
no reports of injury to this airman.

If we can be of additional assistance, please
don't hesitate to contact us.

Sincerely,

George Hamm,
Embassy Representative

Chapter 8
What's Going On?

Glen's next leave was approved and he was eager to get to London to get some answers. His moods had become increasing somber lately. He promised Georgina that he would keep in touch, and he expected her to do the same. She hadn't answered any of his letters in over eleven months. He was preparing himself for the ultimate disappointment and he'd deal with that news when he got it.

On his way out he stopped by Mark Mills' office to inform him that he was headed for London this time. His family needed him too but he used most of his leave to go home to Pennsylvania. "You certainly earned this time off, Glen. You have a safe and happy trip," Mark said.

On his return to North Carolina, Ray needed to figure out a way to explain his lie about Glen's accident. This time he had really gotten himself into a tough situation. He should have checked more thoroughly then he would have known that Glen had been granted leave. Unaware of Glen's impending travel plans, the worst of his problems were about to blow up in his face. He wouldn't be able to return to London for nearly a month. Ray assumed he had some time to formulate another plan to keep

Glen and Georgina apart. He couldn't allow Georgina time to plan a trip to Washington. If she came up with the money to fly to Washington and didn't find Glen, how would he explain Glen's absence to her?

Ray often had a difficult time tracking Glen. The men's paths rarely crossed and Glen's commanding officer was not eager to share any private and personal information about his location. Ray thought if he left Glen in the care of Mark Mills, Mark would keep him posted about Glen's impending leave. Ray knew that as long as Glen was in North Carolina, he wasn't with Georgina, and that resolved many problems. Another obstacle Ray encountered was the mail. He paid people to intercept it so that no correspondence was getting through. He personally intercepted nearly seventy letters in eleven months. Both Glen's to Georgina and Georgina's to Glen.

"I am going to marry this woman, and I will do whatever it takes to keep them apart," Ray thought to himself on the ride back to North Carolina.

Glen arrived in London at eleven thirty PM Greenwich time. It was too late to visit with anyone at this hour. He'd wait until morning to visit the Steiners. It was going to be a long night and possibly a longer day, depending on Georgina's response.

Glen was up with the birds. He just didn't sleep well in anticipation of what might happen. *"Some days just aren't worth getting up for, but maybe today will be a good day,"* Glen said to himself as he checked to make sure his room door was locked on his way out. He walked down the street and headed directly to the Steiner's residence. When Myron opened the door to get his morning paper he saw Glen sitting on the swing. Glen knew everything was going to be okay.

"For heaven's sakes, where have you been?" Myron asked. "Hey, look who's here? Georgina, come. Come now," Myron said.

Georgina ran into Glen's arms. He'd been waiting a long time for this moment, and he had forgotten how good it felt to hold her.

"This is going to be better than I imagined. Unless maybe Georgina has plans to dump me like she did Ray," Glen thought to himself.

"Oh Glen, I can't begin to describe the emptiness that has just been filled by your return. Ray told me you were injured and had been taken to a Hospital in Washington, D.C. I was going to go to the States to be with you just as soon as I figured out a way to get to there. Why would he lie to me like that?" Georgina asked.

"I'm not sure and I don't care. I just want to be with you now," Glen said. He was so happy to be greeted this way. He would follow up with Georgina's information later.

"How did you get here? Why didn't you call me and let me know you were coming?" Georgina asked Glen.

"One question at a time! Since you didn't answer any of my letters I assumed you weren't interested in me any longer, so I—" Glen started.

"What letters?" Georgina said. "I never got any letters, only one about six weeks after your re-enlistment. I didn't understand why you couldn't write just once a month, but I didn't receive any letters," She informed him.

"Are you sure? I wrote you at least twice a week at first. Then when you didn't respond, I cut back to once a week and then once every two weeks, but I have never stopped writing to you and hoped to hear something from you eventually," Glen said.

"I wrote to you all of the time. I never gave up. I hoped when you read my letters you would realize how much I missed you. I assumed you missed me too. I slowed down on the amount I sent you too, but I never stopped writing you," Georgina said.

"I smell a rat here, but I will follow-up on this when I get back to North Carolina. Don't you worry your pretty self about any of this; it is all a big mix-up. Oh, and I really missed you too," Glen said.

"North Carolina? When are you going there?" Georgina asked. "I'm on a two week leave. Then I must return to my base," Glen said. "Are you done in Korea?" Georgina said. "I was only in Korea two months when for some reason I was ordered to return to North Carolina. I was able to get desk duty and some minimal travel duty. Compared to Korea, I really like North Carolina," Glen said. "Ray told me you were in Korea. I don't understand," Georgina said. "I didn't come here to solve a mystery. I will figure all of this out later. If you are interested in me, I suggest we go for a walk and catch up on the last several months," Glen said. "Okay, let me comb my hair and put on shoes," Georgina said.

"Glen, I need a minute with you," Myron said. "I have never seen a woman so patient and certain of her feelings. It's like she had a sixth sense about you. She was certain that you would return. Then when Ray stopped by to tell her you were injured, she was determined to see you. You are a lucky man; she really loves you. We'd consider ourselves lucky to have you part of our family," Myron said.

"Thank you, Mr. Steiner—ah Myron—I appreciate your sincerity. I have been going crazy wondering why I didn't hear from Georgina. I'm sure someone is up to no good and I will get this mess straighten out when I return. This man will not ruin our relationship any longer. When I didn't hear from Georgina I thought for sure ... well, never mind. It doesn't matter what I thought, I was wrong," Glen said.

"I'm ready. Where do you want to go?" Georgina asked with excitement in her voice.

"Let's just walk and talk to make up for lost time. I have almost two weeks here. That should be plenty of time to catch up," Glen said.

"Are you going to visit your family while you're off," Georgina asked. "Not this time. When I leave here, I will have a little less than eight months left to serve. I'll still have enough time left for a few weekend visits. Once I'm discharged I'll return home to visit with my family. Then I'll come back to spend the rest of my life with you. I can't describe how happy you've made me. My heart is healed because I thought for sure you weren't interested any longer," Glen said staring at Georgina with passion in his eyes. "Glen, let's not waste time. My feelings for you won't change, so why don't I come back with you and we can get married in North Carolina," Georgina said.

"What about your family? I think they would want to attend the wedding. I will be back soon. Time will fly by quickly and we'll be married in no time, you'll see," Glen said. "Well okay, but I thought we could put an end to waiting. I'm sure Ray is doing everything possible to keep us apart. The sooner we marry the less chance he'll have accomplishing his devious tricks," Georgina said. "Don't worry, I won't let him come between us ever again," Glen said.

Ray returned to his base in North Carolina and started working on a plan to keep Georgina from coming to the United States. First he needed to pay a visit to Mark Mills.

"Mark my friend," Ray said. "I have a problem, and I'm hoping you might have a solution to help me."

"Mark became very guarded when Ray asked for a favor. He was always trying to make someone else look bad. Ray was not the most personable guy at the base and certainly not the most trusted. Every promotion or perk Ray received came through favors. Mark avoided Ray like the plague.

"What problem might that be, Ray?" Mark asked. "I have a woman friend in London. We had plans to get married," Ray said.

"Congratulations." Mark said. "Well, not so fast. Plans have changed. I have to tell you a story. Unfortunately this time, my plans might have backfired on me and I need someone to help me to formulate a plan to bring her back to me. Are you with me so far?" Ray asked. "I don't know yet, tell me more about your situation?" Mark sighed.

Ray spent the next hour telling Mark about the events of the past five years. When he was done, he asked Mark again. "So do you think you can help me?" Ray asked. "Nope, you're too late. Glen's on leave visiting her in London, probably as we speak. He left here two days ago. I'm sure you have already been exposed by now. There's not much I can do to help you now," Mark said.

"Oh, man, you're kidding me. How am I ever going to look at her again?" Ray asked. "I don't expect that will be a problem after this week," Mark said. "She won't ever want anything to do with you again. If that is where Glen went—and I am sure that it is—he might just come back married to that gal. Then what will you do, Ray?" Mark said. "That won't happen. I have connections in London, and I've got to leave now so I can make some calls. Thanks for the information, Mark. I've got to run," Ray said running out the door.

Ray headed to his room. His stomach was churning and he was in terrible pain. He wrote down some notes and made sure he included every important mistake he made in the past several months. He couldn't afford to leave out any details now. He thought about it for a while and then started to dial the phone to call a person he hoped would have ties to helping him recover from his dumb mistakes.

"May I speak with Gordon Miller," the stern voice said. "May I ask whose calling?" the rough voice on the other end asked. "Lieutenant Buckley," Ray said.

"Lieutenant Raymond Buckley I presume," Gordon Miller said when he answered the phone. Ray could hear the disgust in his voice. "You must need a favor, Buckley." Miller said in a stern voice. "The only time I hear from you anymore is when you're in trouble and dug yourself deep in crap," Gordon said.

"Well yes, as a matter of fact I have, and I need your expertise again," Ray said. "I need to you to come up with an emergency right now that would place an enlistee from North Carolina in China or the South Pacific," Ray begged.

"Do you know what you are asking? You know I can't do that. How about enlightening me in your latest travesty?" Gordon asked.

"Look," Ray said, "I have made a terrible mistake. I got caught lying to the love of my life. I only did it for her best interest. She thinks she's in love with some loser. He'll never give her what I can. If she figures out what I have done, she'll never speak to me again," Ray informed him.

"Actually, I have a better idea. Why don't you come up with some sort of an emergency back in North Carolina?" Gordon Miller asked.

"I need to get this guy as far away as possible. I have to find a way to keep him away from my woman while he is on his leave. He's interfering in our relationship. My girl is infatuated with him and she keeps getting sidetracked by him," Ray said.

"Maybe you ought to re-evaluate your relationship with her. If she can't stay loyal to you now, how will she be later?" Gordon asked.

"I just need to find a viable reason to get Glen out of London. Can you help me or not?" Ray asked.

"I have an idea, but I can't be associated with this plan. I need your word that no one will ever know that I helped you with this plan, do you understand?" Gordon said. "You've got my attention," Ray said.

"There are new recruits in a special forces camp in Geneva, Switzerland. The corporal training them was injured on Friday and I need a temporary replacement. If Glen has the background, maybe—and I mean maybe—he could replace Barry for a few weeks until he returns. That's the best I can do until you come up with something better," Gordon said.

"That will work. What paperwork do I need to complete to send that loser to Geneva?" Ray asked.

"I will get it started right away and get back to you tomorrow," Gordon said. "I'll be waiting to hear from you," Ray said relieved. "I really appreciate your help. I will begin to work on my own plans in the meantime," Ray promised.

The next morning Georgina and Glen met for breakfast. Georgina arranged to take off a few days from her job at the hospital so she could spend time with Glen.

"Glen, I haven't been able to sleep a wink. I am so afraid of what tactics Ray Buckley might be planning to keep us apart. I just do not trust him. He was here just a few days ago telling me about your injuries. He thinks I'm ready to move on with our relationship, but we haven't had a relationship in over three years and he expects me to just forget you. I don't love him. I love you," Georgina said.

"Why are we having this conversation? Why do you keep bringing up Ray Buckley? Are you sure you still don't have feelings for him? Should I be concerned about your commitment to me?" Glen asked.

"No Glen, I am just concerned that Ray has another trick up his sleeve to keep us apart. He's already proved he can't be trusted. He has lied to me a lot," Georgina said.

"How often do you see him? It sounds to me that you spend too much time with him. As long as you listen to him, he is going to lie to you about me. I only have eleven more days here. Let's forget about Ray and enjoy ourselves. I have a surprise for you tonight. I'll pick you up at five thirty for dinner and then we'll attend a show at the theater," Glen said.

"Theater tickets, to what?" Georgina asked. "That's the surprise; just trust me. You'll have a great time," Glen said.

"What shall I wear? Is it formal? Oh, Glen, I don't know if I have anything to wear. I'll need to get a formal dress. Will you come with me?" Georgina asked. "Of course I will," Glen said. The rest of the day was a blur. They had a fun planning for the upcoming evening.

That night Georgina looked like a princess. She was so elegant. Men were turning their heads and staring at this beautiful woman that Glen felt so lucky to be escorting on his arm. To end their perfect evening they stopped for a nightcap after the show. Glen ached to feel Georgina's body next him. He desperately wanted her to spend the night, but out of respect and his better judgment he decided he'd take her home.

The next morning while getting dressed, Glen heard a knock on his room door. *"Must be the maid,"* Glen thought until he opened the door. A tall, thin sergeant in an Air Force uniform pushed his way through Glen's door.

"Excuse me, who are you looking for?" Glen asked. "You Sir," the sergeant said. "Are you Glen Dornstadt?" "I don't know. Identify yourself first. Otherwise, I don't have to tell you anything," Glen said.

"Sergeant Michael Rice, from Special Forces, Sir. I have been sent to retrieve you for our training camp in Geneva. Last Friday my corporal was injured in an accident and our platoon needs a temporary replacement. You have been appointed to replace him until he recovers and gets back on his feet. Your commander gave me your name and your location. How handy it is that you are here in London. I will need you for four to six weeks, and I need you to come with me now," Sergeant Rice relayed.

"No, I am not coming with you. Not this time. I am on leave for ten more days. I am sure there is someone else you can get who is better trained in Special Forces than I am," Glen said.

"There is no one I can get to fill in as quickly as I can get you sir," said Sergeant Rice. "I need someone today and I don't have time to wait. Pack up your stuff and come with me or I will arrange for disciplinary action," he said.

"Do you mind if I ask you a question first?" Glen asked. "Go ahead but I won't guarantee you an answer," Sergeant Rice stated. "Is this another plan to keep me away from Georgina?" Glen asked. "I don't know who Georgina is sir. There has been a request for a temporary replacement at my camp and I've been ordered to pick you up here in London. I was given directions as to where I could find you. So get your things and come with me," Sergeant Rice said in a raised voice.

"First I must make a visit with someone. Is there somewhere I can get in touch with you later?" Glen asked. "No. I'll wait here for you, but be quick; my time is limited. I'm not leaving here without you sir, so don't make any other plans or leave the area without me. The consequences for doing that are more than you would expect," Sergeant Rice warned.

"Brother, it is always something. I just know Buckley is behind this one. I have my work cut out for me when I get back, but he is going to pay for doing this to me again," Glen said to himself.

Glen threw his bags in the jeep and headed to the Steiner's. "Georgina, once again you're correct in your assumptions. I can't believe this, but I have been ordered to go to Geneva, Switzerland. I must leave in the next hour. I haven't been given a choice. I am certain you are right about Ray Buckley keeping us apart. When I get the chance I am going to try and prove his involvement. In the meantime, I want you to know you are the love of my life. I will be back for you as soon as I can; they can't keep me away forever," Glen said.

"Oh Glen, I can't believe Ray is doing this to us again. He's a crazy man. Don't worry, I will wait for you, believe me I will," Georgina said. "Someday we will look back at all of this craziness and we'll be better people for it, I just know it," Glen said.

A few days later the Steiner's phone rang. "Hello," Georgina answered. "Don't hang up, please," the voice on the other end said. "I owe you an apology." "Ray, is that you?" Georgina asked disgusted. "Yes, please listen to me. I made a terrible mistake, and I don't blame you if you hang up on me, but please don't," Ray begged. "This had better be good," Georgina said in her deepest tone.

"I was reading a report on an injured airman and the Air Force ID was provided. Somehow I transposed two numbers when I inquired about the name of the airman, I saw Glen's name. When I was speaking about Glen to another enlisted officer, he corrected me and told me Glen was on his way home for family leave. Glen is just fine. He is home in Pennsylvania with his family," Ray said.

"Don't bother," Georgina belted out. "He never made it home. He was visiting with me when all of a sudden he was called to Geneva for some special forces training. You've won again at keeping us apart, but eventually you'll run out of dirty tricks," Georgina said in a low uncaring tone.

"Well I understand why you'd think that, but I had nothing to do with Glen going to Geneva. Please believe me," Ray said. "Well maybe this time you didn't but you've been behind everything else that kept us apart. Sorry to have wrongly accused you this time," Georgina said. "Oh, that's okay. You don't owe me an apology— not after the mistake I just made," Ray said. "When was he sent to Geneva? That should have come through North Carolina. I will check on that for you. Maybe I can get him released sooner," Ray said. "You would actually do that for us?" Georgina asked. "I'll do what I can and I'll do it for you, not for Glen. I know how much you love Glen. I've learned my lesson. I wouldn't want to break you up now. Remember how I felt about you? Well, I still feel you are a terrific person, and you deserve to be happy. Let me see what I can do. I'll be in touch soon. Hang in there, okay? You have a good day now," Ray said.

Mark Mills congratulated Ray for his sincerity on his phone call. I didn't think you had that in you. You had me believing you really meant that," Mark said. "Yeah, well, I am hoping to use that to my benefit," Ray said. "Why would I think anything different?" Mark said. "As soon as I can get to London, I am going to pay Georgina a visit. This time she will see me in a different light," Ray smiled and winked at Mark.

Glen had just arrived in Geneva when his phone rang. "Glen, it's Mark, I am bringing you back to the States. No one had permission to send you to Geneva. I want you to be able to finish your leave, but you'll need to stay in the country or they will try and send you back to Geneva again," Mark relayed.

"That's okay," Glen said. "I have a lot to do at home in Pennsylvania. I'm sure Georgina will be happier knowing that I am home instead of in Geneva. How did this ever happen?" Glen asked.

"Don't worry about that now. Just go home and enjoy your final days off. I will be sending a Jeep for you. It should be arriving in a few hours. They'll take you to the airport for your flight home. By the way, I've extended your leave another three days to make up for lost time," Mark said.

"You're a great guy. Don't ever let anyone tell you differently," Glen said.

In less than six hours, Glen was on a plane to Harrisburg, Pennsylvania. He sent a telegram to his sister Lona to pick him up at the airport. Hopefully she would have time to take him to the bus terminal for his ride home to Billsport.

While en route to the bus terminal, Lona felt compelled to warn Glen. "You know Mom is not doing very well? Her stomach bothers her all the time, and she's lost a lot of weight. I visit her as often as I can, but I just can't go every week. Betty has been spending a lot of time with her. When you get home, call her, she will update you on some of the procedures Mom has had performed. Glen, are you listening to me?" Lona asked. "Yes but I must admit, my mind is somewhere else right now, I am sorry. I heard everything you said about Mom," Glen said. "Are you still seeing that girl from London? I thought that would pass, or is there someone new?" Lona asked. "Nope, there's no one new, and her name is Georgina. Get used to it; she's going to be your sister-in-law," Glen said. "When is this happening?" Lona asked. "As soon as I can make it possible, but I think we're going to live in London. Her family is fantastic, and they have welcomed me and made me one of them. Georgina is a nurses' aide and she'll make a good living. She wants lots of kids, and I can picture her holding my baby and being a wonderful mother," Glen said. "You will find out soon enough that marriage is never what it appears to be," Lona said as she dropped Glen off at the bus terminal.

Glen walked into his mother's house and found her sitting at the kitchen table with her hand on her head moaning. She looked up at Glen and a smile widened on her face.

"My Glenny, you're home. I've been waiting for you," Kathryn said to her son. "Mom, what's wrong? Why do you look so pale? Tell me the truth Mom," Glen said. "I'm glad you're here. I have not been well. I need someone here to take care of my house and help me so I can rest. Kevin has his school and then he works so he can help me with expenses. This is too much for us," Kathryn exclaimed. "Before I return to North Carolina, I will try to find someone to help you. Just let me take care of you today, okay Mom?" Glen asked. "Yes, thank you son, I knew I could count on you," Kathryn said.

"How have you been cooking? Has anyone been bringing you food?" Glen asked his Mother. "Some days Betty and Howard come with leftovers. Other times they take us home with them for dinner. I don't like going to their house, there are too many steps, so I usually just stay home," Kathryn said.

"You aren't able to cook, are you, Mom?" Glen asked. "Not very well, I open a lot of soup, but cans are difficult for me to open too," Kathryn said.

Later that day while Kathryn took her nap Glen called Lona.

"Have you seen Mom lately? She is so thin. I thought you and Betty would at least see to it that she had food. I think she's starving to death," Glen said.

"I have tried Glen, she won't come home with me, and I don't think Howard wants Mom at their house for dinner every night," Lona said.

"I'd like to arrange for Mom to stay with you until I return in July. I'll help her pack her clothes and her private items, and I'll send them down to you. After I'm discharged I'll bring her home and take care of her myself. I know she is hard to live with, but if we don't do something soon, she will die. I believe with the proper care, she'll be fine," Glen said. "She won't leave Kevin behind, I've tried Glen," Lona said.

"What about Georgina?" Lona asked. "I'll work it out with her," Glen said. "You don't have to do that. We can share taking care of her," Lona said. "You're not doing a very good job now. I'll take care of her myself. As soon as I know when I'm coming home for good, I will let you know," Glen said.

Glen spent the next five days convincing his mother that she didn't have a choice, that she would starve to death or possibly hurt herself if she didn't stay with Lona. He told her how fast time would go by and that he would be home before she knew it. He told her he was going to bring Georgina back with him and they would all live happily together at her house. He hoped Georgina would cook and clean and he'd take care of the animals, shovel the snow, and mow the lawn. Kathryn could sit on her porch swing and relax. With a lot of coaxing Kathryn agreed to move to Lona's house until Glen returned home. Knowing he had a solid plan, Glen was able to return to North Carolina with a sense of accomplishment.

Unfortunately his plan was short lived. Kathryn created such a fuss about returning home that Lona had no choice but to take her back the following weekend.

Once he returned to North Carolina he decided it was time to find out who Ray Buckley knew and how he had managed to get away with so many tricks, reassignments, and transfers. He wanted to know who was helping Ray. He was going to get even. No one should be able to get away with altering the future of another person.

Some records were altered to avoid showing that Ray Buckley pulled off many devious plans during his military career. Many had not yet been changed and showed that Ray's friends and connections had lied for him time after time. He had affected many innocent people's lives. *"How could one man have so much influence, be so devious and get away with it?"* Glen thought.

Glen was stuck in North Carolina for the remainder of his tour. This was the end of his commitment to his Country. He would make that obvious when he completed his discharge papers this time. Once he was cleared for release, Glen was headed directly to London to collect Georgina and her belongings and bring them both back to Pennsylvania. They had written letters back and forth several times a week and they were making a lot of plans. A small wedding would take place almost immediately. It would be just the local family and Glen's friends.

Glen was certain there was no way Ray could mess with him any more. Little did he know that Ray had one final trick up his sleeve? This would prove to Ray once and for all that Glen wasn't the man for Georgina.

Ray hurried back to his barracks; he couldn't be found on the phone discussing his plans. After all, he had a lot of begging to do and reservations to make. Ray had planned to ask Mark Mills to release Glen so he could retrieve a fallen airman from London. Ray was certain Mark would allow the trip. What an opportunity this trip would present for Glen. It would give him a small window to visit with Georgina one more time and finalize their plans before his discharge.

Sunday evening Ray called Mark to his office. "I have a problem and I thought maybe you could help me with a solution," Ray said. "Why do I always shudder when you come to me with a problem? Now what are you up to?" Mark asked.

"I need to have an injured airman escorted from London to Washington. I cannot make the trip myself. I need to send another man over there to escort him home," Ray said.

"Why don't you have a man from the Queenshire base bring him back to the States?" Mark questioned.

"Most of their men are out on special assignments, and they're very shorthanded. Anyhow I don't have any authority over that command. I thought maybe since Glen has his lady friend over there, you could call him and ask him to go," Ray said. "Oh boy, I smell a rat. What are you up to Buckley?" Mark questioned.

"What? I don't understand. I try to do something nice for a change and you ostracize me for trying to be a nice guy. If you're going to react that way I'm not going to be a nice guy anymore," Ray said.

"Okay, if I can get in touch with Glen and if I can make the air connections, I'll do it," Mark said. "I saved you a step. I already called the air tower and made a tentative request for a private jet so we don't waste time—this man is really sick and he needs special treatment he can only receive at Walter Reed. He is being prepped for the trip back, but it might be a few days until he is ready. He can only travel home if he is escorted. You know those are the rules. I thought Glen is very responsible and would be a good person to handle that task," Ray said.

"Yes, you are correct about that. I would have probably chosen Glen myself. It sounds like all I have to do is contact Glen, or have you done that for me too?" Mark asked. "No, but if you need me to, I will do that," Ray said. "No, you better let me do it. I don't think Glen trusts you at all, and he may have a difficult time following orders from you," Mark said.

"Good idea," Ray said. *"I knew I could get Mark to fall for this plan. Let's see how well Glen approves of his girlfriend showing up with another man. That should cause a good fight and a reason to break up,"* Ray thought to himself.

Early Saturday morning there was a knock at the Steiner's front door. "Yes sir, what can I do for you?" Myron asked, as he opened his front door to see a man standing there holding roses. "Is this where Georgina Steiner lives?" the man asked. "Yep, sure is," Myron said. "These flowers are for her. Will you see that she gets them?" the delivery man said. "I've already got them," a female voice answered. "You have a great day now," the man said as he returned to his small street wagon.

"Glen, you didn't have to. Flowers are such an expensive gift. Why didn't you save your money until you came for me?" Georgina thought to herself.

Georgina opened the card and read it slowly to herself.

Georgina,

An evening with you is all I ask,
My presence here will soon be a mask.
My time is soon over, and my service will be done.

So I won't be back to bother you none.
Let's get together one last time,
I know you'll soon be another man's bride.
So for old time's sake, what do you say?
How about meeting me tonight at E-Jay's?

Your friend, Ray

"You sure are a lucky young lady," Myron said to his daughter as she put down the card. "No Daddy, sometimes things aren't always what they appear to be," Georgina said as she turned and walked away from the beautiful and fragrant bouquet.

Myron sensed his daughter's discomfort. Feeling somewhat guilty, he picked up the card and read it. He found Georgina in the parlor looking upset, "you don't have to go," Myron said. "You're so right, Daddy. I haven't decided what I am going to do, but I don't trust this man. I don't believe anything he tells me. After all he's done he still thinks I should love him and not Glen," Georgina said. "Ray adores you and only wishes to have just a moment with you, but as I said, you don't have to go. If you feel a need for closure for some reason, go and have a good time, but be careful," Myron said.

"You know Daddy, you sound like you want me to go," Georgina said. "Nope, you do what you feel is right," Myron said.

As the day wore on Georgina kept thinking that she should go meet Ray. She didn't really know why she felt that way and her initial instincts told her not to go, but concerned about whatever it was that Ray had up his sleeve, she needed to go to avert another possible crisis. If she didn't go, Glen could be the target again, and she didn't want that. Georgina was sure that she was smart enough to watch out for Ray's tricks and smooth talk. She talked herself into having dinner with him just so she could teach him a lesson of honesty and integrity.

Glen received a phone call, just as he had returned to his barracks from his trip back home. "Glen," Mark said, "how would you like to make a trip to Queenshire, London, to escort an ill airman back to Washington, D.C.? I need to send someone, and since you have a lady friend over there, I thought maybe you would like an opportunity to see her," Mark said.

"You're kidding, right? Good things like this never happen to me. They always take me away from her," Glen said.

"Well, not this time," Mark said. "I need an answer. I have a plane waiting for you. The pilot will have an envelope for you with all of the details regarding the injured airman. Please review them on your flight. What do you say? Can you help me out?" "Yes sir," Glen said, "Give me five minutes and I'll be ready to go."

"The sooner you can get to the airport, the sooner you'll get to see your lady," Mark said. "Is there anything I can do for you?" Mark asked Glen. "Oh no sir, I'm okay. I'll be back before you know it, and I'll have your man back for treatment and stay by his side until he gets here. Thank you, sir," Glen said with excitement.

That evening Georgina dressed in her finest dress. She carefully applied her makeup and her favorite perfume and headed to E-Jays. She was ready for Ray. Whatever he had planned, she knew not to trust him.

Georgina walked into E-Jays and realized that she wasn't sure where to look for Ray. There were several coves, private dining rooms and a large backroom. Ray could be in any one of them. She didn't have any instructions as to where to find him.

"Madam, are you dining alone tonight?" the maitre d' asked. "I am to meet someone here but I am not sure where to find him," Georgina said. "No problem madam. What is his name? I am sure if he is here he would have left your name for us to seat you with him. "Ray Buckley," Georgina said. "I am sorry madam; I do not have him listed. Would you like to wait or take a seat at the bar until his arrival?" he asked. "I will sit at the bar, if that is not a problem," Georgina said. "Sure, follow me," he said.

Georgina waited and waited. After about an hour she came to the realization that again she had fallen into another one of Ray's deceptions, and she never saw it coming. *"That man will stop at nothing to embarrass me,"* Georgina thought to herself.

Just as she turned to place a tip on the bar a male voice asked her if she would like to join him as she had obviously been stood up. "Oh," Georgina said startled. "No thank you. I have been here long enough. I must go now," she told the stranger.

"Why are you in such a hurry? The night is still young," the man said. "I don't know you, and obviously the friend I was to meet ran into some difficulty and I must go see if I can find him," she said. "Would you like me to escort you? Maybe this friend could use extra help," the stranger said.

As Georgina reviewed this man's face she was certain that she had met him before. He was a good-looking American man, tall and a good solid build. *"He would be a great catch for someone looking,"* Georgina thought to herself. "Miss is there a problem?" the man asked. "All of a sudden you don't seem like you want to leave," he said. "It's a long story," Georgina said. "I am not sure whether to go or stay. Maybe I should wait a little longer," she said. "That would be fine with me. I'll enjoy your company," the man said. "Let me buy your next drink," he offered.

"I shouldn't be drinking anything. I haven't had dinner yet," Georgina said. "Well then let's have dinner," the man offered. "I would be honored to have you sit with me. What do you say? If your friend shows up now, he can join us, okay?" he said. "I have just one problem," Georgina said. "What is that?" the man asked. "I don't know your name or anything about you," Georgina said. "Oh formalities, I see. My name is George Duncan and I recently moved here from Cleveland, Ohio," he said.

Georgina nodded at George and laughed. "Did I say something funny?" George asked. "No, my name is Georgina—short for George and Gina after my grandparents," she replied. "What's so funny about that? I bet your grandparents are very proud to have you named after them," he said. "Yes, I'm sure they are,"

Georgina said. "It's just that we almost have the same name." "I see," George said.

"Let's get menus so we can order dinner. So who were you meeting, may I ask?" "Just a friend," Georgina said. "You don't sound too sure about that," George said.

"Look, I really would rather forget about him and just have dinner, if you don't mind. It's a long story, and I just don't want to explain any of it tonight," Georgina informed him.

"That's fine, I understand. I have had some of those relationships myself," George said. "There is no relationship," Georgina said rather sternly. "I'm sorry. I am offering too much information and asking too many questions. So tell me about yourself?" George said. "I'm sorry if I seem distant. I have a boyfriend. He is in the United States Air Force and he will be coming for me in about six to seven months. We are not yet sure whether we will be living here or back at his home in Pennsylvania. I was meeting another friend tonight to say our final good-byes. He is in the Air Force too, and he does not expect to return to London again. I will be getting married as soon as Glen returns for me, so I must tell Ray that this will be our final meeting," Georgina said.

"It doesn't sound like you are sure you want it to be a final meeting. You don't sound very convincing that you want to marry the man from Pennsylvania," George said. "I do. I am very positive. Why don't I sound like I want to get married?" Georgina asked. "You hesitated and you don't sound very excited. A bride-to-be should sound secure and excited. I don't detect that in your voice at all. You should sound jubilant, but you don't," George said.

"Well, I am sure I want to get married to Glen. I love him; he is good to me. He is an honest, kind, and gentle man," Georgina said. "What else do you know about him? Do you know about his family background and where he comes from? How about his educational background? Or has he ever been married before?" George asked.

"I get it now. You have been sent to have dinner with me in place of Ray. Ray is up to his old tricks. He sent someone else. I won't fall for this plan. I am smarter than he gives me credit for. He will do anything to ruin my relationship with Glen," Georgina said.

"Wait a minute. I live here now. No one has sent me here or paid me to do any favors. Don't accuse me of helping some loser carry out his dirty deeds. I'm sorry for raising my voice, but all of a sudden, I am the victim here. Maybe I should leave. Here is twenty dollars to pay for your dinner," George said.

"No, wait, don't go. I'm sorry. Ray will stop at nothing to ruin my relationship with Glen. I thought this was another one of his tricks. What do you care? You're not involved in this mess," Georgina said. "No go on," George said. "If you have something to say, to get off of your chest, I recommend you tell me; it is not good to hold back feelings. I got a bit carried away. Please continue. Now what were you going to tell me?" George asked.

"I met Ray first. We dated for over a year, and then he went to Korea. He said he would write me, but I never heard from him. Then I met Glen and he was different. I never met a man like him. Ray was nice, but he was evasive about his background. He rarely opened up to me about his family and he stretched the truth a lot. Then Glen went to Korea and Ray came back wanting to start all over again, but it was too late. I had fallen in love with Glen. Ray wouldn't accept that and he has done everything imaginable to keep us apart," Georgina said.

"You are very special. I can understand that man's dilemma. I would fight for you too, not that I am interested in entering the picture. You already have too many men, so I am going to exit the picture after tonight. Since we are having dinner together, let's have a joyful meal and finish with a happy ending, okay?" George asked. "Yes, let's do that," Georgina said.

Glen arrived in London and reported to Hailey Hospital in the extreme northern part of London. Dr. Orson Smith told Glen it would probably be two days before Joseph White would be ready to transport to Washington, D.C. for the long seven-hour flight. Glen promised the doctor that he would check back on regular intervals. Just in case something arose that they needed to get in touch with Glen, he gave the hospital the hotel where they could leave a message. Once the formalities were completed Glen headed to south London to find Georgina. His first stop was the Steiner's house.

Myron opened the door. "Well, land's sake boy, what are you doing back here so soon?" He said. "I am on a special assignment here in London for a few days. I won't have much time to spend with Georgina, but I am free this evening," Glen said. "I'm afraid she's not here. You'll find her at E-Jay's," Myron said.

"Then I'm off, I'll see you later," Glen said. "Not so fast," Myron said. "I must warn you. Ray's asked her to have dinner with him and she agreed. I don't think she has any interest in him, but every time that man stops here or invites or out, he persuades her to go with him. I do not know what she sees in him, Glen. He doesn't treat her the way you do," he complained.

"Don't worry, Myron, I can handle this situation. I'll have her away from him and with me in less than two minutes," Glen said. "I hope you're right. Now go and have a good evening and stay out of trouble. Hear me?" Myron said.

Glen walked out the front door. He turned back smiling at Myron and nodded. Glen normally walked fast; however he took his time as he thought about his dilemma. "*I need to think of a way to distract Georgina to get her away from Ray. I am sure this is a set up, and I know Ray is going to try and make me look small, embarrass me, or belittle me in front of Georgina. I need to get her away from him before he even knows I am in the room.*"

Glen walked through E-Jay's twice and did not see Georgina. "*Maybe they left,*" he thought to himself. "*Maybe she went home already. I know she has had just about enough of Ray.*"

As Glen turned to leave E-Jay's, he thought he'd better comb through one more time. Then he caught the back of her head over in the far corner in one of the most remote places in the building. "*It figures Ray would turn her around so she would not be able to see me or so that I would not be able to see her. That's just like him,"* Glen thought.

Glen walked up to Georgina slowly, trying not to disturb anyone. As he got closer, he realized that Georgina was not sitting with Ray, but with a stranger. He paused until the stranger saw him approaching them. He was sure that was Georgina, but who was she with? Then the man looked up and spoke. "Are you lost there, Sonny?" he asked. "No I don't believe so. I came to see Georgina," Glen said. Before he finished his sentence, Georgina stood up and faced him.

"Glen what are you doing here?" Are you checking up on me? I can't believe you don't trust me. It was you who set me up," Georgina said angrily. "I don't know what to say. I don't even know this man. He asked me to dine with him so I wouldn't have to dine alone," Georgina said.

"Just so you know; I didn't have a choice about coming to London. "I have been assigned to retrieve an ill airman here in London. While I was here, I hoped to surprise you. Instead, you surprised me. You're out with another man and you told your parents you were going out with Ray. What other surprises do have for me?" Glen asked confused.

"All of a sudden, I feel like the third wheel in your life," Glen said angrily as he rubbed his brow. "I'll just leave some money for my check. You two can work this out. I had a lovely evening, and thank you for joining me for dinner. It was a pleasure," George said.

"Wait. Before you go, I want to thank you for listening. I am sorry for accusing you of helping my dishonest friend," Georgina said.

"Have a good night Georgina, and you too, you lucky fellow," George said.

"Do you want to kiss him good-bye?" Glen asked. "What do you mean by that?" Georgina snarled. "I was waiting to meet Ray. Here is a copy of a poem he sent me. My intentions tonight were to tell him not to bother me anymore, because I am going to marry you. But now I'm not sure. I feel betrayed," Georgina said angrily.

"Oh Georgina, I didn't mean for you to think I don't trust you. I really wanted to surprise you. That is why I went to your parents' house first. Your dad told me where to find you. I didn't have any other intentions," Glen said.   "I'm sorry for that outbreak. I guess I don't surprise well. Let's go somewhere quiet where we can be alone," Georgina said "That's my girl," Glen said.

Glen couldn't help being jealous when he saw Georgina with another man. That man's face was very familiar and it would haunt him for a long time. Glen knew him from somewhere. He'd figure that mystery out later. Glen had an extreme desire to kiss Georgina right at that spot. He was going to hold her as long as she would allow. She finally stopped him when she realized everyone at E-Jay's was watching them. They left and went directly to Georgina's parents' house. Everyone had gone to bed and the two of them were alone downstairs.

"Perfect," Glen thought.

"Would you like anything to eat or maybe something to drink? Tea, coffee, water, or ..." Georgina asked. Glen grabbed her and turned her around to face him. "You, I just want you. I want to hold you and kiss you and take you back to the States with me. I saw you with another man and I was so afraid that you ... well, that someone else had come into your life. All of a sudden, I was beyond jealous," Glen said.

"I am so sorry you had to see that poor display. It's a long story and I don't even know him," Georgina said as she explained the events of the evening to Glen. "Please forgive me? You know I love you and only you," Georgina said.

"Come with me to the living room where we can get more comfortable," Glen said.

He kissed Georgina's neck and then her ears; he slid his tongue down to her shoulders and back up to her lips. She quivered as he slid his hand up her shirt and fondled her breast. He maneuvered Georgina into a horizontal position on the couch. He removed her underwear and then he took off his pants. Georgina felt anxious and exotic at the same time. She wanted the same thing Glen did. However; she found it difficult to relax with the fear of getting caught in her parent's house.

"Stop, my parents—" Georgina started. "Shhh!" Glen placed his finger over her mouth. "We'll be quiet," he whispered as he continued his quest. Glen used variations of foreplay until he knew there was no turning back. He needed to know that she desired him as much as he desired her. Georgina experienced feelings of excitement and anticipation as Glen rubbed his throbbing penis against her thigh. After he instituted such a momentous production, he had to penetrate her.

Glen waited a long time to make love to this woman he adored more than anyone else in the world. He dreamt many times how wonderful she would feel in his arms, how sweet she would smell, and how soft her skin would feel next to his. He wasn't disappointed. She was everything he wanted in a woman. Under normal circumstances he would have taken his time, but the couch in her parent's living room did not make a good environment and he climaxed sooner than he hoped. Their relationship was now consummated.

"Glen, you are such a gentle man. You are wonderful, but somehow this is not the way I imagined our first encounter together. My mother would have heart failure, and my father would kill you if he knew what just took place in his house. If someone would have come down from the second floor, we would never have heard them. We could have been caught," Georgina said.

"Well we weren't, and I'm not leaving you now. I am staying here with you tonight," Glen said.

"I must go to my room. You better stay on the couch. I will explain to my parents in the morning that you had nowhere else to go tonight, so I allowed you to stay down here. Let me get you a blanket," Georgina said. "I don't need a blanket. I'll be fine this way. Your dad will be up in a few hours and I'll get up with him and explain that we came in a very late and I was extremely tired from traveling. I'm sure he will understand," Glen said. "It's not my dad I'm worried about. Mother always thinks the worst," Georgina said. "Like what? That we made love on her couch?" Glen asked. "Stop before they hear you. I'm going to bed now," Georgina whispered.

Glen barely slept those few hours. It was imperative that he be awake when Myron came down for breakfast. When Glen heard noises coming from the second floor he got up and started the coffee.

"Lordy sakes, it smells good down here. That is such a good aroma, isn't it? Myron said. Glen got out the coffee cups and acknowledged Myron's statement. "Mom will be down shortly, and then we'll cook breakfast," Myron informed Glen.

"I suppose you have questions as to why I am here so early," Glen said in a low tone. "Nope, I don't, but Mother will. You might as well save your explanation so you only have to tell it once," Myron said.

Bernice came downstairs later than normal. She attempted to wait up for her daughter's return, but her heavy eyelids eventually won the battle. Bernice still went to bed much later than usual. "Good golly. "I wasn't expecting to see you here this morning. You sure do get up early. Or did you even go to your room last night?" Bernice said to Glen as she came down the steps while she was still pining up her hair. "Well yes, I did," Glen said. Is that all the explanation you're going to provide?" Bernice said. "I would certainly like to leave it at that," Glen said. "Well you can't squeeze juice out of a banana, so I'll leave it alone this time," Bernice said.

Georgina finally got out of bed and joined in the conversation. She listened as Glen explained his Mother's poor health, his plans for his last months in the service and how eager he was to begin his private life. "You sure are quiet this morning." Bernice said to her daughter. "I was just being polite and listening to Glen as he shares his plans with us," Georgina said.

"It's been an enjoyable visit, but I have paper work to complete and people to see so I've got to go now," Glen said

Georgina and Glen walked into the den to say their good byes and then Glen walked into the kitchen to announce. "I will be leaving for the states hopefully early tomorrow morning depending on how soon Joseph is ready to travel. The next time I return, it will be to collect my bride. I'm sure I don't have to ask, but will you take care of my little lady until I return?" he asked

"Yes, of course, we will. We look forward to your return. Myron said, as Glen slowly walked to his waiting ride and waved good-bye.

Ray was preparing for his flight to London. *"I hope I'm not too late. It sounds as if my plan with George might have worked. Glen's going to leave with a broken heart and I'm going to move right in."* Ray thought to himself. Surely the couple had enough time to fight and end their relationship. Ray didn't care about Glen as long as he and Georgina were no longer together.

Chapter 9
The Move

Shortly after Ray began his second tour, his bowel and stomach ailments took a serious turn for the worse. Sometimes getting out of bed and leaving his apartment became a chore for him. Diarrhea plagued him constantly, leaving him drained and weak.

Because of the seriousness of his illness, Ray was able to convince his superiors into allowing him to move to London indefinitely to participate in a trial treatment program. Ray had very good connections at the top. His room and arrangements to move to London were taken care of by his superiors. He was issued a small family apartment in the Meadows building. This facility was owned by the United States Air Force and was set aside for enlisted men with spouses and families. Ray was eager to move to London so he could change everyone's lives, especially his.

He decided it was best to wait a few days before approaching Georgina about his missed appearance at E-Jay's. It would give her time to forgive and forget. In the meantime, he had doctor's appointments to attend and medicines he needed to begin taking to quiet his ailments.

Doctors at the VA hospital in London were confused by the nearly normal test results considering the seriousness of Ray's complaints. No serious disease was evident and only moderate irritation was detected. Unfortunately for Ray he continued to experience very critical bouts of pain, discomfort, and diarrhea. Ray continued to lose weight at an alarming pace and continued to look and feel exhausted. At times, he was much too weak to make the effort he needed to win back Georgina.

Four days of rest gave Ray enough strength to call Georgina. "I owe you a big apology, but I don't really want to discuss what happened over the phone. Can I come over for a short while? I am so much better at apologies in person," he said.

"I don't think so, Ray. I am busy now. I have some chores to finish and then I'm going to write Glen a letter to inform him of some plans I have made for our wedding," Georgina said.

"I understand. I'm not here to interfere, but I thought if I could have a few minutes of your time to explain what happened as to why I didn't make dinner last Friday night, we could at least remain friends," Ray coaxed. "Well, if you really must. When should I expect you?" Georgina asked. "I can be there in ten minutes," Ray said excitedly.

Ray immediately headed to meet Georgina at her parent's home. He had a plan that would hopefully win Georgina back. What did he have to lose?

Bernice saw Ray walking up the sidewalk and called to Georgina. "You soon better decide which man it is you are going to marry. These two men both love you and you just keep tugging both men's chains. One of these days, one of them isn't going to take it any more," Bernice shared.

"Mama, I don't know what you mean by tugging chains. Ray and I are just friends now. He has a girlfriend. We were saying good-bye and he wanted to thank me for being so understanding, and really Mama, I wanted to hear his lame excuse for why he stood me up for dinner last Friday night," Georgina said.

"Don't you believe for one minute this man isn't still in love with you?" Bernice said.

"Hush, Mama, he's here. Can we talk about this later?" Georgina asked.

Georgina announced that she'd get the door since Ray was her visitor. She opened the door and invited him inside. As hard as it was for Georgina to trust Ray, the physical attraction was still there. Ray just smiled and somewhere from within her, those old feeling came to surface and exposed themselves again. Maybe it was the power of suggestion since her mother had just told her that Ray still loved her.

"Good day, my lovely lady," Ray said. "Hello. Thank you for those beautiful flowers last week. I must say I was surprised," Georgina said. "Pleasantly, I hope?" Ray asked. "Of course, especially since we're no longer dating, why would you go to that expense?" Georgina asked. "I wanted you to know that we can still be friends, and I am glad that we are. A person can't have too many friends, you know," Ray shared. "Would you like to go for a walk? I thought maybe we'd walk down to the town park. It is such a nice day, and I have something I want to tell you," he said.

"I don't think we need to leave for you to tell me why you stood me up last week," Georgina said. "I just thought it would be nice to go for a walk—get out and stretch and move around," Ray said. "Is this going to take a while? Am I going to regret going with you again?" Georgina asked. "Why don't you trust me?" Ray asked. "You don't really want me to address that question, do you?" Georgina asked.

"Can we just go for a short walk around the block then?" Ray asked. "Well, I suppose, it really is a nice day outside, so let's go," she replied.

Ray got straight to the point, "I know your plans are to marry Glen Dornstadt. I feel as though I've lost my best friend. You and Glen are so different, and we—well, you and I, that is—have so much more in common," Ray informed her. "You are babbling and I don't know what you think we have in common? What are you trying to say Ray?" Georgina asked.

"I am sure if you gave me the chance, I could make you a very happy woman. You see, I haven't been able to get you out of my mind since I met you. You need to know how I feel. If you have second thoughts on marrying Glen, I'll be there waiting for you," Ray shared. "I am flattered. I really am Ray, but I couldn't marry you now. There's been too much bad history between us. Plus you still haven't told me why you stood me up last week," Georgina said.

"I don't know where that comes from. I have been blamed for everything that has gone wrong in your relationship with Glen. I haven't been responsible for any of it. I misread an airman's name one time. Otherwise I think you need to take a good look at Glen. There are too many invalid excuses. I keep hearing from people that I've done it again. I wish I were so smart. You give me way too much credit. I love you and I wouldn't hurt you for any reason. I wouldn't even take you away from the man you love. Please think about what I have told you today. Go home and sleep on it. In a few days if you still don't have any feelings for me, fine, I'll understand. I'll be waiting to hear from you. As for last Friday, my diarrhea was so bad I couldn't leave my apartment. I tried to call E-Jay's to get a message to you, but their staff wouldn't cooperate," Ray sighed.

Georgina and Ray stopped for dessert and walked home slowly without as much as a sentence between them. Georgina still found Ray very attractive. His physical appearance was more to her liking than Glen's, but Glen's personality, dreams, and ambitions were much more suited to her liking. Ray's disposition was so different from what she usually liked. He was way too aggressive and controlling for her. She always imagined marrying someone docile like Glen. Yet Ray had an excitement and spontaneity about him that Glen lacked. Maybe it was time to re-evaluate her relationship with these two men as her mother had suggested.

"Mama, can I talk with you?" Georgina asked. "You can always talk to me Princess," Bernice said. "I'm so confused. Earlier I took a walk with Ray and he brought up our previous relationship. He shared a lot of information with me that really made sense. He said he has been blamed for everything that has gone wrong in my relationship with Glen. He said I should take another look and see that he couldn't have been responsible for many of the events that he's been blamed for. He also said that Glen is responsible for his own tardiness and excuses and that I need to realize this fact," Georgina relayed.

"Let me just say I don't trust Ray like I do Glen," Bernice said. "I believe that Ray will manipulate you to believe what he wants you to believe. I understand that Ray is a charmer, but if you choose him over Glen, you will never forget Glen. You will always wonder what it might have been like, if you choose Ray. However, this is not my decision; you must go with your heart and nothing else. No one else can make this decision, except for you," Bernice said.

"I guess I have a lot of soul-searching to do to clear up my confusion. I thought for sure I wanted to spend the rest of my life with Glen, but now after talking with Ray, I question our relationship again," Georgina sighed.

Myron overheard the last part of the conversation and interjected, "Princess maybe it would be best not to rush into any decision. Take your time. Spend some time alone. This will help you clear your head and hopefully you will make a good decision. I know which man I prefer for you, but I will not tell you. I do not want to sway your decision in any way," Myron said. "Thanks Dad, I appreciate that," Georgina said.

Later that week Joanna came home from a date with her boyfriend Joe Walker. They surprised the family with their announcement of an impending May wedding. Joe a Marine from Texas was training to be a doctor. Joanna's relationship with Joe was not complicated like Georgina's. Joanna began planning her wedding immediately. Joe had plans to return to Texas to begin an internship and Joanna was going with him. She had a little over four months to put together her wedding. Georgina would be her maid of honor. The girls needed to find gowns and get fitted right away. On Saturday, they left early to shop for their dresses and warned their parents they might be several hours and not to expect them back for a while.

They spent most of the morning trying on dresses. They also needed to find matching accessories like gloves, veils, shoes, and jewelry. After several hours they felt comfortable with their selections and headed to a new restaurant in London to meet Joe for brunch. The Pink Palace was the new hang out. Joe was seated when the girls arrived. I hate to ask, but did you have any success? You look exhausted. Trying on clothes and spending money must be very tiresome for you," Joe joked. "Oh stop, I see how it's going to be," Joanna scolded.

As soon as they finished eating, Georgina announced, "I'll leave the two of you alone. I have some stops to make before I go home. If Mom or Dad asks about me, I will be home shortly," Georgina said.

Georgina was determined to stop and see Ray. She had some unanswered questions and needed to resolve them before she could make any definite choice between the two men. She took a bus to the Meadows where she expected to find Ray. "May I help you?" the concierge asked. "I am looking for Ray Buckley," Georgina said. "I am sorry. He doesn't have anyone listed on his visitor's log for today," he informed her. "Could you call him and announce my presence?" Georgina asked.

"Yes, I can do that. What is your name madam?" the concierge asked. "Georgina Steiner, can you ask him to come to the lobby to meet me? I don't feel comfortable going to his apartment unescorted?" Georgina said. "Yes, I will do that for you, madam," the concierge announced.

"Mr. Buckley you have a visitor, Miss Georgina Steiner is in the lobby to see you," the concierge said into the intercom. "What a surprise. Please send her to my apartment immediately," Ray said. "Sir, she has requested that you come to the lobby to greet her. She does not want to go to your apartment unescorted," the concierge said. "Please send her to my apartment. If she wants to see me today, she will come here unescorted," Ray said. "Yes sir," the concierge acknowledged. "I am sorry Ms. Steiner. He said he will not come to the lobby, but you are welcome to go to his apartment," he relayed to her.

"Hmm, I see. Well, I am not prepared to go to his apartment alone, so I will leave. If he calls, please inform him of my decision," Georgina said. "Yes madam, I will," he said nodding his head in disbelief.

Georgina continued her walk home. She was more confused than ever. If Ray really had such strong feelings for her, he could have at least come to the lobby to greet her.

"That's it. I've decided he's out of my life. He's disappointed me too many times. Glen would not do this to me and I'm not allowing Ray to embarrass me like that," Georgina thought angrily.

Joanna and Joe were just returning home when they saw Georgina coming from the other direction. "My goodness you look like you've lost your best friend," Joanna said. "I do? Well, I can't describe what I'm feeling now," Georgina scowled. "I went to see Ray at his apartment, but he wouldn't come down to see me. I thought we could talk, but I must have misunderstood our conversation from the other day. I guess he's not as sincere about our relationship as I thought he was. Whether he knows it or not he just answered a lot of questions for me. I won't be seeing him again. I'll wait for Glen," Georgina stated emphatically.

"Amen, I was afraid you were going to hurt Glen's feelings for that slimy bum. Ray doesn't deserve you, you know," Joanna said. "Well then you won't be happy to know that I am baffled about information that Ray shared with me about Glen. I am just not sure about him anymore either. I will wait for him to come back before I make any further decisions regarding our future," Georgina said.

"You are such a sweet girl. You deserve someone like Glen who will cater to you. Why would you listen to anything Ray had to say about Glen?" Joe asked.

After a fitful night's sleep Georgina woke questioning whether to believe all those accusations about Glen. She was positive about one thing; she was not going to marry Ray. All of a sudden her love life had become even more complicated. Georgina's attachment to two men was her own fault, caused by her own actions. How could she have let this happen? It didn't matter anymore; she was through with Ray and no longer sure about her future with Glen.

Later that morning, just as she thought her decision to avoid Ray was definite, the doorbell rang.   No one was home except Georgina so she answered the door. "Ray, what are you doing here?" She questioned him with disgust. "Where did you go yesterday? Why didn't you come up to my apartment?" Ray asked. "A proper and decent woman does not go into a single man's apartment unescorted, at least not in this country," Georgina said.

"I was having a bad day with all of my ailments yesterday and I didn't want to take a chance on an embarrassing situation. Please forgive me when I tell you my symptoms are acting up, know that I have reported them to my superiors and I am directed to stay indoors. I cannot disobey those orders," Ray said.

"You expect me to believe that? You know, I don't know what to believe from you anymore," Georgina said. "You must believe me when I tell you that I have moved here indefinitely, because of my illness. The Air Force has a lot of money invested in me. I don't want to be here but in order to find a treatment for my condition I must be where the Air Force places me. I also want you to know that my condition is so bad at times that I have considered taking my own life to put me out of my discomfort. Because you are the highlight of my life and I have someone to look forward to loving me in the future, I have not committed that act. It appears that my illness is not curable, just treatable for now. No one knows what the future holds. The best doctor in the world for treating my condition just happens to be right here in London. If you are not interested in seeing me anymore, that's fine. I'll be on my way," Ray said as he turned and walked down the sidewalk.

Georgina thought for a moment, and it struck her that she could not live with herself if Ray took his own life because she rejected him. Then she thought again. "*This is part of his plan, and I am falling right into his lies again. Either way, I can't chance it, and I better go after him.*" Georgina told herself.

"Ray! Stop," Georgina said. This time Ray did not stop. He was still feeling very weary and headed back to his apartment. Georgina went after him. She was feeling a lot of emotions and needed more information. "Ray, I'm sorry. I didn't know. Please wait. We can go sit in the park and talk if you'd like," Georgina said. "Yes I would like to talk, but not in the park, not today, I'm still having some issues from my last episode and I can't be too far away from a bathroom right now. We can go to my apartment or your parents' house. Which will it be?" Ray asked.

"Since we are almost to your apartment, if it's okay with you, we can go there," Georgina said. Ray was pleasantly surprised and nodded his answer.

Chapter 10
Realization

"Wow, nice apartment," Georgina exclaimed. "You like it? This is the way I would like to live once I have a family. Not in a cluttered small house, like my parents, but a spacious and modern home, filled with the latest gadgets—yet somewhat simple. Let me show you around. Where would you like to start?" Ray asked. "That could be a tough decision," Georgina said. "Well then, let's start with my favorite room: the kitchen," Ray said. "That sounds good to me. I like a man who's not afraid to spend time in the kitchen," Georgina giggled. "If I knew you liked a man in the kitchen, I would have had you over for dinner," Ray replied.

Ray showed Georgina his entire apartment except his bedroom. He didn't want her to feel uncomfortable and was uncertain whether to take her to see his exotic décor. He learned from other women that the fancier the bedroom decorations and furnishings the better the sexual performance and endurance was for both genders. His decorations were very expensive and current. He certainly wasn't frugal when it came to his apartment.

"Would you like to see my bedroom? Ray asked questionably. "I'll understand if you feel uncomfortable entering this room since we are not a couple," Ray said.

"I would definitely like to see your bedroom. One can learn a lot about a person by the colors they sleep in and by how neat they keep their room," Georgina said.

"Oh really, I didn't know that. Maybe we'd better save this room for later. I don't want you to find out too much about me at once," Ray said.

"Did you forget that was part of the reason I chose Glen over you? You never wanted to share information about yourself. I'm not sure I want to go in that room anyhow," Georgina said.

"You are so right. I need to learn to open up and reveal myself to you if we are going to have a relationship," Ray said. "No, we're not going to have a relationship. I shouldn't have come here. I'm engaged to another man. How would Glen feel if he knew I was here?" Georgina stated.

"Georgina, wait. Don't go. I will tell you every secret and piece of information about me that I can remember. I am crazy about you. Don't you understand you are what I want most? I can't eat, sleep, or function without you in my life. I need you to give me another chance," Ray said. "I want to win you from Glen. Look, I know you claim to love Glen, but I can give you the life you deserve. I don't think he can," Ray said.

Georgina paused and thought for a few moments and then replied to Ray's comment.

"Ray, I'm so confused. I have feelings for you, but if I marry you, then I will always wonder what I might have had with Glen. I hope when I marry him I'll be able to forget about you because right now, I wonder what it might be like if I marry you. I want to be with both of you, and I know that can't have it both ways," Georgina said.

Ray kissed Georgina like he never did before. He held her so tight she thought she'd never break free. I know you are planning to marry another man, but he is not here. I am not proud to steal you away from Glen, and I know how bad he will feel when you break his heart, but are you aware you will break one heart or the other?" Ray asked. "I can provide you with a wonderful life if you stay. You will never want for anything. We will have as many babies as you want, and they will be well provided for. Has Glen ever discussed this with you? Can he promise you all of these things, or don't you know this information yet?"

"I am not going to discuss my conversations with Glen. However, I do know that it feels so right to be here with you. I don't know if I feel this good in Glen's arms?" Georgina sighed.

"Then I think you need to re-evaluate your decision to marry Glen," Ray said. "I love you and I want to marry you now. I don't want to wait," he said as he kissed her again.

Georgina pulled back and thought about the night she just spent with Glen. How wonderful and caring he was with her. How could she do this to him? How could she have those same feelings for another man?

"What's wrong with me? I shouldn't be kissing you. Poor Glen," Georgina said. "What about, poor me?" Ray asked. "You said yourself, when you are with Glen you think of me. So are you going to go back and forth between both of us forever until one of us tires out and gives you up for someone else? I want you, and I want you now. Glen isn't here. Marry me and you will never regret it, I promise you," Ray shared.

Ray kissed Georgina again. He gently maneuvered her body onto his bed. He ran his fingers through her hair, across her forehead, and down her cheek to her mouth. He stroked her back and sides. Then without hesitation, he slid his hand under her shirt and slowly worked his way to her breasts. Ray was so sexually excited he ached. He hadn't planned to pursue Georgina in this manner when he invited her to his apartment, but now he wanted to have his way with her. He couldn't let her leave now. Tonight he was going to show her his magic. He removed each piece of his clothing hoping to entice Georgina into wanting the same thing he did. He needed to show her what he had to offer her. He wanted Georgina to want him as badly as he wanted her. Slowly he rubbed the inside of her thigh with his hand until it would go no further. She winced a little so he pulled away. Startled by her reaction, Ray said in a sexy tone, "tell me to stop and I will."

Georgina slid her body further back on his bed. Ray unbuttoned her blouse exposing her breast and began to suckle on them. He waited for her response. When she didn't pull away he accepted her obvious enjoyment as a sign to continue. She kissed his ears and slid her tongue down his neck. Slowly he glided his throbbing penis along her thigh. Georgina attempted to undress herself, but Ray took over. He knew now that she wanted the same thing he did. He no longer feared her reaction when she positioned herself to accept his gift.

Her body was soft and responsive to his needs. She quivered as his strokes and her pleasure increased. She then took command and they changed positions. She kissed his nipples as she tangled her fingers in his chest hairs. This was more than he had expected from her. He was prepared to give her his gift of life; but he was in no hurry to end the adventure.

Finally, neither could restrain their pleasure any longer and they climaxed together consummating their relationship. It was the best experience Ray had ever had with a woman. He knew she wasn't a virgin. She was far too experienced to have never been touched before. As they were getting dressed Ray expressed to Georgina, "This is what it will be like the rest of our lives. You don't want to miss out on this, do you?" Ray asked. "I don't know what to say. I feel so guilty. I was with Glen just a few days ago told him that I would marry him. How do I go back on my word?" she sighed.

"You had sex with Glen?" Ray asked. "Yes, you make it sound so cold and dirty. I'm not proud that I had sex with both of you, and I would like you to call it making love. I was hoping to save myself for that one special man, but that just shows you how much restraint I have with men. Sleeping with both of you just complicates my situation even more. Ray, can you walk me home? I have a lot of thinking to do," Georgina said.

"I know you've had this experience before. I wasn't expecting you to say you had it with Glen," Ray said.

"I had a boyfriend before both of you. He taught me how to please a man. Don't credit Glen for your pleasure," Georgina said.

Ray and Georgina walked silently down the street. As they approached her home, Georgina walked faster and heavier and seemed in a hurry. "Will I see you tomorrow?" Ray asked. "I don't know. I will be in touch with you. Give me a few days," Georgina said. As they approached Georgina's home Ray turned her to face him and he gave her a kiss good night. With that, Georgina turned and ran into her house.

"Good heavens, young lady, where have you been?" Bernice asked. "We expected you home hours ago," Myron said.

"I'm sorry. I need to go to my room. I need to be alone right now," Georgina said.

"This is not good. She has been with Ray and I don't care for that man. Every time she is with him, she comes home upset or in a bad disposition," Myron said. "The poor child is going through something we don't understand. Maybe I should go talk to her," Bernice said. "Do you think that would be wise right now? I don't think she needs reminded that she is engaged to a wonderful man. However, I don't feel she should be spending any more time with Ray," Myron said. "I'll let her rest now and tomorrow we'll discuss her situation between Ray and Glen," Bernice said.

The next morning, Georgina was her perky self. "Joanna, let's go shopping tonight after work to get the decorations you'll need for your wedding. We shouldn't wait till it's too close to the wedding to get them. We will have so many other items to attend to as it gets closer. What do you say?" Georgina asked.

"I don't really have the money tonight. I wasn't prepared to purchase decorations just yet. They will have to wait a few more weeks?" Joanna responded. "I was looking for something to pass the time until Glen comes back. I was looking for something to pass the time. If we must wait, then that is the way it shall be," Georgina said.

The Steiner's were surprised by Georgina's upbeat attitude. What a different girl she was from the evening before.

"Maybe a good night's sleep was all she needed. She sure seems confident that Glen will be coming for her shortly and she will be joining him in Pennsylvania," Myron said.

"Yes, I know. Maybe she was saying good-bye to Ray last night and it was a difficult time for her. I certainly hope that is what happened," Bernice said.

Back at the base, Glen was keeping very busy passing the time until he would return to London and marry the love of his life. *"Whenever you have a goal, time just seems to stand still,"* Glen thought to himself. Between Georgina and his Mother, Glen was confused as to where his first stop would be when he finally left the Air Force forever this time.

Glen left his youngest brother with a lot of responsibility and felt that he should probably return home first to make sure everything was in order. On the other hand Georgina was foremost in his mind. He knew he was needed at home and he should go help his Mother. But his heart was telling him something else. He focused on what he was going to say to Georgina when he finally saw her again.

Glen couldn't help but wonder about what Georgina did while he was gone. He felt confident that she was busy helping her sister with her wedding plans and that she had no time to participate in other activities.

Georgina made every attempt to keep a low profile so she wouldn't run into Ray. She'd hoped that if Ray didn't see her, he would forget about her, but Ray had other plans. When he did not hear from her in a week, he decided to pay her a visit at home.

"Hello, Mrs. Steiner. Is Georgina home?" Ray asked. "Actually, she is out with her sister this evening. You know, they are busy making plans for Joanna's wedding and I am not sure how long they'll be out," Bernice said. "Would you mind if I stayed here and waited a while for her to return?" Ray asked. "Don't you think it's kind of late? I don't know when to expect her, Ray," Bernice said.

"Okay, well obviously she's going to be a while. Would you let her know I stopped by?" Ray asked. "Sure," Bernice replied. Ray took about three steps down the sidewalk and decided to go to the back of the house to sit and wait where no one would see him.

He waited only a short time when he saw Georgina's bedroom light come on. "*That's odd, no one resembling Georgina walked by, nor did I hear any doors open or close. I'll throw a pebble at her bedroom window to get her attention,*" Ray said to himself. When Georgina did not respond, he went and knocked on the front door. "What can I do for you at this late hour?" Myron asked. "I was wondering if I could speak with Georgina," Ray asked. "Oh, she's been in bed for a few hours now. Come back tomorrow," Myron said sternly. "But your wife said she was out with her sister, and I never saw her come home. Her bedroom light just came on," Ray said. "Oh, well, she … uh, let me check," Myron said. Myron walked through the kitchen near the open stair case in the living room. He looked up to see Georgina acknowledging that she was aware of Ray's presence. Myron said to his daughter in a quiet tone. "Ray is downstairs asking for you. Do you want to talk to him? I can tell him you are sick or asleep or anything else you wish me to tell him," Myron offered. "Could you tell him I will call him tomorrow? Please Dad," Georgina said. "She's ready for bed. She will call you tomorrow," Myron said. "I've been told that before, but she doesn't call me back," Ray said. "Well then, I would take that as your answer. She's obviously not interested in talking with you. I will remind her tomorrow to call you, but I cannot make her act against her wishes. Do you understand?" Myron asked.

"Yes sir," Ray said. "*I don't feel like I'm getting anywhere with Georgina. Last week I thought for sure she was mine. Something must have gone wrong. I need to talk to her to find out what that might be. I need to find a way to spend more time with her,"* Ray thought to himself.

The girls were working on wedding decorations joking and laughing when Bernice announced to Georgina, "Ray is here." "Mother, tell him I'm sick and I will call him tomorrow," Georgina said. "Too late! You look like you are having a lot of fun," Ray said.

Georgina stood up and brushed herself off. "Sorry Ray, it's been a long time since I've had this much fun with my sister. I really didn't mean anything by that other than I want to continue working on her decorations. We have a lot to get done and not a lot of time to accomplish our task," Georgina said. "I will accept that as a positive response and justifiably a good reason not to see me today," Ray said.

"Would you like something to drink?" Joanna asked. "No, thank you. I didn't come to drink or to interrupt your fun. I am checking to see if you have a date for the wedding?" Ray asked. "No, but I'm hoping Glen will be back by then; however, I don't know of his plans yet," Georgina said. "I'm not surprised, but I am disappointed. If you change your mind, let me know," Ray said.

Ray's visit prompted Georgina to look at the last letter she had received from Glen, which had been almost two weeks. *"I wonder how he is doing. I'm sure I will be receiving another letter any day now,"* Georgina thought to herself.

Glen went to the train station to catch his ride to Harrisburg so that he could make what he thought might be his final flight home before his discharge.

Kathryn was Glen's strength. She had taught him and his siblings how to be kind and considerate of others. She taught all of her children how to clean, cook, and care for each other. Selfishness was not in their vocabulary. She taught them morals and values that they would carry with them the rest of their lives. No once could replace Glen's mother except maybe Georgina. If Kathryn ever got to meet her, she would understand why Glen was planning on spending the rest of his life with her. Right now he needed Georgina by him more than anyone. Georgina could comfort him while he faced his fears of his mother's impending death. Glen was going to be with Kathryn until she took her last breath. He was planning to postpone his next trip to London, but that might be premature.

On the train ride back to Harrisburg, Glen put his thoughts into Georgina's next letter.

> Georgina,
>
>   I can't wait for us to be together forever. I need you now more than you can imagine. Mother's illness is such a strain on my family. I wish you could meet her. I know the two of you would get along great. If you think you might be able to visit, let me know. I will make all of the arrangements. I'm afraid of missing Mother's last minutes and I might need to postpone my visit to London depending on her condition. I know you'll understand, and I love you for being that way.
>
> Love,
> Glen

Glen really didn't expect Georgina would be interested in visiting Billsport now with her sister's wedding in the near future.

"Mother, I wouldn't normally ask you this question, but I need your advice. Glen's mother is dying and he would like me to go to Pennsylvania to meet her. Glen said he will make all of the arrangements. I think this is important to him and I would like to meet her before she dies," Georgina shared in a concerned tone.

"My dear, have you definitely decided that you are going to marry Glen? I wouldn't recommend this trip unless you are certain," Bernice said.

"I want to say yes, but I am unsure as of yet. I am hoping this trip will help me with my decision," Georgina said.

"You are certainly old enough to make the trip on your own. I cannot make this decision for you. I do need to caution you. When in the right situation, your heart can lead you to a place that you might not be wise going," Bernice said.

"I know where you are going with this, Mother. You have no need to worry. I really want to make this trip to get some answers," Georgina said.

When Glen returned to his base, a letter regarding Georgina's decision was waiting for him.

Glen,

I will come to visit with you and your mother as soon as you can make the arrangements. I must get this visit in before it gets too close to Joanna's wedding. Meeting your mother and helping you with her care is important to me.

I have never flown before, so if you can instruct me on this new endeavor, it would help me immensely.

I will be waiting to hear from you.

Love,
Georgina

Glen was so excited to get Georgina's news. He could hardly wait to tell his family he was bringing her home on his next visit. Just one problem remained. He didn't know if had any more time to take off for a visit before Joanna's wedding. Somehow, even if it was after his discharge he would coordinate Joanna's wedding with Georgina's visit, the first chance he got.

"Mark, if I have any remaining leave, I need to schedule it as soon as possible. My girlfriend Georgina is coming from London to visit with my family. I will need to make flight arrangements and travel plans for her. I believe that I have four days left. How about it? Can you help me with this?" Glen pleaded.

"First I'll need to research your leave. This is something that the Air Force is very strict about. You know how careful we have to be Glen. Let me get back to you tomorrow," Mark said.

"I am going to need to make reservations for Georgina, and time is of the utmost importance, right now. How can I turn her down?" Glen asked.

"I will try to get back to you tomorrow, okay, Glen? That's the best I can do," Mark said. "Thanks so much, Mark. You don't know how much I appreciate this," Glen said. "Not so fast Glen I'm not certain that I can approve leave for you again so soon," Mark said.

Georgina hadn't heard from Glen and was beginning to get worried. Maybe she wouldn't be making a trip to Pennsylvania after all. Maybe it was getting too late and too complicated with Glen in the States and her in London. *I'll give Glen a few more days, and then I'll forget this trip.*

Just as Georgina made her decision, Ray knocked at the door. "Hi Ray," Georgina said. "What a beautiful sight. You look ravenous today. Let's go for a walk, my beautiful lady," Ray said. "Please don't call me your lady. No one owns me. However, I could use some company today. Let me go get my coat and we'll go for a walk," Georgina said.

"What's on your mind? I can tell something is bothering you," Ray said. "I had hoped to go to the states to meet Glen's family, particularly his mother. The woman is dying and I want to meet her for Glen's sake, but I haven't heard from Glen. Sometimes he seems so indifferent. It's very difficult to maintain a long-distance relationship," Georgina said.

"You've finally figured that out. I never thought I would defend Glen, but he is not in control of his time off, nor can he respond as quickly as you would like. There's a lot of paperwork involved in getting time off. Be patient. However, if you don't go to the states with Glen, I will take you with me on my next trip, if that's what you want," Ray said.

"Thanks for the offer, but I'd really like to meet Glen's mother before she dies. I think that would mean a lot to Glen," Georgina said.

"Do you really want to go? Are you sure you're going to marry him after everything you shared with me? I'm not sure I want to hear your answer, but I need to know," Ray said. "Is it necessary that I answer these questions now? You are not the first one to ask me this question in the past couple of days. I am hoping this trip will solidify my decision. If I don't go, I might not ever get the answers to the questions that will help me with my final decision," Georgina replied.

"I know how you think you feel about Glen, but have you thought about the feelings you still have for me?" Ray asked. "Yes, as a matter of fact I have. I don't feel the same way about you that I do about Glen. I'm sorry Ray, but you must know that I miss Glen so much it hurts. I really need to see him. I want to be part of his family. This is the final step I need to take to assure myself that I've made the right decision to marry Glen," Georgina said. "Then you should go to Pennsylvania and meet his family. Maybe I'm self-centered but I'll be willing to bet that you don't feel the same way when you come back," Ray said. "I need to go and I hope you are wrong. Even if you are right, that doesn't mean I will want you," Georgina said.

The next day while Georgina was at work, Bernice signed for a special delivery envelope. Bernice paced in anticipation of what might be in it. She hoped it held Georgina's travel plans. Bernice was nervous about Georgina going to Pennsylvania. However, if this is what Georgina wanted, this is what Bernice wanted for her. As soon as Georgina walked through the door her mother handed her the envelope. "Look Princess, a special delivery from Glen. Is it your airline tickets to Pennsylvania?" Bernice asked.

"Let me get my coat off Mom. I'm sure it must be. I am not expecting anything else," Georgina said.

Georgina opened the envelope to find two airplane tickets inside for various airline connections to get her to Billsport. Instructions on how to make a connecting flight, when Glen would arrive, and where they would meet was included. Georgina felt anxious about flying but excited at the same time to be seeing Glen and finally meeting his family. Her plane left that next Friday morning. She would return home late the following Tuesday night. Four days didn't allow for a very long visit. Hopefully it would be enough time to find out more about his family.

Georgina had a lot to accomplish in just a few days. She had to get coverage at her job. On such a short notice, that could be a difficult task. She rarely traveled and didn't have a suitcase. Her Mother would see to it that all of her clothes were laundered folded and ready to transport. Joanna loaned her a suitcase. Fitting everything into one suitcase was nearly impossible. "*Oh, my, this is too much to organize on such a short notice,*" Georgina said to herself. "*If I weren't such a perfectionist none of the minor details would matter to me.*" Friday arrived quickly. Thanks to her mother and sister she was easily ready the night before her departure.

After the plane took off and leveled out, Georgina heaved a sigh of relief. Hopefully it would be a quiet ride. Because of the time difference she'd arrive in Billsport around noon. She had already been awake several hours and was ready for a nap when she arrived. "*I hope I don't wear out too early. I need to stay awake to meet Glen's family,*" Georgina thought.

The stewardesses came around with the passengers' breakfasts. Georgina wasn't sure she should chance eating. She was feeling a bit queasy, probably a nervous reaction from all of the excitement. She was also nervous meeting Glen's family for the first time. All of a sudden she had a dreadful feeling. Wonder if his family didn't like her. It was too late to turn back now and she wasn't' sure she was ready for this event.

Their planes landed a few minutes apart as scheduled. Georgina righted herself, got her balance, and headed to the front of the plane. She still felt queasy but she put on her best smile to greet Glen. *"This feeling must go away. I can't be sick while I am here. This will be a great opportunity to meet my future family. I hope they are as anxious as I am,"* she worried. She anticipated her reunion with Glen, which took her mind off her stomach. She stepped off the plane and went to retrieve her suitcase. She waited and waited and finally approached the luggage clerk. "I'm sorry but there isn't anymore luggage from that flight. Maybe your luggage didn't make it on the correct plane," the clerk responded. *"Great,"* she said under her breath. *"What a way to start a trip."*

Just as she headed for the complaint desk, she saw Glen waiting with her luggage. "You should be glad I really miss you or you would be in big trouble for that prank, Mister," Georgina said. "I thought I would get your attention by taking your luggage. You were so focused on finding it, you never saw me standing here," Glen said. "You better hope you got the correct bags or I might be wearing men's underwear all weekend," Georgina said. "Don't worry it's yours, I got some really good inside information. You might look cute in men's underwear. Did you every try them?" Glen responded.

"I can think of better ways to get my attention. I am so nervous to meet your family that my stomach is a little upset," Georgina said.

"Don't be nervous, Mom won't bite you. Anyhow, Lona and Betty need a break, so they won't be coming. Betty is pregnant and suffering from morning sickness. I know you don't know how that is, but I'm sure you have heard it can be pretty bad in the beginning. She has five other children; you'd think she'd learned from previous pregnancies not to do it again," Glen said. "Kevin and Mom are the only two that you will meet this trip. Next time, I'll give everybody an advanced notice. Hopefully you will get to meet the rest of my siblings the next trip. I don't know if you'll ever meet my dad, he hardly ever comes around anymore," Glen said. "Let's get out of this airport and go meet Mom. I know she can't wait to meet you. I've told her everything I know about you. When she is feeling well, she will talk your head off—that is, if you can understand her. Did I ever tell you she has a strong German accent?" Glen said.

"Don't worry. I'm used to those German accents. Your mother and I have one thing in common: you. We'll get along just fine," Georgina explained.

Glen already called for a taxi. It was the only way for them to get home, which was about fifteen miles from the airport. For some reason, this ride seemed to take forever.

"What a beautiful place. Look at those gorgeous mountains," Georgina said. "There's so much more for you to see. I wish we had more than four days. I'm sure I will have time to take you to the river. Thirty miles down the road are beautiful waterfalls. There are several mountaintop lookouts to view the scenery, and so many other places for you to see. Right now I want to go check in on Mother," Glen said. "Of course you do, I expected that. I admire your dedication to her," Georgina said.

When they arrived Betty came out to greet them. "Mother's not doing very well today. I think your friend needs to stay at a hotel. Mother wouldn't want anyone to see her this way. Hi, I'm Betty. You must be Georgina. I've heard so much about you. You are as pretty as Glen said you were," Betty shared. "I don't want to cause any problems. If you think I should stay somewhere else—well, if Glen helps me—I don't have a problem doing that," Georgina said.

"That's ridiculous. There's plenty of room here. She won't be in the way. If Mom doesn't want us around, I will see to it that Georgina is practically invisible. This might be the only chance Georgina and Mom get to talk with each other and I'm not putting her in a hotel," Glen said sternly.

"Have it your way. You will any how," Betty said. "I hope you don't think I don't want you here, but his timing is not very good," she said flustered. "What timing? This is the first chance I've had to bring Georgina home. It's not a matter of timing. Why don't you go now? We are here and we'll take care of Mother," Glen said.

"It was nice meeting you, Georgina. I hope we get a chance to talk real soon," Betty said. She turned and got into an old black car that made all kinds of noise as she drove it down the street.

"That was a wonderful surprise. I did get to meet Betty after all. I know what you're thinking. That she wasn't very pleasant. She's just looking out for your mother's best interests," Georgina said.

"You are truly wonderful and so very understanding. You never see the bad side of anything. I am so lucky to have you in my life," Glen said.

"Glen, do you think it would be better if I stayed at a hotel? I don't want to cause any hard feelings between you and your family," Georgina said. "Nonsense, you better forget that silly idea. You are staying right here. If you go to a hotel and I stay here with Mother, we won't have a chance to spend any time together. I was hoping to set a wedding date during your visit, but I don't have an exact discharged date yet so that won't be possible," Glen shared.

"I guess I'll stay after all. I have no idea where to go," Georgina said. "You are coming into my arms for a big hug, that's where you are going. I can't live without you anymore. You consume all of my thoughts," Glen said. "I'm flattered and feel the same way about you," Georgina shared.

Glen and Georgina spent the next ten minutes hugging, kissing, and just staring at each other. Finally, Glen broke the silence. "Let's go meet Mom. Let me check in on her and let her know you are here. Then I will call you into her room. We'll spend a little time with her then we'll get something to eat. Sound good to you?" Glen asked. "Yes, sure, I want what you want. Don't disturb her if she is sleeping. I have three more days to meet her," Georgina said.

Glen quietly walked into his Mother's room. Kathryn's head was turned away from the door. All of a sudden she sensed a presence and quickly turned to see Glen watching her. "Ah, you're home son. I'm rather tired tonight, I hope you don't mind if I sleep a bit?" Kathryn said

"Mother, I brought Georgina home to meet you," Glen said. "She's here? She came the whole way from London?" Kathryn asked. "Yes, and she came to meet you. She said she understands German accents and said she should be able to communicate with you just fine?" Glen said. "Well then, where is she? Don't just stand there, bring her in here, son," Kathryn said.

Georgina walked through the door and the women's eyes connected immediately. Georgina took Kathryn's hand and held it tight. They were at a loss for words, and then Kathryn spoke.

"You are a lovely lady. You will make Glen a wonderful wife. I can see by looking at you that you are a kind and caring lady. You'll forever be involved in each other's lives. You'll learn what make's each other happy. I won't be around for long so I need to share my thoughts with you now," Kathryn took a deep breathe then continued. "Marriage is never a two-way street no matter what anybody tells you. There will always be a dominant figure. The other person will take on the position of the peacekeeper. That's the one who holds the family together. You will not know at first which one will take on that position, but you will always be blessed with a stable relationship. Remember, you can disagree but never fight. You will almost never want the same thing at the same time. And most importantly, never forget the feelings you have for each other now because it won't always feel this wonderful. As time goes by you'll become bored and almost tire of each other. Just remember what made you fall in love in the beginning, and most of all, what brought you together," Kathryn shared happily.

"Now don't let me keep you from each other. You need to spend some time alone, we'll talk again later. Kevin will be here in a little while. I will be all right till he gets here," Kathryn said.

"Mother, we'll be nearby until Kevin comes home. You shouldn't be alone for too long. I couldn't live with myself if something happened to you while I was out on my own behalf," Glen said.

"Mrs. Dornstadt, I would like to share with you what a wonderful man you've raised. He is so kind and thoughtful—a true gentleman—and you have been a wonderful example to him. I appreciate all of your advice and will not forget one word of it. I pray we get more opportunities like this to talk. I couldn't wait to meet you. Glen speaks very fondly of you. I pray the Lord will make you better. You are so young and have many good years ahead of you and I would love to get to know you better," Georgina said as a tear ran down her cheek.

"Child, don't cry for me. I have fulfilled my reason for my creation. I have wonderful children and grandchildren. I've made great friends and belong to a wonderful church with a supportive congregation and a pastor who has helped me on my journey home to the Lord. The experiences you learn in life stay with you. You learn by your mistakes and you pass them on to your loved ones hoping they've learned to avoid those same mistakes. You will be good for our family. I hope I am able to be here the day you become one of us. Now you two go and spend some time together. I will be okay. Kevin will be here soon," Kathryn scolded.

"What are your plans for dinner?" Glen asked his mother. "There's some chicken and dumplings in the icebox. Your sister dropped them off just before you got here. I worry about her. She should not have any more babies. This one has been very difficult for her," Kathryn said.

"That's funny. She said you were having a bad day, but you seem better to me today and I didn't think Betty looked too bad either," Glen said. "She doesn't want you to worry about her. She's lost weight and sleeps too much. Her husband—he doesn't do enough to help her. She is very tired. I don't say much to her; she gets very sensitive when you speak badly of Howard," Kathryn said.

"Don't either of you be keeping secrets from me. I will be home for good real soon and I will do what I can for both you," Glen scolded.

"You and Georgina should go. Kevin and I will be okay," Kathryn said. "We aren't going anywhere except out to the parlor to wait for Kevin. I want him to meet Georgina. We'll eat and spend some time together. In the meantime, you rest Mom," Glen said.

Glen and Georgina took a walk through what used to be the garden. It had been severely neglected because no one was around to take care of it.

"I want to restore the garden and make it beautiful again, when I come home. It will give us a sense of accomplishment, and we will be so proud of our produce. We can share our harvest with the rest of the family," Glen said.

"Glen," Georgina said. "We're not going to live here at your mother's house when we get married, are we?" "I thought maybe for just the first year until we save money to buy our own place. Kevin isn't going to be here for long and Mom will need someone to help her. I thought we could do that for her," Glen said.

"I was hoping we could start out by ourselves. Newlyweds need time to adjust to each other without the interference of parents. I have nothing against your mother; she's great and I adore her, but we are going to want time alone to ourselves, and I think she would agree," Georgina said. "Yes of course she would, but she doesn't always know what is best for her. We need to help her. I thought you would understand," Glen said.

"I suggest that we wait till the time comes and see what we need to do then. In the meantime, let's go inside and get dinner started," Georgina said. "That sounds like a plan to me," Glen said.

Kevin always made his presence known and today wasn't any different. He slammed the door behind him and then dropped a pile of books on the floor. He looked up to see a strange woman looking at him. "Who are you? I didn't come into the wrong house, did I?" Kevin asked. "No," a very familiar voice said. "Hey, Glen, I missed you buddy. Ah, you must be the lovely Georgina? I've heard how pretty you are and Glen sure wasn't exaggerating," Kevin said.

"It's nice to meet you Kevin. You're as cute as Glen said you were too," Georgina said. "He did?" Kevin asked quizzically. "Well it wasn't quite like that. She exaggerates considerably," Glen said.

Glen took Georgina around to show her the rest of the old farmhouse. It has six bedrooms—four upstairs and two downstairs. The wood in the house was very dark and thick and showed its age. The floors are wooden, and most were covered with area rugs. The kitchen was obviously used heavily at one time. There was an old six-burner, coal-stoked, cast iron cook stove located in the far corner. On the wall next to the stove were several pans, griddles, and pots for easy access. Kathryn had been quite the cook in her younger years. Now most of the pots and pans hung un-used. A recent indoor water closet was added to the house so Kathryn wouldn't need to go out in the dark any longer.

"Outside are several other buildings. You'll find a chicken coup, two storage sheds, a large barn, and an outhouse. The barn only houses an old tractor now. At one time it was filled with feed, straw, livestock, and other farm machinery," Glen shared.

"Kevin, I'm sorry you have so much on your plate. I will be home permanently in a few months and I will help you get organized. I promise. After Georgina and I get married, we will move in upstairs and be here as long as you need us or as long as Mother needs us," Glen said.

"You and Georgina should have a place of your own. That's no way to start a marriage," Kevin said. "Are you two sure you haven't met before? She made that exact statement just a little while ago,"

Glen said. "She's right. You can come around and help out. I miss you brother. I want to see you and your lovely lady, but you need to have your own place," Kevin said.

"Well, if it makes you feel any better, that is my plan. But first, I need to get on my feet. I'll need to live here a short while after we get married in order to save money to buy our own house. Then you can get some well-deserved time away from us," Glen said.

"While you two were talking I heated up dinner and made rolls to go with it. I found the dinnerware and the table is ready. Does your mother have a teapot? I need somebody to eat this food, and someone to help feed your mother," Georgina said.

"Kevin, will you get out the teapot? I will go see if Mother wants to come out or if I need to take her dinner to her," Glen said. "Glen, don't try to get Mom out of bed. She is not stable at all anymore. Because Georgina is here she might overexert herself, and that wouldn't be good. Just take her dinner into her room," Kevin said.

"Why didn't anybody tell me this? So she's not as good as she appears?" Glen asked. "No, she's not good at all. If you saw how weak she's become, you wouldn't say she looks good either. I see her every day, and she's gone downhill really fast. I'll admit I was a troublemaker until Mom got sick. Now I am a maid, a cook, a housekeeper, a gardener, and a nurse, and I don't know anyone else who can do all of that for Mom. When school is over this year I am going to get a job and take care of her as long as she needs me," Kevin said.

"Where is Dad, he should be helping her now when she needs him?" Glen said. "He sends a little bit of money every month, but who knows where it comes from? He doesn't care and never did. The last time he wrote home was to whine about Uncle Wayne asking him to leave. He sent us his new address in case anyone needed to contact him. I just can't respect a man who would abandon his wife in this condition," Kevin said.

After dinner Glen kept his promise to Kevin. He and Georgina went into the parlor and closed the doors. They were in there for the remainder of the evening discussing everything from jobs, to kids, and their marriage plans.

"Wow it's getting late. I should have shown you your room a long time ago," Glen stated. "I'm sure you would have liked to have freshened up earlier. I'm sorry. It has been a long day for you. I'm not a very good host," Glen said.

"Don't be too hard on yourself. I've had a wonderful time. I am young and adjust well to new situations. I am going to turn in early though. You're right, it's been a long day and I am very tired," Georgina yawned.

"Of course, but first I must give you something," Glen said. "Oh? What is that?" Georgina asked. Glen reached into his pocket and pulled out a little silver box with a black and silver bow. He handed it to Georgina and said, "Georgina, I love you. I adore you, and I want you in my life forever. Will you marry me?" Georgina paused a few seconds, and then responded.

"Of course I will Glen. You know I love you," Georgina said.

"Wow! You worried me there for a second. You hesitated. Are you sure? I guess I expected you to be more excited." Glen said. "I love you. I am just tired. It's been a long day. I'm sorry if I ruined your surprise," Georgina said.

"I will let you sleep on that tonight and tomorrow we'll tell Mom and Kevin our news. You get some rest. I love you," Glen said.

While Georgina was in Pennsylvania, Ray had a follow up appointment at his doctor's office. Tests indicated he was exhibiting gradual improvement. With continued treatments, he might be able to return to Pope Air Force Base soon. Ray was planning on taking Georgina home with him. He felt very secure with his plan. No one was going to take her away from him.

Chapter 11
Faltering Revelations

Glen woke up early like he was use to doing. He knew Georgina was exhausted so he left her sleep. He didn't know Georgina's sleep patterns. Hopefully he would get an opportunity to learn a lot more about her both intellectually and physically during this visit. Glen scolded himself. *"How could he think such thoughts? You didn't bring her home to take advantage of her How embarrassing, not to mention what a poor example I would be, if Kevin were to catch us.*

Glen decided to check on his mother. Kathryn appeared to be sleeping comfortably, but she would wake up soon, and expect her morning coffee. Glen no longer knew what to feed his mother for breakfast. Her food intake was barely enough for a bird to survive. *"I feel so removed from the family. I will be happy to get back home for good. Betty and Howard can barely handle their own family's needs without the added responsibility of taking care of Mother too, and it's not fair to expect Kevin to continue her care."* Glen thought.

Glen discovered that thinking about his mother's needs distracted him from his sexual desires. It only took a few moments for Glen's thoughts to return to Georgina lying in that big bed.

She looked vulnerable and he wanted so badly to crawl into bed with her and warm her up. He ached to feel her soft body next to him. Just that simple thought aroused him again. Having Georgina here with him 24 hours a day was more difficult than he expected.

Soon he heard footsteps in the hallway and assumed that Georgina was up. When she didn't come out to the kitchen he decided he better check on her to make sure she wasn't confused from being in a strange place. Just as he made the corner he found her coming out of the bathroom.

"You look pale. Do you feel okay?" Glen asked. "I think it must be the time change and being somewhere different. I really haven't felt very well since I left yesterday morning. Give me a few minutes to get dressed, and I will be right out," Georgina said.

Glen couldn't resist knowing that in a few moments she would be naked. Sexual thoughts returned to him and he found he was aroused again. "Let me walk you to the bedroom" he said.

When they got to the bedroom Glen turned Georgina to face him and pulled her body up to his and he began kissing her. His strong male emotions and hormones were working overtime. He began to rub her back and then he caressed her buttocks. Slowly his hands moved to the front of her and he began to caress her breasts. He thought he should stop but he was so aroused that he could no longer contain his desires. Georgina felt his excitement and knew what to expect next. Since he had already professed his love to her, did he need to pursue the issue any further? Would she get upset if he continued to make moves on her?

Georgina started to pull away, but she wasn't fighting him either. Glen backed her up until they both fell onto the bed. It was still early and hopefully no one would be up for a little while. Glen wanted to go slow this time. He wanted time to explore her body. Their last encounter was awkward and didn't allow that opportunity. This time he was going to find out what turned her on.

"I don't think we should be doing this, Glen. What about your mother?" Georgina asked. "She's still asleep, I just checked on her. My darling, it will only be a few months until we are married. I'm alone every day and ache to be with you. In my mind I can feel you, smell you and just imagine what it would be like to have my way with you. You are here and I want you so badly, please don't deny me now," Glen said as he pulled her night gown over her head and exposed her entire, naked, slim body.

Glen proceeded to undress showing Georgina just how excited he was. They became consumed in each other's emotions. Glen never felt this way about anyone close to his own age. His previous sexual partners had been older woman or prostitutes. Guilt and shame were playing with his emotions. He knew how much he wanted to please Georgina and show her how wonderful making love could be, yet he struggled to maintain an erection. Eventually, he relaxed and was able to become consumed in the moment.

Georgina moaned with pleasure. "I'm not hurting you, am I?" he asked. "No, not at all. I feel guilty about enjoying this and where we are doing it. Plus, we're not married yet," she said.

"How can something so beautiful be wrong? Don't feel guilty. Everyone does this. Some people wait for a license. Don't worry we will have one very soon," Glen said.

The couple repeated this activity every morning and evening during her visit. All of a sudden Glen became needy and insecure in this relationship. He thought he was bonding with her and in reality he was pushing her away. Georgina was not very excited about this ritual. Fortunately her time with Glen was limited. She wanted to savor every minute she had with him, but something just wasn't right.

Glen had no idea about Georgina and Ray's matinee. He didn't know the magic she had already experienced with Ray. Georgina felt like a tramp having sex with two different men in such a short period of time. Now she was completely confused. Glen's love making didn't compare to Ray's. Maybe in time she could teach him and he could satisfy her like Ray did. Eventually it could be good, however, Ray already knew how to please her, and she couldn't get him off her mind.

Georgina experienced guilty feelings like never before. How could she be thinking about Ray when she was with the man she loved? Ray had lied to her time and time again. He had this arrogance about him that she didn't care for, and he certainly didn't care about women the way Glen did. *"That's right; keep thinking of Ray that way,"* she told herself.

Glen borrowed his brother-in-law's car for an afternoon and took Georgina to view the best local sights. He took her downtown shopping and introduced her to some friends. The rest of the time they spent with Kathryn and Kevin. In no time, Georgina found herself packing for the return trip home. Glen and Georgina said their good-byes and promised to keep in touch by mail or Western Union, if the need arose. Memories from the trip would stay with Georgina forever.

Glen stayed until Georgina's plane was out of sight. He was taking a bus back to Harrisburg and then flying on to Raleigh. These last few months were going to be very long. Staying focused on completing his final project was going to be difficult. His every thought was of Georgina.

Georgina was exhausted upon her arrival home Tuesday night and was eager to get to her room and relax. Her work week started at seven AM Wednesday morning so she needed to get some sleep.

Bernice was concerned when Georgina seemed blasé about sharing details of her trip. "I'm really sorry Mom. I'll share everything with you tomorrow. I am exhausted from the flight and I just want to rest tonight," she told her parents.

Georgina didn't sound like someone who just spent four days with the person she was planning to marry. Something's wrong," Myron said. "I have a bad feeling about this trip. I hope nothing bad happened between them. She isn't herself, don't you agree Myron?" Bernice asked. "All she wants to do now is to sleep in her own bed. She'll probably be better tomorrow," Myron said.

"Let's follow the leader and go to bed," Bernice suggested.

In the morning Georgina returned to work. She felt somewhat better and brushed off her queasiness as nerves and jet lag. *"Everything will be better tonight, I'm sure,"* Georgina told herself.

That evening Georgian shared with her parents the events of the last four days. She elaborated about the time she spent with Kathryn, Kevin and Glen. You could hear the excitement in her voice when she talked about the sights she visited and the people she met. All of a sudden the tone of her voice changed. She sounded like a little girl again. She built up how wonderful she expected her life to be with Glen and how she couldn't wait to start her life with him in a few months. And then the final surprise. She uncovered her hand and showed them her ring.

"Oh my, he really loves you Georgina! That's absolutely beautiful," Bernice exclaimed.

Georgina was excited about planning her own wedding this time. The only thing missing was the date. A few weeks wouldn't matter to her but her parents were planning to make the trip to Pennsylvania and they needed to know a date as soon as possible in order to make travel arrangements.

"This is going to be a special summer. Both of my girls are getting married. I'll be a new grandma before you know it. I only hope you girls are as happy as your father and I have been," Bernice shared happily. "Why Bernice, that's so nice of you," Myron replied.

On Saturday Georgina went with her mother shopping to help her look for a dress for Joanna's wedding. When they finished, they decided to stop at the farmer's market to buy fish for dinner.

"Whatever you do, don't eat that tonight," said a voice from behind them. Georgina turned around to see Ray standing there. "I was going to stop over later to see if you would like to go to dinner with me tonight," Ray said.

"She can't go out with you anymore Ray, just look at her ring. Georgina and Glen are getting married later this summer,"

Bernice said. "Congratulations! This calls for a celebration!" Ray said. "I better not Ray," Georgina replied with a scowl.

"Oh come on, let me show you how happy I am for you. If I were a woman you would celebrate with me, wouldn't you? Because I am a man, you become prejudice," Ray said.

"If I was already married, you wouldn't ask me out, would you, Ray?" Georgina asked.

"But you're not. So I'll be over at seven PM. See you then," Ray said as he turned and walked away, not giving her a chance to refuse him.

Georgina wasn't sure how to get out of this mess. She had definitely made up her mind. She was marrying Glen, so she should not be going out with Ray. Georgina knew where a night out with Ray could lead her and she would never get over her feelings for him if she continued seeing him.

Ray arrived precisely at seven PM as promised. "I can't go with you. I must stay faithful to Glen. If we are going to be married, I can't be going out with other men," Georgina said.

"You don't sound positive yet about marrying him. You are still saying 'if I marry Glen. Let me take you out tonight to celebrate. I promise I won't bother you after tonight, if you don't want me to. Somehow, I don't think that is what you want," Ray said.

"Give me a few minutes to get changed," Georgina said flustered. She could just kick herself for not saying no. Discipline was not her best strength. She was just too passive. That weakness must change tonight, especially if Ray tried to get her to his apartment. He was so attractive and he knew it, but his attitude could be cold and offensive when he didn't get his way. *"If Ray was just as sincere and kind as Glen was, I would be marrying him instead. If only I had never slept with Ray, I wouldn't be having second thoughts. Glen's sexual skills need improvement and hopefully he'll be as good as Ray in no time. He just needs some experience,"* she thought to herself. Georgina hesitated, she wasn't sure she wanted to do this. *"Make up your mind*, she said to herself.

"Ray, how late do you think we'll be?" Georgina asked. "I will have you back whenever you want, my lady. I will adapt to your schedule," Ray said. "I want to be home early, like nine or nine thirty," Georgina said. "Why that's hardly long enough to eat dinner. It may be a little bit later. Okay?" Ray asked. "Okay, but not much later," Georgina hesitated.

Ray had a cab waiting. Georgina didn't know it yet, but they were going to his apartment.

"Where are our reservations?" she asked. "I never told you we had reservations," Ray said. "Where are we going? You said we were going out for dinner, so I did not eat with my family. I am famished and I was expecting dinner," Georgina said. Oh, so you were expecting me! Ray said. "Calm down, we are having dinner at my place. I have a friend preparing dinner as we speak. Wow, I didn't know that you had to eat on such a strict schedule," Ray said. "I'm sorry. I can't explain it, but it seems if I don't eat lately, I feel sick. You must know I am not thrilled about going to your apartment," Georgina said. "I'm going to send you back home if you continue whining and complaining. I can't seem to do enough to make you happy tonight," Ray said.

"I'm sorry. I am blaming you for my own shortcomings. Let's start over, okay?" Georgina asked. "It's sweet of you to take the blame. I should have told you I was planning on bringing you here. I wanted to surprise you with a special dinner. Considering the circumstances, I shouldn't have done that," Ray said.

When they entered Ray's apartment a wonderful aroma filled the air. Ray had timed their arrival perfectly. Dinner was ready. All Ray had to do was serve it.

Georgina looked around his apartment. He had candles lit in every corner. The furniture was new, not warped. His décor was modern and matched perfectly. This was how she wanted to live. She saw that old farmhouse in Pennsylvania and knew she preferred Ray's taste over Glen's. Let's dig in so that we can spend some time talking. I'm sure you'll want to fill me in on your trip and plans," Ray said.

After dinner, Georgina thanked Ray for his sentiments, his graciousness, and his concerns about their relationship. She didn't know that he was going to use that information to his advantage.

"I just want to make sure you're happy. I'm concerned for you. You just don't seem certain about this marriage," Ray shared.

The two of them made small talk for most of the evening. "Let's have dessert. Follow me to the kitchen," Ray said. "What are we having?" Georgina asked. "Forgive me for this comment, but I'd like to have you. I know you are spoken for. Glen is so lucky; I don't think he realizes what a gem he has in you. I ache every day just to hold you," Ray said.

"Ray stop, you are making me very uncomfortable," Georgina said. "Just hear me out, please. I can give you so much more than Glen. I will make you rich in ways Glen could only imagine, but you won't give me a chance. Postpone your wedding for six months. Let me prove my love to you. That's all I ask," Ray said.

Georgina started to cry. "I can't believe I am in this predicament. I love you too Ray. When I'm with Glen, I think of you. When I'm with you, I think of Glen. I keep telling myself I'm better off with Glen. He is so sincere and a true gentleman. He has never lied to me about anything. I've caught you in several lies," Georgina said.

"In defense of myself, let me tell you, it was all for your benefit. I wanted you to realize life could be so different if you marry me. There's no way for you to know what I have in store for us if you don't give me a chance," Ray shared. "Let me ask you a question. Since you opened up to me, what do you plan to do now? You aren't going to go ahead with this farce of a wedding, are you? I can't imagine a marriage working with such uncertainty. I think you should postpone it," Ray said.

"I can't. I mean … well, Glen gave me this ring. I'm committed. I met his mother, sister, and brother. How would it look to them if I broke Glen's heart?" Georgina asked.

"But you are not sure you love him. You said so yourself," Ray said. "Oh no, I'm sure I love him, but I love you too. I can't have both of you and I committed to him first," Georgina said.

"No, that's not true at all. Four years ago you committed to me. Because I was in a combat zone and I couldn't correspond with you like you wished, you dumped me for Glen. You committed to me first. Do you remember that commitment?" Ray asked.

"I have had enough for one night. Take me home. I need to think about this, but don't expect me to change my mind. I am still going to marry Glen," Georgina said.

Back in North Carolina, Glen was completing the requirements and skills description that were needed to fill the position of the barracks record keeper. He was going to miss this job. It was easy, not at all stressful, and at the same time, very rewarding. He still had to train his replacement, and then he'd be a free man again.

Glen knew that Georgina and her parents were not able to plan a wedding in London that was to take place in the United States. He also knew that the responsibility was going to fall on him. He was looking forward to the challenge. If he could teach men to jump out of airplanes, he could plan a wedding.

As the weeks passed, Georgina was able to avoid Ray. She stayed busy with her sister's wedding plans. She wrote to Glen every day and told him that her life was confusing but that she was functioning well without him. She was holding out for the day they would be together forever. She still had a gnawing feeling in her stomach about Ray. She just couldn't forget him, which bothered her.

Friday night one week before Joanna's wedding the ladies went shopping to complete last-minute details. As the evening progressed, Georgina's stomach was very unsettled and she felt extremely tired. Maybe she was coming down with something.

"Don't do this to me now. We'll go home tonight but I must finish this shopping trip—with or without you tomorrow," Joanna said.

The ladies returned home. Georgina went directly to her room. She took off her clothes and crawled under the covers. She was having a difficult time falling asleep. Her stomach continued to churn and ache. She started rubbing her stomach thinking this would provide her with some relief. All of a sudden she discovered the small hump.

Now as she thought about it, she had not had a period in quite sometime. A few days earlier she had not felt well either, as a matter of fact she felt queasy a lot lately. She even threw up in the bathroom at work twice in the last month. While in Pennsylvania she worried about getting pregnant but put that thought in the back of her mind. Maybe now she should address her illness and see if that was what was causing her frequent bouts of sickness. She was obviously gaining weight.

She jumped out of bed and tried on the bridesmaid gown she was to wear the next week in the wedding. It was tight—very tight—but she could still fit into it.

Georgina sat for several minutes, trying to put her thoughts together. She was trying very hard to deny what she suspected. It all made sense now. Several mornings at work, she couldn't drink tea without it upsetting her stomach. She had a bloated-looking stomach. Then all of a sudden the revelation came to her. Who was the father? *"Oh, no, what do I do now?"* Georgina thought to herself. *"I can't believe I've let this happen."*

She tossed and turned that night in a fitful sleep. The next morning when she got up the entire family commented on how bad she looked. "Maybe we should get you to a doctor dear," her mother suggested. "Let's give it a few days, Mom. Don't rush into anything. I will be better soon, I'm sure," Georgina said, knowing that was probably far from the truth. *"I am not going to ruin Joanna's wedding. This is her day and no one will know my secret until after that day."* Georgina promised herself.

Georgina scheduled a doctor's appointment without telling her family. Dr. Cooper performed the examination. "I suspect you are correct young lady, but before we jump the gun on this diagnosis, let's perform a urinalysis to confirm our suspicions. You can stop by my office on Friday for the results," he said.

That evening Georgina felt better after she took a long afternoon nap. She was restless with her speculation and needed to talk to someone.

"I am going for a walk," Georgina announced. "Do you think you are up for that?" her mother asked. "I will be just fine Mother. I need some fresh air," Georgina said. "Don't be long, you shouldn't push yourself too soon," her mother said.

Georgina walked past Ray's apartment three times. She decided it wouldn't be wise to tell him of her predicament until she knew for sure. Just as she decided to leave, Ray came around the corner.

"Hello. Imagine meeting you here. You avoid me for weeks and then you show up on my doorstep. To what do I owe this visit?" Ray said. "Well actually, I was just leaving," Georgina said.

"Don't go so soon. You just got here," Ray said. "I've been walking around the block for almost an hour now trying to gather the courage to talk to you. Then I decided this was a mistake and I had better leave. I've had a change of heart," Georgina said.

"Boy, now that's just not fair. I didn't even get a chance to make you mad, and you are leaving. Obviously you have something on your mind. Come in to my apartment and we'll talk," Ray giggled. "I'm already in enough trouble I probably shouldn't come inside, can we just walk? Georgina said. "I would rather talk inside where it's drier and more private. I won't bite I promise. Remember you came to see me this time," Ray said.

"I don't know where to start," Georgina said. "How about the beginning, hopefully I'll understand what you are trying to tell me," Ray said.

"Thanks. I really feel welcome now," Georgina sighed. "Don't be so hard on yourself," "Ray said to Georgina as he gave her a quick hug.

"I haven't seen you in weeks. You look charming as ever. Please, let me take your coat, I want you to be comfortable. Ray poured himself a drink and asked Georgina, "Can I get you a drink before we get started?" he asked. "No thank you I don't want a drink," Georgina said as she handed Ray her coat. Let me get straight to the topic of concern before I chicken out: I'm pretty sure I'm pregnant," Georgina said. Ray dropped his glass and it smashed into a hundred pieces. He then gulped air and sat down quickly. "Okay, well, I guess my first question is: when are due?" Ray asked. I don't know yet. The doctor will tell me later this week. I don't even know whose baby it is. I want it to be Glen's, but I can't be sure. This changes everything," Georgina said as she started to cry.

"He doesn't deserve you. I don't care whose baby it is. Let me marry you before anybody figures out you were pregnant before you were married," Ray said. "I can't do that to Glen. He needs to know. He doesn't know about us. He thinks you have been history for a long time and that he is the only one I have been with. He would surely raise this baby and never question its paternity," Georgina said. "Then why did you come to me?" Ray asked. "I needed to talk to someone, and I can't tell my family—not yet. Not until after Joanna's wedding. I have been to a doctor but I won't know for sure until I stop by to get the lab results on Friday. In a way, I hope there is something else wrong with me. But I truly doubt it," Georgina said crying.

Ray took Georgina's hand and sat her down on the sofa next him. He looked her in the eyes.

"I love you," he said. "The one night we shared was wonderful. We've known each other a long time, and I think we could have a beautiful life together. I want this more now than ever. Let me be your baby's father," he begged her.

Ray placed his lips on Georgina's. It was the most passionate kiss Georgina could remember with either man. He pulled her closer and just hugged her till he could feel her heart beating against his chest. Silently, he gazed into her eyes. Nothing needed to be spoken as they both sensed the depth of their relationship at that moment. Ray kissed her again until she came up for a breath.

"Don't, do that, please. You are just complicating matters," Georgina pulled away frustrated. "I don't think you mean what you are saying or you would not have come here tonight. Please don't fight me. Let me have my way with you tonight. I want you to experience the most erotic feelings you have ever felt. Let me remind you of how wonderful it can be forever. I know how to please you, and there's so much more for you to experience," Ray said.

"This is so wrong. Why can't I stop you, Ray?" Georgina cried. Because you are too stubborn to admit you love me more than Glen," Ray said.

Confidently and slowly he began to remove her blouse, button by button. He took off his shirt and rubbed his chest against hers. Her skirt and panties came off next. He kissed her in places where she had never been kissed before. The foreplay he used was magical. She climaxed within a few minutes. It was the best and most sensual experience of her life. Ray was pleased with her response. Georgina had an ache in her pelvis that she had never experienced before. It was a good ache. She couldn't hold back any longer and proceeded to undress him. They made love for a long time. Ray definitely knew how to please her. She never once thought of Glen. When they finished, they fell asleep in each other's arms.

Georgina woke in the middle of the night and jumped up out of bed. As fast as she stood up, she had to sit back down. Queasiness filled her stomach. She needed to run to the bathroom. When she returned, Ray was ready for the most heart-filled conversation of his life.

"I must go now," she said. "Whoa there lady, I think it's time we had a real heart-to-heart talk," Ray said. "Isn't that what we did last night?" Georgina asked.

"Not like the one were going to have now," Ray said. "I'm not pleading with you anymore, and hopefully you will come to your senses. I want you to think about last night and how natural it was to spend the night together. We are perfect together. I honestly believe if you loved Glen the way you say you do, last night would not have happened. There is something missing from that relationship and you refuse to admit it. I admire you for staying with him because you've committed to him, but you are not faithful. How do you think he would handle it if he found out what we did last night? I already know that you have been sleeping with someone else," Ray shared.

"After you fell asleep I rubbed my hand over and over you're growing belly. I have seen pregnant women before. You don't need a doctor's diagnosis. I know by the small hump that you are carrying a baby. So what about us? What about last night? I don't care if the baby is his. I wouldn't be the first man to raise another man's child. We will have more babies together that are ours. You don't even know for certain that the baby is Glen's. I will walk you home when you feel better. Just think about what I said. After Joanna's wedding is over, tell me your decision," Ray pleaded.

Bernice was worried about Georgina and was thinking out loud. "Where could she have spent the night?" "Don't worry about her. She is a big girl," Myron said. "Wonder if she is in a hospital. She wasn't feeling well yesterday," Bernice said.

Just as she finished her sentence, Ray and Georgina appeared. They were walking up the sidewalk holding hands. "Oh for heaven's sake! Just look at this," Bernice coaxed Myron to look.

Myron went to the window. "I don't believe she's completely made up her mind about Glen, but don't you say a word to her, Bernice. I don't like this any more than you do. She's a grown woman, and she's got to make her own decisions," Myron said.

"Good morning. I suppose you want to know where I have been?" asking questionably to her parents, Georgina turned to address Ray. When she turned around he was walking away from her down the sidewalk. Quickly she ran to the door and called to him. "Ray, come back. I think you'll want to hear this," she said eagerly.

"Mom, Dad, I am so ashamed of myself. I've gotten involved with two very different men. I have swung back and forth between both of them for over four years now. I have never been able to rid my mind of Ray. Not once. Last night, I spent the night with Ray and I never once thought of Glen. I didn't wish I were with Glen, nor did I feel that I owed him an apology. What I am trying to say is I'm going to send back Glen's ring. Ray and I have known each other for nearly six years and I feel like I belong with him. I will write Glen and explain everything to him. I am no longer confused, I am certain of what I want," Georgina shared.

"Let me be the first to welcome you to the family," Myron said to Ray. "I can't say I'm surprised. I've felt for a long time this might happen. Glen will be okay. I really like the man. He's tough. He'll get through this and move on. I'm sure you two will be very happy together," Myron stated.

Georgina was feeling queasy again and excused herself. She was wondering how much longer she was going to be able to hide her secret. Ray wouldn't tell anyone; he didn't want anyone to know this might not be his baby.

Georgina sat down later that day and wrote to Glen. She told him so many things and apologized to him for everything. She told him how she wished it could be different, but that this was for the best, at least for her. The most important part was that she was able to avoid telling him her secret. That he was going to be a father. She felt it was best this way.

The day before Joanna's wedding Georgina stopped by the doctor's office to get the news she had suspected all along. She was definitely pregnant. The nurse informed her that she was due approximately October 9. This date confirmed that she was already pregnant before she left for Pennsylvania and the possibility that Ray could be this baby's father.

Joanna's wedding day was a perfect occasion. The guests had a wonderful time. Joe's family thanked everyone for joining them in this wonderful celebration. The Steiner's had saved up a lot of money so they could give all of their daughter's expensive weddings. It was certainly a day to remember.

Ray escorted Georgina to her sister's wedding. He was sure they would have their own wedding shortly. Ray was eager to begin planning their special event. He was not planning on inviting any of his own family.

Georgina had hoped he'd invite his family. She wanted to meet his sister and brothers. She couldn't recall him ever mentioning his parents. She didn't even know if his parents were alive. He certainly wasn't the family man that Glen was. If she were going to marry Ray, she'd leave behind everything she loved about Glen.

The Tuesday after Joanna's wedding, Georgina visited with Dr. Cooper. He shared his concerned for her because she was unwed. He didn't waste anytime asking her about her future plans.

"Georgina, I know a very nice family looking to adopt a baby," Dr. Cooper said. He barely completed his statement when Georgina replied, "My boyfriend and I will be getting married very soon." "If you change your mind, I can help you place your child in a good home," Dr. Cooper relayed.

She went home and looked at a calendar. If her calculations were correct, she was already over four months pregnant. Either way she was already pregnant when she went to Pennsylvania. That explained the queasy stomach, the overwhelming tiredness, and her lack of appetite during her trip. She no longer had that problem. Food was on her mind all of the time.

Glen received Georgina's letter just three weeks prior to his discharge. He couldn't believe what he was reading. Before he could travel back to London to try and determine what went wrong, he had to return to Pennsylvania to see his mother. No way was he going to allow this breakup without a face-to-face explanation.

Meanwhile, Ray was planning a wedding as fast as time would allow. Ray was well aware of an impending transfer back to Pope Air Force Base. The wedding had to take place before he returned to North Carolina. Hopefully he'd be able to finish his treatments before his return. We'll need to be married in order for you to return to North Carolina with me. You will have the baby in the states," Ray informed her. "As long as we are together, it doesn't matter to me where we are located," Georgina said.

Ray couldn't allow Glen time to try and change Georgina's mind. He knew she had received a disturbing letter from Glen and Ray was afraid she would go back to him. She certainly didn't show that she was over Glen. She spoke of him often and Ray knew he had to be patient with her.

A wedding needed to take place before Glen could get to London to stop this event. Ray requested Glen's discharge date from Mark Mills. Once again Mark felt he was being used and refused to disclose this information to anyone. Then Ray remembered a friend who owed him a favor, and he probably had that important information on hand.

"Thomas, how are you are doing, buddy?" Ray asked. "Ray, is that you? I can't believe my ears. What are you up to, and how are your treatments going?" Thomas asked. "I couldn't be better. I am responding well to these new treatments. Everything is happening much faster than we expected. It is true that Great Britain has fewer restrictions on experimental medical treatments. If it wasn't for these treatments, I don't know what I'd be doing right now.

Hey, I need a small favor." Ray said. "Shoot, I hope I can help you," Thomas said. "A friend of mine, Glen Dornstadt is getting discharged in the next month or so. I just want to send him a card and wish him well, and I don't want it to be too soon or too late. Do you think you can find out his discharge date for me? I sure would appreciate anything you can do for me buddy," Ray said.

"Let me see what I can find out for you. You know that is privileged information and I must be careful about what information I offer you," Thomas said. "Sure, I understand and

I don't want to get anyone into trouble. Either way, I'm always glad to speak with you," Ray said. "Yes, and the same to you," Thomas said.

"Hopefully, I'll know real soon how much time I have before Glen makes his return. The sooner I can make Georgina my wife the better," Ray thought to himself. He hoped to be able to work around Georgina's due date. If he slowed down his treatments maybe he could postpone his transfer until after the baby was born.

Glen's heart was aching. There just weren't enough details included with Georgina's explanation. He didn't know what he had done wrong or what caused Georgina to change her mind so quickly. Maybe while visiting Pennsylvania she decided that this lifestyle wasn't for her. Did my family offend her somehow? Something just doesn't make sense here. If Mom's health issues aren't any worse, I will go straight to London after my discharge. Until then, this is just going to drive me crazy. I need to find something to distract me," Glen thought to himself.

Ray's phone rang. "I have that date you need. That would be May twenty-first," Thomas said. "Wow, that doesn't leave me much time. For some reason, I expected he had a few more weeks until his discharge. Thanks, Thomas. I owe you," Ray said. "No, I think that makes us even," Thomas said. "Well, either way, I appreciate your time. I'll have to stop by and pay you a visit when I return to the states," Ray said.

Ray went to see Georgina and her family that evening. Without mentioning Glen or the baby, he explained to her parents why he thought it would be best to have a small, quick, private wedding. Georgina was actually thrilled with his announcement. However, the cat was out of the bag.

"Ray," Myron said sternly. "I know about my daughter being in the family way. I expect you'll do your best to have others believe this was an early baby and that it was conceived on your wedding night. Are you with me on this?" Myron asked sternly.

"Yes sir," Ray said. Ray assumed that Georgina's morning sickness had exposed her condition. Ray didn't want to put any more pressure on her so he didn't quiz her on how her parents found out.

"I expect your wedding will be an official church ceremony with a small family gathering?" Myron asked quizzically. "Sure, why not. Will we be able to have it in the next two weeks?" Ray asked. "Two weeks? I was thinking more like six weeks," Georgina said.

The days events didn't go as well as Ray had hoped. He thought by now they would have set a date, but there was too much conflict. Ray could feel his stomach churning and knotting up for the first time in weeks.

"Okay my princess, whatever you want. I'm going back to my apartment. I need my medication. Hopefully, I'll be better tomorrow. We will continue our plans then," Ray said.

Bernice waited for Ray to leave until she approached her daughter. "Go ahead Mom say what's on your mind. I can tell you're not happy about this situation," Georgina groaned.

"Personally I don't see how you could marry Ray over Glen. You accepted Glen's ring. You are moving too quickly on this wedding and I think you're making a bad decision," Bernice said.

"Mother, you don't know how hard this has been on me. I feel terrible about sending back Glen's ring and calling off my marriage to him. He wouldn't want me once he found out I slept with Ray. I truly believe I was meant to marry Ray, and that's what I am going to do. Please don't continue to bring up Glen. I need to put him out of my mind," Georgina said. "Ray left in such a hurry, I wonder if he might have been offended by your demands, Dad?" Georgina said.

"My dear, I was just testing him. I see right through him. There is a reason for his haste. I want to make sure he is up-front with me," Myron said. "Georgina, I need to ask you a question and I expect you to be honest with me. Ray is not the father of that baby, is he? He wants to get married before Glen returns and finds you pregnant. He knows if Glen finds out about the baby he will try to stop this marriage," Myron asked her.

"Glen doesn't know that I am marrying Ray. I am so embarrassed. I am in love with both men. I don't know how I got into this situation," Georgina said.

"I'll tell you how, young lady. You slept around. I thought I raised you better than that. Once you have sexual relations with someone it changes the content of a relationship. That's just one reason why it is best to save yourself for marriage. Then you know that you married for love, not passion," Bernice said.

"I didn't just sleep with anybody. I love both of these men. I could marry either of them. But I am doing the right thing by marrying the baby's father," Georgina said.

"We will do what you want, not what Ray wants. If you want to wait six weeks, that's fine by me, but when you walk down the aisle, everyone will know you are with child, and that would disgrace our family. The sooner the better Princess," Myron said.

"Daddy, I'm sorry to have disgraced our family. I don't think a few more weeks will matter. People will figure this out for themselves. I've often dreamt of how I wanted my wedding to be and I would like to have a similar affair. I cannot plan that in two week," Georgina said.

"She is right, you know Myron," Bernice said. "I don't agree. She should have thought of the consequences when she laid down for those men," Myron said.

Chapter 12
Wedding Woes

Glen kept in close contact with Lona regarding his mother's health situation. "Glen, you'd better come home before you run off to London. Mother's been crossing off the days on her calendar when you will return. I don't know for what reason, but she will be very disappointed if you don't stop here first," Lona warned him.

"You're right. I can't believe I would put my own selfish needs in front of Mother's. Do you think she'll understand when I leave for London?" Glen asked.

"You know Glen every woman gets a little nervous about marriage. If she was just nervous I don't think she'd call off a wedding so fast. I think you should just stay here and forget about her. You said yourself you don't have any more money to make unnecessary trips," Lona reminded him.

"Well I need answers! I cannot let our relationship end this way. Money does not make me happy. Love does. I can earn the money back later," Glen said sternly.

The couples wedding date was set for June 14. The Steiner's decided only a few close friends and relatives would be invited. Bernice knew how quickly her family would spread Georgina's secret. She also knew that some family members would be upset by not being invited to the wedding. Georgina's predicament was embarrassing enough. The fewer people who attended the wedding the fewer questions they had to answer. It was the best solution as far as Bernice was concerned.

Glen had made arrangements to fly to London on June 10. With a very late arrival he thought it best to wait and go to the Steiner's first thing in the morning. There was no sense waking them up late at night. Myron was an early riser like Glen. He'd visit in the morning with Myron and get some coffee.

Glen had a bad feeling as soon as Myron opened the door. Myron did not welcome Glen with his usual greeting. All of a sudden he felt very uncomfortable. "Sir, if I could just ask you a few questions? You have always been up-front and fair to me," Glen said. "I will try son, but I'm not sure what I can tell you," Myron said.

Just as they started to talk, Georgina came around the corner in her tight nightgown. Her expanding belly was an immediate giveaway. She saw Glen and ran to her bedroom away from him and pushed her door closed.

"Excuse me Sir. Please let me go talk to her. I think I already understand what is going on here," Glen said. "I will let you in, but it's up to Georgina to decide if she wants to talk to you," Myron said.

He knocked on her door. "Georgina let me in. We need to talk. Now I know why you don't want me around. Are you going to give up our baby? I assume you didn't want me to know, so you had to end our relationship," Glen said. "No, that's not it. Just go Glen, I can't talk to you. You shouldn't be here. Why didn't you write me and let me know you were coming?" Georgina cried. "If I told you I was coming you would have found a way to avoid me. So I decided to surprise you. As usual, I am the one surprised. Please open your door. You know I won't hurt you. I can see that you are pregnant. Your secret is out," Glen said.

"It's not that easy. Please, just go. Whenever I see you all of my feelings come back. It tears me apart knowing what agony I am putting you through because of my mistake," Georgina said in a squeaky voice. "That would be our mistake. I'm glad you still have feelings for me," Glen said. "I brought your ring with me. We can have a small ceremony here and you can come back to Pennsylvania with me," Glen said.

Georgina opened her door with clothes on that hid her condition. "How long have you known?" Glen asked. "A couple months," Georgina said. "When you went home with me, you were already pregnant then, weren't you?" Glen said. "I'm so sorry this happened. I know you asked me to stop, but I love you and wanted to express my love to you. You know, I'm not sorry this happened. We will have a beautiful baby and we'll raise it together, and all will be fine," Glen expressed.

"No we can't….stop, Glen, please" Georgina pleaded. "There'll be no wedding. You can't raise this baby. It's not yours," Georgina said. "What are you talking about?" Glen asked hesitantly. A voice from behind him answered, "Because it's mine," Ray said as Georgina started to cry.

"I am so sorry, Glen. I wanted to marry you, but when I found out I was pregnant, I did the math. This is Ray's baby, not yours," Georgina said.

"I see. So you've been sleeping with both of us. How many times were you with him?" Glen asked as he walked toward the door, shaking his head. He turned and looked at Ray with disgust and then back at Georgina. "I can't believe what I am hearing. There's a name for what you have done," Glen sighed.

"Stop right now. Name-calling won't get you anywhere," Myron said. "You need to leave now. You've upset enough people for one day. We're getting married on Saturday," Ray said. "I'm not leaving yet," Glen yelled pushing Ray away. "I need to spend a few minutes alone with Georgina. I have something to say to her, and I don't need an audience. Why don't you get lost? I want her full attention and she doesn't need you distracting her," Glen said, angrily.

"I'm sorry, Glen, I don't want to do this," Georgina said. "Come, please, I just want to tell you a few things. I need closure. It'll just take a few minutes," Glen said.

"I have plans this morning and I can't do this now. I promise if you come back around four this afternoon, we'll go for a walk then. Please Glen," Georgina said. Glen turned and headed for the door, "Yeah, sure, this is the story of my life," he said.

Glen looked at Ray and said in a muffled voice as he walked through the door, "you won you bastard. It obviously pays to have friends in high places."

Ray and Georgina attempted to finalize their wedding plans that morning, but Glen's visit made it difficult. Georgina was not handling Glen's surprise visit well at all. Ray quickly became upset and shared with Georgina that she was going to marry him and not Glen and not to mention Glen's name any more because it caused his stomach ailment to flare up.

It was imperative to Ray that he be part of the wedding plans. He went with Georgina to pick out their wedding cake. He ordered the flowers and picked out his tuxedo. It was supposed to be a happy time for both of them but it certainly wasn't turning into a happy occasion for Georgina.

Glen made Georgina feel guilty. Was she marrying the right person? Why was she lying to everyone? Her heart ached and she already missed Glen.

"Georgina you don't have to meet with Glen you know. If you will be more comfortable, he can talk to you with me in the room or he cannot see you at all, if that is what you want. He's a disaster waiting to happen, and I don't want you to break down and tell him something he doesn't need to know. Do you understand?" Ray asked. "Yes Ray, I understand," Georgina said.

"It's not your fault that idiot needs closure. Let him get it out of his system, but I'd prefer you not go by yourself. I think you need me there with you so he can't poison your mind with his sad story," Ray said. "No, I need to speak with him alone. He would never hurt me, I know that and I won't change my mind now," Georgina said.

Georgina and Glen met that afternoon as planned. They walked through the town park looking as though they belonged together. Glen took Georgina's hand. "This feels so natural," Glen said as he touched Georgina's stomach and ran his fingers along the top. "I wish this were my baby. You'd be marrying me on Saturday instead of him. So how long were you sleeping with both of us?" Glen questioned.

"I hate the way you say that. It was just once but it was too close for me know which one of you is the father," Georgina said. "You were still my girl. Why did you sleep with him?" Glen asked.

"I can't answer that. I got involved in a moment, I suppose," Georgina said. "Glen, I feel terrible about all of this. I had to lie to you at my house in front of my family. They all think Ray's the baby's Father, but I don't know for sure that it isn't your baby," Georgina sighed. "Then why are marrying him?" Glen asked. "Because he pressured me, he doesn't want anyone to know that he might not be the father. He told me you were not to know that this could be your child. He is willing to raise it as if it were his own," Georgina said. "And I would do the same. You still love me, I can tell. It's not too late to change your mind. Marry me. You already said yes once," Glen said.

Georgina started to cry. "Glen, you are making this so hard. You are a wonderful person. You will find someone else and she will make you happy. I have my reasons for marrying Ray. You have to let me go, please," Georgina said.

"I don't know what to say. I want to see your baby after it's born. I'll always wonder if it is mine. Every time you look at your baby, you'll think of me," Glen said. "I think it's a boy," Georgina said. "Don't change the subject. How are you going to live with a child who will never get to meet its real father? How do you think I will feel wondering the rest of my life about my child?" Glen asked. "Ray will be in the same predicament if I marry you. He thinks this is his child, with a slight chance it might be yours," Georgina said.

"I have a comment that might help you when you walk down the isle with Ray. I don't know if I want to marry you now. If I were to go away would you sleep with another man? Would you continue your relationship with Ray? Glen questioned Georgina with a sigh.

Georgina was sobbing now and responded, "I love you both. When I am with you, I think of Ray, and when I am with Ray, I think of you. Time heals all wounds, you'll see, I will forget you eventually. I will have more babies with Ray, and then we will have a real family connection," Georgina said.

"He's not right for you. You really need to think about what you are doing," Glen said. "I have, Glen, I have," Georgina sighed. Glen pulled Georgina to him and kissed her. "I don't know how I will live without you. You have been my rock and support for the last four years. You have consumed my every waking moment. It is not true that time heals all wounds. They may dim after sometime, but I will always love you. I ask that you never speak badly of me. I am going to step out of the picture, but not until I talk to Ray first. There are a few details I need to clear up with him," Glen said.

That evening Georgina sat and stared at the walls for hours. "Princess why don't you come out and join the family, we are playing checkers in the parlor. Maybe that will help take your mind off of your problems," Bernice said.

"Mama, am I making a mistake?" Georgina asked. "Only you can answer that," Bernice said. "I have made a mess of my life. I hope Glen can forgive me," Georgina sighed. "Glen is a good person. He will meet someone and his life will turn around. Because of your relationship, he will make someone else a good husband," Bernice shared.

Glen went to Ray's apartment building. He announced himself through the speaker system and asked if he could have a few minutes of Ray's time. "I don't have anything to say to you," Ray said. "I have lots to say to you and I'm not leaving London till we speak. If you want to get rid of me, you'll come down here and face me you bastard. You won what have you got to lose?" Glen said.

"Okay, how about we meet at E-Jay's in a half hour," Ray said. "Fine I'll see you there. Don't be late," Glen groaned.

The men chose a table right in the center of the large dining area. "This was your idea you idiot. Tell me what is so important that you couldn't tell me through the speaker system. Glen made some strange facial expression and then paused. Ray stood up and announced "either spit it out or I'm leaving. Now what do you want?" Ray asked. "You are despicable. We were engaged to be married and you coerced Georgina to sleep with you," Glen said. "That's a pretty big word for you, airman. That's not true at all. She's in love with me, and we are having a baby to prove it," Ray said.

"You are having my baby. If you look at the calendar, she conceived when we were together; I am sure of that," Glen said. "How do you know she wasn't with me the night before and the night after you were together? Neither of us knows for sure who that child belongs too, but it is mine now. Listen Mr. Know-It-All, she's marrying me, not you, you loser. Why don't you go home where someone misses you?" Ray announced.

"I need to make sure you won't ever hurt her. You'll always take care of her and my baby and make sure no harm ever comes to either one of them," Glen said. "What do think I'm going to do to them? I love her and I feel the same way you do about her," Ray said. "I want you to forget about this being your baby. I am raising him or her and I am never going to question its paternity," Ray said.

"When your marriage doesn't work out, she can always find me. I will never leave Billsport in case she needs me. She will always know where to find me," Glen said.

"She will never need you, and our child will never need you. You said what you had to say. Now go home," Ray said. "What's the matter? Don't you like competition?" Glen asked. "You're not competition any longer. Now get out of here," Ray said.

"I'm leaving, but I'm going to stop by the Steiner's to say good-bye. They have been part of my life the last four years. I want to thank them for their hospitality and friendship. My flight doesn't leave until Saturday morning. I will visit with other friends while I am here. Don't worry; I won't bother you anymore," Glen informed Ray with a deep sigh.

Ray returned to his apartment. His stomach was in knots. It was burning so bad even his medicine wasn't working. Stressful situations caused his ailments to flare up more than anything else. He had hoped he'd learned to cope better than he did tonight.

Glen wasn't aware that he caused the worst stomach episodes that Ray ever experienced. Glen was still going to be in London the morning of their wedding day and that worried Ray. He had to find a way to calm down so he could make it through the wedding. "*Damn that Glen. Look what he's done to me,*" Ray said to himself.

Saturday was a perfect day. Family and friends came to town for the second family wedding. Molly was married now and served as Georgina's attendant. Molly shared with Georgina that she felt that she would marry Ray. Molly was so excited to see this day finally happen for Georgina after everything she'd been through.

Ray felt like rocks were lying on the bottom of his stomach. He feared Glen had plans to ruin the day, but as the sun set and darkness fell, the day ended well.

Once again Ray's treatments had become ineffective and he was hospitalized after the wedding. "Boy, some husband I am. I can't even consummate my wedding," Ray said to Georgina. "Ray, the doctors here are excellent. They'll have you better and out of here in no time, you'll see," Georgina said as she spent hours at his bedside.

Ray couldn't believe his bad luck. He had just spent the last couple of weeks planning and imagining the wonder and splendor of his wedding night with Georgina. He had even gone so far as to spend a few nights with hookers hoping to perfect techniques to please his new bride. Those women were the best in the business. He was not proud about the time he had spent with them, but he had needs, and in Georgina's delicate condition, he couldn't chance something happening to the baby before they said their vows. Georgina didn't need to know how Ray obtained his talents. After the baby was born, Ray planned to use these new skills on his wife.

Pope Air Force Base in North Carolina received the report of Ray's hospitalization from London. "If he can't do any better in London than he can here, we may as well bring him back," his commander said. "There is a similar experimental program at Macgregor Medical Center in San Antonio, Texas near Lackland Air Force Base," Mark Mills said. "Let's send him there and he can continue his treatments while he continues to serve his country," Mark suggested to his Commander.

Commander Morgan agreed. "I'll request his transfer to Texas. You notify Ray about our decision. Give him a date to report to Texas. I'll take care of the paperwork," he said. "Yes sir," Mark Mills said.

Ray was released from the hospital Tuesday after the wedding with orders to take it easy.

He would then need to return for a follow up to determine when he could resume normal activity. The doctors never mentioned anything about sex, and as a newlywed, he had only one thought on his mind.

Ray couldn't keep his hands off of Georgina in the back of the cab during the ride home from the hospital. It didn't matter that she had a protruding belly. He wanted her and he couldn't wait. Now that he was feeling better he was more than ready to consummate his marriage. It was legal now, and she was finally his. Nothing Glen did now would matter. Maybe that was the medicine Ray needed to improve his illness.

Ray had his hands all over Georgina. The cab driver feared they were going to have sex right there in the cab. Georgina laughed as Ray fumbled for his wallet to pay the driver. She knew what he wanted, and it was taking entirely too long to get to the apartment.

Ray paused and then picked up Georgina and carried her over the threshold. "Don't laugh. I'm just keeping with tradition," Ray laughed. "I was afraid you were going to drop me. I'm at least ten pounds heavier than I was just a few months ago. You just got out of the hospital and you're to be taking it easy, remember?" Georgina said. "Stop already. Go directly to the bedroom," Ray said as he put her down.

Georgina opened the door to a thousand red roses. They were a little wilted, but they smelled great. Ray had gotten his point across. He pulled Georgina up to him and started undressing her. "Ray, don't over do it? We haven't had sex in over a month and my belly is much bigger now," Georgina said. "I know, and that is such a turn on for me. I can't explain it. Maybe its' knowing that we made this baby together and Glen is finally out of the picture. Now as your husband, I need to prove my love to you again," Ray said.

Ray undressed his new wife for the first time. When he began to get undress he was suddenly overcome by extreme weakness and exhaustion. He couldn't lift his leg high enough to get his pants off. It was like someone had turned off his power switch.

"Ray, what's the matter? See, I knew you were overdoing it," Georgina exclaimed.

She called for an ambulance and then proceeded to get dressed. Before the ambulance arrived, Ray began to recover. "Why did you get dressed, I'll be okay in a minute. I can't explain it but I feel much better now. Just nerves, I guess," Ray said.

When the ambulance crew arrived they ran the usual tests on him, but nothing appeared out of range. "Mr. Buckley, I suggest we take you back to the hospital and let them review your stats, check your medications and let them decide if you can stay home. Maybe you had a quick drop in blood pressure. You're not diabetic are you?" the driver asked.

"No, I have an unusual stomach condition. They recently gave it a name. They call it ulcerative colitis. I am not returning to the hospital tonight. We just left there," Ray said.

"I wouldn't do anything too strenuous tonight. Take it easy. You should be seen by a doctor tomorrow," the driver said.

Ray practically pushed the ambulance crew out of the door. Once they were clear he pushed the door shut, locked it then started taking off his clothes. He headed directly for Georgina. "Oh no, you don't mister. Not tonight! You're not doing that to me again. If you pass out, I can't pick you up," Georgina said.

"Baby I have longed for this night for years. Just knowing we are in the same room together makes me crazy. If I don't have you, I won't sleep. I have been patient and waited until we took our vows and now it's time for me to prove my love to you. I will take it slow and if anything at all starts to hurt, I'll quit," Ray promised. He reached for Georgina as he finished undressing. The newlyweds kissed and just held each other. Georgina was happy he was okay and Ray was relieved he was able to stay home with her. Ray learned from other women that kissing is very important. To begin a good marathon you must start with a simple kiss and slowly work into other means of pleasure. Ray used techniques on Georgina that she never experienced before. She began to quiver and pant—a good sign for Ray. He knew his technique was working and soon brought Georgina to a climax.

There was that nagging thought that Georgina had been with Glen. Ray wondered how his performance compared to that loser. "You always amaze me. You are so good in bed. No one could ever make me feel the way you do," Georgina said panting.

What a confidence booster. Ray felt like a conqueror that night. He had heard from his new wife what every man wanted to hear from his woman. Ray was hoping for more than one sexual marathon that night, but he had already exerted himself too much. Exhaustion overcame both of them and they collapsed in each other's arms and slept like babies.

Georgina had to go to work in the morning and a good night's sleep was very important in her condition. It was already difficult for her to make it through a complete day. If they were going to continue these sexual marathons like newlyweds do, they needed to start earlier in the evening. After all, she had to think of her baby's needs too.

Glen returned to Pennsylvania to find Kathryn's health even more delicate. Glen didn't want his mother to find out that Georgina was no longer part of his life. His forbid his family to discuss his heartache around her. More than anything, Kathryn wanted her son to be happy, and as far as Glen was concerned, she was going to die thinking he was.

"How's Georgina?" Kathryn asked. "She's doing real well, Mother. I told her that it would be best that she stay at home while I'm here with you. I'm sure she's better off with her family now. She's going to continue working for a while and I'm going to stay here and care for you until your condition improves, Glen said. "You know son, I'm not going to improve. You should go and be with her," Kathryn informed him.

For over a month, Glen and his siblings shared time at their Mothers bedside during her declining health. On a cool summer morning Kathryn passed away peacefully in her sleep with three of her children by her side. Glen was heartbroken about his Mother's passing, yet other's we're relieved since the quality of her life for the past year was practically non-existent. Kathryn's entire family including Niles and her brothers from Germany attended her services.

"Dad, it's been very difficult for us to maintain your house. Most of our time was spent taking care of Mom over the last year. The house is in serious need of many repairs and we were hoping you'd stay and help us fix it. We've spent so little time together in past several years; it would be nice to have time to catch up.

How about hanging around awhile? Give us a hand. Now that Mom's gone you shouldn't have any reason to leave. Kevin will need somewhere to live after he completes his two years in the Marines. I would like to stay here for a while, if you don't mind," Glen shared.

"I heard you're getting married, son. If this is what you need to get yourself started, then go right ahead and live here. Where is your future bride?" Niles asked. "Dad, let's not talk about her right now, okay?" Glen said. "You're not very happy for being an engaged man. I sense a problem. Maybe after this thing is over, we can talk about relationships," Niles said.

"I wouldn't call this a thing. It's Mom's funeral. You should be grieving too," Glen said. "I am in my own way. I was just wondering what happened to your lady friend? Niles said. "We'll talk about her later," Glen said.

Twenty three days after their wedding, Ray received a Western Union from the United States Air Force.

Raymond W. Buckley: You are being transferred to Lackland Air Force Base in San Antonio, Texas. Report to report to Lieutenant Commander John Morgan upon your arrival on August 1, 1952. Your headquarters and bunk will be assigned to you upon your arrival.

"There has got to be a mistake; they must have me confused with another Ray Buckley. That's a pretty common name," Ray told Georgina.

Ray visited his commander in London immediately. "Sir," Ray said, "this has got to be a mistake. When I am well and ready, I am to report back to Pope Air Force Base in North Carolina. What can you tell me about these orders?"

Commander Fritch told Ray to take a seat. He'd have his office clerk send a telegram to get some answers.

In less than two hours Ray had his answer. There was no mistake. He was needed in Texas, and he was to report there immediately.

"That's only a week away. What about my treatments?" Ray questioned. "The message says you'll continue treatment at Macgregor Medical Center in San Antonio, Texas. You'll need to pack your bags, move out of your apartment and report to Lackland by next Friday morning," Commander Fritch said.

"Sir, I got married a few weeks ago. What about my wife? I am not leaving her behind. She is pregnant," Ray said. "You will need to leave her for a little while until you are able to set up family housing in Texas. Once those arrangements have been approved then she can join you and not a day sooner. Do you understand, sergeant?" Commander Fritch asked. "Yes sir. I will tell her. She will be able to stay with her parents, I'm sure," Ray said.

"So she is pregnant. You know the Air Force frowns on that sort of thing," Commander Fritch said. "Well sir, I did the right thing and married her. We have been together nearly six years. This wasn't a one-night stand sir," Ray said. "Good thing. Now, be on your way," Fritch said.

Ray went home and passed along his disappointing news to Georgina. She barely seemed fazed at all. She was prepared to follow Ray no matter where he was sent. It didn't matter to whether it was Texas, North Carolina, or Pennsylvania they were all new to her. She had little knowledge of any of them.

As soon as Ray arrived in San Antonio he applied for family housing. His approval was almost immediate considering his wife was pregnant. Georgina joined him as fast as she could pack her clothes. The flight was terribly long for a pregnant woman. She developed swollen ankles and could barely walk off of the plane. An Air Force medical center doctor examined her immediately and checked her vital signs. Even though she continued to have swelling problems, her other vitals were normal.

Georgina's doctor was evaluating her condition on a regular basis. She continued to retain fluid at a dangerous level. Her kidney and heart functions were strained. Georgina's condition became serious enough to hospitalize her. She remained there until she delivered her baby a month early.

Chapter 13
An Early Arrival

Gary Alan Buckley was only three pounds, twelve ounces when he entered the world. Healthy but small, he proved to be a tough little guy. He was able to come home after only three weeks in the hospital. Georgina's ankles and vital signs returned to normal but her kidneys continued to plague her with unusual ailments for weeks after the delivery.

By the time Gary was released, Georgina was prepared to start her new mothering job. It didn't take her long to discover she was suffering from lack of sleep. She was angry and frustrated most of the time. Her patience wore thin with Ray but she tried as hard as she could to have patience with Gary. At times she found that to be a difficult task too. Every night Ray helped her clean and do the laundry. Occasionally he'd surprise her with flowers, candy, or a simple little trinket. These gifts of kindness only irritated Georgina.

Doctors ignored her symptoms of postpartum depression. Ray thought she wasn't adjusting well to her new routine. Georgina blamed Ray for not helping her more with Gary. She was homesick and wanted to go back to London. Ray tried to appease her but also told her she had to stay here for now as he couldn't get leave and money was rather tight. When her condition improved, they would all go to London for a visit with her family.

Glen was having difficulty focusing on his new job as Georgina's due date got close. He wondered and worried every day about Georgina and his child. Then he received a telegram.

Just a note to inform you that Georgina had a baby boy on Sept 12. He was early, small, but healthy.

"Now I wonder who sent me this? It's not marked and it doesn't mention how Georgina is doing?" Glen thought to himself.

Glen had to see the baby. Unaware that Georgina and Ray had moved to Texas, he called the Steiners to see if they would make arrangements for him to meet Georgina and the baby while Ray was gone. Myron informed Glen that the coupled had moved to San Antonio. He advised Glen to stay away because Myron was unsure how Ray might respond if he found out Glen were to visit.

It took a while but he was able to locate Ray and Georgina through the post office. Glen quit his job and headed to Texas. One morning soon after he arrived, he decided to pay Georgina a visit. Boldly he knocked on the apartment door. Georgina peeked through the curtains and was startled to see Glen looking back at her. Georgina opened the door and quickly warned Glen to leave. "What are you doing here? If Ray sees you here he'll kill you," Georgina said. "That's a rather strong statement don't you think?" Glen asked. "No, it's not! You have no idea how much Ray hates you," Georgina said.

"Can I see my baby?" Glen pleaded. "No, if Ray comes home early you don't want to be found here? Georgina said. "I'll deal with that if it happens," Glen said. "It's not a good idea. I can't take that chance. I don't think he'd hurt me but he would carry on for days about your presence, I can barely tolerate him now when your name is mentioned," Georgina informed him. "I came all this way to see my son and I'm not leaving until I see him. I can handle Ray if he catches me here. I have ways of confronting him. Remember I am the one who lost their son. Ray can't be as mad and upset as I am right now. He won the war and I am the injured one here. One way or the other I am going to see my son. You might as well let me in. I will tell him that you didn't allow me in, but that I insisted. I'll take all of the heat. So how about it, can I please see my baby or do I have to move you and find him myself?" Glen threatened.

"Well, okay, but only for a few minutes, then you better leave. He's down there," Georgina pointed as Glen walked down the hall away from her.

Glen walked the short hallway and instinctively walked directly into the baby's room. Gary was wide awake and laying contently on his back and listening to his own sounds. Glen couldn't help himself; he had to pick him up. "Hi there little guy. "I'm sorry you don't know me," he said. Finally seeing his son brought tears to Glen's eyes. He turned to Georgina and said, "We should be together. Why did you marry Ray? This feels so natural. Did I do something?" Glen said begging for answers.

Georgina turned away from Glen. She walked down the hallway and went into the kitchen. She must have been getting ready to cook because all of a sudden she was banging pans and slamming doors. Glen went down the hall after her. "I didn't mean to upset you. I can't get you out of my mind. I think of you every day. Our family is finally together." Glen said with a cracking voice.

"I don't know what to do, Glen. Tell me what to do. I'm sorry now that I didn't marry you," Georgina said.

Glen didn't have any plans as of yet but he hoped to stay in the area for a while. He sensed that there were problems in the marriage. *"Maybe if I stay long enough, I can convince Georgina to leave with me,"* he thought. Every morning for two weeks Glen waited for Ray to leave for work and then he'd visit with his son.

Ray began to sense something was different. One morning he made arrangements to stay home from work. Georgina was edgy, but that didn't seem all that unusual anymore. Then the doorbell rang. "I'll get that," Ray said.

The men just stood staring at each other until Ray finally broke the silence. "You're at the wrong house, aren't you, or did you get lost on your way to hell?" Ray asked. Glen paused and started to walk away. "You coward, you won't even stay and face me," he yelled.

"No, I won't. You're not worth it, and I don't want to upset Georgina. I wouldn't expect that you'd want that either," Glen said. "What do you want?" Ray asked. "I thought you could've figured that one out for yourself," Glen said. "I've come to take my son and the love of my life back home with me," he exclaimed.

"Well, forget that! I'll make sure that never happens. She doesn't love you. We've talked about your bad relationship. You couldn't sexually please her and she was never physically attracted to you either. She told me herself," Ray said.

"You talk like a juvenile teenage boy. Does it make you feel better to put me down?" Glen asked.

"Face it, Dornstadt, you're a loser, and I came out smelling like a rose," Ray said. "Yea she told me she wants out of your rosy marriage already," Glen said. "She doesn't know what she wants. Since she's had the baby, she's been different. She can only focus on the baby. You won't come back here again now will you?" Ray yelled shaking his fist at Glen. "I can't promise you that Buckley. If Georgina wants me back, then I'll be here for her," Glen said. "No you won't. I'll have you arrested for trespassing," Ray threatened. "We'll see who ends up smelling like a rose. I might not win, but you'll be holding the thorns. I'll go for now, but I'll be back," Glen said as he turned and walked away.

Ray turned to see Georgina standing behind him, holding Gary. Tears were running down her cheeks. She was definitely upset. "You're a pig, Ray. Why did you tell Glen those things? You don't physically excite me either. At least Glen gave me physical contact. Unless you get sex, you won't even touch me. How do you think I feel about that?" Georgina asked.

"Since you had that baby, you've changed. There's no reason to want to touch you. You shake and tremble every time I get close to you. Why would I want to touch you?" Ray asked.

"What went wrong, Ray? Just a few months ago we were so happy and close. Now look at us. I thought I loved you. Now I dread it when you come home," Georgina yelled.

"I'm going to my doctor's appointment. Why don't you try to relax and calm down? I have the rest of the day off. When I get back we'll talk. I want to fix this as much as you do," Ray said.

As Ray was preparing to leave for his doctor's appointment he spotted Glen sitting in his car down the street. He was obviously waiting for Ray to leave so he could visit with Georgina and the baby.

"I thought I told you to leave?" Ray said. Glen attempted to get out of his car, but Ray held the door shut. "I'm going to say good-bye to Georgina. I am doing what you asked. I am leaving today," he said as he attempted to get out of his car. "Well they're not home. If you get any closer to my house you'll regret that you came here you loser," Ray said.

Just then Glen sensed a presence at his passenger door. He looked over to see two large men standing near his door. "If you do anything accept head directly out of town, you'll look like you were in a violent accident. When you go home I want you to leave believing that Georgina and Gary were killed in a violent car accident and you were the sole survivor. I don't care who you tell. I don't care if you tell anyone that I stole her and the baby from you, and then they were killed, but as far as you are concerned, she and Gary are dead. Do you hear me?" Ray demanded.

"No, I don't, especially not the baby. I want the opportunity to meet him someday. I wouldn't agree to such a horrible lie," Glen said. "How do you expect to pull that off? If you and Georgina had a baby together and now she's dead, who has the baby? You will agree to this story or else," Ray said.

"You might have to kill me, but the baby is not dead until I am. I'll think of some way to deal with this situation while I am driving home. What happens when you two break up and she comes looking for me?" Glen asked. We're not going to break up and she doesn't love you anymore, so why would she look for you? Now get out of here," Ray said screaming, doubling over in pain. The two men walked along side the car until Glen drove away.

Ray returned home with lunch for both of them. "How was your doctor's appointment?" Georgina asked. "The Doctor increased my medication. He says, unless I can reduce my stress levels, I may never recover. Our situation isn't helping. I know I can be miserable at times especially when I don't feel well, which has been a lot lately. I know you've been going through a lot of changes, too. Let's try and start over. I thought about leaving you but that wouldn't resolve anything. That would make my condition worse and you would return to London and I don't want that. You've got to promise me no more Glen. I can't go to work and worry about Glen's presence here. He's got to be out of the picture, understand," Ray said. Ray thought for sure that by now Georgina would've been over Glen, but she obviously wasn't. Defeat was at Ray's heels. He didn't know what to do to help Georgina forget Glen but he wasn't ready to give up on this marriage. He wondered if all women exhibit similar symptoms after they give birth.

"I would like to say good-bye to Glen myself and tell him that I have chosen to stay with you, if you don't mind," Georgina said. "I do mind. You are too weak and too sensitive to handle seeing Glen anymore. That idiot will take advantage of your kindness and turn it around to make you think you want him. I already took care of Glen. He'll never be back. If he does come back he'll be sorry. And if he does come back, you stay away from him. Do you hear me? And, oh yeah, I love you way too much to lose you to anybody," Ray said. "Okay Ray, but I can't promise to just get over Glen, it'll take some time," Georgina said frustrated.

After Glen's departure, Georgina and Ray spent weeks in silence. Ray's stomach ailments were not improving and Georgina's silence was not helping his condition. Ray finally decided it would be best to send her back to London to live with her parents. If the silent treatment continued and there was no companionship and no sex, why should he bother to try and save this marriage?

With some hesitation Ray asked Georgina to go back to London. "I tried, and I must say this marriage was a big mistake," he said. "No please Ray, give me another chance, I'll try to improve, but I need you to work with me," she begged. She didn't want her marriage to fail either and she certainly didn't want to return to her parents after only 6 months. She made a conscious effort to work with Ray and improve their relationship. Over several months they took baby steps to improve their marriage. Small acts of kindness, reminding each other when unkind words were spoken and a true effort made by both partners seemed to be working. Unfortunately for Georgina, as soon as they resumed sexual relations, she was pregnant again. Georgina was not happy and rather scared about having another baby.

Chapter 14
Moving On

The next summer Glen met Patty Johnson at a company picnic. Patty was a beautiful redhead with blue eyes and a smile that would melt your heart. Patty was seven years younger than Glen and a recent high school graduate. She was only eighteen and she had a lot of growing up to do. Glen tried to keep his distance from her because of the age difference, but there was a mutual attraction. Patty often showed up on Glen's doorstep and she'd stay until it was very late. Glen regularly took her home earlier than she wanted. Glen didn't want to anger Mildred Johnson in any way.

Glen wasn't sure he was ready to get involved in another relationship. His heart was still with Georgina where ever she was. Patty wanted to help him recover from his broken heart. She knew he needed companionship so she stayed as close to him as he would allow her. She liked to accompany Glen to his favorite sporting events. Glen bowled on evening leagues and Patty was eager to learn the sport so they would have something in common.

Patty began classes at the local business school in the fall. She wanted to work somewhere that her skills would make a difference. All of her friends were waitresses and secretaries. These common jobs did not suit her. Patty wanted a job with more responsibility. She saw what kind of work her father and brother performed in a factory and she definitely didn't want to do that. She was too feminine, and manual labor was not her style.

Patties desire to further her education gave Glen a valid reason to postpone starting a relationship. He didn't want to stand in the way of the career Patty so badly wanted. Glen stayed away from Patty because he feared distracting her from her studies. He told her that maybe they'd see each other around the holidays. Because of Patty, Glen realized he was capable of loving again. He knew he should be pursuing women closer to his own age but Patty was beginning to consume his daily thoughts.

Patty excelled in her studies. She still wasn't sure about her major but knew she wanted a job in a hospital or doctor's office and she needed to take classes that would help her obtain a specialized medical degree. Her advisor suggested she try a few specialized classes to get a feel for the different options available to her.

To her dismay, her father continued to complain about the expense of her education. Harry made several attempts to push her and Glen together. He felt Patty was wasting her time and his money going to a medical business school. Harry made good money and didn't believe that women needed to further their education after they graduated unless they were going to be a nurse or a teacher. He just wanted her to find a good man to marry who would take care of her. Harry Johnson shared with both of his beautiful daughters that girls didn't need fancy educations: "Just look pretty and smile. There are a lot of men looking to find beautiful woman to keep them happy. Do that and he'll take care of you the rest of your life," Harry informed them.

Harry drank every night. Mildred his wife of several years waited up many nights, worrying about her husband's whereabouts. Mildred was a tolerant woman but when Patty her youngest child graduated from high school, she threw Harry out and divorced him. Harry's brother Buzz owned a restaurant and bar on the other side of town. Just about any night you would find Harry at either his brother's bar, the apartment above the bar, or in his car sleeping off his stupor.

Mildred helped Patty as much as she could with her business school expenses but between both of them the financial expectations were too much. Harry paid only when he was begged to help out. He just couldn't see spending his drinking money on something so frivolous.

After Harry met Glen he took him under his wing and started working on him. "Boy,"—Harry referred to Glen, "you need to buy her flowers once in a while," he informed Glen.

"I'm not pushing this relationship Harry," Glen said. "Patty wants an education and I don't want to hold her back. I'm still recovering from a previous relationship and I don't feel I could adequately give Patty the attention she needs," Glen said. "Ah come on boy, she's a beautiful woman. I'll bet she'll meet all of your needs. She's crazy about you," Harry said. Glen just shook his head and walked away from Harry.

As the holidays approached Harry formulated a plan. He'd invite Glen and Patty to a party at his new apartment. Harry didn't need an excuse to celebrate but Christmas was a good reason to have a party. Harry offered Glen several drinks that night in an attempt to get him to propose to his daughter. Once she made that commitment, Harry would be free of any parental obligation tied to Patty's education.

Patty was still under the legal drinking age, but she consumed several glasses of beer that night. She quickly became inebriated. Harrys' plan was working. Patty and Glen became extremely involved in each other both physically and emotionally that night. Harry heard Glen asking Patty if she knew where they could go to be alone. Harry took Glen aside and offered him the spare bedroom. He told Glen to take his time, they could spend the night in there, and no one else would know.

"Patty, I adore you. You are beautiful and it's been a long time since I felt this way about a woman," Glen whispered to her. She was eager to please Glen and she allowed him to fulfill his desires. This was Patty's first sexual experience and Glen wanted her to enjoy the moment. Glen knew he had to be gentle. Unfortunately the alcohol worked against him and Glen climaxed before he had the opportunity to show Patty his skills. When it was all over, Patty seemed indifferent for someone who had just lost her virginity. They rejoined the party and continued to drink. The next morning, Patty was beyond sick. Mildred Johnson was not shy when it came to protecting her children. She threatened Harry about his lack of judgment. "You simple son of a bitch, if you ever give our daughter another drink before she's 21, I'll have you arrested. She's not going to take up your dirty habits," Mildred warned him as she turned and walked away.

Not much else was ever spoken about that night, but Harry got his wish. Six weeks later came a proposal and a quickie marriage. Patty was pregnant and certainly not very happy about it. Glen tried to play along that he was disappointed too, but in reality, he was thrilled. This was his baby. Gary would have another sibling.

When Glen tried to tell Patty about Georgina she became combative and defensive. She knew that everybody had a past and she really wasn't interested in Glen's former relationships. She gave Glen a warning. "If you continue to talk about Georgina you can go and find another Georgina, but I am not her."

Patty focused on finishing her first year of business school. After the baby was born, she'd take a year off and return the next year.

In late August Patty delivered a healthy baby girl. It took four days and two relatives to convince Patty to name the baby Dana. Glen wanted to name her Kathryn, after his mother, but Patty stated that no child of hers would be given that name.

Glen had a good paying job and was comfortable with Patty being a stay-at-home mom for a few years or maybe longer if they decided to have another baby.

After Dana's birth Patty became seriously unstable. When Glen came home from work Patty wanted to sleep. Glen took care of Dana, the shopping and the house work every minute he wasn't working, for almost a year. Glen suffered Patty's brutal attacks on a regular basis. She blamed Glen for having to quit school and ruining her life. She wanted a career and it was Glen's fault that she wasn't able to finish school. Staying home with a baby interfered with her plans. There would be no more babies for now. Patty felt justified punishing Glen by withholding sex.

Eventually Patty took a billing position at the local hospital. She needed a change of scenery and they could use the extra money. She planned to work until she could afford to return to school. At the end of the day Patty picked up Dana from the sitters, prepared dinner for the family and spent the evening with her husband. Patty's personality transformation was a blessing. Glen couldn't imagine such a blissful marriage. Not even with Georgina. Glen was so thankful for this change that he rewarded Patty regularly with simple little gifts to show his love for her. Patty appeared content for several years. At some point Patty lost interest in returning to school.

The old Dornstadt homestead went up for sale after Kevin moved out of town. It sold quickly and the money was divided equally among the siblings. Glen and Patty purchased a new house with their inheritance. Dana had her own room and their house was big enough for more children. The Dornstadt's were living well and enjoying life.

Ray and Georgina had a second son named Terry. Georgina returned to her happy self after her second pregnancy.

Ray was prescribed new medications that made a big difference in managing his Colitis. Once the Air Force determined that Ray's illness was under control, he was promoted to a lieutenant. Soon after his promotion Georgina discovered she was pregnant again.

She was somewhat disappointed at first, but quickly accepted her condition as a blessing and wished for a little girl this time.

Georgina became very involved in Air Force family activities. She was happy in Texas and hoped she'd never have to leave her community of friends. Ray had often refused promotional opportunities to avoid uprooting his family and leaving Texas. Eventually the opportunity of a lifetime was offered to Ray and he just couldn't turn down this promotion. He needed to move his family to Pope Air Force Base outside of Fayetteville, North Carolina.

No time is ever a good time to relocate and Georgina was having another difficult pregnancy. Her doctors were concerned and knowing her past history, determined that the activities involved with moving would be too stressful for her at this time. They insisted she stay where doctors were familiar with the seriousness of her condition. Again Georgina would require several weeks of hospitalization. With no other family to take care of the boys, Ray had to get leave to go home and take care of his children until Georgina could resume their care. Once Georgina was well enough, Ray returned to North Carolina while his family remained in Texas.

Rays illness was returning with a vengeance from the stress of all of these expectations. He felt everything collapsing around him. As soon as he returned to North Carolina from a visit home, he received a telegram informing him that his wife gave birth to a stillborn baby girl. After everything she had been through, she now had to plan a funeral without Ray's help. Georgina quickly returned to her fitful past and informed Ray she was not moving to North Carolina for any reason. Texas was home now and she was staying there. She came here for Ray and she was staying for her kids. As far as Georgina was concerned their marriage was over.

Ray took this promotion for his family and he thought everyone would be happy. Unfortunately it soon became obvious this was promotion was not in his best interests or his families. Ray didn't have a choice now but to stay in North Carolina. Baffled by his situation, his commanding officer suggested that Ray get Georgina to counseling quickly. Ray hoped to convince Georgina that every Air Force wife understood her feelings and how empty their life seemed when they left their friends behind. Many of the wives stated that they'd help her pack and be supportive in order to make a smooth transition, but she refused to cooperate.

Ray shared his cubicle with Jeannie Bartell. Jeannie knew how badly Ray was suffering and quickly warmed up to him hoping to ease his pain. They were both suffering from family separation and needed companionship. As badly as he wanted more from Jeannie, he couldn't cheat on his wife unless he knew there was no hope in reconciling his marriage. Jeannie was charming, but she wasn't as beautiful as Georgina. Ray appreciated her companionship, but he informed her that if she wanted more from him than just his friendship, he wasn't interested and she should move on. Ray soon discovered that Jeannie was the best medicine a man could find. She was very understanding and helped Ray through one of the most difficult separations of his career.

Even though Jeannie was in love with Ray she helped him persuade Georgina to move to North Carolina. He called her every night and reminded her of how much he missed her. He promised her anything she wanted as long as she came back to him. He made regular trips to Texas when his schedule allowed.

After spending several months with only young children, Georgina realized how much she missed Ray's companionship. She decided it was time to give in to her true feelings and join Ray in North Carolina. She missed him and loved him more than she allowed herself to admit.

While unpacking Ray's personal belongings, Georgina found a sealed box stuffed inside a larger box. Carefully she pulled away the seal. She opened the box to find a bunch of unopened letters addressed to Ray and a few addressed to her. The name was all too familiar: Glen Dornstadt. Georgina opened one of the letters. There were pictures of Glen with his daughter Dana and his wife Patty. Georgina was sure Ray never wanted her to see these letters and she was going to make sure he didn't know she had. Carefully she closed the envelopes and returned them to the box. She continued to unpacked the remainder of Ray's other personal belongings. She discovered those letters had much less impact on her than she expected they would. Hopefully she was finally over Glen.

Dana definitely resembled Gary. They had the same cute little noses and bright blue eyes. Dana looked like her mother as much as Glen, so how could she resemble Gary so much?

Georgina wondered if Dana had any talents. Both of her sons seemed to be musically inclined. Gary loved to poke around at the piano and Terry, although very small, liked to beat on the sofa with big wooden spoons. Georgina thought for sure he was going to be a drummer.

Georgina was eager to settle into her new home and lifestyle. She wanted the past to be exactly that—behind her. She wanted her marriage back on track. She had spent way too much time away from Ray and now she needed to make up for lost time. Ray came home early one afternoon with intentions to show his wife how much he loved her and missed her. Both Ray and Georgina were ready to heal their wounds. It had been along time since they had spent any quality time alone. Georgina was finally returning to her very sensual self. All she had to do was enter a room with the right stride and she had Ray's attention. If nothing else, Ray and Georgina's sexual appetites were equal. Just a certain look would send them to the bedroom.

One day Georgina called Ray at work and asked him to come right home after work and not to work overtime if he could help it. "There's no emergency and if you have important business to handle, this will wait," Georgina said.

"Are you all right? Are the boys okay?" Ray asked. "Everything is fine, just come home as soon as you get the chance. I need to discuss something with you," Georgina said.

Georgina told Ray her news; she was pregnant again. Ray was relieved. "That's wonderful. I didn't know what to expect," he said with a sigh.

Georgina had a very easy pregnancy. She finally got her little girl. Rebecca Jean Buckley was a healthy eight and a half pound baby. She made her presence known everywhere she went. She rarely fussed and was usually very talkative. She smiled at everybody and became Daddy's little girl. She looked just like her daddy. She had dark brown hair and brown eyes. Her brothers were very protective of their little sister. Both boys resembled their mother with their fair complexions, but Gary had blue eyes and Terry had brown eyes. None of the children really resembled each other much. All three could have had different fathers.

Glen and Patty had talked several times about trying to have another child, but the timing was just never right for Patty. As Dana approached seven years old, Glen begged Patty again to have another child. "I'd really like to have a son," Glen pleaded.

Patty used sex as a reward or punishment. If Glen wanted another child, he was going to pay. Patty wanted all of the latest gadgets. She wanted a washer and dryer, a new electric stove, and a color TV. Glen obliged but it took months to pay off those debts. As they got closer to being free from the lenders, Glen asked Patty one more time for another child.

One weekend while Dana was staying with her cousin, Patty approached Glen. "Let's go and see if we can't make a baby!" Patty said excitedly. Glen and Patty made love the way a couple should when trying to make a baby. Glen found himself totally consumed in Patty's needs and desires. Unfortunately, that night would not produce a baby.

Patty was ready for another child. They tried for six months to get pregnant. Glen was often heard saying it was the best six months of their marriage.

Patty finally gave Glen the news he was waiting to hear. She was expecting a winter baby. Other than morning sickness and a little ankle swelling, Patty's pregnancy was uneventful.

Late February 1964, Glen and Patty welcomed Darren Albert Dornstadt into their family.

Dana was a very proud big sister. She wheeled Darren all over the neighborhood in his stroller. When he got too big for that, she held his hand and they walked together.

Just when Glen and Patty were finally getting some free time for themselves, Patty discovered she was pregnant again. Patty was certain that she would need to leave her job, and finances were getting tight with one new addition to the family. The company Glen worked for changed hands and it didn't take long for the new owners to bankrupt the business and close the doors. Glen took a new job earning only half of what he had been previously bringing home. This situation put a lot of stress on the family.

Patty left her job sooner than she planned because the strain of standing for long hours was causing serious complications with her pregnancy. Her doctors continued to battle with her pregnancy related health issues. On a very hot day in July, Patty went into labor. Late that night, Patty gave birth to a baby girl, but to everyone's surprise, she wasn't done. Lorraine and Elizabeth Dornstadt joined the world on two different dates. Elizabeth's name was shortened to Lizzy, and Lorraine was Lori.

Glen and Patty had gone from having one child to four children in twenty seven months. Glen either had to find a better paying job or take a second job to support his growing family.

In an effort to assist Patty with child care, Glen spent as much time with his children as possible. Glen soon discovered he was wearing out from lack of sleep. Four children were taking a toll on their time together and their marriage. Patty became distant and neglected Glen's needs. He prayed life would soon return to normal. He wondered how his mother handled nine children. Glen was proud of his beautiful children and wondered if his mother could look down and see what he had created. Glen knew his mother wouldn't have understood Georgina's decision to marry Ray. Glen had to forget about Georgina, and focus on the beautiful family God gave him.

Patty was a good mother. She spent a lot of time with her children reading books, putting puzzles together, and playing with cars and dolls. Patty's children always came first.

Ray and Glen were both so busy earning a living they both missed many of their children's accomplishments and activities. Ray felt it was the mother's place to go to parent-teacher conferences, plays, and school related activities. It was his place to earn a living so they could continue their expensive activities. Ray's children would never want for anything except for their father's attention. Glen fit as many of his children's activities into his schedule as possible.

Gary grew up resenting his father's absence. He drowned his resentment by taking music lessons. He learned to play the piano and guitar and discovered he could forget his disappointments and frustrations with his musical creations. He even took saxophone lessons, but mouth instruments weren't as easy for him to learn.

Terry liked the drums and played them for fun, however he wasn't the musician that Gary had become. Georgina hated the drums, but if she allowed Gary to play the piano and guitar, she had to let Terry play the drums.

The Beatles made their debut when Gary was eleven years old. He wanted to play music just like they did. He soon became consumed by their music. He didn't like sports and really didn't care for drama. He just wanted to play music. This didn't sit well with his parents. Georgina's family attended the opera and theater and this new style of music was horrible. Georgina and Gary fought constantly about his choice of music. If Gary was going to spend his time playing that rock music crap, Georgina felt he was wasting his time. She was proud of his talent, but he certainly wasn't going to make a living playing that stuff.

Gary's family pleaded with him to get more involved in school activities. His grades were high enough that his parents urged him to pursue other interests that would help him get accepted into college. Gary had no interest in furthering his education. To avoid confrontation Gary left his parents believe that college was a possibility. He loved British rock music and that's where his heart was.

Terry tormented Gary with his continuous snide remarks about being a sissy. He told him he wasn't man enough to take on tough sports like other boys his age. Gary avoided Terry as much as possible. His own brother made him feel uncomfortable about his love of music. Gary felt like an outsider in his own home.

The boys lost that brotherly closeness they had had when they were small. Terry pursued sports, girls, hot rod cars and he had lots of friends. Gary only had a few friends and didn't have time for girls. His goal was to be a rock star like Paul McCartney and the Beatles. He liked basketball but he didn't have the time or discipline he needed to play on a team.

Chapter 15
An Unhappy Return

Georgina knew Ray's moods, so when Ray came home looking strangely happy one day she couldn't help but ask, "You look too happy. Would you care to share your excitement with us?"

"I hope you're not disappointed when I tell you I have received a promotion," Ray exclaimed. "That's wonderful, why would I be disappointed?" Georgina questioned.

"Well, I'll have the final say on all lower-class promotions from over thousands of recruits from our airmen and women living in Great Britain which means, we have 30 days to move to London. I wanted this same position for the south central states, but for now, I'll have to settle for London. Since I am already familiar with London, they offered me this assignment. I hope that you're as excited to return to London as I am," Ray said. Georgina's facial expression was difficult to read. Ray wasn't sure but he wasn't sensing her approval. Ray liked power and this promotion gave him that. The higher your rank the better your opportunity becomes to work with dignitaries and attend events that most other people never get to experience. Ray had four more years until he could retire from the Air Force and he was going to go out big.

Georgina was cautiously optimistic about this news, but worried about her children's reactions. Becky Jean was distraught about moving. "What about all of my friends? That's so far away, they won't be able to visit with me," she said harshly. "Dad, can't you go without us?" Terry asked. "Gary, do you have any concerns?" Ray asked. "Not really Dad. You do what you need to do for your job. I like British rock and roll. Maybe moving to London would be inspiring for me. It might be the break I need. I think we should look at this as a new experience or a new chapter in our lives. I suggest we go with an open mind," Gary said.

"We only have a month to pack and say our good-byes," Ray said sternly.

Georgina headed to London immediately to find adequate housing for her family. Air Force houses were very small abodes. She wasn't willing to skimp on size. She needed to find something roomy to please her family. A week of viewing mediocre homes frustrated Georgina. The Buckley's weren't wealthy by any means, but the houses the real estate agents showed her were in no way suitable for a family of five.

Georgina tossed the agent and went out on her own. She scanned the newspapers and drove up and down the streets looking for private sellers. Finally, after two weeks of not finding anything suitable, she found a very nice house just outside the city limits. It was a cedar-shingled, two-story, very roomy, four-bedroom house with a large patio, a two-car garage, and a swimming pool. It had a separate room above the garage for projects or privacy. The kitchen was large enough for several people to move around in easily. The basement had potential too. Maybe one day they would finish it for an extra room. Many houses in London don't have basements large enough to finish and even less have pools. The house was perfect, except for the price. Georgina decided she wanted it and knew it didn't matter to Ray what it cost as long as she was happy.

Upon her return to North Carolina, Georgina was pleased when she discovered Ray hired a moving company to pack and ship their belongings across the ocean. Everything was already just about packed and ready to go. This was too tedious and time consuming to handle any other way.

Georgina's parents were gone now and her sisters were in the States. Cousins and school friends were still in London but it just wasn't the same. Georgina was excited but sad to be returning home under these circumstances. She had raised her children in Texas and North Carolina and she suddenly realized that her friends and her children's friends were in the United States—that was home now. This was going to be an unhappy return.

Becky Jean spent the next year shedding lots of tears and locking herself in her bedroom. Terry became rebellious. He was miserable and wanted to make sure everyone around him was miserable too. He stayed out late most nights and often returned intoxicated. He discovered he got a lot of attention by breaking furniture and screaming obscenities. His mother patronized him and tolerated his outbursts just to appease him. His father was very upset and much less tolerable with this new behavior. Gary on the other hand didn't express his feelings about the move. Ray and Georgina assumed that Gary's lack of communication was a positive sign.

Ray continued to have limited time to spend with his children and he didn't want to spend it enforcing curfews and asserting punishment. He stayed away more and left Georgina to handle these situations at her discretion.

Terry continued his troublesome behavior for several years. He claimed he was seeking his individualism like other teenagers and young adults. Both boys' hair needed serious attention. They wore it long and stringy and it certainly didn't become them. Terry was one of the first of his friends to pierce his ear. He dressed worse than individuals living on the streets. His gloves had no fingers and his pants were torn in many places. His parents pleaded with him to clean up but Terry wanted to start his own trend. It was

Terry's way of getting attention. When he met the girl who would eventually become his bride, she was able to slowly restore him to a cleaner and neater individual. Soon after they married they moved to the United States.

Chapter 16
Tragedy

Glen found a better paying job as a delivery driver, and worked less hours. He was now able to be home every evening allowing him more time to spend with his children. Some months there was even a little extra spending money for special adventures. Patty liked having Glen home in the evenings. Between his work and children, Glen rarely had time to think about Georgina or Gary. Occasionally he'd have a flashback and reminisce about what his life might have been like if he and Georgina had married.

Glen's enthusiasm at his new job earned him a promotion in a relatively short period of time. He was given a company vehicle and his own service route. Then tragedy struck. He lost control of the company van, rolled it over and hit a tree. He was taken to the emergency room where a nurse was told to notify his family immediately. He had so many broken bones the doctors couldn't count them all. His body was covered in blood which made finding all of his wounds very difficult. His wounds and lacerations were so bad that doctors feared he'd bleed to death first. If he made it through the night it would be a miracle. Glen prayed for strength to fight so he wouldn't leave his wife and children behind. Patty knew of his stubbornness and coaxed him to hang on.

He endured many hours of cleaning and repairing superficial abrasions all over his body. He was finally taken into surgery to be put back together. Ten hours later he was wheeled to recovery. Only Patty was allowed to join him. Doctor's told Patty that the next operation might possibly require them to amputate one and possibly both of his legs. Glen begged his wife not to sign anything that would give anyone the authority to perform that sort of operation. Without all of his limbs he preferred death over life; he wanted to die whole. He reminded the doctors and his wife that he made it through Korea with all of his parts, and he was going to die with all of them. Patty was advised of the seriousness of his injuries. No guarantees were promised. It was going to take months for him to recover if he managed to hang on. In spite of all of the warnings, Patty granted his wish. She pushed away the paperwork that would have allowed any amputations.

Patty was the night shift admittance clerk at a different area hospital. At least all of the children were now in school which allowed Patty the necessary time to spend at Glen's side without searching for a babysitter. Patty wanted to be there to take them to school in the morning but most mornings she stopped to see Glen before she went home to get a few hours sleep.

Dana put herself in charge of her sibling's morning routine and made sure they had lunch money, their back packs, and all of their classroom materials before she drove them to school.

Once Glen came home from the hospital, he needed months of physical therapy. After several operations and a year of physical therapy, Glen could barely maneuver two steps. After two and half years of therapy, he was able to walk his daughter down the isle to give her hand in marriage without any support.

The police determined that Glen was at fault in the accident. The owners of the company had to replace him. They couldn't get by without filling his position. He was relieved of his duties immediately.

Dana was a petite, blue-eyed, blonde with simple features. She had lots of friends and no problem attracting boys. She had a subdued yet bubbly personality. Dana was a senior in high school when Glen's accident occurred. She decided to quit school and find a job to help take care of the family's expenses. Since her father's income was going stop, the family was going to need money. She was prepared to work to help support her family and any expenses her father incurred. Glen was livid. His daughter was not quitting school. They would manage somehow. Dana was an exceptionally good student. Glen called a family meeting at his bedside before he went into his next surgery. He told his entire family that none of them were to change their lives because of his carelessness. The Dornstadt children were all required to help around the house. Most of all they were to make sure that in no way, Dana felt the need to quit school. Glen had hoped Dana would attend college and get the education that her mother wished she had achieved years earlier.

For nearly a year Dana was the glue that held the family together. Whenever her siblings needed a ride anywhere, she played chauffer. She put her life on hold, stopped dating, and rarely attended school events. She spent all of her spare time studying, working in the evenings, or taking care of her siblings.

Dana's friends became distant and unsupportive of her situation. Contact between them was minimal. The few occasions Dana ventured out, she had a difficult time enjoying herself. She was committed to her family and promised to be home in time for Patty to leave for work before ten thirty PM. Her friends teased her about her early curfew, but Dana didn't care what they thought. They just didn't understand her situation. Dana gave up trying to explain to them the severity of the crisis in her home.

Under the exceptional care of his doctors; many hours of strenuous physical therapy, and a lot of love and support from his family, Glen's recuperation was amazing. No matter what Glen needed his family by his side. Glen was determined to walk again. He had to make this effort for his loved ones who were so dedicated to him. The doctors never told him any differently and encouraged him in every way. He knew he was never going to be as good as before, but he was going to manage the best he could. Being dependant on others was not a lifestyle he pictured in his future.

Glen made several friends during his long stay in the hospital. His favorite was Lewis Porter, a spunky young salesman with an incredibly upbeat disposition. Lewis had fallen off a ladder while roofing his parents' house and suffered from a broken back and collarbone. He and Glen worked through hours of physical therapy together.

Lewis worked from home as a sales rep for a nationwide corporation. He made frequent trips to his regional headquarters located in Boston. Before his accident he frequently attended trainings and seminars at various locations out of the area. Quarterly sessions were held for interested and new representatives. Lewis continued to watch Glen's progress, and when the time was right, he approached Glen about considering a position with his company. Lewis invited Glen to attend an introductory seminar with him at the Boston headquarters. Lewis hoped to persuade Glen to come on board as soon as he was strong enough, but before he had time to pursue other interests.

Chapter 17
Starting Somewhere

Gary worked very hard at becoming an accomplished guitarist. His guitar rarely left his side. He wrote a lot of the music he played. All he needed now was a band to play his songs. Finding the right talent wasn't easy. He went through forty musicians before he was able to put together a band that suited him. It took some time to come up with a unique name. They eventually agreed to call themselves the White Ravens.

Their families were very financially supportive. Parents helped them purchase sound equipment needed to play for large crowds. They quickly became a success at pubs and nightclubs in London. Their songs were full of harmonizing and long guitar solos. They got many of their ideas from the Beatles. The Beatles' sound was enlightening, exciting, and different. The White Ravens wanted a similar sound. In no time at all, they were booked months in advance. They hoped to be part of the British invasion but quickly realized they were several years too late to be part of that trend.

The band was persistent and continued to book every show they could possibly find. Groupies started to follow them all over. It didn't take long to build a solid fan base. Band members became so involved with their music that they rarely took time from their schedule for family or any other outside events.

Soon overspending, transportation costs, and equipment break downs, along with consuming too much alcohol and marijuana, took its toll on the band. With no money and poor transportation, they fell fast and hard. Their families joined forces and decided that tough love was the best treatment for them. They needed to learn to become more responsible. The five young men had a difficult time maintaining one apartment between them. As fast as they had become a household name, in no time at all they were flat broke and out of the music scene.

Weeks later, determined not to breakup, they hired an agent to help them reorganize. That decision was the beginning of a fantastic career that would span over many decades. They weren't an overnight success worldwide, but in a year their name became a household word among teenagers all over Europe. Their dream was to get their music to the United States. With patience and perseverance their wish would eventually come true.

It took Glen a long time to recover from his accident. Physically he made miraculous strides, but his finances were a mess. He borrowed money from every relative, friend, and bank in Pennsylvania. Like a wildcat, Lewis saw an opportunity to pounce on Glen's vulnerability. Lewis shared very little information with Glen about his company yet he managed to make it sound much more lucrative than it really was. With his unique power of persuasion, Lewis convinced Glen to travel to Boston with him to attend a presentation to entice interested individuals to become new colleagues.

Lewis told Glen, "The benefits that my company pays should be enough to pull your family out of debt in no time. What do you have to lose? There's no strings attached. Just attend this seminar with me; I'll pay all of your expenses. We'll have a great time, you'll see. People come from all over the world to attend these seminars. They are anxious to welcome you and you'll love the hospitality," Lewis said.

With much reluctance Glen agreed to join Lewis at the seminar. Hesitation and procrastination were Glen's worst foes. He'd hesitated too many times before, passing up good job opportunities. If this was as easy as Lewis made it sound he wasn't going to pass up one more chance at making a good living.

Ray was very content with his new classification. He accepted this transfer so Georgina could stay at home and take care of the kids and the house. Georgina and her friends had the time to do almost anything they wanted. Unfortunately, Georgina found herself bored and in need of something to keep her busy. A new acquaintance of Georgina's, Mary Jo Roberts invited her to attend a seminar in Boston. They'd have fun and maybe Georgina would find that she was interested in pursing a career with this company. Mary Jo convinced Georgina that this seminar would be a good opportunity to build their new friendship.

"You can make easy money just by referring other people to our company and getting them to buy our products. Put as much or as little time into as you wish," Mary Jo told Georgina.

"That almost sounds to easy, kind of too good to be true. I'd like to find out more about your company. It sounds like something I might like to do," Georgina told Mary Jo. "Great, then we can go to Boston together. I can't really tell you much about it until you attend a presentation. You'll learn so much more there than I can explain to you," Mary Jo said excitedly.

Georgina's biggest challenge was when she had to tell Ray, "I am going to attend a sales presentation in Boston with Mary Jo Roberts. I know you don't want me to work, but I'd like to find something to occupy my time and soothe my boredom," Georgina announced. "Boston is so far away, and you don't need to work," Ray pleaded. "My mind is made up. I will be leaving on Wednesday," Georgina told him. "I don't understand. You have everything you need. If you must go on a trip, well go ahead, but I don't understand why you need to work?" Ray said disappointed.

"What do you know about this company? I've never heard of them and if it sounds too good to be true, then it probably is. It sounds rather shady to me. Let me just caution you not to sign anything. You are always here for us. It will take some getting used to when you are gone. Please consider our children's needs when you make your final decision. And remember, this business better not involve me in any way because I can't help, nor do I have the time to pursue a family business," Glen informed her.

The White Ravens finally booked their first United States appearance at a nightclub in Boston the same week Georgina and Mary Jo were visiting. They made arrangements to meet the boys for dinner and then Georgina and Mary Jo went to watch the band play. They played to an audience of 1200 people and closed with a standing ovation. Georgina was so proud of her son. She had never imagined that his guitar would take him so far.

Glen and Lewis drove to Boston. It was an excruciating trip for Glen with his injuries. Yet the pain was minor compared to what he had endured before. He thought to himself that he should be ashamed for whining. He could handle this. He needed to get back on his feet financially and if this was what it would take, then he was going to do it.

Lewis was fifteen years younger than Glen and was completely into the rock scene. The first night in Boston he invited Glen to attend a concert with him but Glen was in such pain that he declined. "I'd love to go with you, and if it were tomorrow night, I would probably go," Glen said. "Good enough. We'll attend our presentation in the morning, go to dinner and then go to a show in the evening for entertainment. Maybe you'll feel like dancing," Lewis said. "Whoa, wait a minute. I said I'd go to the show; there'll be no dancing for me," Glen said. "Boy oh boy, your wife has you wrapped around her finger, doesn't she?" Lewis asked. "This has nothing to do with my wife and everything to do with my legs. They just don't move like they used to. I could fall and injure everything that has just been fixed. I'm not taking that chance," Glen said.

Glen didn't want to be unsociable, but he was very uncomfortable. The last thing he wanted to do was attend a dance. He wanted to attend the presentation and then return to his room to rest. Dancing was not part of the plan.

Lewis suggested they arrive at the arena early in the morning to secure good seats. He knew how quickly they filled up and it was important to be near the front. Glen was feeling much better and wanted to scout around before the seminar started. Coffee was a mainstay in Glen's diet so he stopped to get one more cup before the seminar started.

Out of the corner of his eye he spotted a familiar face. *"My mind must be playing tricks on me."* He looked again. *"How could she be here?"* He walked up to the absolutely stunning woman in front of him. He offered his hand and reached out for hers. Just as she was going to put her change into her purse, she saw him. Their eyes met. They could have lit up a room with the amount of energy flowing between them. They stared at each other for what seemed like minutes and then Georgina spoke. "I'm sorry, have we met before?" Georgina asked. "Oh come on Georgina, it's me, Glen. Don't play this game," he exclaimed.

Georgina was trying to refrain from speaking to him. Her heart was racing and she didn't want to say something she'd regret later. She had thought of him often throughout the years but she never imagined running into him like this. Now there he was, right in front of her. She wondered what information she should share with him. *"Should I keep it simple? I'll keep my conversation to a minimum. That way, we'll part in a few minutes, and it'll be like we never saw each other,"* she thought to herself.

"Life has been good to you. You're as beautiful as you were the last time I saw you nearly twenty years ago," Glen said.

"You look good too," Georgina said, not really sounding like she meant it.

"Don't lie. I haven't been as lucky as you. My hair is almost gone, I've gained some weight, and then I had an accident a few years back. I may never completely recover, but I have been lucky.

I overcame many serious injuries and am living almost normal now. No more wheelchairs, crutches, or canes. The good news is that my vision was not affected and I know you are still fabulously beautiful," Glen sighed.

"Are you married?" Georgina asked. "Yes I am, and I have four beautiful children. Dana, my oldest, is seventeen. Darren, my only son, is eleven, and the twins, Lizzy and Lori are eight. My wife Patty has been great through all of my health problems. I am very lucky to have her. How about you? Are you still married to Ray?" Glen asked.

"Yes, and we have three children now. Of course, Gary, who will be nineteen in a few days; Terry is seventeen, and Becky Jean is thirteen. We're living in London again. I came here with a friend to find out about this business. She suggested I try this because I mentioned to her that I might be interested in pursuing a career. I find myself bored at home all day alone and I want to do something meaningful with my life," Georgina said.

"I don't know what I am doing here. I don't think this is the kind of work I am looking to pursue, but I came along to see what this business is all about. I have been a route salesman for the last several months and inside sales for years prior to that. This Company sounded like it would blend in with my past experience. Unfortunately I haven't worked steadily since my accident and I really need to find a job that I can perform that won't bother my legs," Glen said.

"How is our son? Who does he look like? Is he healthy? Was he a good student?" Glen asked. "Wow, wait a minute. One question at a time! Gary is here in Boston. Maybe I can arrange for you to meet him so you can answer your own questions. Glen he doesn't know about us so watch what you ask him, please. He won't have a lot of time. He is here with his band, the White Ravens and they had a few shows scheduled here in Boston. Tonight is their last show here. The band is doing very well and I suspect they will become a big name in the near future. I am going to meet him here for a quick dinner after the seminar. Would you like to join us?" Georgina asked.

"Yes, I would like that. Does he resemble me? Will I be able to pick him out of a crowd?" Glen asked. "When you look at him you can judge for yourself. Now I must get back to my seat. I'll meet you right here at six thirty," Georgina said.

Glen heard very little of the presentation. All he could think about was meeting Georgina and Gary. Who would have thought that his dream of meeting his son would finally happen on a trip he didn't want to make? Meeting Georgina like this couldn't have happened this well if it had been planned. Glen often wondered how he was going to find Gary, if ever. This was perfect.

After the men returned to their room Glen confronted his roommate. "Lewis I have never told anyone about a very private situation in my life, not even Patty. I must confide in you now. I'm not sure how to react to my immediate situation, but I am not going to let an opportunity like this pass me by. I have lived with this secret every day. Today I have an opportunity to change my past forever," Glen shared emphatically. "Wow, I'm honored to be the first to learn about your secret," Lewis said.

Glen told Lewis about his past with Georgina. He elaborated on his probable love child with her and how the relationship had ended. The two men talked for an hour and almost missed dinner. Lewis was astonished by this new revelation. "I would have never placed you in a love triangle. Nor would I have thought you to have an illegitimate child. Don't take this the wrong way but this information changes my whole opinion of you. I thought you were pretty stiff, a follow the rules type person. I guess I was wrong," Lewis said.

Glen told Lewis that he was going to meet with Georgina and Gary at six thirty. "Gary is of age now and I think it's time he knows about his real father. What an opportunity I have been given to tell him," Glen said. "I don't think this is the place Glen. Think about the effect it may have on this young man. He might not be too happy with the information you are about to share with him. Just think; you are telling him you slept with his mother. How do think he is going to respond to that? He might already know about you. I believe if his parents wanted him to know about you, they would have already told him," Lewis shared.

"You don't understand Lewis. I never imagined having the opportunity to meet him. I'm not going to let him leave until he knows about his past," Glen said. "Okay, let me try this one more time. Go meet him, but don't mention his questionable paternity. That should come from his parents. Just wonder if you are wrong and you are not his father?" Lewis said.

"When this does not work out and you go home upset and without a job, how are you going to tell your family about why you are disappointed and sad? Then when he refuses to acknowledge you as his father, you will go home with even more heartache. Why do you want to feel like a loser all over again? Not to mention that you came here to find out about my company, not to chase your past. You realize you'll be going home empty again if you decide not pursue a career with us? How are you going to explain coming home uninformed and without enough information to make a viable decision to your waiting loved ones?" Lewis asked.

Glen had to admit that Lewis was being realistic. He had better think this over before he made a decision he'd regret later. "Okay, you have some valid points for me to consider. I am still going to go through with seeing Gary, but I'll change my approach. I don't expect you to understand where I am coming from. I promise that I will attend the entire seminar tomorrow," Glen said.

"Then if you must, go ahead. I will not be part of your family event. I am going to the free activities provided tonight. I think it is best that I stay as far away from this reunion as possible. Just remember, you might hurt Patty more than anyone else, and I won't defend you. If you don't care about her feelings, then venture on. Please take time to consider securing a position with my business," Lewis said.

Walking down the long corridor to the arena restaurant Glen was shaking and his stomach was queasy. He had no idea how to present himself to Gary or to Georgina for that matter. He no longer had any feelings for Georgina, but confronting Gary in an intellectual way was going to be difficult at best. Lewis was probably right about Gary's response. Glen wasn't sure he was prepared for the name-calling and rejection he was about to receive.

"Hi Georgina," Glen said as he walked up to her and gave her a hug. "Running into you like this has been a wonderful surprise. It's like a reunion. Where is Gary? Will he be joining us?" Glen asked.

"He'll be along shortly. I told him I'd like to introduce him to an old acquaintance and to meet me here in ten minutes. I wanted to speak with you first. Don't tell him Glen. I don't want him to know. He's a very well-adjusted young man. He has his life planned out and this is very private information that might interfere with his success. He has a great future carved out for his band and he could possibly be the next Beatles or Rolling Stones. You don't want to throw a kink into that do you? Don't even approach him if you are going to reveal his past tonight," Georgina warned.

"I understand your apprehension. When do you think I can approach him? If not now, when? I never expected to have this opportunity, but now here it is. This could be the most important moment of my life and Gary's. I beg you to allow me this opportunity. Could I tell him before he leaves? Maybe he'll accept the fact that he has a different father. Please understand Georgina, I've waited all of my life for this opportunity. He has a right to know who his real father is, don't you agree?" Glen asked.

"You didn't hear a word I said, did you? He doesn't need to know this information now. Gary can be extremely sensitive. He may not accept this information well, or not at all. You could ruin his career. I told you, I won't take a chance on ruining his future.

Meeting for dinner is a mistake. I am going to go now," Georgina said as she turned and walked away.

"Don't go, please. I just want to meet my son. I will agree to your request, I promise. I have dreamt of this moment for the past nineteen years. I would never intentionally hurt you or him. You can't possibly understand how I feel. Imagine never being able to see your child. There has never been a day that I didn't think of him," Glen pleaded.

"I will retrieve Gary and be back shortly," Georgina said sternly and scowling as she walked away.

"I'll go get a cup of coffee and wait right here for you," Glen sighed, relieved.

Glen kept rehearsing over and over what he wanted to say to Gary, but he was still unsure as to how to approach him. He wasn't going home until Gary knew about his conception. First he'd wish him a lot of success. His band had the potential to become big. Glen needed Gary to know who he was and that he always loved him. Somehow Glen was going to tell Gary everything.

He saw Georgina and two young men walking towards him. After reviewing the boys he was not certain which one was Gary, but he quickly made his choice. Georgina introduced them to Glen without revealing any more information.

"Boys I'd like you to meet an old acquaintance of mine. This is Glen Dornstadt. He was in the service back when I met Ray. We went on a double date a few times. Did you marry that girl you used to go with?" Georgina asked Glen while winking at him.

"No I didn't," Glen said harshly. He still wasn't sure which one was Gary and obviously, Georgina didn't want him to know yet, either. One young man was fair and the other one had dark hair. Both boys had blue eyes. Either one could be his son.

"So tell me your name?" Glen said to the boys.

A very thin blonde haired young man introduced himself. "Hi, I'm Gary," he said. Then the other young man offered his hand and said, "I'm Lee." *I should have known which one was Gary, he resembles Darren.* Glen thought to himself.

Neither of them had any clue as to why they were being introduced to this stranger. They hoped he was an agent and could help them book shows.

"We are the founding members of the White Ravens. You probably haven't heard of us yet but give us a few months and we'll be a household name in the states," Gary said. "It's a pleasure meeting you. I certainly hope your band makes it as big as your mother expects you will. Your mother is very excited to have a rock star son," Glen said. Gary glanced at his mother and smiled as if to say, "*Thanks for your support, Mom.*"

"We have recorded a lot of songs and plan on traveling throughout the United States to get exposure. Our agent has booked us in several nightclubs in the Boston area. Tomorrow we leave here for a few small venues in different New England towns. Then we'll be going to New York City for a couple of weeks," Lee said.

"Good for you. I'll be keeping my fingers crossed that all goes well. I can feel your excitement, you'll do well. My daughter is about your age. I'll have to tell her about your band," Glen said.

We've really enjoyed talking with you but we have to get ready for our show. It's important that we're not late. It was nice meeting an old friend of Mom's. Good luck at your seminar. Come see one of our shows," Gary said walking away.

"Wow, he is something. If you could just see my eleven-year-old Darren, there are many similarities between the two boys. Darren also plays a guitar. He has been taking lessons for four years now and he's really good," Glen said.

"Now I know where Gary's musical talent comes from. Neither Ray nor I have any musical background," Georgina shared.

"My father could play any instrument you handed him. He was very talented. If it wasn't for his music, I don't know that I would have much good to say about him," Glen said. "Now that you mention it, I remember you rarely ever had much good to say about your father," Georgina shared.

"Glen it has been a pleasure seeing you again after so many years. I'm glad you got to meet Gary, I think he liked you. I really must be getting back to my room now," Georgina said.

While Georgina was in Boston, Ray was busy meeting with training instructors. Ray's years of experience were untouchable. New lieutenants and sergeants flocked to Ray for his expertise. Ray was easy to relate to and very down-to-earth considering his status. He craved perfection and was eager to help wherever he could.

Ray trained Eliza Bower, one of the first women instructors in the Air Force. Eliza was tall with a slender figure and a good build. She had long flowing beautiful blonde hair which she usually pinned up under her cap. This very exciting young woman was not the least bit shy. She approached Ray during a vulnerable time; while Georgina was away. She knew he was lonely. She was extremely attracted to her very well-kept middle-age superior. The Air Force explicitly frowned upon fraternization between service personnel. If caught, their jobs were in serious jeopardy and a possible court marshal could follow. Normally Ray would never have chanced entering such a dangerous territory. Just responding to her advances could get him into trouble with the Air Force. He worried that she could be a plant testing him. Her invitation was just too tempting for a lonely middle-age man whose wife's sexual needs were non-existent.

Ray tried to push her away, but she kept coming back. This beautiful young woman who so eagerly came on to him was the medicine Ray needed to boost his sinking self esteem. His hair was thinning and he had let his physique slide. Ray wanted fireworks in his sex life again and assumed this was probably the only opportunity he would ever get. Ray was certain that he would be sorry either way he chose to resolve this issue. His choice was to experience guilt for cheating on Georgina or sorrow for missing the opportunity to experience some one new. He didn't even know if Eliza was worth the risk and he wouldn't know until it was over. This could be the biggest mistake of his life and he was risking everything just to have a little fun and excitement. Lovemaking with Georgina was bland and routine and technique was not an issue any longer. Seduction was a thing of the past. Did he still have it in him to please a younger woman? Eliza Bower was very serious about her career. Having an affair with an officer was the last thought on her mind—until she met Ray. For some reason she was smitten by him. There was no logical explanation. It wasn't his rank, his authority, or his ability to make her feel weak and insecure. However, his distinguished good looks, that devilish smile and his bright brown eyes melted her heart. She knew what trouble she'd be in if she were caught intimate with another member of the Air Force, especially with someone of his rank. For some reason she was willing to risk it all.

Ray and Eliza purposely walked down a brightly lit street in London in an attempt to disguise their upcoming plans. Hopefully, no one would suspect what was about to come next.

Ray couldn't have Eliza at his house because Terry and Becky Jean were there. He couldn't chance being seen at the base with her so they separately drove out of town to a hotel. Ray was careful not to come home with receipts or evidence of having been there.

It had been years since Ray had tried to please a woman other than his wife and he was extremely nervous. Eliza wasn't shy at all and she made the first move. She skipped all of the foreplay and went straight for Ray's zipper. He didn't have time to unbutton his own shirt. Eliza was undressed and naked in front of him before he had his pants off. Her breasts were firm, soft, and not yet suckled by a baby. Her entire body was very muscular, something that Georgina's physique now lacked. He felt like a teenage boy experiencing sex for the first time. Ray was not familiar with a woman taking charge. He was so excited that he knew that as aroused as he was, this session wasn't going to last very long. He wanted to perform some of the special techniques he used on

Georgina years ago hoping to hold off his impending climax. He needed to show her that he had restraint and the ability to please her.

When their marathon was finished Ray went home and Eliza returned to the base. It was one of the most sexually exciting moments Ray had in years. This experience left Ray feeling like a new person. It brought meaning to his life and now he wanted more.

Ray and Eliza met one more time before Georgina's return. Again Eliza took charge. She excused herself and quickly headed into the bathroom. When she opened the door all of her clothes were off except for a towel. When she dropped her towel she exposed some strategically placed red tassels on her very tight and slender body. Ray shuttered with excitement and quickly lost his shyness. Eliza crawled to Ray from the bathroom and proceeded to climb up his legs. Eliza stayed on her knees until Ray could no longer stand. This night was all about what Ray wanted. Guilt was not in is vocabulary. No woman ever came on to Ray like Eliza had done. When Eliza was done with Ray he had nothing left to offer her. He was so weak he quickly fell asleep.

He remembered to bring protection this time; hopefully it wasn't too late. He scolded himself for not using it the first night. Protection was not what he wanted to be concerned about but a pregnancy with a woman half his age was not in his plans. Not to mention that it could ruin his career and his marriage.

Ray woke up in the morning at the hotel. He left in a flurry, but not without leaving Eliza a note to meet him again on Thursday. Georgina would have returned home by their next planned meeting. She played bridge every Thursday night and probably wouldn't miss Ray for a few hours. Eliza was happy to oblige.

Ray was a new man. Good sex had returned to his life and that made him feel young again. Georgina was still a beautiful, desirable woman, but it never hurts to add a little fun to perk up the self-esteem. Ray justified his tryst with Eliza by convincing himself that Georgina must suspect he was going somewhere else for his sexual needs because she wasn't keeping up her part of their marriage vows.

Ray and Eliza continued their affair on most Thursdays for the next three years. When Eliza was discharged from the Air Force she returned home for good. Ray's heart was heavy. He really missed his young mistress.

A year after Eliza's discharge, a new airman told Ray his sister claimed to have had an affair with him. The airman informed Ray, that approximately seven months after her discharge Eliza gave birth to a son. It was almost as if she had it all planned out. Ray never pursued the child. He thought that if Eliza wanted him to know, she would have contacted him.

Glen returned to his room. "Well, how did it go?" Lewis asked. "You know, I'm not sure. I didn't tell him anything yet. I felt by his expressions that he was waiting for a message or some information. I wonder if he already knows. He wants me to attend one of his shows, but unless I go tonight, I won't get the opportunity. Would you like to go with me?" Glen asked.

"No, the business provides us entertainment so that we don't need to leave the hotel. I suppose you'll miss it. What do you think about the business so far, are you in?" Lewis asked. "I'm sorry Lewis I am somewhat familiar with this business and it doesn't fit with my experience and background. I know I am not aggressive enough to look for sales like you do. I am certain I would not have signed on even if Gary wasn't here. However you have provided me with an opportunity that I never expected to have. I must make the best of it while I can. I doubt that I ever get an opportunity like this again," Glen said.

"I want to get back early and get some sleep so we can head out early tomorrow morning. Go and enjoy your night, but don't get back to late," Lewis said.

Glen headed for the Wild Rangers Night Club in the heart of Boston. He asked the host for the best available seat. He was only a few rows back and could see Gary clearly. His mannerisms were so familiar. There was no doubt in his mind that Gary was his son. It couldn't be an accident that Gary looked so much like Darren. Glen pictured the boys sharing special moments and playing their instruments together. Then reality returned. Glen knew nothing of the sort would ever happen. It wasn't fair that his children would never know each other.

The boys in the band played loud music, jumped on the stage, spun around in circles with their guitars and flirted with all the girls. This was not the type of concert Glen would normally enjoy, but his son was the act and whatever Gary did to earn a living, was fine with him.

Glen vowed not to lose contact with Gary now. He had a few hours to figure out a way to resolve this issue. Otherwise he would lose his son again, probably forever.

Georgina and Mary Jo packed their bags and were ready to leave for the airport for their seven AM flight to London.

"You didn't seem impressed," Mary Jo said. "I don't know, Mary Jo. This isn't what I was expecting. I want a job that seems more like a hobby. I want it to be fun. I don't want a business that someone else owns. I definitely don't want to call on people I don't know. I want one that I own and all of the decisions are up to my discretion. This is too much like outside sales and that's just not me," Georgina said.

In the morning while Glen and Lewis were packing the car for the ride home, Glen spotted Gary and the rest of the band heading for a van.

"Lewis, I need to go talk to that young man. Wait here for me, please," he begged. "I think you should quit while you're ahead," Lewis yelled at Glen as he walked away. "I can't. I need this one last chance. I'll be back in a few minutes, Glen yelled back.

Glen approached Gary and asked, "Can I have a minute of your time before you leave?" "Make it quick. We've got a show to perform tonight, and we don't have a lot of time to get there," Gary said.

"Gary, I don't want to upset you. I'm not here to do that to you," Glen said. "Well then don't say anything you might regret later," Gary said. "Hear me out, please! For years I have had a big void in my life. A child was taken from me many years ago. Until this week I never had the chance to see him. I'm sure you know that I am speaking about you. There isn't a day that I don't worry or wonder about you. Years ago your mother and I had a long relationship, and you were the result of that relationship. I couldn't convince her to marry me. She chose Ray over me and he got to raise you. I don't want anything from you, except acknowledgment," Glen said.

"My parents' marriage has always been guarded because of someone in Mother's past. If you are that person, you interfered unknowingly. Because of you, they always lacked a solid and secure relationship," Gary said.

"I hope I didn't cause any friction between you and your father but in my eyes he is to blame. He left that relationship deteriorate and then decided he wanted back in and he pushed me right out of the picture," Glen said.

Angrily Gary responded to Glen. "Let me tell you something about my Father. Any time your name has been mentioned for as long as I can remember; Dad's demeanor changes in an instant and we all become guarded until he recovers from his anger. He has never said anything good about you. He tells my mother to go and find her sweet little Glen. Just go and see how wonderful your life would be with that loser. He obviously doesn't think much of you. I don't know what to think. I know if my parents wanted me to know that you are my father, they would have told me," Gary said.

"You know what I think? I think you see that we're going to be big some day and that I have an opportunity to make a lot of money and you want part of it. Well you're not getting any. So why don't you go back to Pennsylvania? Even if you are my biological father, you are not my real father. My real father has been out earning a living to support me and my siblings for the last twenty years. Where were you?" Gary asked.

"Gary please, let me tell you that every time I played in the snow or hit a ball with my other children, you were right there with us. I wondered what you might be doing. I wanted to be there, believe me. I worried about your health and if your father treated you the way I would have. Your mother chose Ray over me, or I would have been there. I have since married and have four children. Your sister Dana is just two years younger than you. My eleven year old son Darren looks just like you. Then there are the twins, Lori and Liz, only eight years old, and I know they would all love to meet you. Don't you want to meet them?" Glen asked in a strained tone. "No, I don't. I've got to go now. Don't ever contact me again. This matter is over. I'm sorry Mother shafted you, but my Dad is at home waiting her return. My brother and sister are with him," Gary said sternly.

When Glen returned to the car Lewis confronted him. "That didn't sound too positive," he said. "Actually it went better than I expected. He has heard my name mentioned in his home before. Now he can put a face to my name. The next time his parents fight over me he'll know who I am. I think Gary knew before this meeting that I might be his real father. I wouldn't be surprised if someday he comes around," Glen shared.

The eight-hour drive home took way too long. Glen's legs cramped up again in no time. The men discussed what Glen planned to do next since he wasn't accepting a position with Lewis's company. "You know Lewis I would love to find a position where I am my own boss, but most of those opportunities require some sort of advanced payment and I don't have any money nor can I get any right now. I will continue to watch the newspapers. Hopefully something comes along real soon," Glen said.

Sunday afternoon Glen walked in the front door looking lost and frustrated. Patty was relieved to have him home. She knew this trip had to be difficult for him. "How are you doing?" Patty said. "I'm sorry that I went with Lewis. He works for a company where you find the customer and if that person finds more customers you make money. But if they don't make money, you don't make money and I just don't feel this is the line of work I am looking for. I am sorry Patty, I still don't have a job," Glen said. "Don't worry Glen something will come along soon. I think you are pushing yourself way too soon anyhow," Patty sighed.

Mary Jo and Georgina retuned to their families. "Hello, my pretty. How was your trip?" Ray asked. "Boston just wasn't all that exciting in spite of what I've heard about it," Georgina said. "I knew that. That is why I never took a transfer to that area. I really prefer to be here in London. It has so much more to offer," Ray said.

"I don't understand what it is you are looking for? I have given you everything you could possibly want," Ray said.

"No, you haven't. I feel unimportant and empty inside. People know who you are. They respect you as a leader, a teacher, and a hero. You are so successful. Look how involved you are with our country's security and how you work with other Countries to keep information flowing between them. You have an extremely important position with the United States Air Force. You are one of only a select few with your kind of credentials. I am only important to you and our children," Georgina sighed.

"I am proud of you and the kids, but I need to find something to do with my time that would make you equally proud of me. I have done nothing with my life. I need something to do besides clean the house, cook meals, and do laundry. I want to be able to speak about my own accomplishments. I just don't know what it is that I am looking for," Georgina said.

"You are the mother of my children. I am very proud of what you do. You've done a terrific job raising the kids. I'm not here much; that's why I need you here. I give you a lot of credit. You don't need to work anywhere for me to be proud of you. Have you seen yourself lately? Have you seen other woman your age? You are gorgeous. Most women your age are frumpy-looking and look older than their years," Ray informed her.

"I don't want to be like my mother, that's all. She always wished she could play a piano, paint, sing, carve, or make crafts with her hands, but she never pursued her dreams. There's got to be something I can do well. The kids won't be here forever, and you'll be leaving the Air Force in a few years. I want to have my own business. I want it to be fun, and I don't want it to be regimented like the Air Force," Georgina said.

"You don't want much, do you? I'm not familiar with any kind of work that fits that description. If you find it, let me know. I want to get involved too," Ray said.

"Oh Ray, you make everything sound impossible. There's got to be something out there that I can do to keep me busy, something that will give me meaning and purpose," Georgina said.

"Why can't you just relax and enjoy being a great mother and wife? I remember telling you before we married that you shouldn't ever have to work a day in your life. Now you want to work. I don't understand. If this is what you really want, go for it. I know when you set your mind to something, you make it happen," Ray said.

Chapter 18
The Unexpected Road Trip

The Dornstadt's household's music favorites spanned over many decades. Glen liked good old country sounds: Hank Williams, Eddy Arnold, and Jim Reeves. Patty liked Bobby Darrin, Fabian, Elvis, and Frank Sinatra. Dana was into the latest rock bands like the Doors, the Rolling Stones, Derrick and the Dominos and The Hollies. The younger children were still establishing there music choices.

Darren had a unique talent for his age. He had been offered several positions with local bands. His skills went beyond the guitar. He also played a keyboard, the harmonica and a trumpet. His first love was his guitar; the other instruments he learned were out of curiosity and need.

As soon as Glen returned from Boston, he told Dana about the White Ravens. "I've never heard of them before Dad. I don't know all of the rock bands. If they are bubble gum, blues or contemporary, I wouldn't like them," Dana said brushing off her father's information. "They are a rock band and they are going to be in New York City in a few weeks. Maybe we could make a trip to see them?" Glen looked questionably at Dana. I have a lot to tell you about them, but it will have to wait for when your mother's not home," Glen said. Dana looked strangely at her father and asked. "Does this have something to do with your secret?" "Yes, so we'll discuss this matter later?" Glen said.

"Wow Dad, your accident has had a positive effect on your musical interests. Imagine my dad going to a rock concert. You did say they were a rock band, didn't you?" Dana asked. "Yes, they are a harmonizing rock band," Glen shared. "I like this change," Dana squealed.

Glen purchased tickets and two weeks later they headed to New York City. He still didn't have the stamina to drive long distances, so he and Dana shared driving. By the time they arrived in New York City, Dana was ready to turn around and go home. "I hate driving in this city. Why did I let you talk me into coming here to see a band I've never heard of? You never finished telling me why we're here. Is there something I need to know about this band?" Dana asked. "Yes. Your half brother is a member of the White Ravens. Let's get dinner and I will tell you the rest of the story.

Dana didn't know whether to be upset or elated about finally meeting her half brother. Imagine that, my brother is a rock star. She wanted to tell the world, but if she did, her mother would find out her father's secret. For now she came to see a concert and she didn't want to disappoint her father.

Once Glen and Dana made their way through the door they found a table for two near the wall where Glen's legs would be protected. He was afraid of bumping them and they were already extra sore today. Once he was comfortable Glen and Dana reviewed the poster that hung on the wall behind them. "See the blonde boy on the left, that's Gary. Next to him is Lee the other boy I met," Glen said.

Dana reviewed the pamphlet offered to her when she walked through the turnstile. Paging through the pamphlet Dana discovered family history and booking information. The band consisted of five members: Lee Ridall, Gary Buckley, Richard Betts, Jeff Marx, and Charley Bradley.

Dana was attracted to Gary before he even came out on the stage. She liked what she saw in the pamphlet. It was love at first site. Gary was tall and thin with long straight blond hair, blue eyes, and a smile white as snow. His body language was extremely sexy. He was gorgeous and someone Dana would like to date. How could this hunk be her brother?

Gary recognized Glen immediately. Gary and Lee worked through the crowds during every show. Gary made a special effort to give Dana his attention. He bumped her table, ran his fingers through her hair and even kissed her hand. Gary was successful at upsetting Glen. After the show Glen confronted Dana. "Just what did you call that little episode?" he asked. "Dad, it's not my fault, he came to me," Dana replied. "Maybe, but I believed you played along and provoked him. For God's sakes, he's your brother, remember," Glen said. "Sorry Dad, he's just so cute. If he lived at home, he would just be a pesky brother and I probably wouldn't think of him that way," Dana said.

Dana and Glen waited nearly a half hour to see if the band came out on the floor to sign autographs. Glen decided they waited long enough because they had a long drive home and Dana had classes the next day.

Dana was quiet for most of the ride home. Glen couldn't stand the silence any longer. "You haven't said anything. What do you think of Gary? Did you like the music?" Glen asked. "I hope he isn't my brother. He is so cute. Are you sure he is your son Dad?" Dana asked with a squeal in her voice. "Yes honey, I am. Even Georgina, his mother, admits that his mannerisms are a lot like mine.

So what did you think of the music?" Glen asked. "I actually liked it. They are going to be big, I can tell. Dad he really looks a lot like Darren. This is not exactly your favorite kind of music and you don't like it when Darren plays similar music, why is it okay now?" Dana asked. "Because he is my son and he's probably going to be famous someday," Glen said excitedly.

"Don't you think it's time to tell Mom about Gary?" Dana asked. "That would be very difficult to carry out now. Before we married she shared there had better not be other children in my past. If there were she didn't want to know because she only wanted to raise her own family. You see, when your mother was much younger, she had a jealous streak. If I ever mentioned another woman, whether it was an old girlfriend or a friend of hers, she went into a jealous rage. She turned into an insecure, angry, and combative witch for days. Having children calmed her down considerably, but every once in a while, her insecurities show up. This secret would probably turn her back into that witch. You know how she can be, and we don't want that, do we?" Glen shared.

"The best way to justify my secret is: I lost one woman, I am not willing to risk losing another one. I love your mother. She's been supportive of my bad job choices and my poor financial decisions. I've had many health problems and she's always been there for me. Most of all, she's a beautiful, caring person, and a great mother. If she found out about Gary now, she would want to know why I have never told her. If she wasn't such a hothead when she was younger I might have told her. There is only black and white with your mother and I think she might have left me if she knew about him. How do you propose I tell her now? It's just too risky and I don't want to hurt her. She just wouldn't understand. It's best we keep our secret. Okay, pumpkin?" Glen asked. "Sure Dad," Dana said. "Dad, you said even Gary's mother admits he's a lot like you. Have you kept in contact with her?"

"No. I saw her in Boston for the first time in almost twenty years. What a strange coincidence," Glen said.

Glen and Dana arrived home very late. Patty had waited up for them. "I've never known you to care for rock music," Patty said to Glen. "I heard this band in Boston and had the opportunity to talk to the members. They invited me to a show, and knowing how much Dana likes rock music, I thought she would enjoy seeing them. I just wanted to spend some quality time with my daughter. Is there a problem with that?" Glen asked. "And did you like the concert?" Patty asked Dana. "Yes Mom. The singer is so cute. I like the music too, but I love the singer," Dana said. Glen didn't liked Dana saying that about her brother, but at least she wasn't spilling the beans about his secret," Glen thought to himself.

Dana's good figure, her bright blue eyes and her blonde hair, along with her easy going laid back personality made her a favorite with the college boys. It was often said that Dana was nice to everyone even if she didn't like someone. She would rather avoid someone than be rude and tell them to leave her alone. Dana had a boyfriend when she met Dale Borland. He was outspoken and loud and Dana avoided him as much as possible. Dale knew what he wanted so he remained very persistent. He stood by and waited for the relationship ended. He quickly moved in to console her and heal her pain. Dale knew her boyfriend and he knew that creep only stayed with the same girl for a little while. Once he conquered a woman, she was used material and he moved on to a new challenge.

As hard as she tried to push Dale away, it didn't take Dana long to fall for him. Their courtship was short. After only a little less than two years they said their vows in front of a few friends and family.

The Borland's were very young when they married. Neither set of parents approved of this marriage, but they were both twenty and nothing could be done to stop them. There was no rush to have children. They had a lot of living to do and children would hamper their goals.

Dana and Dale both loved rock music. Dana enjoyed more mellow tunes while Dale liked hard rock. Disco and bubble gum were not allowed to be play on their stereo. The White Ravens music was a variety of sound appealing to both Dana and Dale.

Chapter 19
Chasing a Dream

Dana and Dale moved to Annapolis, Maryland after one of Dale's friends helped him find a construction job. Good job opportunities were difficult to find in his small western Pennsylvania hometown. If he wanted to make a good living, moving south offered more choices in his line of work. The couple planned to see the world and Annapolis was the beginning of their expedition. Dana would have been happy spending the rest of her life in Billsport, but Dale didn't feel there were adequate job opportunities there either.

Dana and Dale maintained a busy lifestyle while in Annapolis. They attended baseball games in Baltimore and frequented museums in Washington, D.C. Dale's sister Nancy lived in Virginia and they often met in Washington, D.C. on weekends. Nancy's home was near the beach. The couple visited Nancy frequently during the hot summer months. Together they attended several concerts. Bands like Santana, the Doobie Brothers, Bruce Springsteen, and Three Dog Night were just a few of the shows they attended.

During Dale and Dana's first year of marriage, the White Ravens appeared in both Baltimore and Washington, D.C. The next summer when the couple visited Nancy, Dale surprised Dana with tickets to a White Ravens concert for their second wedding anniversary.

Dale had now seen enough of the White Raven's and lost interest in attending any more of their shows, but Dana just wouldn't let up. Dale finally put his foot down and told her, "If we are going to travel, you've got to stop spending money on concerts. What's your obsession with this band anyhow?" Dale asked.

Dana never revealed why she was chasing the band. Someday, her opportunity would present itself, and she would get her chance to talk to Gary and reveal her secret to Dale. Dana reluctantly agreed to slow her pace on the concert scene.

A little more than four years into their marriage, Dana discovered she was pregnant. Neither partner was prepared for her news, but it was a pleasant surprise. Dale wanted to move back to Pennsylvania, away from the hustle and bustle of the busy Maryland lifestyle. He took time off from his job in Baltimore to look for work near his hometown. When Dale returned to Annapolis he informed Dana they had three weeks to pack their belongings and find housing in the Greensburg area. Dale was offered a position with a large coal mining company. It was not the type of work he had hoped to find, but it paid well, and he could support a family on his income. He planned to continue to look for other job opportunities once they found housing. Unfortunately it didn't take long for complacency to take over and he stayed in the mines for years.

The couple settled into a two-bedroom apartment while they continued their search for an affordable home. Dana didn't have to work and became adjusted to the domestic housewife routine very easily. Her belly was growing quickly and she was in a hurry to finish the spare bedroom before the baby arrived.

Three weeks before her due date, Dana went into labor. Thirteen hours after she arrived at the hospital, Dana delivered a healthy baby girl named Madeline Renee Borland. Maddy was the Dornstadt's first grandchild and they spent a lot of time traveling the 170 miles on weekends to visit with their new granddaughter. Dale's family lived only thirty miles away and when Patty and Glen weren't visiting, Dana and Dale packed up Maddy with their necessities and stayed in Elksburg most Saturday nights.

It had been years since Dana had talked to her dad about Gary. She was busy raising her daughter. Soon after Dana discovered she was expecting her second child, Glen's first serious heart disorder became evident. He collapsed at work and needed immediate medical attention. An ambulance crew couldn't get a blood pressure reading. Doctors at the local hospital determined that Glen needed open heart surgery immediately. Maddy stayed with her grandparents in Elksburg while the couple drove four hours to the hospital where Glen lay very ill.

Glen woke to find Dana and Dale by his side. Quietly, he spoke the words: "Tell Gary." That statement didn't mean a thing to Dale. He assumed Glen was hallucinating and ignored his request. Dale didn't understand why it bothered Dana so much. She knew exactly what her dad meant. *"How in the world am I going to pull this off?"* She thought. Dana had been suffering with a complicated pregnancy and Glen didn't even know she was pregnant. Her family had enough to worry about and her pregnancy was something she would tell them about later.

Dana had no idea how to contact Gary about their father's poor health. She decided that Gary wouldn't have cared any how. She felt guilty about ignoring her father's request but she was certain this was an impossible task.

Once Glen appeared well on his way to recovery Dana shared her news about her pregnancy. Maybe this time Glen would get his grandson. I'll consider this news my reward for every ache and pain that I suffered," he said.

Later while Dana walked with Glen, she asked her Father to forgive her for ignoring his request. "Honey, I can't get mad at your for that. Just knowing I'm going to have a new grandchild invalidates that request," Glen informed her.

Chapter 20
Making It Big

The '70s started as the most confusing decade in rock music history. Parents assumed their young adult children were going through typical rebellious stages, but in reality they were experimenting with heroine, LSD, marijuana, and other recreational and hallucinogenic drugs. Young adult children, commonly known in the '70s as hippies, were happy away from home, carefree, and heavily involved in spirituality. Not just musicians, but thousands of teenagers and young adults were following the examples the most popular celebrities of the current decade. Drug and alcohol abuse created a lot of uncontrollable tyrants. Parents no longer knew what to do with their children.

Parents of the White Ravens learned to tolerate long hours of practice in their basements and garages. In twenty-two months the White Ravens reached the top of the rock music charts. Their first number-one selling album sold over eleven millions copies. In an attempt to set a good example with their fans, the White Ravens were the first band to show gratitude to all of their family members by listing all of their names on their album covers.

In order to reach as many fans as possible, the White Ravens booked concerts all over the world. In four years they had six number one songs and twelve other releases that made the top ten charts. Over four decades they wrote and produced twenty-nine albums. As new rock bands come into the scene, they push older rock bands into the background. The White Ravens held their ground and remained popular for a long time.

The Band frequented hang outs with the most popular musicians, like the Beatles, Crosby, Stills & Nash, Three Dog Night, and the Beach Boys. These bands influence the style of music that many other bands performed. Members of these bands played or sung background for the White Ravens, just as the White Ravens did for them on their studio recordings.

One of the White Ravens wishes was to remain known as a clean band free from substance abuse. As hard as they tried, Gary made sure they didn't succeed. Most members lived near Hollywood where cars, drugs, alcohol, and sex orgies were prevalent. They had their ups and downs like other bands with these distractions, but somehow for the first few years they managed to stay out of trouble. Eventually, their problems surfaced causing them to fade into a has-been-band, like many other bands from the 70's.

The White Ravens were able to fight off drugs for the first year, but Gary succumbed to the temptation quickly. He became addicted to a variety of uppers and downers and eventually hallucinogenic drugs. Other members of the band used marijuana but avoided everything else. Gary was unable to function without his narcotics. He wasn't aware that eventually he'd lose almost everything he worked so hard achieve. Lee pleaded with him to get help. Gary obliged and with the support of his friends who diligently stood behind him. It took some time but he was successful in this difficult transition. Gary made a promise to the band that he would never touch any kind of recreational substance again.

The White Raven's hired a famous guitarist to help improve their sound. He had an obvious drug problem but they desperately wanted to add his name to their venue. He was given a choice; "We'll keep you if you lay off the drugs, but if you don't, leave now," Lee told him. He only stayed a few months knowing that his every move was being scrutinized. The band had suffered enough setbacks due to drugs and alcohol and they were not willing to sacrifice again.

Unfortunately, Gary's recovery was short-lived. He failed to live up to his promises and the bands expectations. In less than a year Lee began questioning Gary's strange disappearances. To his dismay, Lee found Gary passed out again, presumably from a drug overdose. "Man, it's a good thing you came to visit Gary said as he hugged Lee. Something's wrong with me. Help me, please," Gary pleaded. "I'm going to get you help, but you've got to quit doing this to yourself," Lee said as he called for help.

Gary was placed in rehab again. He pleaded with the band and begged them to forgive him. He was very remorseful and promised again, that he would work harder at staying clean.

The White Ravens weren't normally destructive, but occasional fights broke out usually after someone had too much to drink. They didn't want any problems associated with their name so all extra charges were paid before they checked out of town. Just like other famous bands, once they became better known to the rock & roll world, their good examples and responsibilities to others declined. They hired an attorney to clean up after them.

All of the band members had married except Gary. His love life continued to be a tangled mess with one bad relationship after another. Most relationships ended because of jealously and mistrust. Gary definitely had a sexual addiction. If his girlfriend wasn't present he'd have sex with the best looking female who threw herself at him.

Lee married his high school sweetheart. Even though he promised his new bride fidelity while touring, he discovered life on the road was lonely. Lee had no problem finding women to soothe him and he quickly forgot his vows. Young men in their twenties need that sexual release to perform better. That revelation gave Lee the excuse he needed to participate in regular sexual encounters with women who managed to find their way back to his room. In the early years the band members became involved in sexual encounters after most shows. Orgies were a regular part of the bands activities. Years later as they settled down with their own families most of them changed their habits.

Gary finally met a woman who was different from the typical women who chased after him. Beth was marriage material and someone he'd want his mother to meet. They met at a banquet in Hollywood. She was a petite, brown-eyed, brunette with a charming personality. She didn't throw herself at Gary. Nor did she fill him full of empty praises. After a rocky two-year relationship, Gary proposed to Beth. Their lives were very different and Beth hesitated a few weeks. She soon discovered she couldn't imagine life without Gary so she gave in. She was up for the challenge of combining their different lifestyles. No other woman had ever left as big of an impact on Gary until then. To prove his love and how much he wanted her to fit into his lifestyle, he smothered her with gifts from all over the world. In less than a year, they were married.

Beth was inexperienced in the bedroom and it took Gary a long time to get her to relax and enjoy what should have come natural to her. Her inexperience intrigued and excited him. She lacked the boldness displayed by other women. It must have been her innocent and somewhat shy personality that gave Gary the patience to teach her how to please him. She wasn't a disappointment, but she never became a great lover either. Ordinary sex was out of the question for Gary. He liked it exotic and Beth needed to learn those techniques. Gary's growing discontent in the bedroom eventually caused havoc in their marriage. When Gary toured without Beth, he'd find a partner for the night. Some of them were good, others were okay, and some were a waste of his time. He didn't practice safe sex and was regularly treated for sexually transmitted diseases, a very common ailment among Hollywood rock stars.

Beth Andrews had her own career as a well-known real estate broker for Hollywood's rich and famous. She had a unique talent of finding the perfect property for the next Hollywood mogul and their family. Beth made a very good income and didn't need Gary's money.

Even though Gary loved Beth, she was never able to satisfy his sexual appetite. He continued his poor sexual behavior with every woman who made herself available to him. Beth had a difficult time being intimate with a man who would carry on with other women, while he was married. She was still crazy about Gary and wanted him to desire her and not other women so she made an effort to learn the techniques that he preferred. In one of their experimental bedroom trysts Beth got pregnant. Once she was pregnant, she wouldn't chance contracting a sexually transmitted disease and shut Gary off completely.

Gary was on tour when Beth gave birth to his son. He bragged about his new infant to his fans, yet he wouldn't take time off even once to go home to see him until they had a break in their schedule. He'd be home in a few weeks. He called Beth every night to re-enforce his commitment and love to her. She pleaded with him to come home and bond with their baby but he refused to postpone a show to go home and see him. After a few weeks Beth was losing her patience. How could Gary be so uncaring?

The road and nightlife just didn't fit with Beth's career aspirations. Staying home and being a husband and father didn't agree with Gary's lifestyle either. Fighting about sex and money had become routine. All Gary wanted from Beth was love and affection on the few days a month he was home. Beth reminded him that she had the responsibility of taking care of their home and son while he entertained the world. She conveyed to Gary that she might as well be a single parent since the road and his band were more important to him than his family.

"Why don't you quit your job and accompany me on the road. Having my wife and baby with me makes for a good appearance to the fans and to those interested parties looking to book us later.

If you travel with me I promise won't sleep with other women. I know you can fulfill all of my needs. I don't know what else to do to make you happy. If you don't come with me on the road I can't be there for you and Michael," he urged her. Beth was appalled by Gary's request. "You are joking right? You can't expect me to sit on a bus or an airplane all day with a child while you're out entertaining the world," she told him. Staying home alone while the White Ravens toured wasn't working for Beth either. Gary didn't know how to handle Beth's combativeness any longer. He stayed away longer and longer, till finally he just didn't bother to return home.

He adjusted to the single scene quickly. He had toured before without a woman by his side, and he could do it again. For Gary, home was a place to get clean clothes and an occasional good night's sleep. Rarely was he ever home more than a week at a time. He convinced himself that living alone wasn't so bad. There was no fighting and he could walk around his apartment naked, leave the curtains open, or drop a towel on the floor without getting yelled at. He didn't even need to flush the toilet if he chose not to.

Soon after their separation his finances fell into serious disarray. Beth froze most of the money until the divorce papers were signed. Gary refused to sign any document that didn't meet his financial obligations. That choice left him without money for months. Gary was homeless. Often friends and acquaintances utilized his talents and musical advice in return for a free place to stay. In no time at all Gary was back on drugs and alcohol. White Raven concerts started an hour late and some didn't happen at all. Most performances were terrible. Gary provided a steady supply of jumbled phrases, graphic obscenities, and insults to fans during the show. The band lacked bookings. Ticket sales were weak and shows were cancelled.

Lee finally had enough. He'd hoped the White Raven would help him display his talents, but no one noticed him. Fans only focused on Gary's terrible performance. His displays of ignorance and uncaring attitude had a very negative impact on all of the band members. Unlike the calm person everyone knew, Lee walked out in a fit of rage. Once Lee left, the band was finished. One way or the other he was going to find a band where his talents were displayed and appreciated.

Glen couldn't wait for Dana's next visit home. He'd heard from Georgina and she had informed him about Gary's disturbing behavior. "Georgina called me last week," Glen said to Dana as she took off her coat. "Really, did something happen?" Dana asked. "You could say that. I never once heard from Georgina since our break-up. When I received a message to return a phone call to Mrs. Steiner I assumed I knew who was calling. I also feared what message she might have to relay. I knew she would only call me if there was an emergency. When I finally reached her, she began sobbing. She begged me to call Gary. She was desperate and hoped that someone could make him come to his senses. I'm sure I didn't accomplish anything. She gave me a number that he could be reached at only momentarily. She begged me to call him immediately and relay to him how worried she was and that he was much worse off than he realized. She already talked with him and he brushed her off and proceeded to tell her to leave him alone. I called him right away. Your mother must have been suspicious, because I rarely talk on the phone for any length of time, except to you. Gary acknowledged me and said he was told I would be calling. He was a mess. He was crying and told me how badly he had screwed up his life and marriage. Then he bragged to me about the number of women he was sleeping with in exchange for drugs and a warm bed. He has no willpower and his spending is out of control. He'll sell or exchange whatever he can to support his habit. All of his money is tied up until his divorce is final and financial issues have been resolved," Glen relayed, looking extremely concerned. "Poor, Beth. I'd throw him out too," Dana said.

"Those are just a few of his problems," Glen said hanging his head. "Before they split up Gary didn't come home for days and no one knew where he was. The band broke up because of him. He's so consumed in his habits that he can't perform. The band broke up because it's Gary's band, and legally they can't go on without him." Glen said. "Most of the shows in the last six months have been cancelled. Gary doesn't bother to show up. I'm worried Dana. If he doesn't get help soon, it will be too late. He is going to end up dying from an overdose. I asked him if he would meet with me or someone his own age to discuss his problems, someone unbiased, of course, and he said no. He emphatically told me unless this person has been in his shoes, they wouldn't understand his problems."

"I ended up telling him who I was. I gave him your number and told him to call you. I assured him how understanding you'd be, but he said he didn't want to meet you or your siblings. He became threatening and warned me that all of us are to stay away from him or he'll have us arrested for stalking," Glen said with fear in his voice.

"I really like the White Ravens, Dad. I can't believe they've broken up. It's difficult for me to picture Gary a drug addict. Doesn't he know how many people he is hurting? Doesn't he care about those who love him and want to help him? Knowing my own brother can be so hurtful and uncaring is sad. This changes my whole opinion of him," Dana said.

"I never had time for drug users. They choose their own medicine, but this involves my brother. I need to re-think my opinion of drug abuse. I wish he'd give me a chance to help him. There is nothing he could tell me that would make me turn against him. I don't want any of his money. Do you have a phone number where I can reach him? Maybe I can convince him to talk to me?" Dana asked. "Not any longer, I'm sure he has moved on and is probably impossible to locate by now," Glen said.

Georgina hired private detective Eric Riley to find Gary. Eric called Georgina one morning to inform her that Gary was under his surveillance and hopefully he'd apprehend him soon. "I haven't approached him yet because these people are paranoid and

I don't want to scare him away. I can involve the police, and they will gladly apprehend him, but they will file charges against him if he possesses drugs. Or, I could keep watching him and hope that opportunity will soon be on my side," he said. "Please don't involve the police yet. If it becomes a matter of life or death, then do what you feel is necessary," Georgina pleaded. "Mrs. Buckley, it is a matter of life or death. Gary doesn't have any common sense right now. He'd die for his next fix. I will do what I can, but if I don't apprehend him soon, I will involve the police," Eric warned her.

Eric finally apprehended Gary without involving the police. He was so strung out he was unable to fight back. Georgina had already pre-arranged for Eric to deliver Gary to a rehab treatment center 60 miles from his former home in California.

When Gary arrived he was in serious need of another dose of narcotics to keep him from convulsing. Gary was placed into detoxification immediately. Once his system was stable enough for treatment, he'd begin rehabilitation again. Gary woke from his stupor to find his mother staring at him. He bolted upright and almost fell over.

"Mom, where am I, and what are you doing here?" he asked angrily. "You're in a drug rehabilitation center. I can't let you kill yourself, and if you continue to live on drugs you'll quickly succeed at that," Georgina said in a harsh tone.

"No, no, no, not this time. I'm a failure. Just let me alone. You can't keep me here against my will," Gary said. "I'm sorry, son. It's for your own good," Georgina warned.

Two men appeared and quickly sedated Gary before he knew what happened. Instead of saying good-bye, Georgina had to turn away. It was a terrible situation for any parent to watch. Now that Gary was admitted Georgina left him under the care of the professionals.

Gary settled into the new facility much better than anyone would have expected. As his normal personality evolved, he became a model patient. Eventually he was allowed to have his guitar to entertain the staff and patients. He went through all of the regular phases of regret and anguish for what turmoil he had caused others. Once he was released to go home, he mended fences and begged his former band members for one more chance. Lee was very reluctant and wouldn't commit. He had been in this situation before and had enough of Gary's empty promises. However, finding suitable work had become difficult and he was very unhappy. If Lee didn't return to the White Ravens, Gary would have no choice but to replace him with a new voice. Lee wasn't prepared to hear someone else singing his tones with Gary.

In order to entice Lee's return to the band, Gary had legal documents drawn up stating that if he returned to his previous state of habitual drug use, his portion of royalties would be equally divided between the current members. He would forfeit his portion. This was an impossible offer for Lee to turn down. Lee agreed and returned to the band. Former affiliates and friends assisted in finding them bookings. They were on the road again in no time.

Touring bands regularly have difficulties holding their families together. Life on the road is much more tedious than anyone can imagine. Lee was raised in a very religious family and he wanted the same lifestyle for his own family. He had two small children and resented the fact that he was missing the most important events of their lives. This situation placed a lot of guilt and hardship on all of the band members, but especially Lee.

These absences took a toll on marriages and other relationships as well. Spouses who stayed home with babies and small children were resentful towards their partners. It was up to the wife or girlfriend to raise the children and make important house hold decisions. Parents and siblings suffered from these absences too. At one time or another they all had sick family members, pregnant wives, and other unexpected events causing an occasional concert postponement or cancellation. Gary didn't always understand his co-workers excuses, but he wasn't an uncaring person; he just felt that if someone committed to a job, it should come first.

After playing over two hundred shows a year, for five years, the band decided it was time to take a well-deserved break. Gary really didn't want to do this, but he was outnumbered. Determined not to slow down he recorded a solo album. Unfortunately without the White Ravens name, only a few knew who he was. Gary's solo release performed terribly. Sales were mediocre and the album never hit the charts. Gary's solo career was short-lived.

Former band members were not finding suitable work either. Gary was relieved that most of his band was ready to get back together because he had feared what his life might be like without them. Every one wanted to have a say in the dates of scheduled performances. Bookings were scheduled closer together, with bigger breaks between sessions. The band had finally worked out a schedule that was suitable to everyone.

Chapter 21
A near death event

Dana's second pregnancy was very difficult. She was plagued with bouts of middle back pain and severe vomiting. Her blood pressure rose way above normal and the baby was showing signs of distress. Doctors watched her closely for weeks. They refused to perform tests because they were known to cause birth defects and early deliveries. Her doctor didn't want to be responsible for either problem. Dana remained sick and unable to eat causing her to get thinner and thinner. Her doctors continued to monitor her closely but they still refuse to test her or prescribe medications to help her cope.

Dana suffered through most of her pregnancy. Her doctors knew this was not normal and as soon as it was feasible, they were prepared to induce her. Two weeks prior to her projected delivery date, her doctors determined it was safe to perform tests to determine what might be causing Dana's illness. Her doctors were concerned that she might have a form of internal cancer, but every test was negative. An older doctor with years of experience suspected gall bladder disease. He knew of the potential infections and risks that needed to be addressed once her baby was born.

He knew one thing for sure; most of her internal organs were infected and if they didn't deliver the baby soon, Dana and the baby would both die.

The next day her doctors decided it was safe to induce her. After seven-hours of labor, Dana gave birth to a healthy seven pound baby boy. Bryan Alan Borland was spared any kind of serious infection.

At a time when everyone should have been happy, Dana's illness put a damper on the celebration. The doctors informed the family that her intestinal track and organs were completely infected and she probably wouldn't live through the next twenty-four hours: "Most people don't survive one of these illnesses and live, let alone survive multiple infections." The internist told them.

Glen was livid. In this day with all kinds of medications available, how could her doctors let this happen? Dale was scared and certain that Dana was going to die and leave him with two small children. "Isn't there something you can do to save her? Why didn't you take the baby sooner?" Patty asked the doctors. Every day Patty begged the doctors to administer stronger medications. "How can you just let her lie in bed and not attempt to save her? Some hospital this is. I wouldn't bring my dog here. My daughter is a new mother and I'd bet she's like to raise her baby," Patty yelled at the nurse's station, with everyone looking at her.

Patty and Dale eventually convinced the doctors to put Dana on the strongest medicine her small body could tolerate, after all what did she have to lose. Doctors spent days trying to regulate Dana's vital sign to keep them as close to normal as possible. That was imperative before any surgery could be performed. Dana's family spent twenty-four hours a day at her beside so she would never be alone.

Ladies from the church prepared meals and cleaned the house for Dale so he could continue to work and spend time at Dana's bedside. Between family, friends, and church members, the children had wonderful constant care. Maddy was enjoying making new friends and seemed to like the extra attention she was receiving.

The Dornstadt's spent the first two weeks after Bryan's birth at Dana's bedside waiting for her doctors to make a decision on her treatments. When their allotted vacation time ran out, they had to return home. The drive home was terrible. They knew what the other was thinking. Would they ever see their daughter alive again?

Glen hated leaving Dana in such a horrible situation, but his options were limited. Glen's past illness was probably considered more serious than Dana's and his death could have been justified. If her illness had been treated earlier, they might have been able to prevent this situation. Regrettably Dana suffered worse than Glen had during his heart surgery. Glen was certain his 27 year old daughter would never get the opportunity to raise her children.

Dana was alert and knew her condition was grave. She wanted to live and put up a brave battle. Her doctors were afraid to operate on her knowing that when oxygen infiltrates an infection, it usually spreads and contaminates the remainder of the organs. This happens in a very short period of time and Dana would probably die on the operating table. One, two, and then three weeks passed. Dana's illness was not improving but she continued to hang on. She was put into isolation. All she needed now was a cold, and her already compromised system would shut down.

It was her persistence and strength to fight that helped her doctors decide that they were not going to let Dana suffer any longer. They were going to perform surgery to remove her gall bladder, spleen, her appendix and part of her colon. These were the only organs they could remove that would let her function somewhat normally. She might die on the table, but she would be free from her pain and probably from a life of constant illness. There was no way Dana was going to get any better without surgery. It was a huge risk but the doctors couldn't wait any longer. Before the surgery her doctor held a prayed session for guidance to save this woman who had been so brave and so determined to live.

The entire Dornstadt family, most of the Borlands, her minister and a few friends sat and waited for the long overdue surgery to be performed. A prayer session was held in the hospital sanctuary and even some of the staff who treated Dana attended this special service. Luckily the surgery went relatively well and Dana was returned to her room eight hours after the operation began.

Doctors were cautiously optimistic when Dana woke up as soon as she did. Her body was responding positively to the surgery. Her vitals signs were slowly returning to normal. Dana didn't have an appetite for weeks and now she was hungry. Her recuperation took months but she was able to go home eleven days after her surgery.

The nurses and staff held a party for Dana the day she was discharged. The head nurse told Dana that it was one of the happiest events they had witnessed at work in years. Dale brought Bryan to the hospital so he could ride home with his mother like he should have weeks before.

Glen and Patty spent the next three weekends at Dana's house until she adjusted to her new responsibilities with two children. Returning home from the hospital to take care of an infant and a three-year-old is not an easy task for any new mother, let alone one who just suffered from such a serious illness. "Miraculous" was Dale's description of her recovery.

Four months after she gave birth, Dana and her family went home to Billsport to visit. Her grandmother, Mildred Johnson wasn't able to make the trip to see Dana while she was in the hospital. Mildred had been dealing with her own health problems. It tormented her that her granddaughter was sicker than she was. She called the hospital every day to check on Dana. For weeks, the prognosis wasn't good. Mildred prayed for a miracle and when Dana's condition finally improved, Mildred thanked the Lord for his help and promised not to forget his miracle.

Dana and Mildred hugged and cried together for several minutes. Mildred couldn't let Dana go. She was ecstatic that her beautiful granddaughter was healthy once again.

"The Good Lord answered my prayers and saved you, my dear. Remember to pay him back every day of your life. Unless someone has been where you were, they won't understand the importance of thanking God. You have traveled a road that many people will never experience." Mildred shared.

Dana's parents had planned a big surprise party for her at the church community center. Most of her aunts, uncles, and cousins, along with some school friends, were there to wish her well. Many brought gifts of encouragement and others came to wish her a continued recovery. Dana was never so touched by such an outpouring of love. Even friends she hadn't spoken to in years came to wish her well.

Chapter 22
The Stalemate

After twenty-eight years of marriage, Ray and Georgina's relationship began to falter. They just didn't have much in common any longer. They made several attempts at rekindling their relationship, but as hard as they tried, they only grew further apart. Georgina asked Ray to leave and she filed for divorce. Ray was devastated. After everything they had been through, Georgina didn't want to work out their differences. Boredom had set in and Georgina wasn't willing to surrender to Ray's needs any longer.

Ray was resilient. He was retired from the Air Force and making a very lucrative living from the consulting business he started. In no time he met a wonderful woman close to his age. They had a brief courtship and married only a few months after his divorce from Georgina was final. Georgina had no desire to date now. She had grandchildren to occupy her time. She maintained her home in London and purchased a small house in Texas near where the family lived in the 1950's, and only miles from her daughter's house. It gave her a place to stay when she came to the States to visit.

While his parents were going through their painful divorce, Gary met the woman who would become his second wife. It was difficult watching his parents split up and divide personal belongings. One never knew their moods. To avoid conflict, Gary was reluctant to introduce his new girlfriend to his family until he was sure she was going to be his bride.

Kate was the administrative assistant at the recording studio office where the band was contracted to record. She didn't act like most of the other women that pushed themselves on him. He was just another artist to her. Kate was witty, fun, exciting, and frugal—exactly the kind of wife Gary needed. He wanted someone he could spoil. He also needed someone to give him the freedom he needed to pursue his musical interests. From working in surroundings that produced many stars, Kate understood and appreciated the solitude needed to write successful music.

Kate was very levelheaded. She kept Gary in line and reminded him that he wasn't God, just a rock star. Gary was convinced she was the woman of his dreams. She didn't need his money, but she wanted children and prayed that Gary did too. Kate was very down-to-earth, and she kept Gary well planted. Gary was looking at possibly recording a second solo album. If Kate took over his household chores, he'd have a lot more time for his music.

First things first, the couple needed to get married. Gary thought a wedding in Las Vegas during the intermission of one of their performances would be the most romantic way to express to his fans how much he loved his bride. Lee's father was now a civilian minister. After his 20 years in the Air Force he returned to school and got his doctorate in religious studies. He offered the vows and performed the ceremony in front of 2,800 fans. The band played wedding music and serenaded the newlyweds for their first dance together as man and wife.

Gary's good income made it possible for Kate to resign from her job and be a stay-at-home wife. All she needed now was a baby to occupy her time. Gary was excited about having another child.

This time he planned to help raise his child and assist his wife in child-rearing decisions.

In the beginning of their marriage, trying to conceive a baby was fun and even exotic at times. Still the couple struggled to conceive. It didn't take long for sex to become a chore, so it truly was a blessing when Kate got pregnant. Two weeks before her delivery date, she developed complications which required hospitalization and bed rest. After a long labor, Kate delivered a stillborn baby boy.

Gary discovered vulnerabilities that he had not allowed himself to exhibit before. Instead of tearing them apart, this tragic event brought them closer. They cried in each other's arms for the loss of their infant son. Kate needed a break away from her daily routine. Her goal was to go somewhere she could be pampered to help her heal both mentally and physically.

Gary approached the band about taking a healing and recovery break. His stress level from Kate's pregnancy was over the top. The band knew Gary's weaknesses and certainly did not want him to return to his previous drug abuse habits. After juggling obligations, rescheduling and canceling shows, they were able to take a well deserved four-month break. After the break, old and new music would play again better than before.

Kate and Gary went to London to visit Georgina. One of Georgina's favorite past times was pampering and spoiling friends and family. She was especially excited about this visit. Georgina knew how losing a child felt. She knew what to say and what to avoid in assisting her daughter-in-laws recovery. Georgina loved Kate like her own daughter and knew that Kate was good for Gary. She read him like a book and understood she his moods better than any one else did.

Visiting Gary's mother was a blessing for the couple. They came back rested and healed. Kate soon discovered that she conceived again under Georgina's care. Kate withheld telling anyone, including Gary about her condition, until she could no longer hide it.

Five weeks into their break, Gary received a disturbing phone call, Charlie Bradley, the band's bass guitarist was found dead. Taking a break had turned into a disaster for him. The evening Charlie returned home from the bands last performance he found his wife entertaining another man. When he confronted Maryann she informed him that she had been involved with this man for many years. She had intended to ask Charlie for a divorce but she relied on his income and kept postponing the inevitable.

Once Charlie knew about the affair, Maryann started divorce proceedings. Charlie loved his wife and made every attempt to repair his marriage; unfortunately Maryann was not interested. Realizing his marriage was a failure, Charlie's outlook on life changed drastically overnight. On a cold dismal morning Maryann discovered Charlie's limp body hanging from the rafters of their storage shed. A note was found that read:

> **"If only I knew how lonely I made you, I
> would have left the band to be with you. I'm
> freeing you so you can be with the man you
> love. I have been made a fool and you have
> been entertaining someone else on my dollar.
> The thought of being away and knowing
> someone else is benefiting from my sacrifice
> tears me apart. If I can't have you my love,
> I can't bear being without you and I can't
> watch someone else take you away from me.
> You are the reason I wake-up every day and
> this has been taken away from me. Divorce is
> not an option, but death is."**

When the band suffered setbacks, such as transportation issues, equipment malfunctions or other maladies, it was Charlie's calm reaction and expertise that resolved many problems. Charlie bailed them out of many last minute situations and emergencies.

There were no signs that Charlie was suicidal. Who could have predicted him to be so vulnerable that he'd take his own life?

The band began looking for a suitable replacement to fill Charlie's position before their heavily booked concert schedule resumed. Charlie couldn't be replaced by just anyone. His special music would never be heard again. He had developed his own style and he had never taught anyone how to duplicate his sound. Gary was sure that Charlie would have wanted the band to continue without him. The difficult search continued. As predicted it took a long time to find an adequate replacement. Fortunately one week before their concert schedule resumed the band hired Kurt Harmon He was an exceptional guitarist. He had never been with a band that spent so much time on the road. He refused to sign a contract because he wanted to try touring with the band for a while to determine if he had the stamina to handle their busy schedule.

The band's drummer, Richard Betts—Betty, as they called him—lived with Margo Cooper for over six years when Charlie died. Margo was a small, cute, blue-eyed, frosted blonde with a joyous personality. Margo was always the comedian. Rarely did she take anything seriously. Richard had contemplated proposing to her many times, but her lack of sincerity and jokes about marriage kept him from popping the question. As crazy as he was about her, he couldn't ask a woman to marry him who just didn't seem to have a serious bone in her body. Charlie's death affected Margo in a way Richard had never expected. He finally saw her serious side. She spent weeks comforting Richard after Charlie's death. Because of her sincere response, Richard asked her to marry him. She was ecstatic about the proposal. In less than a month she became Mrs. Richard Betts.

Soon after their marriage, Margo surprised Richard with the announcement of her pregnancy. Richard was the only band member to be without children, and now he was going to be a father too. He asked the band to cut back on scheduling appearances and try to keep most of them as close to California as possible. Because they were just returning from a 5 month hiatus it was just about impossible to grant that request. Since Charlie's death was still fresh on their minds, they were fearful of taking off too much time. Kurt was still learning their music and he needed to continue to practice with Gary. Gary could feel the animosity between Richard and the rest of the band. They were able to accommodate Richard's request somewhat during Margo's pregnancy, but not enough for Richard to be present for his child's birth.

Chapter 23
More touring challenges

Touring is the only way to remain a top rock band. Many bands tour 30 to 40 weeks a year. Bands spent a lot of money on buses to eliminate transportation difficulties. They carry their personal equipment with them and store them in the bunk where they sleep. A small living and cooking area is in the front of the bus. In the 80's designer buses became popular necessities. Some buses allowed for privacy for families, but most did not. The lack of privacy caused many bands to leave their loved ones behind. Buses were a continuous and necessary expense. If one broke down, it might be necessary to rent one in order to get the band to its next concert appearance.

One afternoon while Gary was home rehearsing for the next set of scheduled shows, Kate sensed Gary was somewhat tired and stressed. "Why don't you take a break? Sometimes you are too hard on yourself," Kate shared. "I have something I'd like to tell you," she said in an extremely sexy and soft voice. She didn't allow Gary the opportunity to stop her as she began to run her fingers through his sweaty hair. She proceeded to kiss his neck and remove his glasses. She then approached him with her news.

"It was wonderful that you were able to join me at your mother's house in London. She's a great hostess and nurturer. I was able to relax and better accept the reality of the loss of our baby. A little pampering goes a long way. I ignored my doctor's orders about waiting six months before conceiving again. When you love someone as much as I love you I couldn't justify using birth control," Kate said.

Gary's body language began to change. "Kate, are you saying you're pregnant again?" Gary squealed with excitement. "Yes, and I've known for a while now. I can't hide my condition any longer, so I thought I better tell you," Kate said.

"I just thought you never lost your belly from the last pregnancy, so I really didn't think much of it. Wait till I tell the band. When are you due?" Gary asked. "Late May, and I want to go to London to have the baby. It was conceived there and I would love to have your mother there to pamper us again. What do you think?" Kate asked. "What ever you want sweetheart," Gary expressed excitedly.

Gary purchased their own private bus for touring to accommodate Kate and his soon-to-be growing family.

Gary never told Kate how concerned he was about her delicate mental state since her last pregnancy. He stayed near Kate as much as his schedule allowed. It was very important to him that Kate had a healthy infant this time.

Glen never attended another White Ravens concert. Dana kept him informed of the band's latest accomplishments. On occasion she'd get the opportunity to approach the band for autographs. It wasn't unusual for Dana to attend two or three White Ravens concerts a year, but she was never able to get Gary by himself. Then one evening in a remote, rural county fair in Pennsylvania, Dana had the best opportunity ever to approach Gary. She stood by and patiently waited for Gary and Lee to finish signing autographs for their fans. Time was on her side and she deliberately managed to be the last fan in line. Finally it was her turn. "Hi, my name is Dana. Could you sign my album cover?" she asked both Gary and Lee.

The men were happy to oblige. Just as they were ready to walk back to their bus Dana stopped Gary. "Would you mind if I asked you a personal question?" she asked. "Sure, go ahead, but I don't know if I'll have an answer for you?" Gary said. "I'm not sure how to ask you this. I don't want you to think that I am prying or being nosy. I've waited for years for this opportunity," Dana said. "Well then, ask the question. I can't give you an answer otherwise," Gary said. "Are you adopted? Is your mother Georgina Steiner? Do you know who your real father is?" Dana asked. "I can't believe you asked me that," Gary said angrily. How do you know my Mother's name? Are you crazy?

Lee watched as Gary changed from relaxed to irritated and upset in just seconds. Gary couldn't just walk away. He needed to confront this woman. Lee approached her, "I don't know why you would ask that question, but I suggest you leave now, you just managed to ruin a good evening," he said. As she turned and walk away, Gary shouted, "I wouldn't tell you if I was adopted or who my parents are. It's none of your business. You're right. I think you're prying and nosey and you can ad crazy to that list," Gary yelled.

Lee put his hand on Gary's shoulder as they walked away from their fan. "We can't afford to make our fans mad," Lee reminded Gary. "They are the butter on the bread," he said. "Yeah, well, I don't need fans like that. She's insane. She's on a high and needs to bring someone down with her before she crashes, and that's not going to be me," Gary said. "Gary, she's just another goofy fan," Lee said.

"Where do these people get off asking such personal questions? Don't they know we have feelings too? I better never see her again. I remember seeing her at other shows, don't you? Why did she wait until tonight to ask that question?" Gary asked. "I wouldn't worry about it. You never know where people come up with their information. Why are you letting this bother you anyhow? You've been asked stranger questions than that one. When a woman told you she had your baby, you just laughed at her. Why don't you just laugh at this lady too?" Lee said. "I didn't find her questions humorous," Gary shared.

Later that evening, Gary remembered flirting with that face before. It took a while but he remembered where he saw her. It was in New York City with Glen. Now he knew who she was. He felt bad to have reacted the way he did, but none of the band knew about his past, and he didn't want to explain it to them now. He really didn't want to know if she was his half-sister, after all he had great siblings that he loved.

Georgina made routine visits to Texas to see Becky Jean. She was expecting her first child any day and Georgina wanted to be present for the big event. Gary and Kate were coming from California to see their new niece or nephew and to visit with Georgina. Gary had more exciting news for his mother, so this was to be a multi purpose visit.

While visiting his mother, Gary decided it was time to confront her with his paternity questions. "Mom, you know Kate and I have had a very difficult year. It's true when they say sometimes only mom can make you feel better. "You know, you did a marvelous job when we visited with you in London," Gary said. "Don't give me too much credit dear, I did what you and Kate needed. Any good mother would do that for her child," she said.

"Mom, I feel you are the only person I can talk to about my personal life. I have some questions that I believe only you can answer. Over the years I felt I was different. Terry, Becky, and I don't look anything alike. It's almost as if I'm adopted," Gary said. "Don't be ridiculous son," Georgina said.

"I've overheard you and Dad talking about how I get special treatment. You always disagreed about disciplining me. I even heard you mentioned Glen would have handled the situation differently. You said he would have been a better father to me than Dad. Glen, the man I met in Boston, is he really my biological father?" Gary asked.

Georgina got a look on her face that Gary had never seen before. "I assume by that look, you just gave me my answer," Gary said exasperated.

"Not so fast, Gary, I don't have an answer. However you are my son. You're not adopted," Georgina said. "I'm sure this sounds terrible and I know how difficult this must be for you. I certainly don't want to say that accidents happen. I don't ever want you to think you aren't loved. I am so proud of you. You kids are my proudest creation." Georgina said with a tear in her eye. "I won't lie to you. Yes, you resemble Glen and you might be his child. However sometimes I see Ray in you too. Your kind demeanor is certainly not your father's. He is a very regimented and controlling person. You're nothing at all like him. You're more like Glen. You have a big heart. You're very sensitive, and you share your wealth with everyone. Unlike your father who hordes his money," Georgina said.

"After you left Boston, Glen cornered me. He summed up his side of the story. I was young and arrogant and refused to believe him. I don't understand why Dad hates him so much if this is the Glen that you often referred to. There must be more information to share than what he was able to tell me in about three minutes," Gary said.

"No too long after that meeting, I encountered Glen and his daughter at a show in New York City. I was mad at Glen for telling me what he did. His daughter was cute and seemed very interested in me. So I put on a show for her. I know Glen was not happy, but I felt I was giving her what he did to me. I know I shouldn't have done that. None of this is her fault," Gary sighed.

"What brought this up now?" Georgina asked. "After a recent concert a pretty young woman came to me and asked me if I knew who my real father was. She new your name too! I was very rude to her. I couldn't believe she would ask such a personal question. I can't stop thinking about her now. I keep seeing her face and how sincere she was. Then I remembered her from years ago in New York City. She resembles me more than my own siblings. If she is my half-sister, then she has every right to know the answer to her questions," Gary said.

"No, I don't agree. Imagine if her speculations are wrong? None of this is her business. As far as I'm concerned, Ray is your father. He might not be biologically, but he has been your father in every way possible. It is not her place to prove who your father might be. She obviously didn't consider what the consequence of asking a question like this could have on someone's life? Imagine if she asked the wrong person? Don't you wonder if you're not the only person she asked about this?" Georgina hinted.

"So are you saying that Dad is my biological father?" Gary asked. "Not at all, however she could be just another crazy fan who has a crush on you or wants to start a rumor to get your attention. Whatever her reasons, you don't owe her any answers. She is out of line," Georgina said.

"I can't explain it, as much as I hated her; I felt a strange connection to her. If you saw her, you'd see how much we look alike. The color of our hair and eyes, the shape of our hands, and we even have the same frown lines. Her expressions and smile are so familiar. It's like looking in a mirror. I have a hundred questions and don't know where to start," Gary said questionably.

"How about thanking your father for being there for you? He knows there is a fifty-fifty chance you are not his child, but he raised you as his own, no questions asked. He never treated you differently. If anything, he treated you better then Terry and Becky Jean. I know how proud he is of your accomplishments. We are both so very proud of you," Georgina said.

"How could you not know who my father is?" Gary asked in a deep and stern voice.

"Oh dear, I knew this was coming and I am not at all prepared. Let me try to explain. I alternated relationships between both men for years. While one was away, I was with the other. I finally decide that I was going to marry Glen. Your Father didn't accept rejection well and continued to pursue me. Strangely both of them were in London just days apart. I waited a long time to become sexually active. I wanted to make sure I was comfortable in my relationship with Glen. Your Father didn't know that Glen and I had made love before. Ray made a lot of excuses and did everything he could to come between us. I told Ray to stay out of my life because I wanted to start planning my future with Glen. Your father was very convincing. He lured me to his apartment and then... well you know the rest. You know how determined and controlling he can be. He knew exactly what he was doing. If he got me pregnant, I was his for sure. I was coerced into marrying him in a very short period of time. I don't think he was counting on the fact that I had been with Glen first," Georgina said as she lowered her head.

"I was with both men just days apart. I am not proud of myself, and of course, if I had it to do all over again, I would not have been with either of them. I am not sorry that you were the outcome of my romantic weaknesses. You were meant to be. I had to be intimate with one of them to get you. Don't ever doubt my love for you. I was ready to become a mother when you were conceived. You filled a void and I can not imagine life without you," Georgina said.

"Tell me Mom, did you love him? Do you really think he is my father? I am sorry to do this to you now. If I don't ask while I have the courage, I might never know. I would be happy to know Dad is my real father, but I have questioned my paternity for a long time. Now this woman comes into my life and throws me this curveball that heightens my curiosity," Gary said.

"In a way I have always loved Glen. I don't think about him like I did years ago, but he is always with me," Georgina shared. Did you happen to get that young woman's name?" Georgina asked. "Dana" Gary said. "If Glen is your father, then she is your half sister. Glen has four children: Dana, Darren, Lori, and Liz. They are all fair, blue-eyed blondes like you. I have seen their pictures. It has been years, but, yes, I saw the resemblance myself," Georgina said.

"When we ran into Glen in Boston I wanted to tell you about your possible conception but when I saw you next to Glen, I started to question your paternity. All of a sudden you resembled Ray as much as Glen. You were very vulnerable at that time and I wasn't certain that I should share what I knew, because I didn't know for sure that Glen is your father. I knew how much you wanted a music career and I couldn't let anything interfere with that. Up until that day I assumed you were Glen's son. Now I don't know. With today's technology, if you wanted to know you could find out," Georgina informed him. "I will think about having that test done later Mom," Gary said.

"Oh, and then there is the other reason I wanted to talk to you. Kate is pregnant again and due in May. She is determined to have a baby and I want so much to be there for this child. I feel sorry for Michael. I must admit that I haven't been a very good father. This time I am going to do it right," Gary exclaimed.

"It's not too late for Michael. Start today and make up for lost time," Georgina said. "I've tried, but he's become very close to his stepfather. I don't want to interfere with that relationship. He's better off with Beth and Dan. We get together every so often and have a good time. It seems the day goes by so fast. We never get to finish a visit. It's always cut short for one reason or another. I've told him to contact me anytime, anywhere, and I'll be there as soon as I can but I rarely ever hear from him. Beth won't contact me and I don't think she allows Michael to call me either. I think she feels Michael might be bothering me," Gary said.

"Why don't you step in and be an adult instead of letting her tell you when you can see your son?" Georgina said. "I'm not sure. She's very intimidating. When Michael was born I had a lot of growing up to do and she's always taken charge of his care. Now I look back and wished I had done things differently, but I can't change the past," Gary said.

Chapter 24
Ending it all

Surprisingly one of the bands biggest challenges started when Lee returned home from a long tour to find everything gone except his personal items. His wife of sixteen years had spent too many lonely nights at home caring for their two children. Love and companionship were long gone from their relationship. The silly and fun young man she married years ago changed into a complete stranger. He stopped bringing her gifts. Phone calls from long days away were sparse and when Lee came home all he wanted to do was write music. His low sex drive was fine with her, but eventually sex stopped completely. Their once very close bond slipped away. Lee loved his music more than anything, even Veronica. She decided to set him free allowing him time to pursue his musical related interests.

Lee and Veronica's marital problems had been escalating for years. When he came home he'd play with the children. The remainder of his time was spent practicing and preparing his wardrobe for the next round of shows. Veronica gave Lee several opportunities to make changes and try to restore their relationship, but he never made any attempt to work on their problems. Lee accused Veronica of being a drama queen. He told her she couldn't find a better life with someone else. He assumed she would never leave him.

Veronica did Lee a favor when she left him and took the responsibility to end their marriage. They were too young when they married. Lee's children understood his job demands and remained supportive, in spite of his long absences. He spent a lot of time with them on his short visits home. David eventually joined the band for a few summers during his college breaks. He quickly learned to appreciate the sacrifices his father had made to maintain their relationship. The demands of touring and living on the road weren't nearly as fun as his mother had described. Lee wanted both of his children to further their educations. He supplied them with everything they needed to be successful while attending college.

Lee was certain that he would never marry again. It was too difficult to keep a woman happy with his difficult schedule, and he was happy as long as he had regular contact with his children.

Just a month short of finishing up a long concert schedule Kurt needed an emergency appendectomy. He urged the band to find a temporary replacement but they wouldn't go on without him. Fourteen concerts during May and June were cancelled or rescheduled for the fall. Gary felt bad for Kurt but what an opportunity Kurt's illness created for him. He was able to be present for the birth of his second child. The couple flew to London so Kate could fulfill her wish to deliver her baby there.

Gary persuaded the band members to enjoy the break. Lee was very skeptical and reminded Gary of what had happened to Charlie the last time they took a break.

Breaks were not good for the band, and this break would turn out to be as serious as the last one. Jeff Marx's wife Cheryl, was found dead floating in their swimming pool. At first Jeff was considered the prime suspect in the drowning because they fought all the time. Neighbors often reported disturbances at their address. Jeff was in New York recording music for a movie. He was completely shocked and disturbed about the news and after an investigation Cheryl's death was ruled accidental.

It didn't take long for each musician to discover they were able to carry on without the band. They broadened their musical experiences far beyond what they had anticipated possible.

In mid May Kate delivered a very healthy Jonathan Raymond Buckley. Gary and Kate finally had the family they wanted. Michael, now eleven, was anxious to meet his new little brother. Michael moved in with Kate and Gary during his summer break. Gary finally had an opportunity to learn more about his son's interests and dreams. Michael and Jonathan bonded that summer. Michael was now excited to spend more time at his father's house. When Gary saw his boys together, he finally understood Glen's desire to bring his children together.

Due to scheduling and financial obligations, the band needed to reform and complete their tour schedule. A few of the members had to place other projects on hold.

Early in the fall Margo gave birth to Richie Lee Betts. During a four day break, the band threw a big party for the new family, and all seemed forgiven. Two weeks after the party, Richard quit—no notice, no replacement, and no reason.

Matt Barton was hired to replace Richard Betts. Although he was aware that he had really complicated shoes to fill, he thought he was prepared to take on the challenge. Unfortunately, Matt never felt comfortable in his new position and when the sound manager's position became available he asked to be considered for that job. His wish was granted and again they needed a new drummer. Seventeen drummers auditioned before they hired Tim Scullin.

The next several summers Michael returned to live at his father's house. Gary was usually on the road and spent very little time with his sons. Michael would eventually move to South Carolina to attend College. His regular summer visits ended. He made brief visits when opportunity allowed. Jon really missed his big brother. Kate often wished she could have another child to give Jon a playmate, but that was not meant to be.

Michael formed his own band after he graduated from college. Just like his father, he learned to live out of a suitcase. Gary had numerous connections and wanted to help his son's career escalate much more quickly but Michael wanted to accomplish notoriety on his own. Michael needed to build his career without his father's interference.

Kate became so involved in Jon's activities that it became increasingly difficult for her to spend time with Gary, even when he was only home for a few days. Gary was often excluded from Jon's events, which caused a lot of strain on the family. Gary felt unneeded and unimportant again. He looked into his glass for companionship. His drinking turned into binges and Gary soon reverted back to his past addictions. He got out of control so easily that Jon was afraid of him and avoided him as much as possible.

Jon was growing up just like Michael. He preferred his mother and rarely spent time with his father. Gary tried to be close to his sons, but obviously, something was missing and he didn't know what to do to correct the problem.

Once again drugs and alcohol became Gary crutch. His problems vanished when he was stoned. At first Kate was oblivious to the extent of Gary's problems. She had heard about Gary's previous substance abuse problem from his younger years, however, she was unaware how easily he could fall back into those old habits. She missed the obvious signs and symptoms. Early in their marriage she made it clear that she was not willing to put up with the drug and alcohol problems exhibited by rock stars. Not ever being directly exposed to someone with such a serious problem, Kate chose to brush of Gary's addictions until she could no longer handle him alone.

Having been through this before Gary knew that alcohol didn't help him forget his problems; it just made him feel worse when he was sober. Drugs had a much longer effect and he thought he continued to function normal when using drugs. Alcohol wore off and then he'd have a hangover. There were no hang over's with drugs. Eventually Gary passed functioning normally and once again was causing havoc in his marriage and with the band.

The band members met without Gary and decided it was time for him to go. Gary must have forgotten that if this happened again, he was automatically out of the band and he would lose his royalties. Kate was unaware of those documents. She didn't understand why their income just stopped. Gary's habits were expensive and since there was no money coming in. They were now living off of savings to meet their expenses.

Kate lacked the tolerance she needed to help Gary so she gave him an ultimatum: "It's me and Jon or the substances," she warned. Kate was not ware that Gary wasn't able to stop his habits without help. Kate threw him out of the house. Shocked and hurt, reality set in. Gary had ruined the two most important relationships in his life.

Chapter 25
Discovering spirituality

The separation was a wake-up call for Gary. He loved Kate more than anything in the world; she was his soul mate. He had to get help for his addictions before he lost her forever.

Kate told Gary that if he went to rehab and succeeded, she would consider reconciliation. Until then, she would not allow her son to see his father in such a miserable state.

Maybe the band would wait until he completed rehab, too. Before he left for rehab Gary confronted the band members. He begged for their patience and shared with them that he hoped that he hadn't caused too much damage this time. Unfortunately, it was too late. Most shows were cancelled due to Gary's poor performances and tardiness. Instead of replacing Gary, the band members decided they wanted to stop touring and pursue other interests. Gary knew he'd never find another band to tolerate his weaknesses like the White Ravens did. Somehow the White Ravens would play again.

Georgina was able to reserve a place for Gary at a rehabilitation center near her in London. He soon discovered his rock star status didn't mean anything to the staff. He had a schedule to follow and he regularly tested the staff when he didn't get his way. Using his line of "You don't know who I am?" was ignored. They reminded him that everyone here is somebody and his celebrity status didn't matter to them.

Gary spent nearly four months recovering from his addictions this time. He didn't like being dependant on chemical substances to cover his inadequacies. His counselors spent extra time with him to help him learn how to deal with rejection and his self-esteem issues.

Georgina visited Gary regularly. She cheered him on and gave him the support he needed to continue his treatments. She was good therapy for him. Georgina was Gary's rock. She never belittled him and always found the bright side of every situation. "You're much stronger for having made the decision to get help and fight your addictions, not everyone can handle the withdraw symptoms," Georgina told Gary.

Jon attended a private school in the United States which limited Kate's ability to visit Gary. She organized as many weekend visits as Jon's schedule allowed during the four months Gary was in rehab. Those visits were short but pleasant.

Kate attended counseling sessions to help her better understand why Gary returned to harmful substance abuse. The counselor gave Kate recommendations on how to repair their damaged marriage. He informed Kate that she and Jon were the reason Gary slipped back into his old habits. His counselors determined that his family regularly chose to leave him behind and avoided to inform him of activities they should be doing together. When Gary was home he rarely felt needed. Counselors told Kate to stop excluding Gary and make sure he was informed of activities and given the choice to participate when he could. Kate was wondering if it was even worth the effort to repair her marriage. *"Maybe we'd be better off filing for divorce."* Kate thought to herself.

Gary didn't want to lose Kate so he followed his treatment plan exactly as his doctor ordered. His visits were restricted because the facility regularly encountered visitors trying to smuggle in contraband. That meant Kate flew all the way to Europe for a few one hour visits.

Every person who has ever had a chemical addiction will tell you their recovery was accomplished by taking baby steps. Recovering addicts live day by day. As they progress into months and years, they brag about the time they have remained clean. Only a small percentage of people are able to do that.

Morris Stonewall was repeating his third attempt at drug rehabilitation when Gary was admitted. Morris was the self appointed holy leader of the Talons Purification Cult. A religious organization located in southern Great Brittan. The Talons believe in a combination of holy practices in both sexual and spiritual prophecy. To save souls you must purify them with chants and sacrifices to clear sins from the soul, not the body. Your body isn't capable of sinning he preached. Morris visited other patients regularly to explain his theory on Christianity and purity.

"Did you know that everyone begins pure and evil spreads into your soul like a disease, striking you and your purity at an alarming rate? In order to live clean and stay pure you must chant to your spiritual leader. Praying and paying earns you purity. Purity is your reward for the forgiveness of sins," Morris informed Gary.

"To become a Talon you must first start out celibate and earn the right to have sex by enlisting as a servant and begging for forgiveness from your holy leader. No sexual satisfaction of any kind is allowed until you are deemed pure. Group sex is allowed only in even multiples. For purification reasons, multiple partners are required once you become active. Individual sexual encounters cause relationship commitments. You can't be committed and be a participating member. Bathing after sex is required to wash away lingering superficial sins before and after encounters," Morris informed him.

Morris was discharged a week before Gary. He persuaded Gary into attending a service after his discharge. Georgina worried that Gary would go right back into old habits and begged him not to make the trip to the Talon temple. "Don't worry Mom I'm not interested in having sex with anyone. Morris just wants to help me with my spirituality. He knows I'm married and that is against the Talons book of rules. I would never make it as a servant, you know that," Gary told his mother.

Morris informed Gary that he was far from being accepted into the cult. Gary needed to take several steps in order to be inducted and he didn't have the time or the interest to sacrifice himself like that, or to participate in their perverted activities. Gary was intrigued by the sermons and the purity chants. Morris recommended that Gary use Talonism as a way to redirect energy and divert attention away from drugs and alcohol. It didn't take Gary long to realize that Talonism was not a good diversion for him.

Before Kate came into his life, Gary thought having sexual encounters with multiple partners was exciting. Sometimes other band members participated too. After viewing an orgy at the Talon Temple, Gary wondered how he could have participated in such a disgusting act. He knew he could no longer indulge in something like that, especially if he wanted to remain with Kate. This was not purity or religion to him. The Talons' beliefs were very cut and dry, and their ideas and practices did not resemble any of Gary's religious beliefs. He quickly determined that Talonism was never going to be part of his life.

Morris's dynamic sermons impacted Gary. "Accept every day as a gift and don't expect anyone to make decisions for you. Cast out those demons who try to alter your beliefs, decisions, and choices. Only you know what is best for your soul. You are responsible for yourself. Blaming others for your weaknesses and poor decisions is the work of the devil. Every step and thought you take is scrutinized by the Lord, so think twice before you act. Remember "*Life Ever After*" can only be obtained through purity," he exclaimed in a loud shrill voice.

Gary feared death and was searching for spirituality to help him find acceptance. The Talons preached to remember the sacrificial son so 'that we might have everlasting life. We must experience death in order to move into the next dimension with our true Father. Death is a reward and not an end to life. It's a passage into the next phase or an extension of life in a dimension that we won't understand until we get there. Gary knew Morris had a grasp on death. So when Gary had a question about death he'd contact Morris for answers.

Witnessing orgies helped Gary appreciate the monogamous relationship he had with Kate. He was glad when he married Kate and made the decision to remain faithful. He still needed to ask Kate for forgiveness from all of the havoc he created over the last year. If begging was what she wanted than Gary was willing. He was never more committed in their relationship then he was now. He had a lot of catching up to do and a lot of promises to fulfill. He now realized that he had hurt the person he loved the most in more ways then either of them understood. Gary was ashamed and remorseful for all of his past practices. "I draw strength from you. It's your kindness and love that'll keep me from returning to my old habits," Gary told Kate on the morning of his return. Kate knew how much she had missed the old Gary and agreed to let him come home.

Gary called a meeting with his former band members to see how soon they were willing to get back together. He wasn't surprised when he received a lot of apprehension. He found himself bargaining again with his future finances if he didn't stay clean. Most of the band members were eager to try one final time. Some shared with Gary that they were interested in retiring in the near future. Gary was excited for this final opportunity to tour and play for his fans. He was eager to get started on the production of a new album the band had been planning prior to his latest episode.

Gary's eagerness and enthusiasm was a welcome surprise to the band members. His demeanor was pleasant and non-combative. The fun and laid-back Gary had returned. Their new release made it to the market in record time. The new album had two top ten hits and brought the band back from near extinction. Filling their tour schedule was easy.

Lee began a relationship with a young woman who he thought was divorced. Lee tolerated regular teasing about the age difference and how keeping up with a younger woman would quickly wear him out. They joked that he had needed to stay away from her days they had a performance because he could only perform once after she worked him over.

Gary 6th sense was working. There was something about this woman that he didn't like. "Please be careful," Gary warned. Lee thought Gary was jealous and ignored his warnings. What a mistake that turned out to be.

Kimmie Harner was married for five years when she and Tom separated. Even though she told Lee she was divorced, nothing was finalized. She went out of her way to keep Lee from discovering her marital status. She feared he'd lose interest if her divorce was not final.

Tom was informed about his estranged wife's affair with the rock star. He was hoping for reconciliation and this idiot was compromising his attempts. Hoping to win Kimmie back, he planned a string of events that almost put the White Raven's permanently out of business. Unfortunately the entire band suffered the consequences.

Most of the shows on the White Ravens new tour appeared to be jinxed. The first sign of a problem was when the band woke in the morning to find their bus and equipment down a hill plowed into a brick wall. Most instruments were damaged, and the bus was totally demolished. The police report said that the vehicle had been left in neutral.

At the next show the steps to the stage had a hard to see slippery substance spread on them. Gary fell and went down on his knees on his opening entrance. He was taken to the back where first aid and bandages were applied to his knees. Painkillers helped him get through the show. He apologized to the audience for his clumsiness and the late start of the show.

Two shows later, Lee opened his suitcase to find it full of sand and Styrofoam. His clothes were gone. "Now I am mad. Who is doing this to us?" Lee asked furious.

Kimmie attended every show and assumed these were normal occurrences in the rock & roll world. She blamed poor planning and tired roadies. Then one night while waiting for a show to begin Kimmie spotted Tom running out from under the stage just moments before the band was to be introduced. Tom couldn't possibly be under that stage for a good reason. She knew he was insanely jealous. He never had any interest in attending rock concerts. His presence worried her. "Listen to me please," she said as she grabbed the nearest security guard and requested that the show be stopped. "My crazy and soon to be jealous ex husband can't be trusted. I just saw him come out of that door directly under the stage. The band has had numerous unexplainable events happen to them in the last several weeks and I suspect my husband is the cause of these events," she yelled while pointing at the stage door.

The show never started. Patrons were informed that the show would be starting a little late to correct a minor safety issue. Security went under the stage to search for anything that might hinder the band's performance. They found liquid and wires connected to several pieces of equipment. It appeared someone had been planning to electrocute the band. If planned correctly, a series of events could cause the whole place to go up in flames. They needed to evacuate immediately.

The show was cancelled and fans were given free vouchers for a future show. Most fans were not happy. They had traveled a long way to see the White Ravens and they didn't want to see another show.

"Lee, I am so sorry. I didn't think Tom would track me down this easily. I'm sure he's been behind all of these suspicious acts. I never thought he would go to these extremes. I should have told you we weren't divorced yet. You are just so amazing and I didn't want to lose you. I don't know what to say," Kimmie confessed.

"You just left him continue to sabotage us and never told anyone of your suspicions?" Lee asked angrily.

Lee ended their relationship immediately when he was informed of Kimmie's connection to Tom. He felt seriously deceived and was convinced now more than ever that he would remain single. It was a long time before Lee was able to trust a woman. He apologized over and over for everything that happened. He remained paranoid and suspicious of anyone who came too close to him for a long time.

Tom's fingerprints were found on the van's steering wheel, Lee's suitcase handle, and many pieces of equipment. Tom was arrested and eventually went to trial. The band lost a significant amount of time from their schedule to attend Tom's trial. The band felt justice prevailed when Tom was convicted and sentenced to fifteen years in prison for recklessly endangering thousands of people's lives.

Even though he swore off women, a few years later Lee met Vicky. "A sweet and divine southern belle he knew he could trust," Lee described her to his family and the band. After only eight months, they married. Since no traps had been set and no serious injuries had occurred, Lee relaxed and began to enjoy life with his new bride.

Finally the band seemed to be emerging and thriving from several bouts of setbacks. Lee announced Vicky was pregnant and asked the band to consider limiting tour dates to the West coast so he could stay close to home. This request might have previously been scrutinized, but Gary was a changed person and accepted Lee's request. The band had enough offers for shows in nearby states to keep them performing for over a year. The guys were satisfied with this schedule and discovered that they liked staying closer to home. They enjoyed having more time for their families.

As a result of being closer to home, more babies were on the way. It was three years until they booked tours more than two hundred miles away for more than one night at a time. The White Ravens got along better than they ever had.

As the White Ravens regained their popularity they were asked to play for kings, queens, presidents, premiers, and other people of prestigious backgrounds. They no longer needed to do the county fair circuit. They performed at many of the world's best known concert halls and theaters. They finally earned their place in the Hall of Fame.

Just when the White Ravens reached their highest potential, Tim Scullin was arrested for providing pornography to juvenile boys. In his spare time Tim volunteered at a juvenile facility for troubled males. He gave free music lessons and entertained the boys whenever time allowed.

When Tim joined the band he was still married, but a divorce was in the works. With Tim's good looks, he could have any woman he desired. The band assumed because he went through a very messy divorce that he was still not comfortable dating and would resume in his own time. After his arrest, additional young men came forth to reveal sexual relationships with Tim. The court found Tim guilty of inappropriate touching and relations with over twenty-five juvenile boys. He was sentenced to 250 years in jail—ten years for each boy.

Once again the White Ravens faced embarrassment. Shows were cancelled and bookings became difficult to find. Record sales floundered and the band members were shunned in their own communities. Recovering from this latest episode was going to be tough. Once again Lee suggested retirement. The rest of the band members were uncertain they were ready yet and convinced Lee to pursue another drummer.

After a lengthy search Troy Wallace was invited to join the band. Because of too many bad choices they demanded he sign a contract stating that he didn't have anything in his past that would harm them any further. Troy had a solid marriage with three children. He prayed this was the break he'd been waiting for. He happily signed the contract promising not to harm the band in any way.

Due to free time caused by cancellations, now was the best time to return to the recording studio. New music was recorded and released for the few upcoming shows that they managed to book. Their new sound was stronger, louder, and somewhat abrasive for them. This was an attempt to attract younger fans. New and old fans were pleased with this sound and the band seemed to be rebounding nicely.

Chapter 26
Nothing but Bad Luck

In 1990 Dana was enjoying her life more than ever. Although she loved being a stay-at-home mother she was ready to return to work. Both of her children were in school, and she found a job at a market in town.

Bryan was diagnosed with asthma. His breathing treatments took a lot of time from Dana's work schedule and his appointments were ridiculously expensive.

Dale's job was being downsized and eventually he was laid off.

Both of Dale's parents developed serious health issues. Just when they needed him the most, Dale found a job 150 miles away.

Dale relocated to the Stuartsville area. The family decided that Dale would stay in a hotel and look for suitable housing. The rest of them remained in Elksburg until the house sold. The move was unfortunate for Dale and his parents, but not for Dana. Stuartsville was only thirty minutes from her family.

Dale returned home every weekend until they were all together again. Dana ran the household in Elksburg. Dale quickly found a nice three bedroom house for his family. Dana loved it and they hoped to make a nice profit from selling their current home in Elksburg. Dale was lonely and wanted his family to join him as soon as possible. He had a lot of time to paint, replace floors, repair the landscape, and improve whatever else he felt needed updated.

Dana had the responsibility of getting the Elksburg house ready to sell. She spent nearly a year in turmoil resolving every possible issue that needed addressed that goes with selling property. During the week she and the kids struggled to maintain all the household chores. As luck would have it, their last winter in Elksburg was the worst in many years. It was an exhausting chore to keep the mud out of the house since it was nearly impossible to keep the drive way free of snow and ice. Fortunately, once the house was on the market it sold in only four months. Both families agreed that the transfer would wait until the school year was complete. Not only did Dana have everything else to take care of, she now had to start packing.

Living 150 miles away places a serious strain on relationships. Once the Borland's were finally living together again in Stuartsville, Dale and the kids argued constantly and he and Dana seemed to be disconnected too. Dana had hoped that when her family finally lived under the same roof again that everything would return to normal. She quickly discovered that was going to take a miracle and a lot of hard work.

Dale felt like an outsider. The kids' interests and activities had changed. Maddy had a boyfriend whom Dale had never met. She traveled back to Elksburg regularly to visit him. Dale complained that the kids avoided him and Dana was neglecting his needs. He thought that after spending nearly a year apart Dana would devote more time to him. However, Dana's priorities were organizing her house and finding suitable work.

Dale was exhibiting signs of a depression. Dana didn't realize that she wasn't helping and failed at every attempt to cheer him up. Their marriage was in big trouble. Dana thought for sure

Dale was deliberately ignoring her, when in reality he was dealing with much more serious issues. Along with his best friends, Dale left his sick parents 150 miles away struggling to maintain their household. He made a few friends nearby but he wanted more attention from his family. Dale liked his job, but he wanted his family back to normal.

Maddy's future plans were undecided. Her grandparents complicated her future even more when they offered her the opportunity to stay with them in Elksburg. She could continue her relationships with her friends and attend one of several local colleges. In return she'd help them with housework, grocery shopping, and other chores. Her room would be on the opposite side of the house affording her a lot of privacy. Maddy was very responsible and her grandparents were not concerned about her reliability, so no curfew would be imposed. Her help was certainly needed. In exchange she would have no financial obligations. Maddy didn't have definite college plans, nor did she know if she was even ready for college. She didn't think it was a good time to abandon her parents either. She knew they were going to need a lot of help unpacking and organizing their home.

Until Dana found employment, she and the kids were planning to travel while they had the opportunity. Dale was left behind once again. If Maddy stayed at her grandparents she couldn't travel with her mother and brother and she didn't want to miss this opportunity.

"*I hate to let down Nana and Pappy but I wouldn't be able to stay here as long as they needed me. I have my own future to consider now,*" Maddy convinced herself.

Maddy's friends were eager to visit her and were looking for excuses for weekend road trips. During these visits the entire house was filled with giggling teenage girls playing loud music and talking about boys. Dale expected to be pleased to see familiar faces but by Sunday afternoon when the girls left, he was relieved.

Dale had difficultly tolerating the noise and activity of two busy teenagers. He needed to re-learn to be patient and tolerant of his teens. The kids quickly made new friends and the house soon had a lot of activities going on just about all the time.

Soon after the Borland's moved to Stuartsville, the White Ravens were scheduled for a show at a nightclub about forty miles away. Dana made plans to go to the outdoor show even though finances were rather tight without a second income. She wanted to make it a family event, but her kids had their own agenda and it didn't include the White Ravens. They had attended White Ravens concerts before and really didn't care to go to any more. The current style of rock music was much different than it had been twenty years ago when Dana first became a fan. It just wasn't her kids' style of music. Bryan claimed it sounded like hillbilly music to him.

After much coaxing and begging, Dana gave up on the kids going with her. Dale conceded and attended the outdoor show with her. A White Ravens show under the stars was the much-needed medicine that helped Dana and Dale reconnect. When the show was over the band stayed and mingled through the crowd signing autographs.

Dana waited for her opportunity, and when Gary and Lee passed her table, she asked them for their autographs. Gary stared at Dana intensely which made Dale extremely uncomfortable.

"Have we met before?" Gary asked.

"Yes, I believe it was at a concert a long time ago. Regrettably, I upset you. I promise not to do that again," Dana said.

"You approached me about being related to you, didn't you?" Gary asked. "You must have her mixed up with another fan," Dale said. "No, I don't think so. I swore I would never forget her face," Gary said. "No, he's right. You must have me mixed up with someone else," Dana said. "No, I don't. Let me ask, did you find your half brother?" Gary asked. "No, I didn't and I don't pursue that anymore," Dana said. "I no longer wish to find him," she said.

"Look, I don't know what you're talking about, but you definitely have my wife mixed up with someone else and I think you are making her uncomfortable. Why don't you move on and leave her alone?" Dale said.

"Well, if you change your mind and you still want to discuss the situation, I am willing to talk now. I don't believe this is a good place to begin that discussion. Here's my card where you can reach me. I hope you'll change your mind. I hope we can get together sometime. I want to hear your story. I have already heard my family's side, and I believe you are probably my half sister," Gary said.

"What are you two talking about? None of this is making sense to me. Help me out here. Once again, I've been left in the dark," Dale said flustered.

"It's too bad she has kept this information from you. I hope you've come into the 20th century and are not embarrassed about our situation. I finally accepted that I have another family in Pennsylvania and I would really like an opportunity to meet them. If Dana is my half- sister, then she is my connection to the rest of my family," Gary said.

"So what you are saying is that you two are related?" Dale asked with a surprised expression. "I think so," Dana said. "I don't have definite proof, but if what Dad told me is true, I have a half brother out there somewhere," she said looking away from Dale.

"We need to mingle with the rest of the crowd. Call me and we'll set up a time to get together," Gary said as he walked away.

"We better get on our way home. I'll only get 4 to 5 hours of sleep now before my feet hit the floor again," Dale said.

Dana drove allowing Dale time to rest. Since he was quiet she assumed he had fallen asleep; but he was just gathering his thoughts. "That explains your fixation with the White Ravens. I always thought you were a bit immature when it came to them. How many other secrets have you kept from me all these years?

We've been married twenty years, and I am just now finding out about this. Don't you trust me?" Dale asked.

"Dad made me promise never to tell anyone his secret. If he happens to be wrong and Gary is not his son then he will have disrupted two families for nothing. Don't feel bad about this secret, Dale. Dad has kept it from Mom all of these years, too. The privilege is not just yours. Most of Dad's siblings are unaware that Gary even exists. I am the only one of his children he has told. I have promised never to reveal his secret, until we can confirm that Gary is indeed his son and Gary is willing to share that information with both families. "From his comments, it sounds too me that he might be ready now," Dana squealed.

"Why doesn't he want your mother know?" Dale asked. "From the beginning of their relationship, Mom has been very jealous of Dad's past. Whenever Dad mentioned other women, Mom went wild with jealousy. When Mom got pregnant with me, she felt trapped and obligated to marry Dad. She really wasn't very happy at all about being pregnant. Mom always blamed me for my existence. I interfered with her college plans. She couldn't take me to school with her, and Dad couldn't take me to work, so she had to put school on hold, get a job, and pay a babysitter. She considered that to be counterproductive," Dana said.

"So what's that have to do with Gary Buckley being your brother?" Dale asked.

"The story behind how he lost Gary to another man is really long and involved. Dad saved himself a lot of questions and grief and decided to keep his secret. That was until his accident. He wanted me to know in case someday, Gary came looking for his other family. Dad knew I could keep his secret. I have known about Gary for many years now. I promised Dad I wouldn't tell anyone including you," Dana said.

"I did try to tell you once at an earlier concert. I mentioned to you how much Darren reminds me of Gary. I mentioned that they both play acoustic guitars with their eyes closed and that Gary's mannerism reminded me of Darren's. You just looked at me and laughed and said I just described about 20 million men. Then when I said that they were both fair, blue eyed blondes with similar frames, you were visibly irritated. I commented that they are both exceptional musicians and you said Darren didn't compare to Gary. So when you laughed at me, I assumed I was better off keeping my secret. If Gary hadn't recognized me tonight and brought up the past, you wouldn't have heard about him tonight either. To be honest with you, I am as shocked as you are. The last time I approached him, he became irate. So I gave up talking to him about Dad. Since he brought up the subject, I'm willing to talk with him about his past. I can't wait to tell Dad," Dana said with reserve.

"You've got to admit, this is something out of a book. This sort of thing doesn't happen to people like us," Dale said.

The following week Dana and the kids went to the beach with Dale's family. While everyone was away, Dale frequented a local bar most nights. The Corner Grill had become his favorite place to drown his loneliness. Prior to their move, Dale rarely spent time in a bar. He discovered he could relax and reflect on his past here. He knew it wasn't Dana's fault he lost his job, nor was it her fault that he took a job 150 miles from his home. He needed to quit blaming her for everything he didn't like about this move. Maybe he should attend church and seek help for his weaknesses.

Chapter 27
Life versus Death

Glen's deteriorating health was a constant distraction to his family. His treatment options were limited. Doctors assured Glen and his family that he wasn't strong enough for another operation. His heart was failing quickly and another operation was too risky? At first Glen didn't take his doctor's advice well. When they informed him that he might be dependant on his family and bedridden the rest of his life if his surgery wasn't successful, he changed his mind. His choices were probably die having surgery or die without it. Glen wanted to be mobile the remainder of the time he had left, so he chose not to have any more surgery.

While Dana and the kids were at the beach Glen's health problems escalated even more. His heart was wearing out faster than his doctors predicted. A pacemaker was implanted in his chest wall, but no promises were made as to the comfort and success that came with it. They warned Glen that this was just a temporary fix and it might give him a little more time.

Dana returned from her vacation early to spend time at Glen's bedside. In just a few days he was ready to leave the hospital. Dana felt that now was the time to tell her father about her encounter with Gary. "Don't give up on him Dana. Any man with any sense of family values will eventually want to know more information about their past. I believe he will want to resolve this issue. He'll come around and I expect the two of you will get this right," Glen said.

"Dad, how do you want me to handle your secret with Mom should something happen to you?" Dana asked. "You know she will never accept Gary. He is not her child; therefore he isn't your brother. Don't let her chase him away. I only hope I live long enough to witness a reunion between my children," Glen sighed.

Glen was on enough medication to stock a pharmacy. Each one treated a different ailment. If he wanted to stay home, he needed to comply with the doctors and take his medicine as prescribed. Glen knew it was time to retire. There were places to see and family and friends to visit. He promised Wayne that he would finally make a trip to California to visit him before it was too late. "Lord knows how much time I have left. If I don't go soon, I will never get there," he announced to his family.

For Christmas Glen's children gave him airline tickets for San Francisco. His plan was to visit Wayne the upcoming spring once the weather was no longer a concern.

On an unusually warm February morning Glen headed out to run some errands. Darren didn't know why but he glanced out the kitchen window just in time to watch his father's body drop to the ground. In bare feet, Darren ran out and picked up Glen's limp body and brought him in the house. When the ambulance arrived it was already too late. The cause of death was cardiac arrest. Glen never saw his five children together.

Dana reminded herself that reasoning with God was not an option. No matter how bad the situation, God was in control. Dana found comfort knowing Glen had passed away on his own terms. He wasn't trapped in a hospital bed, nor had he become a burden to his family. Her father's death was the most difficult event of her life. It doesn't matter who you're burying, it's always an unpleasant task. Dana and her siblings owed this last celebration of life to their Father. He had given them the wisdom to help their Mother with this situation and Dana would make sure it was done right.

"I should probably try to contact Gary," Dana said to Dale crying. "Why would he want to know? He never wanted to know you or your siblings before. Personally, I don't think you should waste valuable time trying to get information to someone who doesn't deserve to be told," Dale said. "If you remember Dale, he approached me about Dad. Don't do this to me now," she said as she wiped away her tears. "Dad would want him to know," Dana said.

Kate received the message about Glen's death and passed it on to Gary. "This must be difficult for Dana; however, I can't imagine Glen as my father. Attending Glen's funeral will just create a lot of questions for those who don't know who I am. Now is not the time to make an appearance and stir up family secrets," Gary shared with Kate.

Dana spent the next several hours with her family finalizing plans. All of the chores involved with planning a funeral were complete. Now Dana had to get through this event. Even though her entire family was with her, she felt all alone. Until that day as far as Dana knew, only she and Dale shared her dad's secret.

In spite of his poor health, Wayne felt he owed this final trip home in honor his younger brother. Glen's death brought the remainder of his siblings together one last time. Glen was the first sibling to pass away since Paul's demise nearly forty five years ago. The family was spread out all over the country but distance couldn't separate the Dornstadt siblings. Nieces, nephews, cousins and friends were present for Glen's final exhibition.

When time allowed, Wayne pulled Dana aside, "I have something to share with you about a lost family member. Someone should know about your dad's past, and I believe you are mature enough to handle this information. I am not sure where to begin. I promised your dad I would never tell his secret unless he died first. Damn him. I'm older. He wasn't supposed to do this to me. Now it's up to me to keep up my end of the deal," Wayne said in a hushed tone.

"What are you talking about? Whatever it is, Dad is gone. Does it matter now?" Dana asked. "It might matter a lot when you hear what I have to tell you. Your father has another son," Wayne said. Dana's eyes lit up. "I can't believe someone else knows besides me. I thought I was the only one he told," Dana said.

"You know about Craig?" Wayne asked. Dana's face went blank. "Craig? You mean Gary, don't you?" Dana asked. "No, Craig. I kept in touch with him for many years until he moved after his last divorce. I'm not sure how to tell your mother. She can be very difficult to talk to at times, and I don't think this is the time or place. Knowing this information has been kept from her for so many years make it's much more difficult for me to explain the reason for the secrecy," Wayne said.

"Oh boy, I'm really confused now. What do you know about Gary?" Dana asked. "Gary who?" Wayne asked.

Dana shared with her Uncle a brief synopsis of what she knew about Gary. "I didn't know about Gary. This is all news to me," Wayne said.

"I don't know anything about Craig. I was hoping when you said I had a brother that you had information regarding Gary. Now the plot thickens. Did Dad know about Craig?" Dana asked. "Of course he did. An acquaintance of mine told me that Glen had fathered Joanne Campbell's son. I couldn't believe what I was hearing. Glen was only sixteen at the time. The man who relayed this information to me was not the most trustworthy person I ever knew, so I ignored his story. The next time I was home on leave from the Navy visiting with Mother, she informed me of the blessed event. She was very upset about it and wanted my opinion on how to handle the situation. She said that a neighbor lady took advantage of Glen at a very vulnerable time in his life. There was quite an age difference between her and Glen—something like fifteen years.

"Craig's parents John and Joanne Campbell lived at the next farm down the road from your grandparents. Joanne wasn't able to conceive a child with John. As a disguise she offered your dad money to help her with barn work and then proceeded to seduced him. They had an affair. Eventually she got pregnant. This woman certainly didn't have very good morals. If she were seducing a sixteen-year-old boy and teaching him the facts of life today, she would have been arrested. When Mother discovered that Glen fathered Joanne's child, she was livid. After Craig's birth, Mom approached Joanne and I'll bet it got ugly. Not too long after your father enlisted in the Air Force, the Campbell's moved away. I'm sure Mom was instrumental in their move. Otherwise she was going to make their lives miserable. Craig was her fifth grandchild, but she never acknowledged him.

"Look, I know you have a lot of questions, and so do I now. Let's get this funeral over with, and we will talk some more before I leave, okay?" Wayne urged.

Glen's favorite statements were common vocabulary with his children. These statements were used heavily throughout his eulogy. Glen applied them to daily events and reminded his children, "always be humble and consider yourself fortunate with the blessings God bestowed upon you; there are always people out there with much less than you. You have no choice, someday we will all succumb to the earth from which we came, so enjoy what time you have left. No matter how bad the situation gets, you must accept what you can't change. God has a plan, and you're not to question the outcome. Reasoning with God is not an option." It wasn't unusual for Glen to refer to biblical quotes when he fell on hard times. He reminded his children, "It doesn't take a lot of money to live a good life." And Glen's favorite comment was, "where is your head?" He'd follow-up that statement with, "do you need help finding it?"

The Dornstadt's graciously greeted everyone who passed by Glen's casket. Many left behind small tokens as they said their final good-bye.

Chapter 28
Acceptance

"Wow, two half brothers. Dad never let on about Craig. I need one more opportunity to ask Uncle Wayne about Dad's past before he departs for California. Keeping a secret like this is harder than anyone can image," Dana thought to herself. Without substantial proof or cooperation from either man it was going to be very difficult to explain two forty-five-year-old secrets. Dana was uncertain about how her brother and sisters would react to this news, but was she certain of her mother's response and it wasn't going to be favorable. She also knew now was not the time to pass on this information to her family. Patty would never accept Glen having children with anyone else. Mom would most likely threaten Dana to never repeat unsubstantiated information like that.

Dana hesitantly informed Dale about her second half brother. "Your father's sexual reputation is lousy. He obviously wasn't raised with very good morals. I thought the world of him, but he made some very bad decisions. He certainly liked to make illegitimate children," Dale said.

"Uncle Wayne told me that Craig doesn't know about his real father, so how would you approach him? John and Joanne moved to Illinois after Craig's birth, and lost all contact with the Campbell family," Dana said.

"Uncle Wayne told me if he were a betting man, he'd bet that Dad didn't want to lose two sons, so he was determined to find Gary," Dana shared.

"I was not aware of Gary's existence, but I knew about Georgina. When Glen announced his engagement with her, I was happy for them. I was even more shocked when we were told that Georgina was killed in a violent car crash. I had no idea that there was a baby involved. Your dad told us that Georgina and a friend were on their way to pick up her wedding gown when they were hit and killed by a train while crossing railroad tracks," Wayne said. Dana was horrified that her father carried out Rays demands. That lie helped Glen justify Georgina's absence from his life.

"Craig has three children to his first wife. After that marriage broke up, he moved around the country looking for that elusive career opportunity. He soon took a new job where he met his second wife. This job required working long hours and making a lot of out-of-town trips. Eventually his absence took its toll on his second marriage and after only a few years he got another divorce. He was living in New Mexico at that time and contemplating his next move. About sixteen years ago Craig told me he was moving again and didn't want to be found. I'm sure I don't have to tell you that a lot of things can happen in sixteen years, but I have not run into him nor have I made any attempts to find him," Uncle Wayne told me. "He said to leave Craig alone and continue to pursue Gary.

The day after Glen's funeral everyone met for breakfast before everyone departed for their home destinations. Wayne approached Dana, "it's time for us to part. I'll miss you, but remember I'm just a phone call away. Don't fret over all of this. We can't change the past and have lived forever without knowing these two young men and we'll continue to do," Wayne winked at Dana.

"I'll take you to the airport," Dana said. "No, you can't. I already told Darren he could take me," Wayne said. "Okay, I'll miss you, keep in touch, please," she told him as she hugged him good-bye.

After Wayne returned to California, attempts at forgetting this new information were frugal. Knowing he had more information to share with Dana about various family situations, he sat down and wrote her a letter with even more disturbing information. If he had not found out about Gary he might not have been inclined to share what he was about to reveal.

> Dear Dana,
>
> I didn't feel comfortable talking about your father's past at his own funeral. Some of the information I am about to tell you has been passed on to me by other family members. Some of it is generalized information you might already know.
>
> Glen's youth started out shady. The fact that he fathered a child at sixteen is evidence of that. Glen was a fighter. I had to hold him down more than a few times. He'd get out of control and become nasty for no apparent reason, especially with the younger kids. His energy level was far beyond normal. Not just Glen was a problem for our parents, but I believe he was the worst of us.
>
> He was excessively aggressive towards women, which resulted in several arrests. Any woman who gave him a passing glance was usually chased down. Your grandfather bailed him out of jail more than once for his poor judgment. He was very lucky because numerous charges were filed against him, but for some reason they were always dropped. After a while, the judge had enough and gave him an ultimatum:

go into a branch of the service or go to jail. I
recommended that he join the Air Force, and
for once, he listened to me.

The fact that Patty was pregnant before their
marriage was not a surprise to me. I advised
Glen not to marry her and to take his time to
assess his situation, but as usual he didn't listen.
Patty was beautiful and I could understand a
man's desire to have her, but your father wasn't
prepared for a wife and new baby. Thank
goodness it worked out.

Our father had a difficult time handling so
many children. I believe that's the reason he
chose to stay away from home so often. It was
unfortunate for us kids that he stayed away
so much because we had a very poor example.
Mother on the other hand, was an angel. She
tolerated all of our undeserved remarks and
pranks, yet she rarely let us upset her. She died
way too young. I wish she had more years to
enjoy life.

Dad moved to San Francisco to live with
us because he couldn't tolerate Pennsylvania
anymore and thought he could depend on me
the most. At that time, no one knew how much
difficulty Dad was having getting around. Being
the stubborn old Viking that he was, he didn't
want to become a burden, nor would he ask for
help. At first his needs were simple, and he was
certain I wouldn't mind helping him. The longer
he lived with me, the more difficult his presence
was on my marriage. All of those years on the
railroad had taken a toll on his body and caused
him to bend like a banana. Thank goodness
he lived only four miserable years after Mother

passed away. What little he owned was left to me. The rest of my siblings are unaware of his singled-out graciousness.

While Dad lived with me he shared a lot of information that I might not have otherwise known. He told me about some of Glen's rebellious acts; like when he and Paul got into a fight. To keep Paul from running away like he always did, Glen stabbed him in the back of his leg with an ice pick. Paul was often the victim of many of Glen's vicious acts. Then Ada got him in trouble for telling a little white lie. In retaliation he cut her hair in her sleep and then proceeded to paint it green. He said if he was going to get a beating then he was going to have a reason for it. Dad shared many more examples about your father and my other siblings. I could ramble on forever, but most of his information is insignificant now.

Hopefully this helps you understand your dad's past a little better. I was relieved to discover how domesticated he became once he had children. I assume he just needed a loving relationship to curb his aggressions.

I honestly didn't know anything about Gary. I knew Georgina came to Billsport to visit and everyone was certain that they would marry. You relayed to me that they met years later in Boston. Obviously she didn't die which meant your dad lied to cover their break-up. Did your father ever tell you why they didn't marry? I would be curious to know what ended that relationship. He didn't hit her, I hope? Gary was the lucky one. He wasn't subjected to your father's tantrums.

Don't bother to search for Craig. He's best off not knowing about his real father. I just thought you needed to know about his existence. I didn't mean to stir up a manhunt on your behalf.

Glen really changed over the years. He certainly didn't live up to his tough guy image once he married Patty. I don't know if it was him or if your mother just pushed all the right buttons. All four of you kids are great people and your Dad certainly did a much better job raising you than our father did with us.

You know where to find me if you have questions.

Love, Uncle Wayne

Some years back Glen had relayed to his family, "Wayne is a wonderer, he was never happy in Pennsylvania. It seemed that staying here only caused him pain. While serving in the Navy, Wayne received an anonymous letter from someone telling him that his wife was entertaining other men in his absence. Wayne was not going to be disgraced like that. He filed for divorce and when he left the Navy he didn't return for years. He met his second wife Verna when he took her to the hospital in an ambulance after she was in a pedestrian/car accident. She was ten years older than him and was no longer able to bear children. That was probably a blessing because Wayne didn't care much for kids."

Dana had difficulty absorbing her father's past the way her Uncle described him. When she confronted her Uncle David he confirmed Wayne's information. He told her about the time her dad was so mad at him that he threw a butcher knife at him and it almost hit him in the head. That was not anything like the father who had raised her. David shared, "that as a young man Glen had an unhealthy obsession with money. He'd approached local farmers for work. They'd give him the dirty chores that no one else wanted. He'd offer to complete those tasks for a hefty donation. If he didn't feel the pay was adequate he'd just steal something. Glen acquired a very bad reputation in no time. One farmer actually chased him off his property at gunpoint. The local farmers eventually got together and had Glen arrested for stealing produce, terrorizing their children, and sexual misconduct with their daughters. That's another reason our dad chose to stay away. Some of those farmers were his friends and he could no longer face them," he said.

Dana was horrified to find out the father she loved and adored, was capable of such terrible crimes.

Lona seemed like the most logical relative to approach about Craig. "Oh I never heard that tale. Your Uncle Wayne, he always seemed to be the story teller of the family. I'm sure he imagined this scenario because I'm almost certain I would have known about this event if it had happened. Don't pursue this story Dana. It's a waste of your time and what does it matter now. Your father's gone. You don't want to reveal any more lies about him now, do you?" She said.

Dana started attending seminars at the local library on "how and where to look for lost family members." It seemed like a good idea but she soon discovered there wasn't enough information to help her locate Craig. Assuming her position at the computer, she spent what seemed like an eternity looking for something that might link her to Craig. She researched adoption sites and postings and various chat rooms but nothing came together. She finally decided to listen to her Aunt and Uncle, and abort her search for Craig. She had found one brother whom she adored, and he finally wanted to get to know her.

Chapter 29
Recovery

The distractions Dana used to conceal her loss was not enough. Her employer recently implemented many new and overwhelming changes that she needed to learn very quickly. She became unable to cope with simple every day tasks and relied heavily on others to assist her, at both home and work., Dana's happy and bubbly personality turned into a rigid, combative, and scornful person.

In a matter of weeks Maddy decided to move into her own apartment. Dana was overwhelmed with guilt that her daughter was no longer comfortable living at home. Dale knew how difficult depression was to overcome. He begged Dana to seek help. He almost lost her once. He was not going to let depression kill her. She refused at first, but eventually agreed once she realized that she couldn't handle her confusion and resentment by herself.

Four months after Glen's death, Dale saw an ad in the Sunday paper that he hoped would change everything for Dana.

Live in Concert: The White Ravens - Sunday, June 29th

"This is it," Dale thought, *"the medicine that Dana needs."*

On the day of the show, Dale told Dana that they were going on a little adventure. He wanted to keep it a secret from her as long as he could. He called her mother and told her to tell the entire family not to mention the White Ravens were going to be in town.

Dale made arrangements for dinner first, and then he told her they were going to the movies. Dale knew Dana had sunk to a new low when she didn't even check the White Ravens concert schedule. Otherwise she would have known where he was taking her. Dana wasn't very excited about dressing up just to go to dinner. It took a lot of coaxing and a phone call from her mother asking when they were going to arrive.

Dinner was a disaster. Patty waited a very long time for them to arrive. Her demeanor was less than satisfactory and caused Dana to get upset. Dana was in no mood for her Mothers sarcasm. Dale needed both of them to calm down so he could carry out his surprise. "Look Dale, I just had to put up with Mom's attitude so I just want to go home. Can we go to the movies another time?" Dana stated. "Where are going? This isn't the way home," Dana yelled. "You know Dana, it's not always about you. I'd like to see this movie, and that's where we are going," Dale said as he was loosing his patience with her. Dale was certain he would need to tell her where they were going so she would go with him, but she eventually settled down and accepted that they were going to see a movie.

When they arrived at the theater Dana immediately saw the marquee on the building. Her face lit up like a spotlight— something Dale had not seen in a couple months. "*Yes, this might work*," he thought.

"Ha. I think I've been tricked," Dana said. "I had to find some way to get you out of the house. I hope you don't mind going to this show with me?" Dale asked. "Are you kidding, I've really missed these guys," Dana said with a big smile on her face.

The old Dana reappeared that night. She was eager to stand in line after the show to get autographs. When Gary saw Dana, his face took on a whole different appearance. Dale thought for sure that Gary was going to ask Dana a question, but he just let her do the talking.

"Hi Gary, remember me? It's been a while, hasn't it?" Dana asked. "Yes, of course I remember you. I'm glad you came. I was hoping to see you here," Gary said. "Really, I was sure you lost interest in meeting with us after the last show, because you never contacted me," Dana said. "You were to contact me, remember?" Gary said.

"Did you get the message that Dad died in February?" Dana asked.

"Yes, I did and I'm sorry. Unfortunately, I had other obligations which prevented me from attending his service. I really wanted to pay my respects, but the opportunity just didn't present itself. I'm hoping we can spend some time getting to know each other later tonight. I have some questions about Glen's past that I hope you can answer for me," Gary said.

"I would love to spend time telling you what I know about Dad," Dana said.

"We're holding up the line. Here is my room number and a key. Meet us there in forty-five minutes to an hour. Can you do that?" Gary asked. "Of course, we can. I wouldn't miss this opportunity for anything in the world," Dana said giving Dale an uncertain look. "Yeah, we'll be there," Dale said. He was just relieved to see Dana smiling again. This was the most positive Dana had been in months. The Borlands left the concert hall and headed directly to the hotel across the street where the band was staying. Dana was so excited she keep shaking Dale's arm. "Can you believe it? He's going to meet with us. This is the best day of my life. Well, except for when I married you, of course. You are great for bringing me here. I love you," Dana said glaring at Dale excitedly.

Dale encouraged Dana to be strong and remain positive. He feared that Gary might reject her if she asked too many questions. Dale knew very little about Gary and worried that he might not show up or he might change his mind and ask her to leave? That would have devastating consequences for Dana. He wanted to take her home now to avoid any unwanted confrontations. Dana couldn't handle another disappointment.

"This is so exciting. I'm finally going to get a chance to explain to Gary how our parents fell in love and how the breakup occurred," Dana said.

"Not so fast. You better let Gary talk first. You should give him a chance to ask questions before you give him answers he's not interested in knowing. You don't want to insult him either. Maybe he already knows what you know," Dale said. There wasn't any way to get out of the situation now. Dale just prayed that Gary would show up.

"Are you sure you want to do this? Are you prepared to handle more disappointment if you ask Gary the wrong question and he tells you to leave?" Dale asked.

"I can't believe you'd ask me that. I have been waiting a lifetime for an opportunity to talk with Gary. He wants to know about his past and I hope I have the answers he is looking for. Dad lived for this moment, and I'm not disappointing him. Come on Dale, where is your head?" Dana asked.

Dale knew how sensitive Dana's condition was, and that was not her talking. Timing was everything and now probably wasn't a good time to remind her that Gary had hurt her before.

Dana waited for what seemed like an eternity before the band entered the room.

"You two get yourself a drink and get comfortable and I'll introduce you to the band. That'll give me a moment to change and time for everyone else to get acquainted before we get into any discussion. Is that okay with you?" Gary asked. "Sure, that's fine with me," Dana said hesitating.

Gary carried out his introductions and explained to the band members why Dana was invited back to the suite. The band members didn't know about Gary's family secret. They were about to learn a whole lot more.

"I have a confession to make," Dana said. "If it wasn't for Dad, I don't know that I would have become a White Ravens fan, but after the first concert, I was hooked. I have attended more than fifty concerts in seven states. My friends don't know the family history part. I have not shared that information with anyone. They all think I am a White Ravens groupie," Dana said.

"Dana's been so patient with me over the years. I've rejected her attempts at connecting me to my extended family. I have avoided her questions because I refused to accept what I suspected was true all along. The father who raised me, supported me, picked me up and hugged me when I was hurt and gave me ten dollars every time I asked, is not my biological father. However, in my heart Ray is my real father," Gary said.

"I'm sure you have the usual father and son bond that nothing can come between. I would never interfere with that connection nor expect anything less. That just proves to me that you are a decent caring person and you have genuine feelings and a deep respect and compassion for the man who raised you. He definitely deserves that respect. I know however that the man who didn't have that opportunity wished so much that he did. He loved you unconditionally. I know how empty he felt because of your absence from his life. I didn't expect we'd jump right into this conversation," Dana said.

"You're right. We should take some time to get better acquainted first," Gary suggested.

"Would you like me tell you the names of my favorite White Ravens songs and you can tell me what musicians have inspired you? Or tell me whatever you feel compelled to share with me. I want to know all about you. I'll tell you anything you'd like to know about me or my family," Dana blurted out excitedly.

"Let me get another drink first. Concerts always make me thirsty. Can I get you another drink?" Gary asked. "I'll have another bottle of water?" Dana announced. "Water? Is she always this boring?" Gary asked Dale. "Yep, pretty much," Dale said.

"Dana, tell me something about your past. Did you go to college?" Gary asked.

"Yes, Dale and I met at college. I took business classes that are now pretty much obsolete. If only I knew then what I know now, I wouldn't have wasted my time and money. I am a secretary now and have been most of my adult life. Today's training and techniques are not what they were when I went to school," Dana said.

"Dale, do you mind if I ask you your occupation?" Gary asked.

"No problem. I don't mind telling you about myself, but I thought you'd be interested in talking with Dana, not me," Dale said.

"Well, I'd like to get to know the whole family," Gary said.

The phone rang, interrupting the conversation. Kurt answered it so Gary didn't have to leave his guests.

"Gary, its Michael, do you want me to tell him to call you back?" Kurt said. "Tell him I've got an interview and I'll get back to him when I can," Gary said. A few moments later, Kurt insisted that Gary talk with his son. "Excuse me, this must be important. He's on the road and might have a problem," Gary said.

"I understand how kids think. What's an emergency to them is not necessarily one to us," Dana said.

Gary tried to speak quietly, but his voice continued to elevate. He appeared agitated and Dana could hear parts of the conversation.

"I can't believe you sometimes. I'm not giving you money for that. I'm entertaining and I am not leaving now. You'll just have to wait. I'll call you back later. Where can I reach you?" Gary asked. When he hung up the phone, Gary apologized to Dana and Dale for the interruption.

"I'm sure you must know how impatient kids can get, right?" Gary asked.

"Yes I do, Dana said. "She has a lot more patience with the kids than I do. I know how quickly they can do something to upset me. It sounds like your life's pretty normal when it comes to family?" Dale said.

"Well, no, not really. I haven't been around very much for my son. My ex-wife raised him. She pretty much lets Michael tell her what he is doing. All he wants to do is spend, spend, and spend some more. She gives him very little money and he has a very limited income so he comes to me. He's over 18 so I no longer pay child support. I often wondered what that money went for. She sends him to me and I won't just give him everything he wants. He told me he needs money to repair his very expensive car which I told him not to buy. Now he is always sinking my money into his car. I might as well own it. When I get home, I'll decide how much to give him, if anything, for his next big repair. This always causes a lot of strain between us," Gary said.

Gary quickly changed the topic. He began to brag about Michael's accomplishments. He was definitely a proud father.

All of a sudden, Dana became very quiet and Dale feared she might need her medication.

"Hey, if we are going to get to know each other better, you need to talk more. I got the impression that you are very vocal and someone easy to relate to. What's going on? I hope I haven't scared you away?" Gary said.

"I'm not scared, maybe intimated. I'm just not sure how to approach you," Dana said. "This is the moment I have dreamt of for years and now I'm so unprepared. I didn't know we were coming here tonight, and when we arrived I didn't know that I would have this opportunity to finally meet with you. Sometime I have a shy side and when something is difficult for me, I clam up," Dana shared.

"What's so difficult about talking to me? I am no different than talking to your husband or anyone else," Gary said.

"Well, I have some very personal questions that I would like to ask you, but I don't want to start off by offending you," Dana said.

"You can't ask me anything I haven't already been asked by fans. Consider yourself lucky; I'll probably answer you. I don't always answer personal questions. As a matter of fact, you probably win the award for one the craziest questions I've ever been asked. You are the first and only person to ever ask me if I were adopted. The shock factor is over, so shoot," Gary said.

"Okay, well, I just wanted to know what it is like being a rock star, I have this famous brother who I have not been able to ever tell anyone about. I don't know your likes or dislikes and if I were to brag to someone about my wonderful brother, what would I say to them?" Dana said.

"I'm not much different than you. The band has had many problems over the years. It isn't all fun and games, as people believe it to be. Equipment failure, sick band or family members, scheduling conflicts—you name it, it happens," Gary said. Face it we're not the Beatles or even the Beach Boys. We can still book a show but we rarely sell one out," Gary said.

"That was easy. Do you have any more questions?" Gary asked. "I'm just getting started. I was wondering about your personal life. How do you maintain a marriage and stay on the road so much? What's your favorite sport, color, animal, car or song? What do you think about the President? Have you ever been arrested?" Dana asked.

"Since I asked you back to my room and you are not asking for an interview I will be totally honest with you. My first marriage ended because I took advantage of my wife—not physically, but emotionally. I expected her to be at my beck and call. If I was going on tour, she was going to go with me. If I wanted to change furniture, it didn't matter what she wanted or liked, it was what I wanted; she had to conform. She was a beautiful woman. I adored her. Unfortunately I was such a blockhead. She had her own life and agenda and I wouldn't allow her to be who she wanted to be. I was a real jerk back then. I had a substance abuse problem during our marriage and there was no dealing with me. It was my way or the highway, and she took the highway," Gary said.

I don't discuss my political views. You can anger too many people that way. My favorite color is blue. I like basketball. I don't care much for animals. As for cars, that's tough because I've had three cars that I really liked.

"You sound like you wished you had done things differently with your first marriage," Dana said. "Darn right, I wish I had, however, my current wife is a great woman, and I remind myself every day how lucky I am to have her in my life. I almost lost her once too. Now, I won't do anything to jeopardize our marriage. That's not the answer you are looking for, is it? Tell me about yourself, Dana. This isn't all about me, you know," Gary reminded her.

"I have two great kids, Maddy and Bryan. They have their own lives now. I have been a secretary almost all of my life, and if I wasn't a secretary, I would do something even less exciting. I like to go to concerts. I love basketball, the beach, and I love to travel. I am a very curious person and feel that somehow, I can change the world. I just need to figure out how to do that," Dana said.

"Wow, that's quite a challenge.

"Tell me about some of the concerts you've attended," Gary said.

"I love the White Ravens, Chicago, the Eagles, Foreigner, Boston, Journey, Kansas, Aerosmith, and a lot of other bands. I like comedy and magic too. I also believe in reincarnation and ghosts," Dana said.

"Ghosts, I'm afraid to ask," Gary said. "I go to places that are haunted, but I am convinced that they can't scare me because I have stayed in the most haunted rooms and I have never seen a ghost," Dana said.

"So you have attended other concerts. Why do you follow us so much when you have so many other favorite bands?" Gary asked. "Because you continue to tour and produce new music. Your name is recognized as a rock legend. Our father was a proud man and strong-willed, so strong unfortunately that he was able to keep a secret that only a few select relatives knew about. He shared a lot with me about his relationship with your mother, but I am certain I don't know the whole story. My father and your mother are our connection. I have a tie to this band that I don't have with those other bands. He kept this secret from Mom because she had a jealous streak that scared him. I can't believe he could keep this from her for so many years. Dad's was never allowed to discuss his past around mom. He didn't tell her about you and his affair when he first me my mother. That's something that you just don't talk about on a first or second date. Nor is it something you share in a new relationship with someone who has a jealousy problem. I think he meant to tell her eventually, but he wasn't prepared to lose out on another relationship. My uncle told me that Dad was wild when he was younger, but Mom tamed him and he was intimidated by her. He wouldn't mention Georgina's name because of mom's reaction. So when they got married, he never told her about you. So even until this day, she's unaware of your existence. If she does happen to know about you, she's never mentioned your existence to any of us. If I tried to tell her about you now, she would accuse me of sticking my nose where it didn't belong and then she wouldn't speak to me for a while. I can't risk that," Dana said.

"So no one cares about my reaction or how I might feel about being totally left out of this family because of one person's reaction?" Gary asked.

"Unfortunately, that's exactly how it is," Dale jumped in. "But, for what it's worth, there was a time you shunned this family and you threatened them to stay away," Dale shared. "You are right, and I am so sorry. Maturity changes all of us," Gary said.

"Gary, you have been ignored long enough. I am going to figure out a way to approach mom and then we'll finally become a family. Now is a good time to tell her," Dana said. "I have a thought. You could tell her that you have proof you're Dad's son. Tell her you believe the reason that Dad didn't tell her before was because he didn't want to risk ruining the best relationship he ever had. She might buy that," Dana suggested.

"Uh, I don't think so. She and I probably wouldn't hit it off, and I have had all of the conflict in my life I care to have. I'm sorry, Dana. You'll have to relay that message to her yourself. She wouldn't care if I ever came around, I'm sure," Gary said.

"Let's forget I ever mentioned that silly idea and move on," Dana said.

"Well, then, its best we keep dad's secret," Gary said.

Hearing Gary call her father Dad gave Dana goose bumps, and produced a big and bright smile on her tired face. It was a dream come true for Dana and she was certain that her Father was cheering her on from his grave.

"I've got to call it a night. It's late, and I'll soon turn into a mushroom. The excitement of finally spending time with you has kept me awake. I just wanted to mention the first time I saw you when Dad and I went to see you in the seventies in New York City, I didn't want you to be my brother. I was so attracted to you, and then you sang to me, Dad was very unhappy with both of us. Dad said expressing those feelings were wrong. He thought you did that deliberately because of the way he approached you in Boston. It took me a long time to put those feelings behind me. Until I could face you without feeling that way, I couldn't pursue the brother-sister relationship," Dana said.

"So what you are saying? I've grown old and ugly and am no longer a heartthrob?" Gary asked.

"I didn't mean it that way! Wow, I feel bad now that you said that," Dana sighed. "Oh, don't worry. I know I don't look like I did twenty years ago, and if you must know, I felt the same way about you. Don't take this the wrong way but I didn't have any self-control twenty years ago. I would have slept with you regardless and regretted it later, so I am glad one of us was able to restrain themselves," Gary said.

"I still love you, but in a very different way now. I have always loved you, and I can say that and get away with it now," Dana said.

"You're right. You're turning into a mushroom. I hope we can get together again real soon. You're getting sappy, and I can't handle that. How about I call you in a few days after we've had some time to mull over tonight's conversation? Maybe I'll make arrangements for you to come to California to meet my wife and family. Do you think you'd want to do that sometime?" Gary asked.

"I would love to do that sometime," Dana replied. "Okay then. I have a lot of room and a private plane. Bring Dale, your kids, Darren, Liz, and Lori if you like. Just let me know how many to expect. I'll take care of the arrangements. I'll be in touch soon," Gary said.

"Just one more childish and foolish request, if I might," Dana said. "Okay, shoot," Gary said. "Could you spare a hug? I'm just living out a dream, and making up for lost time, that's all," Dana said. "You bet, I could use that myself," Gary said as he hugged and kissed Dana on the corner of her mouth.

Dana didn't speak one word the whole way home. Dale would bet his paycheck that Dana wouldn't sleep that night. He knew her well enough to know that her mind was racing from the excitement of her evening. Hopefully, this positive event was the medicine Dana needed to begin her recovery from her severe depression.

Chapter 30
Exiting the Dream

After two nights of no sleep, Dana was exhausted—so exhausted that she had to take a sleeping pill to allow her body to relax. She fell into such a deep sleep that she didn't wake up until nine thirty the next morning. Dale came in to check on her to make sure she was still breathing. When he touched her, she bolted upright with a look of fright that Dale never saw on her face before. She grabbed Dale and hugged him like she hadn't done in weeks.

"Whoa. What's that all about?" Dale asked. "Do you remember Gary said he would fly all of us out to California?" Dana asked.

"Oh boy, here we go. I'm sure there's a story coming out of that comment?" Dale sighed.

"I dreamt Gary was a mean person. He didn't really want us to visit him in California. He accused us of chasing him for his money. He put two parachutes on the plane—one for him and one for his pilot. They jumped out and left us to fend for ourselves. There were a bunch of us on the plane—I couldn't tell you exactly who was on that plane, but most of my family was present," Dana said, shaking.

"You know, I wouldn't blame him if he did feel that way, but he's not a killer. He would have made the headlines by now if he was. Don't you think he would have shared those feeling and told you to hit the road instead of trying to kill us?" Dale asked.

"It seemed so real. I remember Gary announcing over the loud speaker system: I hope one of you morons knows how to fly this machine, because if you can't, you'll continue to fly out over the Pacific Ocean until you eventually run out of gas, and then you'll go down. Sorry it had to end this way, but you can't have my money. I earned it, and I'm keeping it," he said in my dream.

"That's not a dream. You're hallucinating from those sleeping pills. You better not take any more of them. Forget about it already. Come on, I'll make you breakfast," Dale said.

Dana said very little as she performed her regular household chores. Dale knew better than to address her thoughts. He could tell by the scowl on her face that she hadn't forgotten the dream. He was certain Dana was having second thoughts about making the trip to California now.

Dana was still depressed and very delicate. Without her medication Dale had to be very careful about what he suggested to her. The silence worried him. Thank goodness Gary had his concert schedule to complete before he could finalize plans for the Borland's visit with his family in California. *"Maybe by then, Dana would have forgotten her dream, and possibly be more relaxed about making the journey,"* Dale thought.

A few days later Maddy announced that she and Phillip were getting married. Her news was a wonderful distraction and great therapy to help Dana recover from her illness. Maddy was concerned about her mother's mental condition and knew she had to include her in the wedding plans or her depression might get worse.

The White Ravens took a back seat to Maddy's special day. There were invitations and decorations to buy, a cake to order, and they needed to book a place to hold the reception. Maddy and Dana shopped all over the state to find the perfect wedding gown.

They eventually booked a DJ, a photographer, and a caterer. Dana's thoughts were consumed in this wedding. Dale was pleased as his wife appeared to return to her normal state of mind.

At dinner one night Dana announced, "I have decided when Gary call's, I am not going to California to meet his family unless we fly on a commercial airline."

"That is so completely ridiculous. Don't you think you'll hurt his feelings if you don't go on his plane?" Dale asked.

"I'm not going to take a chance on a pilot I know nothing about. I think the best way to go, is with a commercial airline that will have many passengers," Dana said.

"So now you are allowing that stupid dream to interfere with your plans, and instead of having free airfare, you are going to pay. I don't know about you sometimes. You let the dumbest things infiltrate that mind of yours," Dale said.

"Not really, I think that would be taking advantage of Gary. It's not right to expect him to provide our transportation, a free place to stay and food. I was also thinking that we might want to stay in a hotel. It's not fair to expect his wife to clean up after us either," Dana said.

"How do you know they don't have a maid?" Dale asked. "Even if they do, someone is going to have to clean up after us," Dana said.

"You are so frugal, yet now you want to pay for this trip. You don't make sense to me sometimes," Dale said loudly. Dana looked at Dale and after a long pause she responded with, "it's either commercial airlines, or we don't go. We can stay at his house, but I won't fly in a private jet," Dana said.

Chapter 31
A Life-Changing Event

On his way home from a six-week tour, Gary wondered how to explain a probable visit with his pseudo family to Kate. He enjoyed visiting with Dana and in many ways they had a lot in common. Gary felt a definite connection.

"Kate, I invited Dana, her siblings, and their children to come visit with us. I want to show them my instrument collection. Dana told me Darren is a musician too. He would really enjoy seeing my studio. Maybe we could jam together," Gary said.

"Do you remember Gary when your mother mentioned that you should have a paternity test? If you feel so strongly connected to this family then why don't you arrange to have that test to prove that you are indeed their brother?" Kate asked.

"I've contemplated that test many times. I'm not sure how I'd handle finding out that Ray is not my father," Gary said.

"Then you break the news to Dana. Either way, you'll move on with your life, but at least the mystery will be solved," Kate said.

"I love you, and I'm not putting you down when I say this, but I need to approach this situation on my own time line. I know I can't have it both ways, but as long as I don't have that test, it can be both ways," Gary shared.

"I love you too, and this mystery has been tormenting you for a long time. All I am saying is; think about putting an end to this mystery. You mention it all the time now. I would love for you to have closure, and I think you owe this to yourself and your real father," Kate said. "Let me think about it a little more," Gary said.

"So have they informed you of their travel plans yet?" Kate asked.

"That won't happen until I call them and set up everything. I plan to do it soon, maybe in the next month. Is that okay with you?" Gary asked.

"Do you want to get the visit in before you leave for your tour to Japan in January?" Kate asked.

"Let me call Dana and work it out with her," Gary said. "Hi, it's Gary. How are you? I'm calling to see if you and the family are planning to come for a visit? Kate would like to know a head count." Gary asked. "Yes but not until after Maddy's wedding, probably sometime next summer," Dana responded. "I also need to know if you are you going to the show in Pittsburgh next month." Gary asked inquisitively.

"Maddy's wedding is a week away and I have been so focused on the wedding, I didn't even notice that you sent me an e-mail about your Pittsburgh show until a few nights ago," Dana replied.

"I haven't heard from you and time is of the essence. I need to know a head count by the end of the week," Gary shared.

"Wow, I don't know if I can make this show? With the wedding a week away, I haven't had time to think of anything else. Let me check with my siblings and my kids. I'll e-mail you with a count in a few days, I promise," Dana said.

"I know that's a long drive for you. Will you need a hotel room? I can reserve one for you at the same place where we're staying?" Gary asked. "I'll let you know about that too," Dana said.

That phone call made Gary feel somewhat unimportant to Dana. He didn't like feeling that way. He wanted to be the center of attention when he called her. *"Maybe I deserve her attitude. How many times have I given her the cold shoulder?"* He thought to himself.

Insane would not be too harsh describing Dana's disposition one week before the wedding. She reviewed every detail making sure nothing was forgotten. It was almost as if she were getting married again herself. Maddy knew her mother had everything under control.

"Mom," Maddy said. "Please take a break. Everything will be perfect. It has to be. You've gone over your list so many times you couldn't possibly have forgotten anything."

The wedding was a wonderful celebration of the beginning of a lifelong commitment between Maddy and Phillip. The bride and groom looked like royalty. Dana and Dale were the perfect hosts. Friends and family came from everywhere. The wedding was like one big reunion. The weather didn't cooperate as well as they would have liked, but it was a wonderful day in spite of the wind and drizzle. There was enough food to feed an army. If guests left hungry, it was their own fault.

Chapter 32
A Spectacular Spectacle

Dana was finally able to relax and was looking forward to some peace and quiet. She was anticipating the next White Ravens show in Pittsburgh. Dana e-mailed Gary with her ticket and hotel room needs.

Gary's reply to Dana read:
    Kate is flying into Pittsburgh just before the show. She's hoping to finalize your travel plans for your first visit to California. Will four days be long enough? I hope by the show you can tell us how many to expect.
Dana responded:
    Not too many of us will be able to make a trip in the near future. Only Dale, Lori, Bryan and I will be out the first time. Maddy and Phillip will be visiting other relatives later this year and they will try and connect with you then. I don't want to put Kate to any trouble. We will make our own arrangements and I will notify the two

of you when they are complete. Just give me
dates that you want us to come. It's not fair to
Kate to have to clean up after us. If you want,
we can stay in a hotel, just give me the name
and phone number and I can make reservations.

Kate read Dana's e-mail response and shared with Gary, "she seems like a very considerate person. That's so nice of her to take my time into consideration, but if we are going to try and get to know each other, I think they should stay at the house," Kate shared. "I told you Dana is one of a kind. It would break my heart to learn she isn't my sister?" Gary replied. "I will let you know if I agree with you once I meet her in Pittsburgh," Kate replied.

Three vehicles formed a caravan and headed west to Pittsburgh for a new family adventure. Dana never expected to see this event take place. Eleven Dornstadt's, five band members, and the roadies were going to celebrate and bond for two days.

The White Ravens played for nearly two hours both nights to a rambunctious and gracious audience. Just knowing all of those relatives were watching was reason enough to play longer and with more enthusiasm. The band members were on their usual highs after a near-perfect performance.

"They loved us tonight," Matt said. "I can't believe that after so many years, we still get a standing ovation at the end of the show!" he yelled excited. "Hey, come on. Someday the ovation might stop and we'll be standing back here wondering what the heck happened," Lee said.

"Are you always this wound up after a show?" Dana asked. "It depends on the crowd. Tonight, the audience was exceptionally generous. It was a terrific crowd. For some reason Pittsburgh is always one of the best crowds to play for. We don't always have as generous of a response as we had tonight. This was a great show for you to see," Gary said.

"I have been to more than fifty shows now and I only remember one show that the fans didn't respond that way," Dana said.

Kate booked the banquet room in advanced. The hotel set up buffet tables and loaded them with wonderful delicacies. There was enough food and drinks for a hundred people.

"Wow, look at this spread. Let's party," Jeff exclaimed.

This was going to be a celebration to remember. It was important to Gary that he and Kate leave a good impression on the Dornstadt's. Hopefully everybody was hungry and in the mood to celebrate. Gary and Dana rose to the occasion and made individual toasts to the crowd.

"To my new family, friends and especially Glen: No matter where our travels take us, we will always be in each other's hearts forever. A lot of Love fills this room tonight. Cheers!" Gary said wholeheartedly.

Dana followed up in a quivering voice. "To Gary and the White Ravens: Dad is smiling down on us with great pride. Our big brother has finally been united with his family tonight," she said as a tear ran down her cheek.

Gary, Dana, Liz and Lori found a couch in the corner of the room and started talking about past events during their lives. Darren, Tam, and Kate sat at another table talking about Gary's past. Kate shared Gary's turmoil about finding out if he truly was a Dornstadt. Everyone rotated several times throughout the evening so they all got a chance to get acquainted.

Dana shared many details about their father's past and the battles that took place between Ray and Glen. She relayed how Georgina couldn't decide which man to marry and how Ray convinced her to marry him. Gary couldn't believe what antics Ray displayed in order to win his mother's heart. Gary was shocked that Glen exposed his sexual background so vividly. Gary shared, "my parents rarely displayed affection in front of us kids.

"My parents often squeezed or pinched each other in a very loving way. Dad was always pulling Mom close to him and giving her a peck on the cheek. He'd often make provocative remarks, implying his intentions for later; unfortunately for dad, I'm sure mom ignored his advances," Dana shared.

"Dad rarely played games or read to us kids, nor did he display affection with any of us. He was very materialistic. He'd bring us gifts but I would have rather played games or even gotten a hug. I can't ever remember dad hugging me," Gary shared. Gary didn't want Dana to think he had a boring childhood, but he definitely felt he had lost out on a lot of the fun and attention. Ray had little time to attend his children's events. He'd show up when his schedule allowed. Georgina played games, read books, sang songs, and helped with schoolwork to make up for their father's absence.

"I remember when my sister was born. Mom spent almost every night in the nursery. When Becky was old enough to be on her own, Mom often slept in the guest room. I rarely saw Mom and Dad share the same bedroom. Years later Terry and I knew dad had a lady friend, and we assumed Mom knew too. Mom seemed to be okay with it for a while; however I think she finally decided she could live without dad, so she left him," Gary relayed.

"Mom still smothers us kids with attention. She is a great mother and I am so relieved that it's not her that might not be my biological parent. On the other hand, dad wasn't a bad father. He provided us with everything we needed. He'd pat our heads, squeeze our shoulders, or pull Becky's hair. When the Air Force held special family events, we were the first children through the door. Dad liked to go to the movies. He often took one of us with him," Gary said as he walked towards his wife and put his arm around her waist.

"I'm very lucky to have found Kate," Gary continued, "I don't know anyone else who would have tolerated my drunken stupors, my excessive spending, and my tantrums like she has. She helped me realize that I have the ability to help people forget their problems for an evening. I can take an audience out of reality and help them get absorbed in the moment. Fans are able to leave their troubles behind for ninety minutes—that makes me feel good. She reminds me that not everyone who attends our concerts is there for me. She also reminds me that I have a family with the same needs as everyone else and that I must do what it takes to fulfill those needs. I wear clothes, eat food, and excrete body fluids like everyone does. I am no different, nor am I special. She has a wonderful way of bringing me back to earth when I become god-bound," Gary shared.

"I understand what you are saying, but I'm not sure why you are telling me all of this? I'm sure we've all been god-bound at some time in our life," Dana expressed.

"Addictions are my specialties'," Gary said. "It started with sex. I was a late bloomer. When I finally discovered it, I realized that it felt really good. I couldn't get enough. Then a friend turned me onto uppers and sex got even better. It got to the point I felt I needed sex several times a day. I thank God every day for giving me the wisdom to use protection. It wasn't at all unusual for me to have three or more partners a day. The sexual addiction turned into a drug habit because sex only got better when I took uppers. When I was married to Beth, if she didn't go on the road with me, I would find at least one partner and often more after every show. It was so easy; women were always throwing themselves at me. One woman told me that we had met a few years earlier and that she was game for a second time around. For over two years I was either stoned or drunk and many times, I was both. I finally went to rehab and learned how to redirect my sexual desires, break the chemical substance and alcohol abuse habits. After I did that, I wrote three number-one hits in fifteen months.

"Several years after Kate and I got married, I got involved with drugs again. I attended rehab in London. I shared a room with a man who ran a religious cult, the Talons. They have their own book of rules and instructions, but their beliefs are very different. They believe that when a man ejaculates it releases certain endorphins that give off energy. Therefore, it's okay to start practicing intercourse at an early age and have multiple partners. They preach against the Bible's belief of monogamy, and they give substantiated evidence to support their beliefs. That is when

I first sat down and read the Bible. There were way too many contradictions. You could not possibly believe in God and follow Talonism. I made sure if I cheated on my wife it was with someone I really found desirable. The unexpected happened. I discovered that a monogamous relationship was much more satisfying than wondering what you might get from the stranger you slept with last night.

"Not too long ago a woman approached me about fathering her son. I didn't know how to tell Kate, and then it was in the tabloids. Kate asked me if it were true. I told her that it wasn't possible. She advised me to have a paternity test since I had nothing to hide and to clear my responsibilities. The courts informed me it was my obligation to have the test done, so I did. Thankfully, the results determined that I was not the father. I wasn't worried because I hadn't been with anyone other than Kate for a long time," Gary shared.

Gary stopped and thought about what he had just told Dana. "I'm in the same predicament as Glen—what a revelation," he said.

He stopped and looked around the room and got teary eyed. Dana gave him a hug and asked, "Are you okay? You look so sad, I have never seen you display that facial expression before," she said looking at him with sympathy.

"Oh, it's nothing. I was just reminded of another situation I don't care to discuss," Gary said. "Anyhow, I thought I would mention that I have been faithful to Kate now for many years. Kate makes an effort to keep me satisfied and she has definitely earned my commitment," Gary shared.

"What's wrong with you? You've hardly spoken a word in the last two hours," Gary said.

"I'm just really tired and I don't want this moment to end. I'm willing to let you go on forever. I have waited almost a lifetime for this opportunity. I'm in no hurry for it to end," Dana said.

Dana realized it was four AM and they were the only two in the room. Everyone had retreated to their rooms hours ago.

Dana gave Gary a goodnight hug. She explained that Dale was a morning person and if she went to bed now, she would only get a few hours sleep before he got up.

"Wait, I would like to play catch-up if you don't mind?" Gary said. "Play what?" Dana said. Gary turned Dana to face him. The look on his face was easy to read. He bent over and kissed Dana in a way that brothers do not kiss their sisters. He couldn't let her go, and then Dana relaxed and melted into Gary's arms. Finally Gary stopped and Dana took a breath and gazed questioningly into his eyes. "Wow, I wasn't expecting that," Dana whispered. "A lot of siblings experiment that way. I never got my chance, so I owed you that sis," Gary winked, as he whispered in her ear.

Dana was feeling confused about that statement and what had just happened. She thought she knew her limits and wondered if Gary might have crossed them. It had been a long day and she was very tired and not thinking clearly. Since Dale was in the next room, Dana considered Gary's affections harmless.

By noon everyone was up and gathering in the hotel lounge for lunch.

"I sure had a wonderful time," Dana said.

"I'll keep you informed of when we're going to be in the area. I'll provide you with tickets for every show," Gary said.

"I can't imagine missing a show for anything," Dana said. "Oh, but you would miss it for something," Gary said. "Well, sometimes things come up, you know. I'm waiting to become a grandmother. If I was needed to baby sit or if I were waiting for a blessed event, I expect I would miss a concert for that," Dana shared.

Soon it was time to part and everyone was giving good-bye hugs and hand shakes. "Come give me a big hug," Gary said. "That was a fast two days, I can't believe it's over already. Isn't funny how we change. When I was a teenager I had such a crush on you. I would have given anything to have just one minute with you. Now a simple good-bye peck on the check will suffice," Dana said.

"If I were ten years younger, I would have wanted more than a kiss last night, but I've aged and have found my morals, and they kicked in last night and slapped me along the side of the head. If it wasn't for morals, I would have given you an experience that you would never have forgotten," Gary said.

"Thank goodness I was really tired last night. I was almost offended. If you tried something, I might have slapped you, or worse. Amazing how a few hours of sleep can change ones perspective about an incident," Dana said. "Come walk with me for a minute," Gary said. Together Dana and Gary walked down the corridor and then proceeded to walk into the vending room. Gary and Dana embraced one more time and then kissed for almost a minute, finally Gary pulled away. "There's the minute you wanted, don't say I never gave you anything," Gary sighed breathing heavily.

"I could have kept on going. I shouldn't feel this way about my own sister, but I had to get that out of my system. Why didn't you stop me?" Gary said. "I wanted the same thing you did. I know how that sounds, but I have loved you in more ways than one for many years. I would have eventually stopped you," Dana whispered with a sigh.

"Let's get back to the lounge with our spouses. I guess I don't have to tell you not to discuss this with anyone?" Gary warned as he patted Dana's butt on the way down the hall. "Of course you don't," Dana said.

Gary offered his hand to Dale and wished him a safe ride home. He told him how great it was to finally learn about Glen and meet his special new family. Dale thanked Gary for his hospitality and told him he was glad that this event finally took place. Maybe now Dana could relax.

The trip to Pittsburgh was everything Dana hoped it would be. They had a great chance to bond. First they had a sing-a-long, they then they ask questions and told stories about their past. On the drive home, Dana kept running her fingers over her mouth. Gary's kiss had fulfilled a life long fantasy. Dana would never forget the information nor the private moments shared over the last two days.

Dana decided it was time to face Patty. Her Mother had been deceived long enough. The reason for the events of the past weekend needed to be explained. Dana would take on the chore of telling her mother why this very personal and private information had been kept a secret from her for so long.

"Are you sure you want to tell your mom now?" Dale asked. "Are you prepared for her reaction, her possible temper tantrum, the name calling and the denial? Do you know how quickly she will ruin your high? Are you ready to hit bottom again? You've come a long way and worked so hard at maintaining a positive outlook since your dad died. You know, all of that is going to go down the drain when you tell your mom about your dad's past," Dale warned.

"I can't help it, Dale. I want Gary in my life, and I'm tired of hiding this secret from mom. I can't believe she isn't already suspicious. If I don't tell her now, when do you propose I tell her? We don't give her enough credit, you know," Dana said.

"You have been through hell since your dad's death. Maddy's wedding and your job issues have put your stress level almost above manageable. I just don't want you to suffer any more setbacks," Dale said as he rubbed her shoulder.

"Everyone goes through a healing process after losing a parent and marrying off a child," Dana said. "Most people don't have both events occur in the same year," Dale informed her.

"I'll bet you a trip to the beach that your mom shames you for telling her about Gary. I even bet she knows about him, and she'll tell you some ridiculous story about your dad's past to cover up the truth. When your mom makes up her mind, there is no changing it," Dale said. "I know that? I think there is a diplomatic way of approaching her, and if I do it right, she'll have no choice but to admit Gary's connection to the family," Dana said. "I hope you're not disappointed," Dale said.

Since Glen's death, Dana visited her mother regularly. Patty never intentionally became verbally aggressive, but if she disagreed with someone, she could be very difficult to calm down. Dana wanted to avoid confrontation at all costs. Gary had finally accepted their family and Glen would have been ecstatic. Dana wanted Patty to be happy for everyone. She had enough sadness in her life recently and needed her mother's approval now more than ever.

The next morning after breakfast, Dana braved confronting her mother about her father's questionable past. "Hi Mom, I thought I'd better stop and see you since we left you here all alone over the weekend," Dana said.

"How was your trip?" Patty asked. "Real good, but funny you should ask," Dana said. "Oh, why is that?" Patty asked. "Because you don't usually ask when I go to concerts," Dana said. "You don't usually stay overnight and take the entire family with you either," Patty said.

"It was great, Mom. You should go with us sometime. I bet you'd enjoy a White Raven's concert. They don't play too terribly loud, and their music is rather mellow compared to some rock bands," Dana said. "Don't hold your breath, but maybe someday," Patty said.

"If Darren or Bryan were playing you'd go, wouldn't you?" Dana said. "That's different I'm not related to anybody in the White Ravens," Patty said.

That comment left Dana the opportunity to glide right into the subject.

"Dad was the first person to take me to see the White Ravens. Do you remember that?" Dana asked. "Yes I do, and I never quite figured out why. That was so unlike him," Patty said.

"It's a concert I'll never forget. I got to meet the band members that night. It was almost as if Dad had some connection," Dana said. "Don't be silly," Patty said. "He did that for you."

"I was just speculating. Well actually, I wasn't. Dad took me because he knew the parents of one of the band members, and he wanted me to meet him," Dana said. "What are you talking about?" Patty replied. "Dad thought because we were about the same age, we'd like to meet each other," Dana said. "You're not making any sense. Who did he know?" Patty asked.

Dana started wondering about how bold she could get with Patty. Dana was prepared to take a tongue-lashing after revealing her father's secret. She just backed herself into a corner and there was no easy way to tell Patty about Gary now.

"Mom, did dad ever tell you anything about his past?" Dana asked. "Yes, of course he did. I knew about his years in the service and his unhappy childhood and his bad relationship with his father, his failed jobs—what else is there to know?" Patty asked. "Did he ever tell you about an old girlfriend by the name of Georgina?" Dana asked. "Oh, I believe he mentioned her a time or two. What does she have to do with anything?" Patty asked. "Did you ever hear the name Ray Buckley?" Dana asked.

"Yes! He's the guy who was always giving your dad a hard time. I believe the last time he called your dad was about fifteen years ago or so," Patty said. "Really, do you know what he wanted?" Dana asked. "No, I don't. I didn't pry into your father's phone calls.

Why are you asking?" Patty said. "Why all of these questions now?" "Mom, dad is Ray's son's father," Dana said. "You're not making any sense!" Patty said agitated.

"Listen to me, Mom. Gary is dad's son," Dana said. "How can he be Ray's son and be your dad's son? Who filled your head with that trash?" Patty asked. "Dad," Dana said. "Your father would be turning over in his grave if he heard you talking this way. Stop disgracing your father like that," Patty said. "I'm not. Dad wanted to tell you in the worst way, but he didn't know how or where to begin. Believe me Mom, I've tried telling you before, but dad swore me to secrecy. I tried to get dad to tell you, but he was afraid of how you'd react," Dana said.

"I think your dad was dreaming. He wanted that boy to be his son. Then that would have given that tramp a reason to marry your father instead of Ray. But she didn't. She married Ray instead. He made up this story so he didn't look rejected. You don't believe any of this crap, do you? I can't believe he'd fill your head with such trash," Patty said angrily.

"No Mom, it's not a story. Gary knows about dad. It's you who needs to face reality. Gary is your stepson. You've never met him. If you took one look at him, you'd know he is dad's son. He and Darren look a lot alike. He and I have the same hands; his are larger, but they're almost identical. He has the same family blue-green eyes. He is definitely my brother, and I won't believe any differently. Think about the talent comparison. Darren and Gary are both extremely talented guitarists," Dana said.

"Stop now. You can go home if you are going to continue this charade," Patty said. "You could be right about all of this, but he is not my son. I don't ever want you to discuss him with me again. Don't tell your aunts and uncles about this. I suppose you've filled Darren's, Lori's, and Liz's heads full of nonsense about Gary, haven't you?" Patty asked. "Yes, and Uncle Wayne, Uncle Kevin, and Aunt Lona, too," Dana said. "Why would you do that? Unless you have proof, I wouldn't be sharing any of this information with anyone. You are making your father look very bad," Patty said.

"Mom, do you know you are the last one to be told about Gary? We've all known for years, but because dad wanted to protect you, they have all promised to keep his secret," Dana said.

Patty got quiet for a moment. "The Dornstadt must be laughing at me. They all know something that I should have known all along. I'm not sure what to say," Patty said shaking.

"We didn't tell you, because we knew you'd react exactly the way you just did, and no one wants to confront you," Dana said. She felt the need to grab her mother and hug her, but she feared her hug wouldn't be returned. "Mom, I'm sorry dad never told you. That's not my fault. That's why I want you to know now. I kept dad's promise not to tell you, but he's not here any longer, and I want Gary to be in my life. I don't want anyone to get any wrong ideas or suspicions. I don't want you left out any longer. It's time to expose dad's secret," Dana said.

"How much do your siblings know? Have they all met him, and do they agree with you?" Patty asked. "Darren and Gary act like brothers. They were jamming together. Lori and Liz are rather indifferent to him. They are both very protective of you and they didn't want me to tell you about Gary. They didn't want me to hurt you. I felt by not telling you, I was hurting you more. I guess you get hurt either way, but I am tired of hiding and keeping this secret from you. I want to move on with my life, and I haven't been able to since I found out about Gary over twenty years ago. That is a long time to live with a secret of this magnitude. Imagine how dad must have felt," Dana said. "Lori and Liz are afraid that you'll ban me from the family for some reason. I told them to be realistic. I am your daughter and you wouldn't do that to me. Keeping this secret was dad's choice, not mine," Dana said.

"I'll talk with them. I just need time to absorb all of this news. It hasn't' been very easy since I lost your father; I'm not ready to gain a son," Patty said.

"I hope you get to meet him someday. You'd be proud of him, Mom. He has made a great name for himself," Dana said. "Dana, he is not my blood. He's only related to you and your siblings'. He'll never be my son. Your father never told me because I warned him about running around and fathering illegitimate children. I told him that no one would ever raise our children, nor would I raise other people's children. He probably felt bringing Gary into the family just wouldn't have worked, and believe me, it wouldn't have. Let's not talk about this anymore. I've had enough for one day. Okay?" Patty exclaimed. "Sure Mom," Dana sighed, somewhat relieved.

Chapter 33
Reaction and Resistance

"Mom's reaction surprised me. I feel good, but bad, if that makes any sense. I didn't think I would react this way to her response. I thought I'd feel as if a big weight was lifted from me. Now I have created a lot of questions and disgraced mom. Lori and Liz aren't too happy with me either. I'm not sure how I feel," Dana said to Dale

"See? I told you it wasn't going to be easy. What made you think that you could tell her about your dad's past, when he new better than to even try to tell her about it?" Dale said. "I feel she has been betrayed long enough. Dad should have told her many years ago. Any how, I don't think you expected mom to react the way she did?" Dana said. "One can never tell about your mother. I think you're one step ahead of yourself. Wait and see how she responds after she's had time to absorb everything you told her. Remember she said she'd think about it and get back to you," Dale said.

The phone rang but Dana wasn't sure she wanted to answer it. She was sure it was going to be her mother or a sibling ready to lay into her about what just took place. Why couldn't she be happy with the life she had without Gary? What reason did she have to inform her mother about Gary? Did she resolve anything or did she just make matters worse? Dana no longer knew why she felt compelled to tell her mother about Gary. Why did she need to complicate her mother's life? Revealing this information wasn't going to change anything. Maybe it was because Glen felt his life was uneventful and meaningless. Gary was his masterful creation, but his bragging rights had been stripped from him. Out of selfishness, Dana wanted to make sure the family knew that her father had a famous son.

Dana wanted to bring both families together on Glen's behalf. She knew this is what her dad wanted and he would have been pleased with the outcome. Maybe she should have waited, but then she felt Patty waited long enough to hear about Glen's past.

"Dana, the phone's for you," Dale said. "Do you know who it is?" Dana asked. "Maybe, I didn't know I was your personal secretary," Dale said. "Hello," Dana said very carefully into the phone. "Hi Dana, how'd it go with Mom?" Darren asked. "I'm not sure. She's really skeptical. When I told her about the similarities between us and how much you and Gary enjoyed jamming together, I think she began having second thoughts," Dana said.

"I need to share something with you. I know how much you want this relationship to work, but I don't feel the same connection that you do. I knew about Gary too and was sworn to secrecy like you were. Since you decided to pursue the connection, I left you do all of the dirty work. I agree that we look alike and our builds and features are similar, but I feel insignificant and belittled around him. I don't think he's very friendly. His life has been very different from ours. He hasn't been raised with the same manners, morals and values that we have been. However, I do believe that he is our brother, especially when I looked into his eyes. I almost felt as if I were looking at you. Your eyes are identical," Darren said.

"So why do I detect some skepticism here?" Dana asked. "I'm not sure why but I really don't care for him all that much. I think he's a snob. He kept trying to change the keying on my own music. When I played his music with him, he wouldn't listen to any of my suggestions. I reminded him that we weren't doing a show. I was just making constructive suggestions. He got all defensive and told me that his music sold without my help just the way it was, and he wasn't taking an amateur's criticism. If he were really my brother, I'd think he'd be more considerate. I tried to discuss sports, but all he likes is basketball, and I don't know anything about that sport. I just thought you might want to hear my input," Darren said.

"I'm sorry to hear that Darren. He might just need some time to adjust to us. Remember, he met a lot of people and he might still feel a little overwhelmed. I really wish you two would have hit it off better. Just remember, Darren, I'm on your side. I have had you a lot longer than him," Dana reminded him.

Back in California Gary and Lee were meeting with their scheduling agent. "I don't want any concerts booked anywhere near Pennsylvania. Do whatever it takes, but I don't want to run into any of the Dornstadt's," Gary sighed.

"What? I thought you had that all worked out. I thought you and your new siblings were planning on spending more time together to make up for all those lost years?" Lee said.

"You know, Lee, I'm not sure how I feel about them. I was getting strange vibes from most of them. If they were all like Dana, I'd have no problem with them, but they seem like such simple and boring people. They couldn't live our lifestyle. Even Dana is a country hick, but she's intelligent, fun, and thoughtful. I know they are my family, but a lot of people don't associate with their own families because they don't want to be like them. I believe this is the easiest solution. I'm sure we don't have anything in common. Another thing that comes to mind is when a band like ours is successful everyone thinks you have a lot of money. I have worked too hard to get here, and I am not sharing my wealth with any of those people. I understand their mother Patty recently moved into public housing. I expect she would be the first to come at me with some line about helping out the family. I don't want any part of it," Gary said.

"Wow, what an about-face from a few days ago. You've obviously had some time to think about your new relatives. I assume someone rubbed you the wrong way?" Lee asked.

"I can't put my finger on anything right now, but I just don't feel very comfortable with some of them. Dana's a pearl, but I question the rest of them. Dale doesn't like me either. I think he's jealous of me. I just don't want to be around any of them right now," Gary said.

"When Dana starts calling and wanting to know why we're not performing in Pennsylvania, how are you planning on handling that?" Lee asked.

"I don't know. I will address that issue when the time comes," Gary said. "Isn't it strange what paths our lives take and not always by our own choices? If I am a Dornstadt, we probably wouldn't get along very well anyhow. I'm glad Ray is my father. Our lives are so very different. We are on the road two hundred days a year, and we get bored staying home. They stay home and might travel two weeks out of the year, and they get bored with traveling and can't wait to return home. It's too much work, too much stress, and making reservations is too tedious. There is a big world out there and so much to see; I wouldn't know how to feel if I stayed home for very long. I need to spread my wings and experience the world," Gary shared. "You don't need to justify your reasons with me," Lee said.

"I have lived all of my life without the Dornstadt's, so why am I feeling guilty that I am moving on and forgetting about them?" Gary asked. "Maybe it's because you are a decent human being. You probably really care about them. I'm not in your shoes and can't understand the confusion and frustration that you're experiencing," Lee said.

"I think it would be best if we stayed out of Pennsylvania long enough for me to confront my feelings," Gary said. "You know as well as I do that we can't stay out of Pennsylvania forever; we have commitments there," Lee said. "I know, I just need some time to evaluate my situation," Gary said.

"I'd like to ask you a very personal question. You don't have to answer it if you don't want to," Lee said. "Sure we've been friends a long time; you know me better than anyone. I can't even lie to you anymore. So what's your question?" Gary asked. "You're in love with her, aren't you?" Lee said. Gary stared at the wall. He thought for a moment and looked at Lee. "Yes, I suppose I am. I know I can't have her, making her an even greater challenge. Lee I kissed her, I couldn't help myself. I felt sixteen all over again. I don't even feel guilty about kissing her. I can't get her out of my mind. I don't really know her all that well. I can't believe I feel this way about her," Gary said.

"You're right, it's best you avoid Dana as much as possible. I think you'll find you don't want to lose Kate. Keep thinking about how much you'd hurt her," Lee said sternly.

Chapter 34
Somewhat Normal

"Kate and I talked last night. She's still urging me to have the paternity test done. If the Dornstadt's aren't my family, that will resolve everything. If they are my family, I don't have to tell them the results, and I can decide for myself if I want to continue a relationship," Gary explained to Lee.

"Don't you think you should tell them if the test shows there are no family ties? Otherwise, they'll continue to want your involvement," Lee said.

"I thought about that, too. I'm not sure how I might handle finding out that Dana isn't my sister. My feelings for her are wrong and I fear my reaction. Either way I still want her in my life.

I don't want my dad to know that I had the test performed. If I am a Dornstadt he will never know. He's my father and under no circumstance will I ever degrade him like that. When I was a teenager, I didn't like him very much. Now I admire him for never treating me differently. For him to find out now that I'm not his son would crush him. I can't justify doing that to him. I think he would be terribly hurt to find out I had this test performed.

He would want to know what I was expecting to resolve," Gary said.

"Let's finalize our schedule and play list. Once that is completed, I can direct my thoughts into scheduling that test. You know how focused I get when touring. I even have a new song I want you guys to hear. Maybe we can tweak it a bit and get it ready for our next set of shows. If it's well received, we'll put it on our next CD," Gary said.

Living in rural Pennsylvania during the colder months often falls into a monotonous lifestyle. The Dornstadt's and Borlands didn't live glitzy or glamorous lives. An exciting event might be a NASCAR race, a concert, or one of many county fairs throughout the State. The most recent excitement for the family was waiting for the arrival of Darren and Tam's first child.

The visit to California kept getting postponed. Most family members had forgotten about it and some of them never really expected it to take place. They really weren't disappointed by the lack of communications from Gary. That just seemed natural for him.

Darren was hoping that he and Gary might get another opportunity to jam together and maybe finally find peace between them. Gary knew that Darren was every bit as good of a guitarist as anyone he knew, including himself. Unfortunately for Darren, he never joined the right band and missed his opportunity for fame.

Gary had all the contacts Darren needed, but he wasn't up for finding him a gig. Gary didn't want to explain where Darren fit in the picture. Everyone knew that finding a job for a friend or relative came with a lot of baggage. Gary didn't want to owe anyone any favors and Darren wouldn't fit in the Hollywood scene any how. There was just no way to involve him in the rock world without disrupting his life back home. Gary didn't want his father or other friends to know of his connection to Darren, so he would remain unknown.

Gary regularly found work for Michael but he wasn't going to do that for anyone else. Michael was an exceptional guitarist too, just like his dad. In the summer months while school was out, he toured with the White Ravens and played back-up on numerous artist recordings. The audience loved seeing Michael play his guitar with the band. Lee's son David was also a good musician, and he added saxophone and trumpet to some songs and others he played his guitar. David and Michael became so competitive that they took turns playing with the band during the summer months.

Gary was reviewing the upcoming tour schedule when he saw the band had a show scheduled in Scranton, Pennsylvania. Suddenly Gary realized it had been more than a year since he and Dana had any kind of contact. *"That's odd, until recently Dana e-mailed me regularly. I imagine the Borland's are probably expecting tickets to the show and are waiting to hear from me. I hope the rest of the family doesn't come. I can deal with Dana, but everyone else wears me out. I should probably call her and see what her plans are so I know how many tickets I'll need"*, Gary thought to himself.

"Hello," a voice said on the other end. "Hi! Is this Dana?" Gary asked. "No, it's Maddy. Who's this?" she asked. "It's Gary Buckley. How are you doing, Maddy?" Gary asked. "I'm okay. Mom just mentioned the other day that she hasn't heard from you in a while," Maddy said in a harsh tone. "Oh, did she need something?" Gary asked. "She has throat cancer. She started chemotherapy treatments a few months ago. I stay at my parent's house more than I do at my own home. Mom can't talk, and she's unable to do her own chores. I spend most evenings here helping out Dad," Maddy said.

Gary got quiet. Feelings of guilt flooded him. "I am so sorry to hear that. Why didn't anyone call me?" Gary asked. "I called a few times, as a matter of fact," Maddy said. "When?" Gary asked. "I left a message with Sherry once and Jeff once," Maddy said. "You mean they didn't pass the message on?" Maddy said. "I wonder why they never told me you called. I would have called you back right away," Gary said. "Mom would have called you if she could," Maddy said.

"Wow! Could you do me a favor?" Gary asked. "I suppose. You know, it's not about you this time. My mom is very sick," Maddy said. "I understand. I need you to keep me posted. I will give you a phone number where you can reach me any time of day. Will you do that for me please?" Gary asked. "I will have to talk with my dad. He's really very guarded about mom's situation right now. He doesn't share much information about her condition with too many people," Maddy said. "Well, let me give you my number. If you don't call, I'll understand, but at least you'll have my number," Gary said. "Okay, I can do that. I'll put it in a safe place," Maddy shared.

Gary hung up after giving her the number. He stared out the window for a long time and reflected about his decision to avoid the Borlands. *"Because I decided to stop communications with the family, no one passed on messages to me. Now Dana is dying. I could have been there for her. How could I be so shallow?"* He scolded himself.

Dana's health affected Gary's mood for the next several weeks. His performances were lackluster and the band's reviews were suffering. "Gary, do you remember a few years back when we first talked about retiring? You said you weren't ready. Do you think you're ready yet?" Lee asked. "Why would you think that? Absolutely not, this is the only thing that keeps me grounded. I feel like there is a purpose in life when I am performing," Gary said. "Well then, you better act like it, or we won't have anyone scheduling shows in the future. Your performances have been less than acceptable," Kurt said. "Sorry, I've allowed myself to get sidetracked. I promise I will give the performance of my life at the next show," Gary said as he scowled and paced the floor.

"That might not be good enough any longer. I called a meeting with the band. We all think it is time to hang it up. We're ready for retirement. We have several contractual obligations over the next twenty months and then we are retiring. We are not scheduling anymore performances. Our hands are wearing out, not to mention my voice. You'll need to find something else if you want to continue performing, but I think retirement would do you good," Lee said.

"Well, that's okay for all of you, but I will schedule solo performances. I know people who will use me for a backup. I am not ready to retire yet," Gary said. "Do what you want, but I think you are having issues you need to deal with, and not in a year or two, but now," Lee said.

"Lee, you and I have been best friends for a long time. I'd like to ask your opinion in finally resolving my paternity issue," Gary said. "I gave you my opinion before; nothing has changed. You don't need to tell Ray the results, but I think for peace of mind you need to get that test done," Lee said. "Great. That's the answer I needed to hear. Kate agrees with you," Gary said.

After consulting a doctor, Gary discovered it wasn't going to be as simple as he thought. He needed to collect saliva samples from either Ray or a sibling and then one from Dana or one of her siblings in order to determine matches between the prospective fathers. Ray was not to know about the test, so he was out of the picture.

Gary contacted Maddy. "How's your mother doing?" he asked. "She's responding well to the chemotherapy. She just completed four months of treatments. Then if needed, she'll have surgery to remove scar tissue. Her voice might return, but that is yet to be determined," Maddy said.

"I have a proposition for your mother," Gary said. "Go on," Maddy replied. "I am ready to have a paternity test done to make sure your grandfather really was my father. I don't want to get too personal but not knowing the truth all of these years has taken its toll on me. I'm sure your mother would like closure too. Do you think she can supply me with a saliva sample if I mail her a kit?" Gary asked.

"I'm sure she would be more than happy to do that for you, but do you know what she'd like even better?" Maddy asked. "No, what's that?" Gary asked. "She'd like a visit from you. You could deliver the kit yourself and take it back with you.

I can tell mom is feeling better. She has been talking about attending concerts again," Maddy said. "That's great. I'm relieved to hear that. I will think about that visit, but it won't be for at least a month. I have some upcoming obligations and then I'll have about ten days available to visit. Hopefully I can make it then. I'll get back to you on that visit, soon," Gary said.

"Mom will be so excited. You will make her day," Maddy said. "Don't tell her just yet, please. I need to make sure I can make all of the arrangements first," Gary said. The next week Dana started coughing uncontrollably. She had a fever of 103° and wasn't responding to typical medication. Her white blood cell count was erratic. Doctors admitted her to the hospital to try and determine what might be causing her high fever. After two weeks of hospitalization and treatments she was stabilized well enough to have visitors for 10 minutes at a time. Doctors decided it was too risky to allow her to leave and placed her isolation. Exposure to the wrong germs now could trigger another episode, and she wasn't strong enough to sustain any kind of trauma to her system.

In early August Maddy contacted Gary and informed him of Dana's condition. "That's it. I'll be out in a few days," he said. "You need to know that you may not be allowed to visit with her. Anyone who has been on an airplane is considered a risk," Maddy said. "I will suit up," Gary said.

"Gary, Uncle Darren will give you the saliva sample you need," Maddy said. "That's wonderful. He seems as anxious as I am to have closure to this mystery. I still want to see your mother you know?" Gary said. "She's waiting to see you too. So when can I tell her to expect you?" Maddy asked. "I will call you back shortly and let you know," Gary said.

Gary wasted no time getting to Billsport. He paid a friend to fly him out in his personal airplane. Gary informed Maddy of his arrival time so that someone would greet him at the airport. He only had three days to visit, and he was going to spend as much of it as possible with Dana. Bryan picked up Gary and took him directly to the hospital.

When he arrived, Dana was receiving a breathing treatment. Gary was instructed to wait, which allowed him time to get her flowers. The nurse provided Gary with a suit for when Dana's treatment was complete. Gary pulled up a chair at Dana's bedside and took her hand in his.

"Hi," Gary said whispering? Dana had been expecting Dale. When she heard Gary's voice, she lifted her head slightly and smiled. Gary tried not to show how concerned he was by her deteriorating condition. She was much worse than he had expected. Her once beautiful blue eyes were a hazy gray. Her hair was very thin, like a baby's, and her once full face was very bloated and discolored. Instead of expecting to carry on a conversation with Dana, he hushed her when she attempted to talk. Gary sat holding Dana's hand for nearly an hour until the nurse told him visiting hours were over for the night. Bryan took Gary to his hotel to check in.

"Oh my goodness, I never expected … I mean I can't believe what she looks like. I'm so sorry that I didn't get out here sooner Bryan," Gary said. "Well at least you made it, and that's what's important to mom," Bryan said.

"Let me ask. What are the doctors saying? What are her chances?" Gary asked. "I wouldn't bet my paycheck that she'll see her next birthday," Bryan said. "That's only a few weeks away," Gary said. "That's right. I hope I'm wrong," Bryan said as a tear rolled down his cheek. "Gary, you didn't know her like I did. She would have given a perfect stranger her kidney if they asked. Getting you to take a paternity test was the one thing I can remember her talking about since my dad found out about your possible connection to our family. Even when she was mad at you, she never stopped loving you," Bryan relayed, trying to hold back more tears.

"Look, I can't tell you how bad I feel about your mother. I have known for years that she is my sister, even if the tests prove differently. I have adopted her. She is the sister I always wanted. I have a sister; but she's seven years younger than me. We have very little in common. Dana and I just have this strange connection. We would've had a great childhood together," Gary said.

"That's funny because mom was certain you'd never want anything to do with her. She always felt as though she were bothering you," Bryan said.

"I'm guilty. I was so vain when I was younger. I was certain I was special. Not too many people rated as high as I thought I was. I also thought I was rich and that everyone wanted my money. I realize now that I'm not near as rich as I thought I was. I was convinced that I jumped through hoops to make my money. Now I realize that I have lived a pretty normal life. Time changes all of us. I would give all of my money for Dana's recovery. I don't want her to suffer any longer," Gary said. "Tell me, where can I find Darren? I need to get his saliva sample so we can get this test processed and our results back so that your mother can find out the truth before ... something happens," Gary sniffled, as a tear ran down his cheek.

"Uncle Darren works until eleven thirty, but we can wait at his house until he comes home. He knows you're on your way," Bryan said.

Darren was surprised when he pulled into the driveway. "Wow, I thought you'd wait until morning," he said. "I want to be at Dana's bedside in the morning. I thought we could get this over with tonight?" Gary urged.

"So how have you been?" Darren asked. "The band has decided to hang it up. We're going to finish our contractual obligations, and then we're done. I'm going to pursue fillers and personal appearances, but I don't have anything organized yet. This was all decided in the last few weeks," Gary said.

Gary and Darren talked for over two hours about music, traveling, Darren's job, and of course, Dana. Darren was preparing himself for the worst. "I never thought she'd go this way. I guess it doesn't matter how someone dies, you're never prepared," Darren said. "I remember when she baby sat us. She always played games, colored with us, took us on hikes, or cooked with the girls. She always did something fun. I was a rat. Every opportunity I had, I got her into trouble. Now I wish I could take it all back. I can't stand to see her suffer like this," Darren said as his voice cracked.

"Don't give up on her yet. Anything's possible today," Gary said. "The one thing none of us can escape is death, and it is knocking on Dana's door," Darren said.

"So what are your plans if you find out that we are not related?" Darren asked Gary. "I don't know. I want to be your brother. Years ago, I couldn't be bothered with more siblings. Now I want to have an extended family. Ray will always be my father, no matter what the test results say. I never knew Glen. But if I lose Dana, I will be devastated," Gary said.

"Tell me about it. We're both about to lose Dana. I feel so helpless. I can't do anything for her. She was always so trusting. Now, when I look in her eyes, I see her asking for help. If I could change one thing, it would be to have her health restored," Darren said.

"Look, it's getting late, and I want to be at the hospital early. Thanks for the hospitality and the swab," Gary said. "Any time brother—blood or not," Darren said.

Chapter 35
Waiting

Gary now had all of the saliva samples. *"I dread finding out these results. I know I'll be miserable no matter how they come back. If Ray is my father, I can't bear telling Dana that she's not my sister.. This dilemma has given me more mixed emotions than any other event in my life,"* he thought to himself.

Gary headed to the hospital very early in spite of the late hours he kept with Darren. His time was limited with Dana and he was afraid that when he left, he would never see her again. To his surprise, she was sitting up in bed when he arrived. She was so weak she could barely feed herself. A nurse was helping her. The nurse didn't see Gary come in but she knew someone was behind her because Dana's eyes lit up the room when Gary entered.

"When did you get here?" Dana whispered very quietly. "I spent over an hour at your bedside last night, holding your hand and watching you breathe. Do you know when you sleep you whistle, or maybe it's a hum, but it's not a snore?" Gary asked.

"I've never been told that before. Can't you find something more interesting to do in your spare time?" Dana whispered.

"Sir, I need to finish feeding Mrs. Borland. Can you take a seat in the hall for a few minutes?" the nurse pleaded. "Sure, I don't want to stand in the way of her recovery," Gary said.

When she was finished, the nurse allowed Gary to see Dana but warned she'd be back soon to bathe her patient. "Don't you just want to growl at her?" Dana joked. "That's much kinder than what I was thinking," Gary laughed.

The nurse returned and gave Gary a glance. "I know, I'm going, I need to get another coffee anyhow," Gary said. "You can stay. There's not much to see. I've melted away to nothing. Can you believe this body used to be almost fifty pounds overweight?" Dana informed him. "You always looked good to me," Gary said.

The nurse gave Gary another glance. Quietly he turned and left the room. When he returned he watched Dana drift in and out of sleep.

"I'm sorry. I'm not the best conversationalist these days," Dana said. "I understand. You need your rest. Take a break. I'm not going anywhere," Gary said. "Okay," Dana said as her eyes closed.

While Dana slept, Gary found the cafeteria. He hated cafeteria food, but it was the best he could do. The coffee wasn't too bad, but the hotcakes weren't hot, and the eggs were soupy. They would work for now; maybe he could do better for lunch. Gary decided to stay at the hospital all day, even if it meant just watching Dana sleep.

Dana was sitting up in bed reading when Gary walked through the door. What little hair she had was combed, and she definitely looked refreshed.

"Ah, so the drifter has awakened?" Gary joked. "I'll bet I could write a song or make a movie about a very sleepy person called the drifter. What do you think?" Gary questioned. "Didn't someone already write that song?" Dana replied.

"If you were dying, Gary, what would be your last wish?" Dana asked very seriously.

"Boy, you know how to throw a direct hit, don't you?" Gary said. He hesitated and then sat on the side of her bed. Dana shook and quivered. "Oh no, what did I do?" Gary asked. Alarms began to buzz and ring from every corner of the room. Dana's drain tube had been pulled out. Fortunately, this was not a life-threatening event and Dana was unharmed. Gary felt terrible. His intentions were to support her and provide her with healing nourishment, not hurt her.

A nurse came to respond to the alarms. She discovered Gary asking Dana's forgiveness for disconnecting the tube. "Young man," the nurse said, you must be more careful. Her situation is very delicate," she said as she scolded him. "I'm sorry, I made a mess," Gary said childlike. "I never asked your relationship to the patient. She can only have immediate family visitors, you know. I just assumed you're related to her—you look enough alike," the nurse said. "I am Gary, her older brother," he said. "That can't be, I was told she was the oldest of four children?" the nurse questioned. "Actually there are five of us. We have the same father, but different mothers," Gary said.

Just as he completed his sentence, Patty Dornstadt walked through the doorway. She looked at Gary and let out a very large groan. "The famous Gary Buckley, I suppose?" Patty asked. "Yes, and I presume you are Mother Dornstadt?" Gary questioned. "Don't call me that. I heard you've been stirring up my family. Darren's all worked up about your visit, and now you are starting on Dana. How long did you say you are staying?" Patty asked. "I didn't, but the answer is two more days; then I'll be out of your hair. While I'm here there's no need for you to be here. I'm going to stay with Dana all day, and I'll see that she is taken care of," Gary said, slightly perturbed.

"You know when someone is ill they like to have their spouse or mother around for comfort. Since Dale spends very little time here, she needs me with her, and I am not leaving on your behalf," Patty said. "That's quite alright. I can sit in the chair and stay out of your way, but I have no plans until Sunday night, so I'm not going anywhere," Gary said.

"Have it your way, but I'm not leaving her either. Not yet anyhow. You know, I don't believe that you are Glen's son," Patty sighed.

"Our test samples are in the mail as we speak. The results will be available in the next ten days. I didn't know Glen very well, but my mother spoke very highly of him. The one occasion I met him was a very confusing time in my life. I was more into my own needs at the time and refused to accept what he and my mother were trying to convey to me," Gary said.

"You're smarter than I give you credit for. Then why are you here if you don't believe Glen is your father?" Patty said.

"I don't know who my biological father is, but Ray will always be my real father. This mystery has followed me around most of my adult life, just as it has for Dana, and she is the reason I am pursuing this test now. She is the one who insisted that she was my sister. I adore her, and over the years we've built a relationship. I have grown very fond of her. She's such a special person. She's been there for me when I was down, and now I'm here for her— sister or not," Gary said.

"I hate to tell you this and it's against my better judgment but your movements and mannerisms remind me of Glen. You resemble Darren a lot. I guess it wouldn't be so bad if you were Glen's son. I just wish he would have told me when he was alive. I didn't think I was a monster, but many people have told me that I come across that way. So Glen wouldn't tell me in fear of my reaction," Patty said.

"I was told the reason he never told you was that he didn't want to risk losing the best thing that ever happened to him. That's all in our past now. We need to move on for Dana. I'll do whatever I can to help her. I hope it's not too late," Gary said.

"Come with me please. I'd like to have a few words with you," Patty said.

She led Gary down the hall to the patient lounge. He wasn't ready to take a verbal lashing now and he wasn't leaving on Patty's behalf. Patty's tone was somber. Gary never expected to hear what she was about to share with him. "Take a seat, please. Dana won't be coming home. I have prepared myself for the worst. She has been ill before and beat it, but not this time. She is so weak. Her body can't take much more. I just wanted you to know that I'm grateful for your visit. This means a lot to her. I know how much she loves you. She says you are the inspiration that has kept her on a path to find the answer to resolve a lot of people's questions. I don't know if I follow that comment, but she has made that statement a lot in the past year. I believe she has fought off this disease longer than most people could tolerate, just to find her answer. I'm afraid once she knows the answer to your paternity issue, she'll have no reason to hang on," Patty replied as she finally allowed herself to break down and sob. She shook her head and repeated to Gary. "It's just not fair, it's just not fair."

"I don't know what to say. I can't image losing a child. It hurts being so helpless. We can't stop her from passing on. I feel so vulnerable. I wish I would have come to my senses years ago. I pushed her away and rejected her like a fly in my soup. I even told her she was crazy. I finally grew up and accepted what I cannot change. I want her in my life and now this happens. My heart aches for her and all of you. Selfishly, I don't want her to die but I don't want her to continue to be miserable either," Gary told Patty as he took her hand and produced a weak smile.

"I'll be leaving here late tomorrow night. Would you mind if I have her to myself for a while? Again I know I am being selfish but I don't expect I will ever see her again after I leave," Gary said.

"She will have other visitors. You'll need to chase them away too. I will leave her in your care today. I'll be back tomorrow morning for a little while. Promise you'll call me if there is a change in her condition," Patty asked. "Yes, I promise, and thank you for being so understanding. I think everyone was wrong about you. I think you are a terrific person and you are just watching

out for Dana's best interests," Gary said as he waved good-bye to
Patty.

Gary returned to Dana's room to find her asleep. He pulled
his chair up to her bedside and took her hand. She squeezed his
hand and then struggled in a very soft voice to tell him, "I waited
all my life for you to come around. Dad told me a good person
would eventually come around and want to be part of the family.
You didn't disappoint us. I feel that I've known you forever. I have
so much to share with you and not enough energy or time left for
us," Dana said with tears running down her cheeks.

"Don't cry. Watching you suffer like this is tearing my heart
out. We'll always be part of each other. Maybe you'll get better,
and we'll have that time together. Don't give up yet. There's a lot
going on in the medical field that may help you. I'll be retiring
next year and I'll have a lot of time to spend with you. When you
get better we'll do all of those things we should have done together
years ago," Gary said.

"You're such an optimist, but I don't have much time left. I
just want this to be over with. I remember when I feared death.
Now I'm prepared to move on to my next life. There's something
bigger and better waiting for me. I've used up my time here on
earth. My angel has been waiting on me for a while now. She told
me she'll wait till I'm ready," Dana said.

"Oh, come on now. You need to think more positively. You're
too young to think about angels and dying. You need to think
of life," Gary said. "Sorry, I don't mean to disappoint you. I'm
too tired to talk any more. Lay here next to me so I can feel the
warmth of your body. Please!" Dana said quietly.

"I'll pull out another plug or tube or something. I'll have that
nurse in here in no time, and she'll beat me up. I better not," Gary
giggled. "She doesn't scare me. I want to feel you next to me. I
want to feel the warmth of your body just once. I want to make
up for lost time, but I'll have to settle for this one time. Tomorrow
might be too late. Please!" Dana pleaded again.

Gary carefully maneuvered his body next to Dana. She slid her weak body over far enough so that the two of them fit well into the single hospital bed. Gary propped his arm up over her pillow and wrapped it around Dana. She was so small now. Gary felt her soft, weak body mold into the curves of his body. Dana fell into a deep sleep. Gary held her and watched her breathe. He knew now what unconditional love meant. It no longer mattered if there were family ties. He cried as he realized that he could be comforting Dana in her last hours of life. Sister or not he was losing a good friend.

Gary lay with her for a long time. His body and arm were turning numb. He had to get up and move. When he got up, he turned around to discover Dale sitting in the chair behind him. Dale started to get out of the chair and Gary apologized for ignoring him.

"Don't worry. I know you were just comforting her. I've done it many times. She likes to be held. She's been waiting for you to come for a long time. You have answered her prayers," Dale said.

"You know what's strange? I expected resentment and hostility, but everyone has been so relaxed and comforting. I've been an ass all these years ignoring this family. I finally accepted you as my family during one of the worst times of your lives, and you're so understanding and accommodating. I am embarrassed that I didn't come around years ago. Glen should have told Patty about me years ago. Our lives could have been so different. It wasn't fair to place the responsibility on Dana, to tell the rest of the family. We could have had many years together. I just don't know what to say," Gary said.

"There were times I thought she loved you more than me or anyone else. I didn't understand her feelings for you. I thought she was living out some weird infatuation. There were so many times when she couldn't get enough of you. I was very jealous of you. Now when I realize how much of her life you missed, I just feel sorry for you. You could have had so much more," Dale said.

"Is there somewhere we can get some lunch? I'm starving. We'll let her sleep. Maybe she'll be awake when we return," Gary said.

"Sounds like a plan to me, but no hospital food. We'll go down the street to a really good inexpensive restaurant," Dale said. "Oh thank goodness. I don't know how many more hospital meals I can stand," Gary said.

On the ride to the restaurant Dale shared his feelings with Gary about the family secret. "When I first found out about your connection to the family, I thought it was another exaggerated tale. It took me a long time to accept this wasn't someone's story but a real fact. I thought you were Glen's pipe dream. I really liked Glen, but his past is rather shady. He was a great person and Dana's personality is a lot like his. Thankfully Glen and Patty set higher standards for their children than were expected of them," Dale expressed.

"I can't believe she knew that you were her brother when I met her. She kept that secret from me for well over twenty years. She was always very dedicated to her father, but she could never keep a secret, so I am surprised that she was able to keep that one most of all. I thought she was living in a fantasy world and she needed to grow up. I didn't want to believe you could be related to her, but that revelation explained a lot of her behavior. Many times over the years, I had threatened her with, 'grow up, don't you think it's time to drop the rock star idol thing?' She would agree until the time she found out that you were touring within a few hours' drive away. She'd rant and rave about how good you were. Not the band, just you. One time she said how much you looked like Darren. I couldn't believe what I was hearing. Now she was connecting you to her family. Once I discovered the truth, I became even more jealous. Now I had another challenge, I didn't know where you'd fit into her life, but I was always afraid of losing her to you," Dale said.

The men entered the restaurant and ordered sandwiches and drinks. Dale shared a lot of information about their marriage, their travel adventures, and Dana's health issues. Then Dale broke down. He shared how tough she had been through her illness, but he knew she was losing the battle. Once he regained his composure he asked Gary what his plans were regarding the family once Dana passed away. "I don't feel the same connection to the rest of the family, but if the test results show they are my siblings, I am going to make every effort to be part of their lives," he replied.

"The way you explained that Dana reacted towards me when she attends a concert is not unusual. I'm not bragging but, there are women out there who would take me home with them today if I would go. The very first confrontation I had with Dana in New York was typical. But when I ran into her years later when she asked me if I were adopted, I realized that she was different. She was subtle, not pushy, and when I rejected her questions, she left calmly. She walked away and left me hanging. I didn't know how to respond to someone who just walked away from me without a fight. I considered her one of the most disruptive fans I ever encountered. I hated her for exposing the truth again. I blamed Dana, not Glen who cornered me years before about my paternity and not our parents who created this mess," Gary said.

"So you've decided to resolve the paternity issue?" Dale asked. "Yes, and I'm hoping to get the results back before Dana …"Gary choked. "I know it's a tough thing to say. I have that same problem myself," Dale said

Trying to change the subject to something positive, Gary asked. "So what brought you two together?" "At first, it was a physical attraction. Then I discovered her inner beauty, her kindness, and strengths and weakness. We compliment each other. I've mellowed now, but I was rough around the edges for a long time. Dana's rather quiet, but she can be very outspoken when she doesn't agree with someone. She's almost always kind, rarely rude and most of the time she's happy. Now I'm going to lose all of that. Then she insists I find someone else to take care of my needs. I just want her to get better. Is that selfish of me? I won't ever be able to find someone like her," Dale shared with a quiver in his voice.

"I don't think you're selfish. You love her and want to be with her for many more years. Life just isn't fair. She's so young. She could live another twenty or thirty years," Gary said. "I doubt that. Her body has been pumped full of poisons. If she does rebound, she won't last long—a few years maybe. I'm going to miss her so much," Dale said as he started to cry again and covered his face.

"I'm glad I made this trip for Dana, but I'm sorry I had to witness so much heartbreak. I wasn't expecting to encounter all of this sorrow; it really brings me down. My goal was to get Darren's saliva sample and watch Dana return home. I must leave soon and I'm absorbed in this nightmare. I want to stay until the end. Well actually, I want to stay until she recovers and goes home, but I don't believe that's going to happen. Let's get back to the hospital. My time is limited here," Gary said.

Gary and Dale returned to Dana's room to find Bryan and Maddy sitting by her side. Dana was awake and wondering what had happened to Gary. "Now there's something I never expected to see, the two of you together. This is good medicine for me. I can't tell you how important it is that you accept each other," Dana whispered, trying to smile. "Gary, I was worried that you might have left without saying good-bye," Dana said. "I would never do that," Gary said. "We got a bite to eat. Sitting here doing nothing makes a man hungry," Dale said. "Anything makes you hungry. Don't give me that sad excuse," Dana whispered. "See, she's still got some spunk in her," Dale said.

"Dad," Maddy said. "Yes, honey?" Just knowing his daughters tone he knew he wasn't ready to hear what she was about to ask him. "Mom wants to go home. She said she wants to go outside, see her cats and feel the sun again. She doesn't want to die here," Maddy said.

"She's better off here. What am I going to do when she needs a doctor?" Dale asked. "The hospital will arrange for hospice to come twice a day to check her meds and take care of any other needs," Maddy said. "Hospice, that's for—" Dale stopped and realized that this was his wife's last wish and he was trying to take it from her. "This is so final. I don't know if I'm prepared for this?" Dale sighed.

"I don't think there should be any question here. This is her final wish and I think it should be granted. Please forgive me for seeing it her way," Gary shared.

"If that is what she wants, then it's a done deal," Dale said.

Chapter 36
The Final Performance

In late October both Darren and Dale received packages from Gary. They included tickets for an upcoming show and reservation information for a specific hotel near Lancaster, Pennsylvania. The White Ravens had a show coming up November 16th and Gary wanted everyone to attend. He specified who each ticket was for and where they were to sit. He mentioned in a brief note that he had a special announcement to make and wished that everyone could make an effort to attend the show to hear the announcement.

Dale called Maddy immediately to inform her of the upcoming show. She and Phillip would need to rearrange their work schedules. Darren's packet included tickets for him, Tam, Lori, Liz, Bryan and Patty.

Gary pleaded with Kate to understand this final act of kindness. Kate lacked the compassion and understanding that Gary so desperately needed from her. "What is your infatuation with this woman? I wish I were as important in your life as she has become to you. After all, I sleep in the same bed as you, she doesn't. You have been consumed with her for months," Kate said.

"You know she only has a short time to live. I can't explain my reasons. I just know I need to dedicate this show to her. I know you think I'm crazy. Even though she looks terrible, her face lights up when she sees me. It crushes me to know that I've spent years ignoring her thinking she was just after my money. I finally accepted her and the rest of the family in Pennsylvania and now it's all going to be taken from me when she dies. She is my soul sister, even if she isn't my biological sister. She's has had so much faith in me, I can't let her down now. I must make this show the best one she's ever seen. I'm sure this will be her last," Gary said.

The night of the show the band prepared for this special performance. Gary dressed as though he were going to a prom. He wore a tuxedo jacket with tails and a bowtie with blue jeans. He had twenty four roses tied to his microphone stand. He was more nervous than the night before he got married. He was pacing and humming a tune. It had to be perfect.

When the band came on stage, the room was dark. He couldn't see who was sitting in the front row. He could only hope she had made it. When the lights came on the entire family was smiling and waving. Right in the center was Dana. Her desire to go home had proved to be better medicine for her than staying in that drab hospital room. Her doctors were amazed that she had managed to hang on this long. Her wheelchair had all of her life-sustaining necessities, but she was there. This was going to be the best performance of Gary's life.

The band played their usual song list. After seven songs, Gary took time to introduce the band as he always did. This time he had additional people to introduce. "Because of someone's diligence and perseverance I am now proud to introduce you to my extended family," Gary exclaimed.

Gary made the introductions of every member except Dana. He paused, took a breath, and then wiped away a tear as he continued his introduction. "The last person I have to introduce was instrumental in bringing us together. Her never ending quest in convincing me that I am her biological brother and that I have and extended family who wants to be part of my life is to be commended. I'm so glad I've been given this opportunity to introduce you to my younger sister, Dana Borland. "No one knows what tomorrow brings. Luckily she is able to be with us tonight. If it wasn't for Dana's trust and love, my life might have taken a different path. Dana is not able to stand up to greet you, so I ask that you stand up to greet her," Gary pleaded very emotionally.

As Gary was making his announcement Dana cried out, "This is for you, Dad."

The audience stood up and gave Dana a two-minute ovation. Dana was shocked. It was more than a dream come true. "I'll bet heaven is just like this," Dana said to those around her.

"I wrote a song and I have dedicated it to Dana," Gary said.

The band played the new three-minute song called "A Treasure of the Heart." Dana began to cry. She understood the meaning of Gary's words better than anyone else did. The melody was perfect and the audience loved it. Gary finished by repeating these lyrics to Dana: "I have a gift to send your way; my heart, my love, and my soul. I almost passed up a treasure of the heart. What a fool I would have been," Gary sang as he looked out over the audience with tears running down his cheeks.

There weren't very many dry eyes at that moment. Even Dale, who was usually very composed, wiped away a tear. This was Dana's moment of recognition. She finally accomplished her lifelong dream and her challenges on earth were complete.

After the song was over Gary walked off the stage with roses in his hand. He pulled Dana up in his arms and hugged her tight. The entire arena gave them a standing ovation. Then silence fell and tears started flowing. The audience could sense the depth of Dana's illness and Gary's connection to her. This was a very difficult adventure for Gary. He gently placed her back in her chair and handed her twenty-four roses and kissed her on the cheek as the tears rolled down his face.

Gary went behind the stage to regain his composure. He never expected to feel this way. He hadn't anticipated the deep heartache he was now experiencing. He had a show to finish so he had to pull himself together.

Kate gave him a hug and wiped away his tears and said, "You've got more to show her. Go now and let her see what she'll never see again."

"A Treasure of the Heart" might have been the best song the White Ravens ever performed. Dana cried as she knew her time was short and the White Ravens and her father were finally connected. She cried for the years that she and her siblings had been cheated out of a brother. She cried for what might have been and cried for what would never be. She knew she was too sick to establish the relationship she longed for all these years. For the first time in her life, she felt love flowing through her entire family. She knew her father was smiling down on them, she could feel it in her heart.

After the show everyone was taken to a private dining area and fed a wonderful meal. Gary's other two siblings, Terry and Becky Jean came to meet Gary's new family. With the exception of Dana and Dale the rest of the family partied and shared stories all night long.

Finally everyone dispersed. Terry, Becky Jean, Kate and Gary were the only people left in the room. "Gary, why are you making a big deal out of complete strangers?" Becky Jean asked. "Dana's not a stranger. She deserves recognition for her efforts and because I fell in love with her. Not the love you feel for your spouse, but the love you share with your siblings, your best friend, or a close relative. She's such a great person. She is a perfect person in every way. She's so kind, loving, sweet, considerate of mankind, and I have never met anyone who has exhibited so much trust and faith in me when I didn't deserve it. If there were more people in the world like her, it would be a much better place. The world is a better place because of her. I don't ever want her to know the truth. I'm sorry that Glen passed away before we ever got to know each other, but it would have been so much more difficult to carry on this lie if he were alive. Dana will be joining her father soon. I am retiring and the end of an era is near for both of us. I just needed to do this for her. Now I need the two of you to join me when I go tell Mom the results of the tests," Gary said with a sigh.

"I know you're hurting. It must be difficult for you to lose that entire family, but remember, you'll always have us," Becky Jean said.

On the way home from the concert, Dana started coughing. Her heart rate became erratic and weakness overcame her. Dale took her straight to the hospital. "I knew this was more than you could handle," he said to Dana. "I wouldn't have missed this performance for anything. I truly believe God wanted me to live long enough to witness this concert. Do you know how happy dad is tonight?" Dana said between coughs.

Georgina was ageless. She looked as beautiful as ever. Her children arrived and greeted her at the door. They took off their shoes and gave her a peck on the cheek, just as she had taught them years earlier. Then everyone went to the parlor to have tea and dessert.

"Now dear, what is this news you were so excited to share with me?" Georgina asked.

"Mom, I finally took your advice. I had a paternity test performed to determine my real father," Gary said. "Oh dear, I don't know if I'm prepared to hear the results?" Georgina said. "Mom, I believe you'll be pleasantly surprised. The cloud that's hung over me for years has been lifted. My real father raised me. I can't explain the similarities between me and the Dornstadt's, it's almost eerie. I hope you don't mind if I continue this charade with the Dornstadt's until Dana passes away? It would crush her if she knew the truth," Gary said.

"You have a very big heart, my son. You always did, it just took you a while to realize it was there all along. I'm sure you must be devastated. I know how close you've become to Dana. I'm surprised. I was certain that Glen was your father. I guess I didn't marry the wrong man after all," Georgina said.

"I don't know why Dana came into my life. Maybe it was to keep me more firmly planted. Maybe it was to realize that bad things happen to good people. Maybe it was to teach me how to love unconditionally, but she certainly has had an impact on me for the last several years," Gary said.

"Let me make a suggestion. I think you should tell your father about the outcome of your tests. I believe he deserves to hear this news. He earned this reward," Georgina said. "I will, but I'm sure he'll have some sarcastic remark. I will go see him as soon as I get to Austin," Gary said.

Gary was surprised at his Mother's concern for Ray. They wouldn't even be seen together. They are cordial for the benefit of the children, however, when a family event takes place they never appear at the same time. Gary assumed his mother had no regard at all for Ray any longer, but her comment proved that she still cared.

Ray was a patient in an assisted living village near Austin, Texas. His body was consumed by arthritis so severe that walking was impossible now. His stomach ailments from years ago returned with a vengeance. He had heart bypass surgery not long after he moved into assisted care and was now very week from that surgery. Gary seldom visited his father because he couldn't bear to watch him drift into the unknown. On good days he'd go to the day room where various daily activities were available for those who wished to be social.

Ray's mental state varied from day to day. Some days he was barely alert. Nurses warned Ray's visitor about his sarcasm and his nasty hurtful comments. "He's been good today; he must have known you were coming. Some days he seems to understand us. You'll find him in the dayroom. Do you want us to bring him back to his room?" the nurse asked Gary. "No, that won't be necessary," Gary said as he walked into the room to see his father's wilting figure before him.

When Ray saw Gary he started with the first question. "Where have you been, son?" Ray said. Gary apologized for his absence and proceeded to carry on a long conversation about nothing important. Finally Gary told Ray his news. "For so many years I resented Glen Dornstadt. I used to feel like a like a conqueror; now I just feel sorry for the fool," Ray said.

"Dad, I feel terrible for Dana; if she found out the truth, it would crush her. You know she's dying and only has a very short time left. She'll pass on thinking I am her brother," Gary said.

"You know Gary; I've pretended all of my life. I'm done now. I will never run into those people again, thank goodness. If Glen were alive, I'd give him a piece of my mind. It's too bad about the girl; she must have her father's bad luck," Ray said.

Gary remembered why he didn't visit his dad very often. He could easily put you down with his snide remarks and his bold criticism. He rarely showed remorse and was always trying to make someone else look bad. That just wasn't Gary's style. He must have taken after his mother when it came to others' feelings. Gary cared; he wanted everyone to be his friend. His father didn't want friends, nor did he care about anyone's feelings.

"You know Dad, I consider myself very lucky to have met the Dornstadt's. I understand how Glen fell in love with Mom, and I understand not wanting to lose a child. Can you imagine how Glen would have felt if he lived long enough to find out that he wasn't my father after all? I'm sure that realization would have been difficult for him to handle," Gary said.

"He was a fool for thinking he fathered you. I knew all along you were my son. I don't know why you even wasted your time with that foolish test. Did your mother put you up to it?" Ray asked. "No, Mom had nothing to do with it," Gary said. "Did you tell her that her precious Glen is not your father?" Ray snickered.

"Yes, and she told me to make sure you knew of the outcome," Gary said.

"If she would have just gotten over Glen, we could have had a wonderful marriage. She wouldn't let it go. She was sure you were his son. That'll show that foolish woman. I'm glad now you had that test. Now she knows why I hated that man," Ray said loudly. "She was going to leave me for him because she thought you were his son. Now I get the last laugh," he chuckled.

"I'm going to go now Dad. It's been a tough week. I have to call and check up on Dana. I think the show was very difficult on her, but she got to see us one more time. She may not have seen more performances than other fans, but she was my best fan," Gary said.

Chapter 37
Expectations

"Well you're looking chipper this morning," Dale said to Dana at the hospital. "Take me home. I hate it here," Dana said. "Don't be in such a rush. You had a rough night last night. I don't want to take you home only to bring you back later," Dale said. "I'm not coming back. I want to die at home, and my time is running out," Dana said. "Whoa. Who said anything about dying? You've been doing really well lately," Dale said. "Yes, but we all know I've been living on borrowed time. I want to make it to Christmas. I want to buy Gary a Christmas present. It'll be our first Christmas together," Dana said.

"Don't you be overdoing it Christmas shopping. I'm sure Gary is not expecting you to run right out and buy him presents he doesn't need," Dale said. "This will probably be the only chance I get, and I am going to spoil him this year," Dana said.

"Christmas isn't that far away. I'm sure you'll get your chance," Dale said.

Two nights later, Dana woke up with severe pains in her chest. "Dale, wake up please. I can't breathe. Hold me. I need to feel you.

You've been so wonderful through all of this. You won't have me around to worry about much longer," Dana whispered.

Dale jumped out of bed and called for an ambulance. "I'm not going to the hospital. Call the kids, please. If I have time, I want to say good-bye. If they don't make it, tell them I love them," Dana said as she slipped in and out of consciousness.

The ambulance crew arrived and hooked Dana up to oxygen. They started an IV to make her more comfortable until she slipped into unconsciousness.

"I'm afraid this is all we can do for her, Mr. Borland," the driver said. "Just keep her alive long enough for the kids to get here. Maddy's a half hour away and Bryan should be here momentarily," he said anguished.

When Maddy arrived, she told her father that her grandmother was on her way with Darren, Liz, and Lori.

Once the family arrived they sat together at Dana's bedside for what seemed like hours. They held her hand and prayed with Dana and exchanged happy stories from her past. Bryan promised he would start attending church to fill her empty seat so he could go to heaven to be reunited with her again someday. Patty and Darren sat at the foot of her bed, crying and listening to the children talk. Patty couldn't ever remember feeling so bad.

"You don't bury your children; they bury you," she told Dale.

Dana passed on and slipped into the next dimension at 10:02 AM, November 21, 2007.

"That's strange," Patty said surprised, "she chose her father's birthday to pass away."

Funeral arrangements were finalized, and Gary and his family were notified. Gary arrived and asked if he would be imposing if he sang a hymn and performed "A Treasure of the Heart" at her service. "You can sing all you want; after all, she was your sister too," Dale said.

Each sibling got up and shared how Dana had personally affected their lives. Maddy and Bryan both shared precious memories of their mother, but neither of them spoke for long as they were both crying, almost uncontrollably. Once Dale said his good-byes the procession left for the cemetery.

Gary had no intention of informing the family now that he had no ties to them. He knew that he couldn't let Dana die disappointed. Maybe someday he'd come back and visit or drop them a letter, but if he told them now, they would be suffering an additional loss and he couldn't do that to the people who so readily accepted him.

Life continued for the family, as it does when someone passes away. Dale, Maddy, and Bryan often reminisce about the many fond memories they have of Dana.

Gary went on to record "A Treasure of the Heart" and dedicated to the memory of his adopted sister. The message was so strong that the band had their first top ten recording on the R&B charts and their first top ten recording on the pop rock charts in fifteen years. Thirteen months later they would disband as planned. It didn't matter that Dana wasn't his blood sister. She was his sister at heart.

Years ago when Dana first discovered she had a famous rock star half brother, she composed a note which she gave to Gary long before he acknowledged his extended family. Gary had saved the note. At the funeral he offered a copy to Patty and Dale. He knew that a compassionate, fearless, and strong individual had written these words and he needed to pass on her strengths to her family.

> Love comes to us through many openings.
> Whether or not we choose to accept this love is
> up to us. Some people accept it gracefully while
> others just push it away. Just because it isn't
> readily accepted doesn't mean it isn't wanted.
> It's not true that love conquerors all, or I would
> have conquered you. Love is like a disease—it's
> hard to catch, but once you catch it, it can be

tough to shake. I know without a doubt, that I
love you.

Dana died, not knowing how much she had affected Gary.
He described their relationship the following way: "I never knew
how much love I missed until Dana's Death. I bet many people
have experienced this sort of loss. Regrettably with her passing, I
now understand why some people quietly slip into our lives and
then leave with an explosion. Her unconditional love will be with
me forever.